MICKEY COLLINS

~

Kevin Forde

www.kevinforde.com/mickeycollins

Spright Publishing
Drumard
Ballineadig
Farran
Co. Cork

First published in 2022 by Spright Publishing

Acknowledgements

Thank you very much, Mary O'Regan, factotum and encourager extraordinaire.
Also, to Bradley Eagles, Dan Corkery, Jaimie Vandenbergh, Martin Forrest and Lucy Forde. Sincere thanks for all the help and encouragement.

The Author

There is nothing worth saying or knowing about the author. He has some other books listed on www.kevinforde.com. Other than that, there is nothing. We checked.

Introduction

Mickey Collins, from Cork City, Ireland narrates the following true story, transcribed from a series of recorded interviews and set down here, as spoken. Although modified slightly in part for readability purposes, it remains unedited on the whole to maintain perspective.

THE GLORY YEARS

Mr. Mulcahy

They didn't let me go home straight after, the government. They said I had to stay out a while, see what's the matter and if I was a junkie. I wasn't like, but I took a few different things at different times. Mostly for a buzz. The main thing they were all asking me is did my mother give me stuff and I told them all the same thing I told everyone else – 'course not. And she didn't neither. Not really anyway. The way it started, I think, is we both were taking things when we'd find them off the table, me and Cillian. And my mam would be, Did ye see tablets on the table? And we'd be like, No. She might of half-believed us for a while but after that she knew it was us and she said if we were going to be taking them things we should stick to the hash only and she got us do jobs for her so she'd give us hash-only so we'd stay away from the tablets. She never gave us no tabs, like. Not around then anyway. It was the opposite. We earned hash with jobs so we'd stay <u>off</u> the tabs, like, see? But the jobs was mostly getting tabs or bags of hash off one fella, Moxie. Or else we'd be dropping them off someplace else, like, for our mother other times.

Moxie'd give us extra tabs too if we agreed to bring them to a kind of posh fella who lived in Carrigaline, so we got hash and tabs easy enough after a while. And we got our own gang too working with us, like, off and on, more or less. Just delivering mostly, is all. Make a few bob. I was the youngest in the gang. I'd say I was probably five at the time, starting off, Ahahahahaah! Around that.

But at this time I'm talking about now, I was probably around ten or thirteen (something like that, like) and after taking tabs I found in an old house me and Cillian were in, see. Then I collapsed and he brung me to the hospital. I never seen the tabs I got in that house before so that's why I tried them ones.

At this time, social workers and all them was looking to place me in a home for a bit if they knew I wasn't a junkie, so I had to give urine samples every couple of days and do interviews and chats with different people. Beors mostly, like. They were alright too. And I had to go to school all the time and I stayed with Foxy Bill a few days first and then they found a home for me near there with a woman called Bizzy. She hadn't a clue, Bizzy. She'd be like, Oh don't do that now! God bless us! and I wouldn't be after doing nothing bad, like. She had a stairs an' all in her house, Bizzy, so I'd be just sliding down it and she be screaming. Or I'd be climbing out the window just to see the view up above, cos there was a grand view in the gaff, and she'd be screaming at me again, Oh don't do that now! God bless us!

She had a garage with all tools and stuff and I told her I'd make her a house for her dog, Bootsy, cos he was a lovely fella and I love dogs, me, and I done woodwork one time, I was telling her. But she was like, Oh don't do that now! God bless us!

Her husband was dead she told me one time and she showed me a photo of him that was on top of the telly. I thought it was like a funny fillum when she got all sad so I gave her a push and laughed and she started crying for no reason. I didn't push her hard I swear it, like. It was to give her a laugh, like, but she was all bothered or something all the time.

Another time, one time I accidentally ripped the wallpaper – just a tiny bit, like and she was the same, Oh don't do that!

I never even made a hole in the wall or nothing! And one time or two times I had dirty clothes that was full of mud and she was screaming again when she came in and I was lying on the settee. My mother even told me do it when we were on a telephone call cos Bizzy was paid a load extra off the government if she had to clean the settee, but Bizzy didn't even care, she just wanted a clean settee. Every time she'd just be screaming to God. I said it to my mam later that Bizzy didn't like when I dirtied the couch and my mam goes, The gratitude of some people!

I always remember that cos it was funny the way she said it like, all posh: The gratitude of some people!

That woman done my head-in in the end, Bizzy, and I stayed in Foxy Bill's place after for a few days or weeks til they found someone else.

And I went to school a lot of days and I had the odd visit home every now and again to see my brother Cillian and we'd do stuff a few hours, but we never broke into a house together no more or anything like that. Just talked and stuff mostly. He told me he was doing a load with Con (our Uncle, like) and our mother mainly. And it was his birthday one time too so we had a party at home and my urine failed a few times after that cos you need a few weeks to come down, like.

Next, I got a place with a fella called Mr. Mulcahy who was alright, like. That's when I met him, I think, Mr. Mulcahy around then. He was kind of old and kind of foxy too like Bill, or blondie brown hair at least, like. And skinny. He was skinny-out. He had a small beard on him, I think kinda, and probably a moustache too and he smoked a load. His first name was Desmond but I always called him Mr. Mulcahy. I don't remember why, cos mostly I call people by their first name if they're friendly enough, 'specially if they're not an officer or a Judge, like, and he was probably the nicest to me growing up, Mr. Mulcahy, like. I'd say he preferred that name to Desmond. With me anyway. He was a social worker before, but not anymore. Retired, like, but still he'd look after the odd kid now and again for a bit if they was stuck, he said, and if they couldn't find no one else to take them. Like me, like.

He never went out I don't think, 'cept to take me places if I needed to. Nobody really took me places where I wanted before, mostly cos I'd go anywhere, me. He was like, Where would you like to go, Mickey?

And I'd be after getting a shock and say Fota Wildlife Park, so. And he'd bring me there, like! And I chased a giraffe and the guards came and chased me and I was running around the giraffes and they were in their truck chasing me. They took us back to a room, after, and Mr. Mulcahy was mad-out at me, giving out in a whisper. And the main fella in charge goes it was a very serious offence, but Mr. Mulcahy, fair dues to him, got him to chill after a while and said I loved animals and I didn't know at the time I wasn't allowed run around with the giraffes, but I knew it now. And yer man goes it's very dangerous cos they could've kicked me and killed me and Mr. Mulcahy goes we all agree it's best to keep the young lad safe and away from danger. So we got a spin off a fella called George after that, whose job it was to drive us around for the day down there. He took us everywhere in his jeep and he learned us all about the monkeys and things an' we going. That was the best day of my life I'd say, down there. They gave us food an' all for free in the restaurant. I could be a zookeeper in charge of elephants. I'd be good with elephants I'd say. There was no elephants in Fota though.

Another time when he asked, I said I'd go to Sligo, cos I was nearly there one time. But Mr. Mulcahy goes, That's a bit far – let's go to the Mallow Races instead. Cos that's still in Cork, see? He said he liked putting money on the horses, but he wasn't allowed bring me, so if he brung me and if I told on him, he might get into trouble. I said I wouldn't say nothing and until right now I never said it neither. I don't know why I never really, but I just thought of it now. Might've worked better if I did and get away from all the other stuff, now I think of it.

He'd be there with his racing book and choosing his horses and then he goes to me, Here, take this and put a fiver on Number One Son at 2:15 and bring me back the change.

And he gives me a tenner and I'm holding onto it and he's not even looking at me, but he's already studying his racing book and I'm still holding out the tenner, in shock like. I goes, I could just run away with the money! and he goes, You could.

Nothing else like, just, You could. And I goes, What'll ya give me, so, if I put on the bet for you? He looks at me and has a think and goes, If you give me the change, I'll pay you two euro for your work or else you can have ten percent of any possible winnings.

I had a think about that, cos I'm no daw either like, and I asked him what are the odds on the horse he's putting on and he told me 3/1 and I thinks about it again and goes I'll take the bet. And when I'm going off he calls me back and asks if I knew how much I'd get for ten percent at 3/1 on a fiver and I told him One fifty.

I could tell he had a shock when I knew it. And when I got back and gave him his change, he goes, Why didn't you take the two euro if you knew the most you'd win would be One-fifty? And I goes, You'd get a better craic off the One-fifty.

The horse didn't win, but it was good craic. Worth a euro and fifty cents anyway. I'm thinking now though, now I think of it, I could've taken the two euro he was giving me and put that on the horse in the first place and I'd of gotten two euros' worth out of it 'stead of one-fifty! I'd say he even knew that an' all though, cos he was the cleverest man ever from all them books he'd be reading.

I was in Mr. Mulcahy's for a good while. A year around I'd say. Mostly he'd be taking me to school in the morning and he'd be mostly outside and pick me up after that and take me back home, to where he lived, like. We'd be walking back. I was doing that ages and they were always saying I was doing good, most days. And Mr. Mulcahy'd be always saying well done all the time. That school was mostly OK, but I don't want to talk about that place. Mostly talking stuff and sometimes writing. Boring enough.

And my mother'd be calling and telling me get a new coat and I'd have to get a new one or look out for expensive big books, she'd say, like a big Bible in Mr. Mulcahy's, but mostly I only saw old ones nobody'd be bothered with so I left him off like that. And she was inside a few weeks one time, up in Limerick and she phonecalled Mr. Mulcahy and told him she wanted me for a visit so he brung me up there even when I told him forty times I wasn't going. What would I want being in no woman's jail? I goes. I burnt a hole in the seat of his car by accident an' all on the way up cos I was rubbing his lighter off the cushion cos I was mad and giving out to him but he wasn't listening so I was rubbing the chair with the lighter and he didn't even care and then it felt hot and I saw there was a big burn-mark and a hole. He looked and spotted it and didn't even say nothing and I was mad at him more after that and flung his lighter out the window. He was mad at that alright cos he couldn't have no more fags on the way up til we stopped.

Inside then I had to wait on my own til my mother got in the meeting room cos not Cillian or Mr. Mulcahy was with me and all the wans in there was sad-out, just having a fag mostly and talking with their visitors, not bothering no one.

And when my mother came she was delighted to see me and was showing all the guards and the other women me and going, That's my second now! Cos Cillian was up last week she told me and Tara was coming next week and Melanie the week after. Jordan-SueAnne wasn't born yet that time, I'd say. And her friends was cheered up in fairness and even my mam was all happy-out to see me cos she's not usually like, but up there she was all thrilled.

Then we were sitting down and she goes Con was getting a house. Con was her brother, like. A big house and we'd all be living in it. And I was like, Yeah? And she was like, Yeah! He was up in court before me, she goes, And his solicitor tells him he should keep his money in property cos that's how they wouldn't be able to come after you no more, like.

And I goes I bet he made a load off the travellers (cos he was doing big business with them at the time). And my mam was going, He did! but there was a battle going on again now cos the travellers tried to double-cross Con and he had to teach them a lesson.

15

I asked her what happened and she tells me they tried dealing with her separate to Con and Con found out they was dealing with someone else and he got mad at them and started a fight and they wouldn't work with him no more, only with her from now on, but she managed to calm everyone down eventually mostly like, so as long as Con buys the house off them and doesn't give them more grief while she's stuck inside we'd all be well-set up when she gets out and we'll get into the new place then.

I was asking her then about the house and she tells me it's a mansion an' all and we'll be all moving in soon enough and she'll have all her children under the one roof like she only ever wanted. And everyone'd have their own room. And Stacey could stay there too. And Con too maybe.

And I goes would Con be mad at her for dealing with the travellers and she goes no cos he was glad someone in the family was able to keep up the deal so Con'd be working for my mam now soon an' all.

She tells me don't tell anyone about all that now, but I could tell Mr. Mulcahy she'd be taking me back soon enough.

I was thrilled then when I got back to Mr. Mulcahy and told him we'd all be living in a big mansion, all the family, but he only smiled and said we'll see how she works that one through.

It still was ages after that before the house come up. Later, like months later, or years probably. There was all hassle cos the council wouldn't pay Con nothing to my mother for us to live there, see? First they goes Con got no papers for it off the travellers, but then he got papers, and they were going, The family isn't big enough.

16

Cos there was too many rooms for our family for them to be paying for, so they moved another family into it an' all instead and paid them for it, robbing bastards! But Con was giving out to the council cos he said that other family would make shit of the place an' he wanted his poor sister's family in there, but the council were on and on about all the book of rules an' everything all the time. They said my mother only had four children and the children wasn't even living with her mostly and it was a six bedroom mansion Con brought so it was too big for us.

•

Mostly when Mr. Mulcahy'd be home, he'd be sitting around his house reading all the time. Didn't even own a television 'til I got him to get one after a long time. He gave me a book every now and again, still though, but mostly they'd be filled with words only and I wouldn't be bothered and then one time he gave me a children's book with children's pictures and he goes here try that one and I got mad at him cos I thought he was mocking me, but then I knew he wasn't and he was straight about it and I took it and read it to prove him I could. It was called Tiger-Tiger Is It True? by Byron Katie and Hans Wilhelm. I always remember that one cos I read it like a hundred times at least. It was a children's book alright, but like it was a good story about a little tiger who had no friends and stuff.

And after he saw me reading it loads, he asked me one morning if I'd try other ones like that, but I wouldn't be bothered. I goes, Naw, I'm alright with this one, like. Then he asked me why that one was special and I told him I just liked it and he goes, Does Tiger-Tiger remind you of anybody? And I goes no he's just a tiger who was sad cos nobody was good to him and now he's happy by the end. And Mr. Mulcahy goes, Do you feel a bit like Tiger-Tiger feels sometimes? And I got so mad at him I flung the book at the wall an' all and shouted and said of course not, Cillian is my best friend and my brother and I wanted to go for a visit with him and prove it.

So we rang my mother, who was after getting home by now. And I told her we were coming on a visit and she told me I wasn't allowed and wouldn't tell me why 'cept after a while she goes Mr. Mulcahy was probably queer and he was turning me queer too and she couldn't allow me see Cillian no more in case I'd turn him a queer too. I was crying with her for ages cos she wouldn't believe me that I wasn't a queer and then she goes prove it and hung up.

And when I got off the phone I called Mr. Mulcahy all the names and wrecked a load of his stupid books and ran out of the house and then I made it back home to prove it to her I wasn't no queer, which is the same as a bender.

•

That was Mr. Mulcahy anyway. He was sound-out.

But I'd better say first about the dagger and what's all that about. Or probably about all the rest too, I suppose. And why I'm locked-up now too, while I'm on it.

18

Mother's Little Helpers

First thing, if you ask me, is I'm not right in the head. I know that. Now, like. I don't mean it bad, like some people, but for years I'd be fighting anyone who'd say it, including my mother mostly. She was the first to know it and she'd be mocking me over it, like, but tried getting help too, though, going off to social services about it. She went to the courts an' all. Yer wan in the hospital only laughed at her Christmas Eve one time years before that, true as God, an' my mother karting us around with nowhere to drop us. She had a party she had to go to and didn't want to be dropping us just anywhere. I'll tell ya about that later on. Probably. Nobody'd help her though. Not a single person. You'd think there'd be a bit of help for that wouldn't you, like?

We were on the waiting list for a decent house must be ten year or more. She got ones in-between, like, but they were all shitholes you couldn't stay in for long. Sure who could live here? my mam screamed at the social worker one time, pointing at the broken windows myself and Cillian broke. And the doors off the hinges that some of her buddies took down to sell but forgot to take them away after they got baked and my mam kicked them out. And the burns on the carpet and the broken settees and the holes in the walls and the telly didn't work or nothing in any house. Just as well anyway, kids today are ruined from television, isn't that right?

My uncle Con took the copper and lead piping out of two places we lived and he got me and Cillian to help him. And he gave us a box of fags and a six pack of crisps for helping him once. I forget what he gave us the other time. We done it more times in other houses, like, but only two times in our own place. We were his apprentice plumbers, me and Cillian, but my mam kilt him when she caught him afterwards and they went on the batter for a week before she forgot about it again. She was like a demon, though, having to deal with the council after, I remember. They gave her a load of grief for it like it was her fault. Couldn't have been her cos she was in Tenerife – or what's that other one called, begins with T? Santa Ponsa! That's the one! Or Malaga maybe, now I think of it. I think it was Malaga at the time. She showed them the tickets an' all but they couldn't care less. It was around a year at least I'd say before they done anything about it, too. By then the whole place was riddled with rats. They walked in through the holes even after we blocked them up. Con got a van that was full of bags of cement and got us to fill a load of the holes with them, but the rats got in through the spaces between the walls and the bags.

I can't think of the other time now but it wasn't worse than that one. Even now I still know how to do plumbing though, no bother. I could be a plumber in the morning, me. If you learn something when you're a child you never forget it I always say. Like, I got a phone for the first time a few year ago and I still barely know how to use them things. I've been through a load of them since, but they're all the same anyway you ask me. If I had one when I was a child though I'd be shit-hot at it now wouldn't I? Whiz-kid even like yer man Jeremy, probably. They should give phones to everyone when they're born. That way they wouldn't have to waste time. They could look up how to change a nappy or something and learn much quicker that way, isn't that right? Ahahahahaah. Cillian always says he changed my nappies. He's only two years older than me, like around, and I know he changed the girls' but there's no way he changed mine.

Those were the good ole days though. Plumbing I mean. And just after that second time, before we moved into Winchester, we lived in one house a few year where we had one bedroom for me, Cillian and Tara mostly. And Melanie then too. And the other bedroom for my mam, mostly. There was no bed at all in the place when we moved in first, I'd say, but after a while we got a mattress, just. A big massive one. The rest of us slept on those blow-up beds in our own room cos my mother said we'd have to make sure we didn't rip it like we done loads before with other beds. Took up nearly the whole space in my mam's room, that mattress though. We used love jumping on it when she wasn't there. She'd kill us if she caught us, like, but we didn't even care. Tara found a roll of cash under the pillow one time. She was only a toddler though and we got it off her and got Anthony down the road to get us a load of cans and we had a party. I'd say I was around nine. Nine or eight definitely. Cillian was at least thirteen though so technically he was old enough. My mam kilt us when her money was missing. Well she would've really killed us if she knew we took it but she thought Harry The Jinnet took it before he shagged off. And since he wasn't seen for years after, we got away with that one. The Jinnet didn't though, in the end. Ahahahahaah.

Wasn't her fault either like, whatever they tell ya. She done her best but we were wild and no one helped her no matter what they say – an' she had another one on the way a lot of the time.

Cillian was worse than me though, I guarantee ya that. Much worse. I was only doing what he showed me mostly. Wasn't our mam at all. Look at him now you'd think butter wouldn't melt in his mouth. But I won't talk about him now either. Well I will, like, but it's not his fault either in fairness. I'm going to get a job too like Cillian once everything blows over. I'll pack it all in an' get a house an' a mortgage and I'll be like the father of the house that no cops ever even come to or nothing. And I'll take care of my mam too cos Cillian'd never do it and the rest don't talk to her at all no more neither. And nobody minded her when we were growing up, but I'll mind her now. And from now on. Here, I'll mind her! That's all she needs every now and again is a bit of help. And I don't even mean the hard stuff. I mean she'll want to come visit me in my new front room and smoke a fag or maybe a joint at most for her nerves and let me know about stuff and get me to do some job for her. And if the girl I was married to didn't want her in the house well she could get stuffed an' all. She wouldn't be able to stop me I tell ya that straight.

I don't have a wife, like, or a girlfriend at the minute but I'd probably be married with kids and my wife wouldn't be able to stop me doing nothing for my own mother or letting her see her grandchildren even. No way would anyone stop her seeing her grandchildren! I'd make sure of it.

It's me only who helps her. Even now she'll tell you that herself. She can only depend on me. No one else. She told me the same thing and that's a fact: Not Tony, not her lawyer, definitely not the judge or the shades anyway – Ahahahahaah!

22

I was at Mr. Mulcahy's for around for a year or more and he done his best I'd say alright but even he was useless in the end when you think about it. And there was Stacey. She was alright but she ended up ratting on my mother and she done time that time too. My mother I mean, not Stacey. Stacey never done no time the bitch, it'd suit her too. And there was another social worker I remember, can't remember her name now, wasn't too bad. And Foxy Bill a'course.

But they were all useless. Or pointless really. Foxy Bill'd tell you that much. You'd go round in circles with them all till they moved on. There were others in the council or different places I'd say were genuine enough in fairness looking back but mostly they just wanted to take things away from her instead of giving her stuff. They took my sisters, Tara and Melanie off her and later Jordan-SueAnne. And they took me and Cillian off her too a load of times, even before Mr. Mulcahy. We were in different homes and some of them weren't too bad in fairness. Stuck-up bollixes the lot of 'em though. Most of them anyway. At the time I suppose they weren't too bad, mostly, but like they had to know more than you know the whole time, you know what I mean? Do your head in.

But me and Cillian could have helped her more and we weren't allowed cos we were robbed off her. We had to escape whenever she needed us do a job. And we knew when she needed us. The girls were too young, sure.

Alright I might be inside again if they do me for what happened, like. But if not, I'm going to settle down shortly and take it easy definitely. I'll get a job. Probably on the skips is the plan, like, I was thinking. Wasn't my fault, what happened anyway, but I know they don't believe me. I'll have to retire probably though when you think about it. Getting too old now I'm twenty nine or twenty eight, like.

I suppose I shouldn't be saying nothing, but sure what do I care? Might as well, sure. By the time it comes out it'll all be done and dusted anyway, not like I'm grassing on anyone is it? Most of them are dead or in jail. The cops can't do nothing after you're locked up and we were juveniles most of the time anyway and people like Stacey might get a knock on the door for what she done too. How bad? All good news if you ask me. Good news is bad news. Bad news for Stacey anyway, put it that way – Ahahahahaah!

Torneens

Cops caught me and Cillian one time. I don't know what age I was. Ten or twelve. They caught us all the time of course, but this one time we weren't even doing nothing and they brought us home and Stacey was there and they goes, Are you the mother of these juveniles what were caught throwing rocks at traffic? And Stacey was zonked and she goes, Ya. And the cops asked her if she was alright and she stood there with her open white eyes while the police waited for an answer at the door and me and Cillian got the dagger from under our mam's bed and a packet of juicy fruits from the kitchen and when we got back outside the cops were gone but Stacey was still standing there with her mouth open and the front door open, looking at the inside of the back of her head. She done that a lot. I know the feeling in fairness.

That time, while I'm on it, we weren't even throwing rocks at the cars, like I said. We were on the bridge looking at the cars. We never had no rocks that day. There was none there so most we done was spitting. Funny thing is we thought they were doing us for what we done earlier but after we got back home we knew they never even knew about that.

We were exploring down by the river earlier, see, catching thorneels and we climbed over a wall where the fence was broken on top and we were up on a roof, up high like, and we could see down into the quarry at all the lorries and I was spotting them for ages and Cillian was after finding a spot in the roof in the corner where the felt was loose and we couldn't see nothing inside it was all dark so he lowered me in and then left go and I fell a bit but not too far and I still couldn't see nothing and there was no light switch so Cillian dropped down too and the only thing we could both see for ages was the hole where we came in but after a while like we could see a door and it was locked on the other side and me and Cillian were trying to escape into it for ages but got no joy. There was nothing hard enough or pointy enough in the room for to help us. Just a load of papers and a big table but even after we got the leg off the table and used it as a battering ram, we couldn't open the door. It was rock-solid. We could hear there was no one on the other side, like, so there was no bother making noises, but there was nothing worth taking in the room after we searched the place, so we got out the same way. We had to get the long part of the table up against the wall, like, to climb out cos the hole was up too high and when I was up at the top of the table Cillian had to pull me up through the hole cos I couldn't reach and when he pulled me, the table collapsed and made a louder racket than the battering ram and we were sure someone heard it and caught us after on the bridge cos of that.

But then we knew no one heard a sound, after we got a lift home. So when we got the dagger and our dinner, we left straight away to see what's in the other room past the door.

A buddy of Cillian's died a few year before that, now I think of it. They were out with an older fella one night. Cillian, Shazzer and WillaWilla was the older fella. They were up on the roofs by the Mercy Hospital, Cillian was telling me. WillaWilla goes to Shazzer, Willa come on I drop you down in there in the dark and you turn on the light when you get there and we'll see what's in there then. Shazzer goes alright and WillaWilla drops him in but the drop went down for miles. I think it was like a hundred foot and Shazzer died from it. That can happen too like.

The dagger was an ancient one our mam brought home one night. She told us she got it from ancient Egypt or off the old IRA. The hangle was bigger than a big hand. I'd say Con's hand would've easy fit the hangle but just about. The blade was around two times the length of the hangle. It was big enough and just the right size I'd say to be a good one. She got Butcher Murphy to sharpen it for her, my mam. He was alright, like, Butcher. He was called that cos he worked in a restaurant. He went to school with my mam and he offered her fifty quid or a hundred for it straight out and she said naw, but he sharpened it anyway and you could cut anything with it.

I'd say you'd stab someone if you just dropped it and they were underneath, Cillian says when he saw it. Wasn't far wrong either I'd say. We stuck it in the wall in the bedroom no bother even before it was sharpened and you could pull it down and make a rip in the wall easy enough an' all. After it was sharpened she wouldn't let us touch it but hid it under the bed at least two nights and two days. Then we needed it for the door so we had to take it.

It had its own holster too so Cillian strapped that on and we went down the road and Cillian had a kind of a limp when he walked with it so I was going faster and when I got to the shop there was about four fellas come out who were about five years older than me and much bigger and I said here do ya want a fight? I was mad in them days, fight anyone. And the lads were looking at me and only laughing and one of them goes who do you want to fight and I goes the lot of ye like and they broke their arses again at that.

Come on so we fight ya, says one of them laughing and raising his fists and I goes it's not me at all it's my brother. And Cillian limps up and pulled out the big dagger and the fellas all legged it faster than a rabbit at the races. Cillian shouted at them with the dagger in the air but I'd say they didn't even hear it they were faster than the sound barrier.

We couldn't get up to the roof where the room was til later cos there were men working on the road by the river when we got there and they'd've seen us so it was nearly dark when we getting back in there.

Before that though we stuck around by the river or thereabouts and met some other fellas fishing who were alright and Cillian showed them the dagger and one of them caught a fish after a while and Cillian said he'd chop it up for them and then he chopped it. Cut through the fish no bother. He done five pieces and I got the bit with the eyeballs for my piece and Cillian made the fish talk when he squeezed the side of his head and we all broke our arses at that. It was like the fish was talking but Cillian done it. Then he chopped his own part smaller and smaller and the dagger could easy cut it all so I said do mine and he done that and even the mouth sliced easy and he left the eyeballs til last but that was 'scusting. One chop of the first eyeball and it just gooed out, soft like. He used the back of the blade on the second eyeball and there was a small pop sound and it made a kind of a splash. That one was better. The dagger done it all no bother though and the other fellas all wanted to see their pieces be chopped too. One fella wanted to chop his own bit up and Cillian left him do it too. That was some dagger.

Later on, after the fellas moved on and the workers left, the two of us climbed up and got onto the roof and there was no bother getting back into the room, but the light coming in from the hole was darker and we dug the dagger into the wall by the door – the wood part – and it took Cillian ages to get through even with the dagger. It was all dark and we had no matches even, but I could hear him scraping and getting deeper and after a while the door opened and we saw it was a big open room past the door with a bit of light only. You could get an echo off it if you screamed. And there was windows all along one wall and we could see the outside into the quarry but we couldn't make out the bottom cos the moon put light in the hole but there was a shadow down the bottom. We were fierce high up even and we went down the big steps and then down around into the quarry. Round and around and around all the way down to the bottom. We could see where we were going with the stars making it bright, but the big machines were all locked up down the end. After we got the air out of one of the big huge wheels, I found a metal box under the JCB and Cillian got it opened and there was a small bit of change and a packet of fags and a lighter in it, so we had a smoke on our way back up and said we'd scoot on, but the gate was locked and there was wires at the top so Cillian goes we'll have to go out through the room again.

I didn't want to go back that way but I didn't bother telling him I was a-scared cos I wasn't really but Cillian goes we can use the lighter to see, so I goes alright. And when we got up the top of the steps Cillian lit the lighter when we went in the big room and we could see shelves that were all totally empty and that was it.

Inside the room we had to out the lighter to get the table back up against the wall so Cillian lit a small fire with the papers so we could see, like, and we got out that way and by the time we were down by the river we could see there was a big fire behind us up on the roof and it took ages for the fire brigade to get there and when they did they couldn't get in the gate and when they did it was nearly morning and the whole place was lit up and we got in the gate and there was a load of people around and we were all looking at the fire and the whole building collapsed, stairs an' all, while they were hosing it down. That was some night. It was painful walking in circles all the time, down and then up from the quarry. We were totally wrecked from it, like, but in fairness the fire brigade made up for it.

Cob

Con was like a different person different times you'd meet him. He'd be hot and cold and soft and hard. But over the years he had different times too – like he was fun and he was a trickster. And he was the hardest, toughest man, like the big boss, nearly, more or less. Then he got softer and softer. They put me away for a small bit and when I come out, Con was just going in himself, like, around then. And after he got out, he was like retired and couldn't give a shit about nothing and spent all his days watching Judge Judy on the telly drinking cans. That's how he was 'til he got hit. I know nothing 'bout that, but I might tell ya later. Last February he was hit. Three months next Friday. What day is it now? Three or five months next Tuesday or Wednesday I'd say.

I always remember the first time I met Uncle Con. He wasn't there for the first load of years that I know. I think he was inside, I'd have to ask Cillian or my mother that. Well, I won't ask my mother, but Cillian would know anyway probably. We were messing on the street, me and Cillian. I'd say I was around five at the most and we pissed into an empty milk bottle. We had two bottles and he pissed in one and I had a piss in the other one. In them days the bottles were glass and you'd get your money back on them. We were after finding them outside someone's house, but after we threw out the milk we pissed into the bottles and pretended we were drinking out of them while we stood around. Any time someone passed, one of us would pretend to drink it like, and the other would say, Hey you want a sup of lime? We were going to say Club Lemon but there was no fizz in it, see.

Most people wouldn't go near it. Would you, like? But this was years ago. Anyone'd do anything. One fella passed by after a while and Cillian asks him if he wanted some. He was walking fast with a bag under his arm but he marched straight up and took a slug. I was going to say something, it was 'scusting to see him slug it, Ahahahahaah. But Cillian slapped my hand. He didn't drink the lot like, yer man, but he drank a lot of it, put it that way, and he didn't think it was too bad neither. He seemed thirsty and it did the trick. He gave a big, AAHHH! after he finished and looked at the bottle like he was going to ask it a question. We thought we'd get a chase off him then, but we hadn't a clue what to do instead. Next he handed the bottle back to Cillian and asks him straight out if we knew Tanya Collins and where she lived.

I was thinking he wanted to tell our mother about what we done cos that's our mother's name and I was going to give him a kick and run away or something, but Cillian cool as a cucumber tells him where she lived but that she's not there now. He was a big horse of a man even then. Head on him like a rhinoceros in a brown suit. Cob was his name. His name was Con, like, but that's what they called him: Cob. Cob Collins. They called him that, but I never did cos sometimes he'd be happy to be called it and another time he'd kill ya for saying the same thing. He goes to a fella one time why'dja call me Cob? And yer man goes he didn't know any other name for him and Con goes d'ya know what a cob is? And yer man goes no and Con tells him a cob is a traveller's horse is that what you think of me?

32

If you knew one thing about Con it was that he hated travellers nearly more than he hated benders. That fella who called him Cob that time was no good anyway. He wanted a big cut out of a job after he done nothing 'cept open the door. Before the stuff was even sold-on yer man came back calling him Cob and looking for his cut and Con had to put him straight. Later on that day there was a party and there was a big sing-song and another fella even sung a song that he wrote called Cob Collins. And Con was thrilled and everyone had a great night. Better to say nothing though and call him Con just in case. That's what I always done cos that was his name and he was family too, like.

His suit was full of wrinkles, that day anyway when he drank the piss and asked where was Tanya Collins. He stood there a minute kinda listening to the wind blowing, after Cillian told him she wasn't at home. He gave one look to Cillian like he was checking how far away he was, then faced back up the street. Ya gonna tell me where she fuckin is, he says like he was talking to the empty street. Or do I need to stand here any more?

We didn't know him, yet like, but he wasn't a cop and you wouldn't give him shit. We knew that much. We told him the name of the pub and he smiled and said thanks for the drink. That was the scariest part. His smile. His front teeth kinda poked out. One was dark brown and pointed in a different direction to the rest. It was like he was smiling in one way but his brown tooth was trying to leg it in the other direction at the same time. Every time I saw him smile after that I nearly shit a brick. It nearly always meant trouble. At least he didn't smile much.

We forgot about him after that and got a chase off the next fella who took the bottle. I handed him mine and he took a sniff off it and just before he drank it, Cillian goes, That's a bottle a piss ya steamer! And he flung his bottle at him and we both legged it, then. Yer man chased us up the road screaming at us but his pants was soaking. I remember us up the wall laughing at him. Nobber pissed his pants! Cillian shouted when people came out of the shop. That was some laugh. Bursted our arses laughing at him, we did. I'd say though we were doing him a favour and he never thought of it. We coulda let him drink the bottle of piss but we left him off. People never see the good things!

Later on we were at home. I'd say it was a few days later cos our mam was there and she would've been gone at least a week cos her buddy died a few days before and she was at his funeral. She was with Con, having a drink at the kitchen table, an' we getting up one morning. She goes, that's her brother Con, there lah. And he looks at us and laughed and says he knew us. He told her we gave him a bottle of piss the other day and he drank it and then he nearly hit the floor laughing. That's the thing, I'd say, – his laugh was funny. His smile was wicked but his laugh was funny, like he meant it.

I don't know how or when he knew it was piss, like, but he knew we caught him and he left us off. Or else he knew it beforehand and wanted us to owe him. You'd never know what Con was thinking. Always the opposite. Later he'd get us do a job and tell us that's how we could make up for making him drink piss, but in the kitchen we were having a party. We were welcoming Uncle Con home. We had to go out a few times to get more gatt during the day cos they kept finishing all the bottles and cans that were there, like. And more adults would call in all the time. They bought their own, like, but Con and my mother would let them have some of theirs first, then the new

34

people would pay for the rest of it. We got a few quid off it too for deliveries.

The first time, Con took me and Cillian to the off-licence so they'd know the gatt was for him next time. They tried telling him they wouldn't be able to serve us if he wasn't there, but he told them if we came here on our own anytime today then it was for him and they were to serve us or he'd have to come back all the way himself. He didn't even smash nothing, just asked them nice and they served us for years every time after that. Well most times anyway, depending who was on. If yer man with the glasses was on you'd get nothing off that fella and we'd push over a rake of bottles and run out with a six-pack or something. That was before CCTV and all the bigger rules. They're stricter these days. Kids today wouldn't get nothing off an Off Licence. That's better business for me too, Ahahahahaah, isn't that right?

That night though, the last few times coming back we were like the blackies in Africa carrying water on our heads, but we done it with gatt, see? Twenty four pack on the noggin and a bag in each hand. We were over and back all night.

Con gave Cillian a fag back at the party but only laughed when I asked for one too. He said I was too young to be smoking, but he left Cillian give me the ucks of it when my mother went to the jacks. Then I got a loan of a can off the table and when my mam caught me hiding with it she laughed and called everyone take a look. I was after spilling half it down my top they said.

He took us shopping next day, Con. Probably the next day, or thereabouts anyway. We brought Tara too, in the pram, like. Con wouldn't push it of course but Cillian didn't mind doing it when our mother had to wait outside the shop. We never needed no trolley or nothing when we were with Con. Just

35

load up the pram and walk on. Tara would be buried under a mountain of crap by the time we'd be home. We tried it without Con a few times but always got caught doing it that way. Con was the best at it. Nobody'd mess with him, but they didn't know what we knew – Con was soft really. We didn't know it then, like, but the softer part of him grew bigger the older he got. I was talking to my mam the other day on the phone and she told me he was a bender, but I find that hard to believe. Con like!? I'll never believe that long as I live. I mean he never felt me up or Cillian up or anything like that. Never tried to even. He was the biggest hardest man I ever seen. Years ago, like. Nobody'd mess with Con.

He always wore the same brown suit – or something like that. And a proper shirt under. He'd wear a tie with it at funerals or communions. I don't think he ever had a coat. It'd be lashing raining and I remember the water pouring off his head onto the shoulders of his suit like he never even knew the rain was there. That was Con. Not a bender. Couldn't be. If he turned gay I'd say it was Judge Judy what done it, turned him gay if anything. Had to be.

He'd thump the shit out of anyone who'd try to say something like that about him, though. He'd do it to a bender even! I was there myself in a pub with him one night when it happened one time. Saw it myself and it wasn't the only time either. We were sitting inside the pub, a gang of us like, (this was eight year ago at most I'd say) having a bit of craic when we heard the wall collapse in the jacks and the mirror and the whole place was smashed up by the time we got in. Con was in there and a fella tried to get a look off him and he smashed the whole place up. Yer man was rushed to hospital and Con was barred for at least a week but he had to do it when you think of it.

That same bender had kids an' all imagine! There was a chicken supper for him, after, to collect money to pay for some super-duper wheelchair for him. Top of the range electric shit. He was set for life – never had to work again or nothing. They called him Ironside after that. His wife didn't seem to mind he was a bender cos she stuck by him too in fairness. Con even went to the chicken supper to show there was no hard feelings and he took me with him. The wife nearly screamed the place down when she seen him and people were holding her back until Con, without saying a word to the woman, just shrugged and left. I was shocked. She was screaming as if it was Con was the queer and he didn't even deck her. I mean I never decked no woman myself, but nobody'd blame Con if he did that night. He was hard-out, Con. Looking back, that was probably the start of his softness, now I think about it. He left her off and everyone looking. I mean it was probably tough on yer wan to have a husband in a wheelchair who was a bender, but if anything, Con probably done her a favour when you look at it. She'da never known it otherwise. The gratitude of some people!

But that day shopping, we had a new uncle that we didn't even know about and he was treating us to everything. He always treated us great when he took us shopping. He even paid for ice creams an' all most days. Con was never as bad as he seemed to some people. We had the best of everything.

My mother always got us the good stuff – Adidas and shit – but even by then they knew her in Penneys, like, so we weren't in there a lot. Just with Stacey a few times, but she stuck around the bras mostly and you'd come out with just underpantses and vests. In there with Con back then, though, the place was like heaven! See something – pick it up, straight in the pram. Bang!

Even if you wouldn't wear it you'd make a few bob off it. I tell ya I'd wear the jocks and the socks from Penneys any day even now, but I won't wear the clothes.

That day we were upstairs at the front of the shop with the pram loaded up and Con lamped a few of the staff follying us around. They had no cameras but there was plain clothes detectives, like. We knew one fella and showed Con him when we walked in, but Con spotted two more when we were upstairs at the front with no easy way out. There was a woman who kept looking over the hats at us and another fella who pretended to be buying a kettle. They used sell kettles in there in them days. They don't anymore far's I know. Con taught us how to see them. The detectives. Can't say how, but you spot them no bother after a while even if you were never in a place. They were hopeless in them days too. They're better at it now like and they have the CCTV an' everything all over but at the time they'd be pretending to be shopping while they're lamping everything. It'd be funny after a while they're so obvious and wouldn't have a clue. Sometimes they didn't even care if you knew who they were! Those were the dangerous ones.

A fella one time follied myself and Cillian around Dunnes even before we got anything. As soon as we walked in, he walks everywhere we walked. Bold as brass he was. Brazen out treating us like criminals! We had to split up and he follied Cillian around and I only got a packet of vests cos I was still learning and I thought I'd have to hold it tight inside my coat with my two arms so I thought I couldn't carry anything more. My mother had tears laughing at me when I walked in home with my arms tight over my coat with my hands in my pockets. She opened my zip and the only thing in there was a packet of vests. She thought it was the funniest thing ever. Not worth the

38

shoe leather going all the way to town and coming home with a packet of vests, she tells me.

But Con gets a box of something. Cardboard box and puts it on top of the pram – when we're in Penneys that time I mean. I forget what was in the box, socks or something probably. He made-out like he was buying all the stuff in the box and he'd add a few more things on top of it all the time. It was a massive box! At the same time he got Cillian and me, one by one, to sneak a few things out from under the box, down the stairs and bring it around the corner to my mother while he kept them busy. He kept adding things to the box. When I got back, Cillian'd leave and it'd be my turn to push the pram around for a while. After a while we were down by the front door but there was nothing under the box 'cept Tara and her blanket.

Con picked up the box and pretended he was about to run out of the shop with it. All the detectives closed in on him like they were going to chase him once he left, but he made-out like he knew nothing. Then he put the box down on the ground, cool like. He complained to one of the detectives that the place was so busy he couldn't even get a chance to pay for stuff so he had to leave it all after him cos he had a meeting with his solicitor with regards to his neighbour whose hedge was growing onto his lawn. He'd say things like that, Con, to make it believable. You'd believe anything he'd tell ya. He said it like he was talking to another shopper and didn't know he was a detective, but he knew alright. He was sharp-out and had yer man fooled. Then he walked out the door and they were looking at the box, then they were looking at him. They could see he had nothing on him, like. Well probably nothing. Cillian and me were already after

39

leaving with the pram and two detectives ran after us then when they saw what Con done and stopped us in the street.

Here! You can't molest young childern that way! Con shouts when they tried taking the pram off Cillian to turn it back inside. They were shouting back something else and Con says he saw it all and they were trying to kidnap these helpless kids and he was in the middle of accusing them when my mother jumps on. She had two and a half black plastic bags full of the stuff we just got and started screaming at the detectives. Are you the mother of these childern? shouts Con. (*He used say childern instead of children.*) I saw it all! he says, This two were trying to molest them in the street!

Well my mother was mad-out and let them know it. Later-on she sued them and got a few bob for it too, far's I know. Who knows what they would've done if they got us back inside, filthy bastards.

We thought the pram was empty too, but when we got home, a load of clothes fell out from the pouch under Tara's feet. What a laugh we had when we saw all that. Party time!

Stacey

S tacey minded us most of the time for years. Or if she was out with my mother, Mary down the road would take us. She had her own kids, Mary like, but they were older than us and her husband would be around sometimes. He was like a cop asking us questions, that fella, but we'd be wide of him. Mary was alright though. She was like a real person. My mam would say any chance you could mind the boys I have to go to a funeral? And Mary'd be delighted to take us. She'd feed us even and keep us in the house long as she could. She wanted us to stay indoors even and not be running around outside, she said.

She told us one time sit down cos she wanted to read us a story. Some boring shit about a sad boy. He was sad alright. Cillian and me were jumping on the settee when she was reading it, but she carried on as if we were listening. Didn't even stop us jumping or nothing. When she was finished she asked what bad thing the boy done. I wasn't listening but I told her what he done (can't even remember now what I told her). She was shocked though. She asked how come he done that. I told her, Cos Cillian's dad went to prison and he had to break out so the boy helped him smash everything and beat them all up and when Cillian saw his dad was out he forgot all about the boy who helped his dad and he went away with his dad and the boy had to do it all on his own then after that.

It wasn't true, like, any of it. Cillian and me have the same dad, ask anyone, and he's not in prison. Never was, far's I know.

41

I don't know where the story I made up came from, but Mary was delighted with it. After that, for years seemed like, she kept asking me for stories and I'd tell her. Cillian used to laugh an' I telling them. Then he'd call me a fool and say the opposite, but Mary was delighted with that too and wrote it all down. One time I told my mother I told Mary something, and my mother was raging. And she was raging more then when Cillian goes, An' she wrote it down too!

My mother goes are you a grass or what, just like that and stormed out the door. It was like, late at night and I was after falling asleep and waking up and it was still dark when I told her during the party – my mam was having a party, like, that night when I told her.

I said it cos she was telling everyone the same thing like what I said to Mary that day and they were all having a laugh off it. And I remembered saying it an' I was laughing too, so I goes, I told Mary that too!

Straight away she was mad-out but didn't hit me or nothing but then Cillian told her, And Mary wrote it down an' all!

And my mother bolted out the door and said, Are you a grass or what? she goes an' she going. And she didn't come back for ages and half the party left to see what she'd do and I smashed a glass off the table then and went to sleep again cos I was mad that she called me a grass, 'specially over-right all her friends.

Next day Mary knocks on the door with her husband and we opened it and she asks if our mother was in and I said she was in bed and she said she was sorry for asking us questions and she gave us all of her pages and said she wouldn't ask us no more questions but we could still come to her house if our mam was at a funeral and if she left us come. Her husband walks over to say something then but Cillian took the pages and shut the door and we went in for a cuddle with our mother. She wasn't mad at me no more. Cillian was on one side and she put her arm around me on the other side. When he gave her the pages she goes, Who was at the door, Murder She Wrote?

That's what we called Mary after that: Murder She Wrote.

•

But Stacey was my mam's friend, who my mam minded and helped for years. She was mad, Stacey was. Off her head worse than my mother most of the time. I mean you could talk to my mam sometimes and she'd talk straight with you. Even now she'd be like that most of the time.

But Stacey would forget things. That must be twenty year ago, like and she'd be like that. Only the angels know what she must be like now. Or the doctors probably, Ahahahahaah.

I was in the hospital myself lately for a few weeks. Was checked in after I got out – *before* I got out really but I was still in the hospital when I got out. I was in there a while cos I'm not right myself sometimes, but Cillian visited me anyway and he's all posh now and goes look at yer wan over there, lah. And I looked over and it was an old wan with black hair that was all grey. Her face was all sunk like she sucked the dregs out of a fag and kept going. She was walking around the corridor with her arms folded in a pink dressing-gown blabbing away to herself. I hadn't a clue who she was.

That's Stacey, Cillian goes. And we were both shocked but I said that's not Stacey, Stacey's a blondie. This mad woman

43

was around ninety, I'd say – much older than my mam. Wasn't Stacey at all. No way, couldn't've been. Cillian goes it's her alright and he called and waved at her but I told him my mam would have her killed if it was her and he forgot about that so he stopped waving. Yer wan didn't even see us anyway or anyone else. Away in her own world she was. Nothing new about that for Stacey. I'd say it wasn't her though.

Still, makes you think…

Stacey'd be talking about one thing, back donkeys' years, and then she'd be talking about a different thing at the same time and she'd be after forgetting the first thing like it wasn't there and you'd go what about the other thing she'd be like what are you on about? This was all the time. She'd take you to town for apples and ye might end up on the bus to Youghal and she'd be calling your mam to pick us up cos her fake bus pass got robbed by the inspector and they threw us off at Midleton and called the guards but my mother wouldn't have no lift cos she doesn't drive and Stacey would tell the guards drop us back and my mother would tell her don't forget the apples on the way and the shades would stop for apples but Stacey'd be after forgetting them again and say she got no money and the shades would buy the apples and give me one and I'd be eating mine when they got to the door and my mother pelted the shades with them cos they got green ones instead of red ones and I'd take a last bite out of mine and hit the back of the squad car with the ucks.

That's how Stacey was. She'd be doing the gonge all the time. During the day, like for a chill. Later on she'd be taking her medicine, but during the daytime back then she'd be chillin' on the gonge. You'd see her without it sometimes and she'd be up to ninety screaming and roaring worse than us. Saw her one or two times getting blood off her wrist with a spoon. My mam mostly hid the sharp things under the bed in case she had to fight anyone so Stacey used spoons to cut herself and one time or usually like, my mother would give her a clatter and get her the gonge and light up for her. To calm her nerves, like. She'd look after ya that way, my mam.

Stacey'd be chill after that and she'd take us to the park if there was a funeral on or something. We were at the park all day one time an' Stacey looking-after us. Well she was minding Melanie mainly – she was in the pram. Later on we were back at home and I was having a sangwitch and my mother goes where's Stacey and Melanie? And we goes back to the park and Stacey was still there on the seat minding us even though we were gone home. Tara was gone home too with me and Cillian. Melanie was in the pram in the dark, cool-out with Stacey. Jordan-SueAnne wasn't born yet that time. Your arse would break from laughing at this shit.

Mostly my mother would mind Stacey and Stacey minded us. Unless they had a job on without us or if they were on the batter and we didn't want to stay in the pub with them the whole time or if there was a scatter and they had to escape or something. They'd leg it together then. They done everything together: Booze, drugs, men, you name it. Stacey'd ride all round her but she never got pregnant. That's why she lived at home with Mrs. O'Connor at that time, but mostly she lived in our house. A fella might call to the door sometimes and Stacey'd go, Why don't ye go out and play? And we'd go, OK. And Cillian'd put Tara in the pram and we'd go out and then come back in and we'd have a laugh listening to Stacey and yer man in the bedroom having it off. After yer man would go away Stacey'd say not to say to our mam that she used the bed and she'd give us a fiver and we'd keep it a secret until there was a fight. And sometimes it'd be Cillian, but mostly it'd be me who'd tell on Stacey, alright. Not on purpose, like, but it'd come out cos Cillian might be hitting me or Stacey might say you can't finish all the Corn Flakes or my mam was being all cuddles. Then my mam would kill her and after Stacey paid her for the bed and they made up, she'd make her promise not to be bringing men back to the house no more and using the bed like that, over-right the children.

Con called one time when Stacey was at it and he was shocked. Busted down the door cos he forgot how to open it with the shock and thumped yer man for what he done and Stacey ran down the road with nothing on and we all chased her all the way, laughing til she got home and when we got back, yer man was screaming and after a while Con dragged him out by one leg and his langer flying all over the place and he flung him out the front door and he staggered away and we started running behind him too for a laugh but it wasn't as fun cos he was moving slower and bleeding all over and it looked like he was bleeding down the back of his leg even, so we went home and Con was throwing his clothes out the back window after checking his pockets to pay for the damage. Cillian goes you gave him a good batin' there Con. And Con goes, Shoved a stick up his arse too he won't be back raping no one soon dirty bastard! And we all broke out laughing. Con could be sound-out in fairness. He'd stick up for you when you wouldn't even be expecting it. I never even seen him speak with Stacey when you think of it, but he looked after her, alright like.

On Our Holidays

It was in the paper an' all about the fire in the quarry that burnt down. There was a big colour picture of the massive flames on the cover of The Echo with all the people looking on and you can see the back of Cillian's head an' all in the photograph, down on the righthand side, like. You can't see me but I was standing next to him at the time. My mam sent Stacey into the Examiner office to get a copy of the photograph and they wanted twenty quid at least for it and my mam had to go down herself and set them straight that it was her son in the photo and he gave no rights to be on the front of the paper, selling their paper for them and she got no royalties and now they wanted to even charge her money for a photo of her own son that she never asked for. And I was with her and we were told come into a back room away from the public but my mother knew her rights and refused to go to no room until the manager with a baldy head on him came down to her and gave her a photo that was page-size of the same photo that was in the paper and then we left. You have to stand up to these people or you'd be walked all over.

When we got home, she put the photo on the table where Con was after spilling his drink and he kilt her for spoiling the photograph, but it was mostly alright later on after it dried. She asks us then for the first time when she was picking up the wet photograph if it was us who lit the fire and we said no it wasn't us at all and she knew we were telling the truth.

47

The sad part of the story though is that we left the dagger at the bottom of the quarry, but my mam didn't know it was gone for ages. It wasn't news or nothing. No one in the paper said it was there. We were after using it getting the box opened and Cillian put it down when we were lighting-up and we were at the top of the quarry before he remembered it and by then it was too late so we left it there, like. We didn't need the holster for it no more either so he tossed that too before we were around with the crowds.

Thing is though, we didn't know it was worth millions, probably. At least a thousand pound anyway I'd say. It was Michael Collins' Scian, the paper said a bit later. He's world famous for saving Ireland. It was stoled out of Fitzgerald Park Museum the week before the fire, but my mother told us the real story and they left that one out too. Lying bastards were already after stealing it from my family cos Michael Collins was my mother's dad's uncle and he gave it to him when he was dying and told him keep it always under your bed in case you got attacked. An' only we needed it for the door that's where it would've stayed too. They took it off my grandad when he got arrested that time and when he got out they robbed it and never gave it back to him and she only collected it back the week before and it was gone again now straight away. That's why I'm called Michael, she told me then: In the memory of your grandfather.

Since then there was always a Michael Collins in the family. He was the bravest soldier who ever fought for Ireland and won us a bit of peace.

She kilt us when she couldn't find the dagger and then someone told her it was in the paper about a week later when it was given back to the museum and they said it was found in the quarry that time. And she knew then it was us what was in the

48

quarry that night and she asked us what we got and she wouldn't believe us we got nothing out of the place and kicked us out til Cillian found a big rocker and we lifted it back to the house with a wheelbarrow we found and dumped it at the front door and the rock broke the door a bit and my mam had a canary and goes what are ye doing? And Cillian goes we got that in the quarry and she starts bursting laughing and we were left back in then.

The paper couldn't figure out how Michael Collins' Scian got in the quarry either though, on the same night the fire burnt the main building down causing a hundred thousand pound worth of damage. It was pounds in them days before the euros. No way was it a hundred grand though when you think of it. Especially back then. There was only a big room – two rooms – up at the top of a big tall stairs and there was nothing in it. Insurance job I'd say. They're all at it.

Con was around the next day, around. This was around a week or two or maybe more after the fire I think and he took us all on a holiday in a car he brought and we drove to Limerick and every pub we stopped in on the way had a pool table and me and Cillian had a great laugh all the way up. In one place Con played a fella for money in pool and the fella won and Con gave him twenty quid and goes I'd say you think you're shit-hot at darts an' all and yer man plays him in Shanghai and beats him at the darts too and Con is getting really mad, you could tell it and the fella goes to the jacks and comes back and says he was sorry he didn't mean it but he wants to play doubles or quits to give Con another chance and Con said no I'll play ya for a hundred notes, so they had one game of poker for a hundred notes and Con had Ace-High and me and Cillian were standing behind yer man and he would've beat Con too 'cept he hadn't a clue how to play cos he burnt a Ten, a King and an Ace (and he already had another Ten). And he didn't let anyone see what he got next, cos he thought he was so good at it. But Con's Ace-High bate him in the end and yer man tossed his cards into the deck and handed over the money while Con's brown tooth was pointing at the bar. But just when he was taking it off yer man, he locked onto his hand and had an idea. Con kept hold of the man's hand with the money in it and turned over the cards at the top of the pile to see that fella had Ten, Seven, Jack, Five and Seven! And Con is in a shock.

What does that mean!? He goes to yer man who's in a shock too. Sure you had a pair of sevens so you must've won it, didja? And Con's tooth tucks in, cos he thought he was being tricked, but yer man goes, No, it's not like that – this was my card and it got mixed-up when I threw them in. And he turned over another one fast and it was an Ace. And then he goes, No it wasn't that one either..

But Con seen that his own Ace-Queen beat yer man's Ace-Jack anyway, so he left him off and took the money off him, cos Con'd be very fair about things like that. You thought you had me didn't ya? he smiled again, but his tooth wasn't showing this time. And yer man said well done to him and ran off like a coward. Then Con brought my mother and Stacey a drink and himself a drink and he got a Coke and Taytos for me and Cillian out of it too. He was some card shark, Con.

The girls were after being robbed off the government by that time so they weren't on the holiday. They were living in other places. Other houses mostly by then. Jordan-SueAnne wasn't born then either.

Con goes, later on then, we're on our holidays til the smoke blows over and I goes OK cos I was after seeing the smoke still coming off the building when the fire brigade was done and it lit up again a few days later (wasn't us at all that time, like) and I thought that's what Con was on about. Then my mother goes thanks Con for protecting my boys and he goes, I protect those childern like they're my own and I'll get those others back for you too, true as God, and I won't see you go down for no museum robbery too.

I was surprised to hear that bit and my mother laughed at it and said we were mostly on holidays cos the boys needed to escape but we found out later off Stacey that the cops were onto the two of them already about the museum and they were trying to pin it on them cos they had no one else to blame for it and mostly the museum stuff they got was a load of crap too that was good for nothing anyway. But Con goes there'll be none of ye do time cos I'm taking ye on holidays instead.

We were already in the hotel we were going to be staying in when he said that. In the bar, like.

After that we checked in and there was a bath and a shower too in the room where Con and me and Cillian was staying and we had our own TV. Con wasn't there til late, like, cos the pub was still opened and the two of us ordered a hamburger and chicken nuggets and two Cokes on the white telephone and they brought it up to us an' all and we were out on the balcony an' everything. And Cillian got different people on the ground with the chicken nuggets and we got locked out there by accident but we were having a laugh so we didn't care.

All the nuggets was long-gone and we were still outside and Cillian was climbing over the bars to make a jump to the other room when Con comes into the room and opened the balcony door and kind of whisper-shouted at us come in out of it and he caught us and flung us back into the room, onto the bed. Cillian would've made it too to the other balcony. I would've too after him, but we forgot about it. There was another man there too with Con in a uniform who we didn't know, standing by the door. Con said he was scarlet embarrassed cos the manager told him there was childern in their room throwing chicken nuggets down and he didn't think it was his boys a tall, but now he knew it was the two of us who done it and it was a terrible thing to see it. And Cillian said we only went out to view the view and a seagull robbed a chicken nugget and dropped it and the manager goes loads of people came into the hotel to say we thrun the chicken nuggets deliberately and we said we didn't and he said we did and Con was like the judge and goes, Hold it a while now, let's get this straight now first – first of all, where did these chicken nuggets come from?

And we told him and Con was stunned and the manager was waiting til Con gave out to him about supplying us with chicken nuggets so late after dark and no wonder we were all sugared-up and couldn't even sleep and who was supposed to be paying for these things anyway? Con had good experience how to judge like a judge and he was good at it too, like. He made the manager give us the nuggets for free and the hamburger and Cokes too cos no way should they be supplying stuff like that to "childern" (Ahahahahaah!), he says, and blaming them on top of it too for what their Limerick seagulls'd be doing.

After the manager went away we gave Con a big cheer and he gave us both a flaking and said he was scarlet embarrassed and couldn't even enjoy his drink in peace and our mam and Stacey had to run off when the manager told them there was chicken nuggets being thrown, they were so embarrassed and they won't be back now til late.

When he went back to the pub, me and Cillian ran around the corridors playing hide and go seek and up and down the lifts and we got locked out and Cillian went down to the bar to get the key off Con and he was scarlet embarrassed again inside the bar, over-right his new friends and told Cillian get a key at the desk cos he won't be able to get in later-on otherwise, so Cillian ordered another key and they gave it to him too.

After we went back to the room, we done chasing more and on the top floor of the hotel I found another lift at the back and I called Cillian and the lift went up just one more floor to a massive room that had a big view of everything. There was no one around the whole place. It was empty, like, but there was plenty of stuff around including a massive bed and a full bar with gatt and everything and there was free bath robes and slippers and silver ash trays. And then we found the swimming pool and we couldn't believe it. In the bathroom! A swimming pool, like! Up on the top floor in the hotel and no one there and we discovered it! It had a bubble machine and everything.

We were swimming in it for hours but it was freezing cold and there was a stink off it. Con said it was chlorine next day when we told him about the pool. He said we were stinking of it and made us show him where it came from and he told us it wasn't a swimming pool at all, it was a jacuzzi. He got a load of stuff there and bottles of whiskey too. They were all small doonchy ones, about a hundred of them and we helped him bring it all back down to our room. Then he banged on the door of my mam and Stacey's room and when Stacey opened the door he walks in and there was another fella inside and my mam goes

Jarlath couldn't get a lift home so he had to stay in our room and Con goes I'm pleased to meet you Jarlath did you have a good night. And Jarlath didn't say much and my mother goes Jarlath had a very good night and they all enjoyed themselves at the disco. And Con told her the manager was giving out last night regarding chicken nuggets of all things, but we cleared it up after a while.

Could you imagine, Jarlath? he goes, And myself below pouring money behind the counter!

And they carried on talking a while and the word Jarlath was in nearly everything they said and me and Cillian couldn't stop laughing every time someone said it, like. It was Con said it the most I'd say.

Then Con goes he only came in to tell her her childern had to be scrubbed and if Jarlath wouldn't mind he'll borrow his sister and ask her to tend to this matter. Jarlath didn't mind. He said he was just leaving anyway and Con gave him a good clap on the back to let him know he was alright.

Then when my mother was bringing me and Cillian back to our room I heard Con tell Jarlath how expensive it was to stay in this hotel and I knew then Con was rich to be treating us all on this holiday and I asked my mam how rich was Con and she said he was very good to us all. And he was. Always in fairness. We were lucky Con was our uncle. Before he died, like.

There was a phonecall, anyway, from the front desk an' we getting dressed after our shower. Con got my mam to answer it cos they kept ringing back when we didn't answer and she said we were coming down shortly to them. We were supposed to check out at twelve o'clock they told her and it was now half-past four. Some people don't half be getting their knickers in a twist don't they? They upset Con an' all, they were complaining so much. He was only giving us a holiday and he had to be listening to all that. When the phonecall was over he gave out to my mam for delaying us and said we need to hurry on so she went back to her and Stacey's room to clear out stuff and we helped Con load up the car in the carpark.

It was a big estate he got and room for dogs an all in the back. He didn't have dogs with him on that holiday though and before we put anything in the boot he opened a trapdoor and there was a wood shoebox inside and he goes to Cillian hold that and Con and me packed up the car. We left that box up in the room when we went back down and packed up more stuff and then we packed up my mam and Stacey's stuff. We had a load of more stuff an' we leaving, but we fitted it all in. It was really the best hotel I ever stayed in, long as I live. That's as true as God. The best hotel.

We went back to our room and Con tells Cillian open the box and Cillian opened it and screams, Jesus Christ! and flings the whole box in the air and a rat flies in the air too and hits the ground and Con was shocked that the rat was dead. He said he must've had a heart attack cos he was alive only yesterday, he says. Then Con flung the box over the balcony, didn't even look or nothing, and said we'd have to do a change of plan. He picked the dead rat up and jammed him down the back of the hot rad til only his tail was sticking out, then he called my mother and told her get the manager up and she did and he told him he felt choking all night cos there was a bad smell in the room and he couldn't figure out what 'twas and it wasn't healthy for childern to be breathing that in and it was only after we packing everything up we discovered this dead rat body was behind the rad an' we breathing it all in the whole time. And the manager said the rat wasn't there when he was up here last night and Con says that's even worse if the rat was alive and died while we were all sleeping in our beds. And then my mother joined in and gave the manager stink over it too.

Stacey took me and Cillian to wait in the car after a while and after a while my mam and Con got back and we drove on, on our holidays. We done all the West Coast that time – we were up as far even as Galway and stayed with our Galway cousins for two nights. My mam had a fight with her aunty Nora though when Nora accused her of stealing her money years and years ago and Con didn't like the look off the fella his cousin Julie married while he was away, so we went back down to Tralee before there was a scatter, and after a few days, onto Killarney even. We stayed the longest in Killarney and Con made friends with a gang of yanks and he sung them songs and we stayed in the bar all night and they all cheered Con on and he drove them on a bus up the mountains next day and we all went too and they all gave Con loads, but when we got back with the bus, a busman who was mad-out was waiting and Con had to have a word with him and he paid him for the petrol, like an' all. He made a good few bob off the yanks too, like. Con knew how to do business, I tell ya. It was some holiday in fairness!

As good as that was though, after ages away, it's always better to be back in Cork, don't you think? I mean, there's nowhere like it really is there? Where else would ya get it, sure?

We were back only an hour at most I'd say and the door that was already a bit broke, got smashed in by the cops and Con flung his can in the air with the fright the same way Cillian flung the dead rat. Me and Cillian hopped out the back window before we knew they weren't chasing after us at all and we went around to the front door to batter them if they were taking away our mam but they were still inside and there was around ten of them on top of Con, who was on the ground and he still had the better of them and they couldn't cuff him until a big sergeant strolls in with a big truncheon and knocks him out with around three or four hard blows to the head. Then they cuffed him and they had to call another Paddy Wagon full of cops to be able to cart him off in the Paddy Wagon like a giant dead animal.

They said he was being done for theft of salt and batteries. That's what I thought my mother was telling me and I thought they were catching him in a trick cos why would Con steal a load of salt and batteries? But I know now it was Theft and Assault and Battery but I didn't know it at that time, like. He was accused of beating up the manager in a shop, we found out later, and they pinned some robbery on him too. The manager was a liar Con knew who owed him money, but the shades were waiting for him to get back to Cork so they could arrest him anyway. He never done it but they were waiting to blame him soon as he got back after our holidays.

Later that night me and Cillian went to town and we were mad-out at the way Con was treated. They wouldn't treat no fella who wore a suit and stole a million pound that way, Cillian says and I goes yeah. Then Cillian smashed the window of a car with a brick and we didn't even try to get anything out of it. I got stones and battered them at parked cars and made holes in some of the glass til there was a load of alarms going off and we legged it. And we done other stuff I can't remember and then we saw a fella who looked around Cillian's age walking around in town in the dark with a beor and she had a long coat on like she was posh and they were holding hands and Cillian pulled on yer man's shoulder and goes could you give me a loan of 20p to make a phonecall and yer man goes no and tries to walk-on without looking and Cillian asks him if he even has 20p and yer man goes yes and Cillian says why don't you give it to me so, I have to make a phonecall and yer man, brazen-out, goes he didn't want to and then I jumped on his back and he staggered off the footpath and fell over and I was thumping him. And his ou' doll was screaming and I was just about to thump him in the face when yer man looks at me and goes, Hey don't ya remember me? he goes. I met you fishing!

I was never fishing, I tells him and gave him a smaller thump, but I wasn't sure. Yeah, he goes, And we cut up the fish with your brother's knife!

Oh yeah I remember you! I says and I laughed. What were the chances we'd be beating up him of all the people? He was alright, that fella. He was the one who caught the fish that day. You were alright, I told him. You chopped up your own bit! I remembered. He looked older at this time but he was probably older that time too or Cillian'd of never given him a chance on the dagger.

That's right, he goes and I stood up and put out my hand for him but when I was pulling him up Cillian ran over and gave him a dig right in the eyeball and I swear I saw it burst and there was the same pop sound that was made when Cillian popped the fish's eyeball with the back of the blade, only louder. And yer wan was screaming non-stop. I was kinda frozen myself cos there was blood and I didn't expect to see it, but yer man hit the ground and Cillian goes, You never saw the two of us nowhere and we're not even brothers anyway and I don't even know what's the dagger you're referring to!

We legged it away and yer man was screaming on the ground and yer wan was screaming in the long coat worse and I wasn't feeling right after we stopped running, so we went home and we didn't say much but Cillian asked every now and again if I was alright and I didn't say anything to him and we were lying down and he goes what's wrong and I said, Naw'hin. And after a while he kept asking and I didn't know how to say it. He was after saying to that fella we weren't brothers and I knew he only said it so he wouldn't know we were brothers, but it made me funny to hear Cillian say it and I kinda felt dizzy and far away, like. We are brothers, like, and it made me sad even if it wasn't true when he said it. Cillian'd of only laughed and made a laugh off it if I told him what it was, so I said there was nothing and after a long while when the room was dark and all quiet, Cillian goes, You know I only made up to yer man about us not being brothers? And I said I do and then we went to sleep.

Next day there was around four cops at the door and Stacey ran in while my mam was keeping them busy and Stacey goes, Get out the window they're here for ye this time! So we both jumped out in our underpantses and there was cops outside too and this time they were there for us and they nabbed us straight away like. Cillian got over the fence and down the road a bit alright, but one shade was fast out and he caught him and brought him back. And there was a few Bean Gardaí there too cos we were juveniles and they had to go easy on us a bit. My mother made sure they knew that too, in fairness.

Yer man with the eyeball did know us and he knew we were brothers and he even knew our names. His mam and dad reported it to the police when Cillian burst his eyeball, not him. And when the cops heard we had a dagger and that we were there that day at the river and that that's how yer man knew us, they knew then it was us who had Michael Collins' knife and it was us who burnt down the building, accidentally like.

In a funny way I felt better when I was being questioned cos the guard goes to me yer man knew ye were brothers and he knew yere surname was Collins, although it was his parents who squelt on ye, like, not him at all. And I was like, yeah?

So he never thought we weren't brothers at all and I got mad cos I was feeling happy and I told the guard the knife belonged to us anyway cos Michael Collins was my grandfather and he gave it to my grandfather (I got confused, like) and the guard laughed and said I was full of shit. He goes did your mother tell you that and I goes what of it. Then the fella who was with me there in a suit, my solicitor like, tells the guard go easy on me or something and they stops and that's all I remember about that.

Foxy Bill

That night we were sent down to a home like a prison. It was a house, like, but not for families. There was a foxy fella working there with a big beard on him. He'd scare the hell out of you if you saw him in a dark room, but he wasn't the worst of them in fairness, he was alright. He asks us if we were fed and we were, but Cillian goes no we weren't so he gave us our dinner again. The poppies were massive! Yer man made them an' all himself. I never seen a fella cook food before. Not proper stuff like. His name was Bill. He didn't talk much, only wrote down when we did anything, but he spoke soft, like, and didn't shout or nothing and when Cillian asked him for a fag he gave him one an' all.

Everyone had their own separate room in the place, so I wasn't allowed stay with my brother. His room was across the hall. There was a phonecall down below after we got to our rooms and it was our mother. Cillian got there first and says hello and she's talking to him and he goes no, yes, alright, alright, yes, alright. Like that, he was talking and nodding and then he goes alright and hands me the phone. Did ya say anything about the museum, she goes to me when I said hello. No, I told her, They stopped asking me stuff when I told them Michael Collins was my grandfather cos they were a scared of me then I'd say. She goes you're a stupid shit for talking about that and I goes the cop said that too. I said that so she'd shut up cos I thought she wouldn't like to be agreeing with no shade, but she didn't shut up.

She goes don't mention the museum and don't tell them it was her what done it cos she didn't even do it and she never even seen no dagger. If they ask where ye got the dagger, she goes to me, tell them ye found it by the river – or … she gives me a rake of stuff to remember and I goes yeah yeah alright ok alright. But like how am I supposed to know all that really? I'm not thick, like. I knew what not to talk about to the cops even then. Well mostly. And I didn't hear anything more she was on about but I stayed on until she said put Cillian back on and I did and he was going yeah alright, yeah yeah and I went back up to my room. The Foxy fella was at the end of the hall, not listening like I don't think, but he started writing down when I went back upstairs.

See, until I said about Michael Collins they didn't ask if we stole the dagger from the museum. They were only questioning me about the fella we bate up. They were going alright, Where'd ye get the dagger? But they were waiting for me to say where first. When I said Michael Collins, yer man with me got me to stop and that was it.

Next day *I* was, only, taken back to the Bridewell. Not Cillian. There was a different Guard there and a woman and my solicitor and a Bean Garda too who looked like Pretty Woman in the movie. She was alright, like.

She did most of the questions at the start, the Bean Garda. She asked me a load of the same stuff as the day before, about the batin' we gave yer man mostly, but then she goes where did we meet yer man before and I said I didn't never meet him and she goes ye did and your brother had a knife where did he

62

get it? I said he found it like by the river and she goes was it a good knife? And I lashed into telling her all about the knife and how it cut the fish. And she goes where did ye leave the knife after? An' I remembered I was tricked into telling then so I said nothing more about that and she goes were you ever up the park and I says yeah and she goes did ye get the knife in the museum up there and it all goes on and on like that for ages and they were saying me and Cillian robbed the knife off the museum and I told them no we didn't and the other garda who was a man started asking questions then and making me all confused and I think I was saying we got the knife under my mam's bed after a while, but I didn't know what I was saying like. It was just cos they were saying we done it – the robbery in the museum, but I knew we didn't, like and I kept forgetting what I was supposed to say or not.

And then after a while they brought me back to the house with Foxy Bill and he gave me more dinner and even said I could have a fag. And he wrote down what I ate and I asked him if he wrote down that he gave me a fag and he goes no and I goes what if I squelt on him about it and he goes nobody'd believe me and even if they did, nobody'd care. And I knew that it was true and Bill knew it too, but he didn't mean it bad, like. We kind've had a smile at it, both of us, and I said they're all full of shit and Bill laughed soft and said, Ain't that the truth!

There's a difference, see? Some people'd be full of crap and they pretend like their shit smells of Lynx. Other people just don't give a damn cos they know everyone else is full of it and I knew Bill was like that. We both knew it, like.

63

One time me and Cillian used be going to this place out the country. Years before that, like, most weekends when we was young. I'd say I was around four at the most. Or six, like. A car would come and pick us up. Think it was a social worker. And she'd take us to this house like, out the country for the weekend. And it was an old biddy's house and her husband. Madge was her name and I can't remember his name, but he never said much to us anyway 'cept carry them bags over to there and get two buckets of coal and go on away out now and play with the buses.

And Madge would be all smiles to the social worker and nodding away at the instructions about what type of food we'd like and how to wash our clothes so they'd be fresh when we go home, cos our mother never washes anything (the social worker was telling Madge all this, over-right us). And Madge was smiling and nodding and being all nice. And as soon as the social worker'd be gone Madge's smile would be gone and she'd go, Fuck off out now, come back at six for ye're dinner. She'd go all red an' she saying it, like she didn't say fuck often enough, but she'd tell it to us alright.

Me and Cillian'd be happy-out to be free out the country and the fields were massive and we got a jockey off a cow one time and a chase off a farmer plenty of times. And Cillian joined the soccer team out there, cos we were around for most of the matches at the weekends and he was brilliant at it and if anyone'd tackle him bad like he'd take them out no bother next time and mostly he'd get sent off cos the ref would have it in for him cos they'd say I know who ye are and ye can't come out here with that gurrier attitude and I'd tell him fuck off and we'd be both sent off, even though I wasn't even playing cos I was too young anyway. And Madge, who wouldn't even be there would tell the social worker that Cillian got fired off the team again. But Cillian was their best player, like, so next time, or the time after that, he'd be left back on but he'd be on his last warning. And I'd be waiting to join the team too when I'd be older, cos I was a better soccer player even than Cillian, me. But when I got old enough we weren't calling to Madge's anymore.

But that time, when we was going there like, if we were back at six o'clock Madge would cook us sausages for our dinner. We both liked sausages and Madge did great ones always. We both liked poppies too but we'd only get those on a Sunday with our sausages before we went home. Anyway, after dinner she might say we could watch telly til 8 o'clock or 9 o'clock if there was something on and then we'd have to go to bed. If we did all of that, she'd write it down. If one of us didn't do something, she'd write that down. If Cillian asked for a biscuit, she'd say no and write that down. Or sometimes she'd say yes, like and give us a Rich Tea or two Mariettas between us. Then she'd write that she gave us a treat. She'd have a packet of Chocolate Biscuits too, like, when we'd be watching a movie, but they'd only be for her or for her husband, like. She wouldn't be bothered writing that.

Foxy Bill was the opposite to Madge. He pretended to be shitty but he was alright. He still wrote everything down, like, cos that's his job.

Madge was told wash our clothes before we went back, but she only brushed them with a wet sponge all the time before the social worker would come and we'd be standing out at the front door. One time on the way home like Cillian told the social worker that our clothes weren't washed and she looked at them when Cillian showed her the dirt and she goes, You probably

65

dirtied it since, but it don't matter anyway. And when we got home the social worker goes to our mother, I think they might be getting fed up calling to Madge. And my mother goes they don't know what's good for them. We weren't fed-up mostly, like, just she wouldn't be the nicest most days and there wasn't a load to do out there all the time, but it was good too, though, to be there sometimes.

Just, well I didn't care myself like if we never went out there, but I knew Cillian did want to be, so he goes, No we're not fed up at all! (He said that like he meant it. And he did mean it too.) And my mam goes, Well ask if you can still go so. And the social worker stood there waiting for Cillian to ask and he did. And my mother goes, Say please! And Cillian said please and the social worker goes to my mother yes of course they can still go if you consent to it. And my mother hit Cillian on the back of the head and told him piss off now and behave. Then the social worker left.

Cillian wasn't anywhere around, that night when I got back to Bill. I was after asking him where was Cillian and Bill said he'll be back tomorrow. That's when I had my dinner, after that and smoked a fag too with Bill and then I walked around into the front room where there was a telly that I could've watched if I wanted to an' all, but it was broke.

After a while two other shades brought another fella into the house. And yer man who was cuffed to one of them started screaming and kicking everything and kicked the shade and spat at Bill and goes to me when I looked down the hall, What are you looking at ya fucking prick!

I said nothing to him cos he was mad-out. The other guard told me go on away to your room and I just goes up, like

66

that, and I heard that fella screaming and shouting all night after they locked him up. His room was locked but me and Cillian didn't have locks on our doors cos we agreed not to try to run away and we didn't neither. Well Cillian wasn't there that night but on the night he was, he didn't.

Then another fella in another room who I never seen starts shouting at the other fella to shut up and the two of them had a big fight for hours and they couldn't even see each other. I'd say the other fella's room was locked too.

The two guards were gone away by then an' the two fellas kept on and on. Bill never said nothing to them but I was betting he was down in the kitchen writing down that they were fighting and he might've been writing what they were saying to each other an' all even, but it was all total shit. Even I knew that and Bill even knew it too.

It wasn't my first time being locked up, like, but it was my first time being locked up two nights and I was never in this house before and it wasn't the worst of them. Bill was alright at least. I met him a few times in there later on, like, Bill. And I met him in the pub one time years after. I thought he knew me and I was speaking with him and he was talking away and he was still alright, but when I thought about it after I knew he didn't remember me at all and didn't give a shit who I was anyway and you know what? He was dead-right too!

Usually my mother would get me out of wherever the cops would have me locked up – or at least be around, off and on, giving out to them. On the phone even she'd be giving out to them and she'd call me loads of times. This time she kept away and didn't call no more.

She kilt me later on, like, next time I saw her, for grassing on her. I told her I didn't (and I didn't grass on her neither, far's I know), but she said only for Cillian admitting he done it she'd've been locked up herself and there'd be nothing done on us anyway cos we was minors of course and I should've known it, she says. She told me that on the phone that day, she goes. And she called me all names and Cillian was her favourite after that, not me.

She gave him a big hug after he got out an' all and brought him a laptop computer and a pony. She said I wasn't allowed up on him cos I was a fuckface and I never was up on him, 'cept one time much later. Well two times, around, but she never knew it or she'd've kilt me. Or killed me even. She said she'd name the pony after me though and then she called him Fuckface. That was Cillian's pony's name. That was all much later, like, weeks or months or maybe a year later. After he got out.

That night though in the room (it was more like a room in a house than a cell) there was a wardrobe and drawers for stuff if you had stuff and the bed was a proper bed and the window was like a normal window with no bars or nothing, but you couldn't really fit out, like, cos it didn't open that much. But that night in the room when the fellas were fighting each other from their own rooms I wasn't really listening to them mostly but I was kinda sad and it was mostly about Con. I was thinking about my uncle and he'd be locked up in a place like this (I thought anyway – I didn't know til much later what kind of place he'd be locked up in). And I was thinking Con would hate this and he'd go mad, the size of him in this small room, and that made me sad cos Con was sound-out, like, when you got to know him.

Then I was getting mad cos he done nothing wrong and I done nothing too.

Next day I was left go home, Bill said an' he smiling when I ate my breakfast. I said tell them I finished my toast and finished all my tea too. And he wrote that down and we were both laughing. I was taken to the Bridewell first and Stacey was there and she took me home. There was no news about Cillian and I asked Stacey where was my mother and she goes she's locked up for questioning and Stacey stayed in our house that night and her boyfriend Charlie too. They had a party and had cocaine and I was making them laugh saying Charlie was doing Charlie and stuff like that and I asked them for some but they wouldn't, like, cos it cost too much and after a while they laughed so much they said I could have a go too and I was buzzing after that and I ran out the door after a while and I was all round the city smashing things all night. I remember for a while I was running around looking for Cillian and when I'd spot someone who I thought might be him I'd attack them when they weren't Cillian at all and I'd run-on looking for him more. AhaAhaha, I was out of it. I forget what age I was then. Ten or twelve I'd say at the most. Or thirteen maybe, max. I was mad then, Ahahahahaah. Kinda small, but I was strong out. Stronger than I'd be even now I'd say. I'd've fought anyone at that time and I'd've probably bate them too.

When I got home it was nearly bright and the two of them – Stacey and Charlie – were bollox-naked in the front room, fast asleep. He was on the settee and he had a horn on him the size of a donkey, I'll never forget, and it took me a while to spot Stacey cos I was looking for her in case he was the only one there. You wouldn't know what a nobber like that might do. She was there too though – down the back of the settee, like, curled up in a ball like she was hiding and fell asleep. So I went to bed. I remember thinking my own bed wasn't as good as the bed in the prison cell I stayed the last two nights (I was still thinking I was in a prison then, Ahahahahaah!)

That was the first time I think I knew I had no proper bed at home. Or felt it, like. We had ones like that a short while a few times, like, but they always got ripped to bits when we was younger. We were pure animals, like. We weren't living in Winchester yet then either and we were still too young so my bed was a mattress that you blow up. They'd last a week or a month or a few days before I'd have to find another one, but far's I cared at the time that's what real beds in your home was. Or were I mean. For children at least.

Then my mother got back and she was odd with me for days and days and wouldn't talk to me even cos she said I tried to get her sent down and I was a grass, but I was telling her I wasn't and she still wouldn't talk to me and she thrun me out for two nights, but left me come back when I brought some fancy jewellery to her for a present, like, that I found in Murder She Wrote's house. I slept there the second night. I didn't sleep anywhere the first night cos I was mad and mostly ran around town. Then when I was hanging tired next day I was back by our house and Murder She Wrote spotted me and goes come in for a glass of milk and she was sound-out and gave me food an' all cos I was starving. Then when she heard my mother thrun me out she was going to call the cops or someone but she was a scared and I said don't bother I'd be allowed back in again next day anyway. And I was too, after I found the jewellery like. I never took nothing off her place before that, but I knew my mother would like it and I knew where it was.

She still wouldn't talk to me like, my mam, but she said I could sleep in my own and Cillian's room, but it was all my fault Cillian got done for what I done. And she was right too, I know. I was a stupid shit and she made me say it over and over 'til I knew it. Then I said sorry again but my mother could be fierce mad at you for ages sometimes.

They kept Cillian for ages too. I forgot to ask him where he was when he got back and I couldn't ask my mother cos she'd've never told me, but when I got her more presents she started talking with me again and after a while I was her favourite again cos there was no one else there like. And Tara came back for a while and Melanie. And they were her favourites and they left again and she was friends with me again, so I didn't miss them so much cos I was cheering up my mam and made her laugh and she was bringing me with her to the pub an' all. We were like buddies, the two of us.

One time she got a call off the shades to tell her I had a motorbike and they wanted it back. They said they just wanted the bike and they wouldn't do no more to me cos I was a juvenile. Just meet them at the traffic lights at the end of our road, they said, at 10:30 next morning and hand over the bike and nothing more would be said or done about it. She was an XR 600. Lovely bike. Honda. You could go anywhere on her, like.

My mother tells me all this about the cop when it was dark and I had her all night to ride around and have a think about what I wanted to do, like. They said if I damaged her or burnt her out or whatever, the deal was off and I'd definitely be going down this time. A load of kids and mams and dads in the area heard about it and when we were all around the bonna that night they were all asking me what I was going to do and I told them all I hadn't a clue what I'd do and we had a great laugh. What a bike! I was up and down steps an' everything on her. And Timmy McGrath who was around double my age goes he couldn't even do that on a bike like that and I went up and down again to give him a thrill, like.

Next morning I said I might as well bring the bike back and get off the heat, so I got the bike from where I kept her (alright she was in my bedroom, but they'd've needed a search warrant to find her there so it was the safest place when you think about it, like) and I drove down to the traffic lights. The Sierra was parked down there on one side of the road and there was a white van on the other side opposite, belonging to the bike shop for them to take her away. I drove up and stopped in front of the Sierra and Garda Mick, who had the same name as me like, started walking towards me slowly. He was after being speaking with the owner of the bike, or some fella who was probably the owner anyway, and he kinda waved to him go away when I got there and then the Guard walked slowly up to me.

All the neighbours was lined up at the top of the grass hill above us to see me hand it over. They all said the night before give it back cos I could always get it again another time but if I kept it or burnt it I'd be in worse trouble than Cillian even. My mother even was up at the top of the grass when I looked and she shouted, Go on, give him the bike Mickey!

And the Guard was nearly up to me, with his arm out and I shouts out, I will in me mickey! And I revved the engine and drove up the front of the Sierra and down the other side, with Garda Mick's rookie partner sitting inside, looking at me an' his jaw open. I stalled a minute to give him a chance to turn the squad car around, then shot off for a thrill with the two cops in the car chasing me. They were all screaming and roaring up on the hill, including my mother.

After I went around the blockie I tore back up the same street again and they were still there waving an' laughing an' cheering me on. What a laugh. My mother was in stitches and I knew she forgot she was odd with me then and I was her favourite. I tore up and down that road for ages and I could see after a while Garda Mick looked like he was fed up and was gonna leave so I drove away out the country an' all. I ran out of petrol, then, out by The Lough and I phoned my mother and told her tell the cops the bike is out by The Lough and when they turned up I said I was minding it for them to make sure it's not damaged and could they give me a lift back home cos I had no spin. And they did an' all, bunch of langers that they are! When I got home I got a big cheer again from my mam and all her buddies who was in the house having a party by that time.

And I was at the parties mostly an' all after that, doing jobs for her an' everything. Until, then Cillian gets back eventually and she remembered what I done and she had his laptop computer waiting for him and brought him his pony the next day and she wouldn't talk to me again for ages 'cept to call me names and say Cillian was her favourite. It wasn't his fault at all, like. Cillian knew how she'd be and he was always the best brother to me, growing up. Unless we was fighting, like.

But Cillian was different then too I think, looking back. We had good fun again and we done all stuff together same as always, for about a year I'd say, but more or less overall I'd say he was sad, like. He didn't say it but I knowed it, like at the time,

73

and tried to get him change his mind with all messin' and things. He never turned on his computer even and sold it after to a fella he knew cos Cash Converters wouldn't give him nothing for it cos he had no receipt or nothing, even when he told them it was a present. And it was, like.

And I loved Fuckface the Pony more than Cillian and I fed him most days too, but Cillian only pretended he loved him when our mother was around and he'd be up on him, riding up and down outside and she'd be laughing and waving at Cillian. And she'd laugh at me then cos I couldn't have a go cos I was a grass.

One time then, ages after, over-right my mother, Cillian goes to me, You could have a go on him! And I was hopping on, but my mother started screaming and told us no way. And Cillian even wouldn't go on him no more after that and said he wouldn't be bothered. That was the night I snuck a go on Fuckface the first time when no one knew and when I got home Cillian was there and I was telling him again about me on the bike. He was after hearing all about it, like already, but I told him again and he was listening and laughing and then I told him I was gonna take Fuckface on a jaunt next day and ride him up and down outside over-right our mother an' everyone and she'd have to let me ride him after that.

And Cillian got mad and goes no way and he told me he'd bate me if I tried it cos our mother would kill me if I did it. And I said OK but then I said I was gonna do it and we had a small bit of a scatter in our room, but mostly it was me saying I was gonna ride Fuckface for a laugh and Cillian bating me til I said I wouldn't and then when he got off me I'd carry on saying

74

it again and he'd be bating me again until I'd stop then he'd stop. He gave me a black-eye an' all that time too. What a laugh!

A Day-Out In Midleton

Next day we were out on the field, me and Cillian. And Fuckface was there but I wasn't saying anything about it. We both knew our mother would be in bed that day til late, like, so there'd be nothing happen til after that. Cillian was looking to know if I was still going to ride Fuckface over-right her. He wouldn't say it to me, like, but I knew that's what he was waiting for, so I wasn't saying nothing either.

I was walking up and down and we were jumping off a roof onto another roof and onto the ground to practice, just doing nothing really like until the right time came. Cillian wasn't saying nothing but I knew he was getting mad cos I was saying nothing. But it got late enough after a while and Cillian was still getting madder and I knew I didn't have a chance to get away but I hopped on anyway and Cillian was straight over and shoved me off and I hopped on again and nearly got away but he ran after me and pulled me down again and he got on himself then and tore off up the hill on Fuckface. And I was screaming, Ya langer Cillian! But he didn't stop cos we both knew.

I didn't see him for hours and I was down outside the baths with the two Davies when Cillian comes along again. I was around with the two of them a bit before that, mainly when Cillian was away, like. It was Davie Gonad and Davie O'Brien. I wouldn't say I ever knew Gonad's real name, but he was called that cos he was playing hurling at school one day and a fella gave him a lash with the hurley and knocked out one of his balls. Far's I know he still had the other one. Davie O'Brien was more like in our gang than Gonad. He'd only be giving out to us when he'd hear about something, Davie Gonad like, and going on about it all the time, so we wouldn't bother with him mostly.

Anyway Cillian walks up and says Fuckface is gone and I start shouting at him and he goes the travellers hopped him and kidnapped the pony. I didn't believe him cos I knew it, but he kept saying it over and over. And he followed me back home and telling me don't say anything and we'll tell her he was robbed and we don't know by who. But when we got there Con was in the house sitting at the table and we gave him a big cheer and he hugged the two of us and told us stories about how he was the boss in the prison and all the guards were afraid of him even. I forgot to tell him shut up, but I remembered when he shut up and I goes the travellers robbed Fuckface! And Con hopped up and goes, The dirty bastards I'll fuckin kill them! Where are they? And Cillian goes they're miles away − not the travellers over the field but ones he never even seen before. And Con was mad-out and shouted how many travellers was there and how old were they and what kind of clothes were they wearing (cos he says they all look the same otherwise) and what did they say when they was robbing him? And who's the fuckface anyway?

Con didn't even know. I'd say he thought Fuckface was Cillian or Cillian's friend or someone. When he heard it was the pony he got mad again and goes, I'll get that pony back for you, true as God. There'll be no traveller take naw'hin from a Collins!

And me and Cillian starts screaming we'll get the bastards and the two of us raced out to go look for Fuckface so we could tell Con where he was.

I started up the hill outside, but Cillian goes no the travellers who robbed Fuckface is from Midleton I think. He wouldn't believe me either when I told him which way he went earlier on the pony, so we goes into town instead and got on the bus and went to Midleton. The first bus had a prick driving and he wouldn't budge til we got off cos he said we got no ticket, but the next one we snuck on when a load of people were getting on and it was a woman driver and she didn't even see us so she drove away down to Midleton and no inspector or nothing got on.

On the way down, I knew Cillian was telling the truth cos he was getting madder at the travellers an' he saying it again about how one fella jumped up and pushed him off Fuckface and another fella rode off on him and about five of them was kicking him an' he on the ground until he got the mads and jumped up and bate them all, but yer man on the pony was long-gone by then and the others were saying, Come on we leg it back to Midleton. So that's how Cillian knew where they were from.

Down there anyway, I found a big long stick and we were all around the place looking for travellers but we couldn't find any. We spotted a few traveller horses alright in a big field outside the town but none of them was Fuckface and we had a laugh around the shops and I stuck my stick in a letterbox and a fella ran out and started chasing us and Cillian hopped over a wall and when I was getting up the same wall, yer man ran up behind me and gave me a big kick up the hole and I went tumbling over and my arse was sore and Cillian battered yer man when he was walking off but he didn't bother coming back. What a laugh! There was a gang of lads there a bit later and we had a battering match with them then and one fella ran home crying to his mammy when Cillian got him on the forehead with a rocker. And we moved on after a while.

We hitched it home later I remember, when a fella in a builders' van stopped to pick us up and he was sound, that fella. I ate a strawberry out of a carton on the seat next to us and Cillian gave me a belt and told me not to do it and yer man who was driving goes, Ah that's alright, eat away. And Cillian and me ate one after the other and I ate the last one. Then Cillian gave out to me again for eating it and he tells me that he's scarlet embarrassed, but yer man goes, Ye enjoyed them, how bad? He was really sound-out. He dropped us in town an' everything and we got home from there.

When we got there, Fuckface was tied up outside the front door and when we went in Con was inside with my mam and a few others. Con was after finding the pony at the traveller site up the road, he told us. They had him up there and they were telling him he was their own pony what they had for years but he knew as soon as he seen him it was Fuckface. I don't know how he knew it cos he never seen him before, like, but Con is no daw. He knew him alright and he got him back.

He said we'd have to mind the pony for a few days cos they'd be back to kill him or to rob him off us again and that's why he got the gang around to tell them all what to do in case the travellers came back. He said he broke one fella's leg, but they won't forget it an' they'll keep coming back til we teach them proper.

Then Cillian goes, They can fuckin keep Fuckface if they're gonna be like that about it! And my mother got mad at Cillian. And Con goes, No, it's gone beyond all that now. These fellas know it and they'll be back for revenge!

Timmy McGrath was there and Scanny and Johnny Silver and Kanturk, who was from Kanturk originally, like, so we all just called him Kanturk. And there was a few of the women there too and Con gave a big speech like Braveheart and they all goes, Yeah! And they all agreed they'd be on the lookout for travellers in the area and we'd be ready to jump-on if they tried kidnapping the poor pony, cos if we let them off with this the whole area would go down and these fellas only understood one thing. And Con was all for taking it to them and fighting them at their place to keep our streets safe for "the childern and ung uns!" *(he said ung uns instead of young ones and it sounded like onions, Ahahahahaah!)*

But the rest of them said it was better to see if they'd come back and Con was fierce mad that they were too a-scared to fight them and he said he'd go fight them himself or there'd be no rest and it took ages, but my mother calmed him down and said we'd all jump-on and give them a right batin' when they come.

They had a party after cos they agreed the plan and they were all legless by the time the travellers came. Con was the only one who was able to fight them but they waited till he was in the jacks before they stole back the pony and threw a rock in the window. Con ran out after them while he was still tying up his pants, but they already had Fuckface inside their HiAce and they tore off down the road. We never even seen them or nothing.

•

Me and Cillian'd have better things to be doing than go to school most days. Like, we were still at school, like, most days nearly, but mostly we wouldn't go, like.

80

The day after the pony was robbed back by the travellers, Cillian all of a sudden goes c'mon we go to school and I was like, Wha? I wanted to hang around and ambush the travellers with Con and the boys, but they were all still asleep or not around when Cillian goes, Yeah come on we weren't there in ages!

After a while I said OK, but I didn't want to go, still. But Cillian was annoying me too much so I was going. But on the way I found a door that was left opened. A front door to a house, like. It looked like it mightn't've been closed and I just pushed it a bit and it was wide opened! Cillian had a new teacher and he said he didn't like her but I knew he liked her but I didn't say nothing cos I knew it and that's why we was going. She gave him a gold star one time, the last week before that, or a month before maybe, for Bravery and he was happy-out with himself showing my mam an' all until she was mocking him for being all goody-goody. And we all had a laugh off him when she said stars is only for babies. That was the last time we went to school before that.

So when I found the door that was opened I knew we was saved and we went in and there was no one in there in the whole place an' all.

We took our time looking around first cos there's no point getting the first things if you can't carry no more when you find something better, like, so we were just walking around downstairs and upstairs a bit. The place was old but there was a few things that were good. Mostly old though. Then Cillian was downstairs and I was in the toilet upstairs and I found a load of tablets. I hadn't a clue what they were but I took some in case I'd get a buzz off them like and I didn't so I had another one off another bottle and I felt tired in my belly and dizzy in my head, like, and I knew it was a trap and I goes to Cillian, Cillian! And then I think I hit the ground in the toilet.

I was out of it for a few days I think. Woke up in the hospital and the nurses were asking me what happened to me and I hadn't a clue. They said they found tablets in my stomach and asked what did I take and where did I get them but I told them nothing cos I'm not a squealer. Different doctors and people came round and one fella was wearing a suit and he was asking me if my mother had tablets at home like what I took and I set him straight I didn't take no tablets until he believed me and he went away.

Next day Cillian came to visit me and brung Davie O'Brien with him. And we had a laugh at it. Cillian said he thought I was dead and carried me to the hospital before someone stopped their car and brought the both of us. He told them at the hospital that I just collapsed on the way to school. We got nothing off the open house in the end. I was telling Davie then about the tablets and he was laughing and next Cillian goes about the pony, Fuckface is dead! He got chopped by them travellers!

That made me sad-out. Like, who'd want to chop a beautiful animal like Fuckface? Travellers is who! I could see why Con hated their guts. I got the mads then at the travellers til Cillian goes, No it's alright! It's all taken care of – they're doing jobs now with Con and they're all friends. They're alright actually.

And I goes, Actually!? Cos I never heard Cillian use a posh word before and around then he seemed to be starting saying things like "Actually" and I mocked him over it and we all had a laugh, but I was still surprised between Con and the travellers.

I never really got the full story of it and when my mother came to the hospital later on, or next day she wouldn't say nothing. She'd only nod yes or no like she had no voice when the doctors was there and after they went away she only whispered to give out to me and wouldn't tell me nothing. She said I told them I got the tablets off home and I was telling her I didn't but she wouldn't believe me. Grass again she was calling me.

Fuckface was chopped and Con and the travellers was friends and working together. My mother was calling me grass again and nobody was bothered about the poor pony! They all do my head in sometimes and that was one time!

Bridie

Later I knew why Con and them travellers got friends. It was cos they were after getting stuff from the same place Moxie got stuff – or even straight in from outside the country, like, but they couldn't sell it cos nobody'd pay travellers that much cos they wouldn't trust them like. So my mother got Con to do a deal and they all became friends.

But all that was later-on, when I was back at home. First I was back in Foxy Bill's for ages. And different homes for me to stay in then, see where I could go. Mr. Mulcahy was the main one around then for at least a year or more. That's when I was staying with him and we done all stuff. We never went to Sligo, like I said, but Museums and Fota Wildlife and the Racing and the Pictures all the time. A load of things and reading books an' all. But after my mother needed me and filled me in that he was a queer, I was back at home again. After I busted up his place, like.

•

That day when I got back on my own, after running away from Mr. Mulcahy's though, I remember Cillian was at home and there was loud music everywhere so we couldn't even be talking, so we went up around the field to Moxie, who was mad chatting with a few others and he goes I have a job for ya Cillian.

So we went down around town after that and got on the bus to Carrigaline cos Cillian needed to bring stuff to yer man, Trevor, and I was his bodyguard. After we dropped that off, anyway, we carried on down to Crosshaven and walked up the hill to Graball for a walk along the rocks to catch catfish for a bit and then I went for a swim too, not Cillian, but it was freezing and my underpants was soaking wet the whole way home and soaked my pants and the bus seat an' all.

And my mother and Stacey was home when we got home and Tara too even, back on a visit and they were all mocking my wet pants, Cillian an' all. I went in our room and slammed the door and knocked a few holes in the wall cos they were mocking me still through the door. And I remembered the music then cos there was no other noise when I was inside my room for a while 'cept from the speakers my mam had out the window, playing music full-blast non-stop, but inside the kitchen you could hear it only softer.

When I comes out later, I goes how come the speakers is outside and my mam goes so the neighbours could enjoy the party an' all. And I goes what party? And she goes Cillian's gone to the chipper and we're having a party. And I asked her why aren't the speakers inside so and she goes they're too loud to be in the kitchen.

And we had a massive dinner with batter burgers and battered sausages and everything. And Stacey goes, I wonder could you get battered chicken? And Cillian goes the Chinese batter their balls and Stacey goes, Oh I'd say that'd be sore. And we all starts laughing, Stacey too, but mostly we were mocking Stacey cos Cillian whispered to me he was talking about chicken balls, but Stacey thought it was their Chinee men's balls, like. And Stacey kept going on about it asking if they'd need to shave them first and then she was making a face and saying she wouldn't like it but she'd give them a go, like. And we were all breaking our arses.

Tara didn't say much but Stacey was asking her about where she was living and Tara'd be like "it's alright" or "yes, sometimes." Stuff like that. She wasn't mad or anything. And my mother was giving out then about Bridie, who was minding Tara, like, mostly, saying Bridie was fierce bad to her, locking her up every night in a cage and giving her a batin' all the time and everything. And she fed her nothing too even though the government paid her thousands every week to make sure she got the best of eats. That's why we were having this party now so we'd fatten Tara up before she went back to that place, it was so bad.

We were all mad at Bridie and I goes to Tara is it true? And Tara just shrugged and goes yeah. I got mad and told her I'd save her off Bridie and off the government, true as God, cos nodoby'd be allowed treat a Collins that way. And then Cillian and my mam mocks me and called me Young Cob. But Tara didn't laugh at all and Stacey didn't neither, only smiled. My mother goes to her then, would you like to come home to live with your family, Tara, and we'd all have parties like this all the time an' all? But Tara only said naw she'd stay at Bridie's like. And I got mad with Tara over that cos I couldn't understand why she'd want to be there in a cage instead of at home having parties and chips with her own family, like.

A bit after that, Bridie, who was minding Tara, came to the house, bold as brass like she done nothing wrong. All big smiles and loud talk. She made sure she was heard louder than the music even. And I was mad at her and goes, I bet you won't

86

be smiling like that when you take Tara away! And she's only laughing and talks about the weather and the traffic with my mam, who I can't believe isn't even ganging-up on her, like.

My mother's only all shy and nice with Bridie, like she's a scared of her or something, but I wasn't a scared of her and neither was Cillian. She turns down the music outside then an' all, my mam like. It was our first time meeting Bridie, me and Cillian's, and we went outside after a while cos our mother pushed us out like we wasn't standing up for our rights and Tara's. And she goes make sure Bridie's car isn't robbed when she gets out with Tara. And we found the big fancy yolk she parked down the road, Bridie's car, that she got off the government with all the money they paid her for minding Tara and we got others to help us get blocks under it and we had a tyre wrench and got one wheel off and rolled it away down the hill before she came out, cos we were refusing to let her take our sister back to that place.

And she spotted us after she came out with Tara and our mother and she wasn't smiling no more. She goes she needed the wheel and we said we hadn't a clue what she was on about and after ages a Tyre Truck van came with a new wheel and they stuck it on and she took Tara away anyway. And my mother left her take her. And Tara went too even when I was banging on the window and trying to get her out of the car, like. I was mad-out and sad for Tara that she'd be locked up in a cage in a house like that and you wouldn't think Bridie'd be the kind of wan who'd do it, but my mother said she was and I remembered Madge from years ago, only worse even. And the music started up even louder after that and everything was mad-out in my head even.

My mother told us after that, that the government made her sign a piece of paper on all of us to say they could take us whenever they liked. And the only thing she could do was get a visit or something every now and again off any of us. It made me mad-out to see her all sad how they'd be messing with us all the time like that, just to get us back even if we done nothing. An' we was so happy just a while before that when we was all just left alone at home, the whole family together like. 'Cept Melanie wasn't there and Jordan-SueAnne wasn't born then neither.

The Proof

Next day or two later, or a week maybe, cops come and my social worker too, and I thought it was about Bridie's tyre or about not going to school again or something like that, but it was about Mr. Mulcahy and how I run away. The social worker, whatever this one's name was, was like to my mother, Turn that music down! So we all turned it up. And then she goes Mr. Mulcahy was speaking with my mother the other day and I was supposed to go back to stay with him, but I never went and she never told me that, like, neither. I didn't know he'd still let me go back after I smashed loads of stuff at his house. He was sound enough for that when you think of it.

And my mother goes that fella's a faggot and the social worker tells her I don't have to stay with Mr. Mulcahy but they have to take me away now and my mother shouted out that he molested me, Mr. Mulcahy, like, cos the music was all loud. And they all looks at me just in the quiet bit between that song ending and the next one starting and I was in a shock and I didn't even know what to say, like.

•

I was back in Foxy Bill's the day after that cos I was supposed to be in Mr. Mulcahy's but they couldn't send me there in case he'd feel me up and I was caught that night by the shades and they said I was smashing things around town again, but they never saw if it was me, but just said it was me cos I wasn't even in the same street where the cars was smashed when they caught me so they had no proof but they pinned it on me anyway so I had to stay in Foxy Bill's, 'cept it wasn't Bill who was on. It was the other person who worked there sometimes 'stead of Bill. She was on that night cos it was Bill's day off. Well, sometimes there'd be a guard stay there too or sometimes there'd be just one on. That night it was yer wan only. She done a load of writing all the time and gave me no fag like Bill would any day and she'd write I didn't eat naw'hin and that I thrun my dinner on the floor and that I shouted for a cigarette and I was abusive and that I spat at her and she had to call for assistance when I wouldn't go to bed. She'd write all that. Say nothing, like, but just write and then they locks the door after I went in, an' all. Bill never locked no door. He told her before not to lock no door on me neither but that night she locked it cos she probably thought I was a queer an' all, over Mr. Mulcahy and what they all thought he done.

I don't know why I said it happened cos I got nothing but grief over it, but my mother said it did and she's my mother, like. And I felt worse even cos they all mocked me and wouldn't talk with me and my mother too even. She made me all funny about it and told me say he felt me up and that we done queer stuff all the time. Why would I want to be saying that?

It wasn't her at all really when you think about it either, I know that now, obviously like. And my mother only told me that herself too the other day when I asked her on the phone. I goes, Remember Mr. Mulcahy? And she made-out like she didn't, but I knew she did. Why did you make me say he done that to me? I goes. And she made a joke of it first, but then I kept asking and she goes she was a scared about Cillian, see. She thought I'd turn Cillian a queer too, see, if Mr. Mulcahy turned me queer. She was looking out for my brother at the time, cos they was fighting mostly cos Cillian didn't want to live in our house no more, not even in the new house we were going to be moving into. And that's how mothers think, see? They're all like that.

In fact Mr. Mulcahy never touched me up or anything like that, like, at all. And that's a fact. He never turned me a bender neither. My mother even now if you asked her says, He did for a bit, till I seen to him.

But I definitely was never no bender, me. I had a girlfriend an' all for ages. Ask anyone.

•

But anyway, I was back at home soon enough cos there was nowhere else to put me, like, so I got back and Cillian wasn't allowed stay in my room cos they all said I was a queer or a bender. They was running away for ages when I walk into the room, Cillian too. Messing, like, but serious too in case they caught it. Stacey was alright, but Cillian and my mother was like, I have something to do!

And then they'd run out the door laughing. They got good friends then, the two of them, like, but they wouldn't say much any other time neither to me, like. And I saw Con one time or two times at that time and he had all tears in his eyes an' all and rubbing them and he goes he was fierce sad about what that bastard Mulcahy done to me and that at least my mother was going to be screwing him more than he ever done to me. Getting her own backs on him.

Like, Mr. Mulcahy never screwed anything far's I know. I never even seen his langer and he definitely had a canary anytime he nearly saw mine. One time, after I stayed with him first, I remember, I had a bath cos we never had a bath in our own house and there was all bubbles in it. Mr. Matey, an' all. And I was there lying in it for hours and I got out and got a packet of Tayto that was on the table cos Mr. Mulcahy let me eat Taytos and he never wrote it down or nothing. And he nearly hit the roof screaming with his hands up to his eyes, telling me get back in the bath and don't be walking around the shop balls-naked! Like, if he was a bender he'd've never been like that, sure. He never had no friends even 'cept me I'd say and he never went down the docks feeling fellas up long as I was there too, 'cept my mother heard that's what he was up to all the time.

I suppose you never know, cos she heard too he was sucking fellas off and he got arrested for getting a rake of queer magazines in the post. That was the proof alright I suppose. She had it, cos she had to sue him to get a few bob for it, but he died before the case come up about a year later or something and she sued the government too cos it was all their fault really.

Cancer's what I heard is what Mr. Mulcahy got. He died, like, and I never seen no more of him after. He'd of been probably better off too when you think of it, cos he'd never be right for prison at all, Mr. Mulcahy.

But anyway, I was mad-out at my mam and Cillian the first few months or weeks when I got back that time, and they'd pretend like it's not cos I was a queer when they run away from me, but I knew it was like, cos they kept it up so long.

She goes to Cillian he better sleep in her room an' all, just in case like, so he got the big soft bed and he was happy-out with himself for one night at least. I was sad-out and I was so mad I didn't even bother sleeping at home most nights cos they was doing my head in, the two of them. 'Specially with all the music you'd hear non-stop from our bedroom, from the speakers outside the window. That was doing my head-in an' all, but it didn't seem to bother no one else, like. Cillian was back in our room most nights after that, if he wasn't gone out, but when I'd see him there I'd just go on away out again.

And I'd say I tried more drugs around then too, different ones like – all different ones, around then than ever. And I didn't bother with school no more at that time and I'd fall asleep in different houses at parties and in parks an' all sometimes cos it wasn't cold or nothing. I couldn't even feel it anyway cos I'd be out of it, me.

And after a while I'd be back at home for a bit and I got a rake of stuff for my mother all the time, presents like. And she'd take it off me and go, That'll pay for my therapy. And nothing else.

Davie O'Brien was around with me mostly around then, cos Cillian wasn't. Davie was alright about the other thing he said cos he knew I wasn't no bender anyway. But my mother'd still only stick up for Cillian and be all nice to him but Cillian wasn't nice with her all the time, but she'd still be nicer and nicer with him and buying him things, even though he was only fighting with her most days, all cranky-out, like, he was with her. But he wouldn't be on my side neither. We'd be all fighting all the time around then and it was fierce sad when you think of it.

Stacey was the best about it though and she helped me get the proof too after a while. One time she came over to me like, Stacey, all soft-like, and put her hand on my knee and goes, What you need is a woman.

And I hadn't a clue what she was on about. And then I got an idea of it and I had a shock. I wasn't sure if she meant it like I was thinking, but I was in a shock alright. Like, she was a lasher mostly alright, to be fair, Stacey like. 'Specially when she'd be all dolled-up with lipstick and shit. But Cillian said before that she was probably riddled with diseases and the AIDs. So there was that too to think of too, like.

And I goes, But I'm *not* a bender!

And she goes she knows cos she knows how to spot them and I goes how do you know? And she goes, Cos if I done this they wouldn't like it. And she flashed her tits at me and I laughed and she laughed and said, See! That's the proof!

Then Cillian and my mother walks in and spots us laughing and he goes what are ye laughing at and I said Stacey proved I'm not a bender and he goes how and I said cos she flashed her tits and made me laugh. And he goes that's not proof. And then Stacey rubs my cheek and goes, That's not the proof. And then she rubbed my hard knob with a pure feel-up and goes, That's the proof!

I swear I nearly exploded. Cillian was laughing his head off then and said he never thought I was a queer anyway, but my mother had a shock. She gave out to Stacey for flashing at me and said she should be ashamed of herself, but Stacey only had a smile an' she walking away all happy-like. I was scarlet embarrassed over-right my mother, but kind of happy too, like.

Benalmadena

There was a court summons for me to be in court one time around then. They wanted to lock me up cos I was caught in a car with another fella driving. I was only walking down the road one night when Davie O'Brien's older brother, Shane, done a mad-skid over-right me and sticks his head out the window and goes get in Mickey we go for a ride. So I hops in, what else would ya be doing, like? There was two other fellas in there too that I only barely knew, but we was having a laugh and got a chase off the cops an' all for a bit only but they ambushed us and I tried to leg it, but they caught me and after that they found some drugs in there too, like, in the car, but it wasn't mine at all and I didn't even know if it was in there.

And there was other stuff too, like, on CCTV around then when I was pinned on the ground in a garage by this fella. There was no one even behind the counter when I went in to buy fags cos yer man was out the back and when he come back he saw me getting stuff and he pinned me down, but all's I was doing was serving myself til he got back. He never thought of that, like. And another one was when I was with Cillian, but he was fighting with me, again like, so I only hopped over a wall to get away from him cos he was annoying me cos he was saying we shouldn't be doing what our mother'd be saying all the time. Like he knew better than anyone or something. So I hops over the wall to escape him. And there was a massive back door wide open to a big house that I never even know was there and I was

95

walking up to the door of this place when a fella stuck his head up. He was working in the garden, see, and he looks up just when I was looking in the back door, only, to his house and he chased me into the house and bate the shit out of me and he still shopped me to the guards after that cos he was a guard himself an' all. And there was one time more, or a few like maybe, when I was caught around cars after that too, but it was mainly just hanging around, like. And that was it in total. More or less.

•

But anyway I was up, supposed to be, on Thursday and my mam was saying the judge was a right langer who was definitely going to send me down this time. So the day before, she goes to us all, me, Cillian, Stacey, I'm not letting them take you to no court tomorrow!

And Cillian goes what are you going to do about it and she says she got a holiday for us all and we was going to Bellamadena. She got the tickets an' all and we was going straight away and collecting Tara and Melanie on the way. And we were all buzzing from that – all of us together on a holiday, like!

'Cept Cillian goes then, don't you think Mickey should go to court? And my mam kilt him, saying he only wanted me to get in trouble. And Cillian said no he wanted me to get better and I goes to him, get better from what? And he was saying I should go to school and shit and he was going to school more than me around that time, cos I wasn't going no more. And it was all this shit for ages off Cillian, an' he putting a damper on everything like a dryballs and my mam packed Cillian's bag and told him he's going and Cillian goes no he's not and Con collected us.

We went to the house Melanie was staying at and my mam told us all stay in the car and she got out to speak with Melanie's social worker, who was there waiting with Melanie. And Melanie had a bag, packed an' everything. I'd say she was around four or five at that time, but she looked like a proper woman, ready for an'thing. You'd just look at her and want to give her a big squeeze, she was so cute!

Anyway, next we goes to Bridie's house where Tara was staying and it's a massive mansion! And I asks my mam can I come too. Sure, she goes, Ye might as well all come. Except you Con. You can wait in the car.

Con has no bother with that. I'd say he wasn't planning on getting out anyway. And Stacey is only dreaming away to herself like she doesn't even hear it.

So I'm holding Melanie's hand and Cillian came too and my mother knocks at Bridie's front door. Bridie opens it after a while and she has a shock when my mam tells her we're here to take Tara on her holidays. She says to my mam she got no notice of it and that my mam (*Tara's own mother, imagine!*) has no right to grab Tara like that. And my mother then has a shock over that cos she said she filled in the form to take Tara on her holidays ages ago. And Tara was behind Bridie and she had a shock an' all cos it's the first she heard of it too. Come on we'll take ya to Bellamadena, Tara Love, my mam goes, Would you like that? And Tara goes, Ya! And she's delighted, like, to be going. Who wouldn't be, sure!?

And Bridie is like, I have to ring the guards now Tara, this isn't right at all! And she tells Tara she's sorry an' all, but she doesn't give a shit cos Tara is crying even, but Bridie has Tara locked-up behind the door and it's fierce sad. And I was mad-out and walks up to kick in the door, but my mam holds me off

97

and goes, It's alright, dear, I was afraid this might happen. We might have to leave Tara behind this time.

I was in a shock. And Cillian's just standing there like he hasn't a clue. He's nearly crying, but he's doing nothing about it. I was screaming and roaring at Bridie and then I goes, I'm gonna get Con so! And my mother stops me and goes, Naw that's OK Mickey – Tara love, I have your two brothers here and your sister and we're going on our holidays to Bellamadena, see? But we'll have to leave you there this time with Bridie, OK? Cos it's all the rules now that I can't bring you on your holidays with your brothers and sister when you're living with Bridie. It's a pity you aren't living at home no more at the minute, but you can return to you own mother all you want soon if you'd like to, and I'll take you on our holidays the next time too if you're good, OK love?

And Bridie is getting mad-out, cos she knew she was caught-out and she goes she's ringing the guards, but my mother told her for what? Cos we was leaving on our holidays without Tara and there was no hassle. And Bridie said she got no permission to have a visit even. And my mam goes she's not visiting and she never even saw Tara anyway, cos Tara was still behind the front door and behind Bridie.

And Con and Stacey was sitting in the car the whole time, like there's nothing happening. And Bridie starts then on Cillian cos Cillian was crying that he didn't want to go neither. And Bridie tells him he doesn't have to go if he doesn't want to and all this shit was going on and on.

After ages anyway we got back in the car without Tara and we was all bawling our eyes out by then and my mother had to hold Con off and said Bridie would get us in fierce trouble if we didn't just take off without Tara.

And when we got to the airport, Con left us out and we were all inside and Cillian goes again he's not going and my mother told him fuck off so and he owed her four hundred euros for the ticket and Cillian was fucking off and I was like, Come on Cillian we'll have a laugh.

But he said then we were only going anyway cos our mam was up in court too on Friday and he saw the summons. She was supposed to be there the day after me, he goes, and that's why she wants to go on the run, cos she was caught fighting in town and other things too.

And my mother kilt Cillian when he said that and told him he was lying cos yer wan she was having an argument-with got a bottle in the face and they pinned it on her only cos Stacey was unconscious by the time the cops got there. Stacey was in stitches laughing at that and said it was a mad night. But none of that had nothing to do with the holiday, my mam said, and Cillian was only trying to spoil it now for the lot of us.

So he had to get out of the airport on his own cos we all took off to Bellamadena and Con was already gone and he still refused to go even though it was for free, but he had to pay my mam two hundred and eighty five for it later cos he didn't go at all, like.

●

The first night over there, Stacey and my mother went out on the piss so me and Melanie had a laugh by the apartments and we found a pool in the hotel down the road. It was all lit up but there was no one swimming in it and when they saw us swimming the manager ran out screaming at us in Spanish or something like that and we got a chase off him and he caught Melanie and I had to go back and give him shit. Like, there was plenty of room for us or anyone else, but there was no one even swimming in it. And he told us in English he wouldn't call the cops if we didn't come back no more, but we should go home and have a wash when we got back to where we was staying but I told him fuck off cos the cheek of him! I told him he should go and have a wash instead cos he was blacker than us!

Next day Melanie was coughing non-stop and both our eyes was fierce sore, but I wasn't coughing at all, only a small bit. My mam was after finding a new boyfriend and she was gone away with him for a few days up the mountain, so it was just me and Stacey and Melanie. So Stacey gave Melanie a load of ice cream to cure the coughing and I got some too. It was good stuff, but it didn't work for Melanie's cough, mostly. We had a laugh anyway, like, and I was asking Stacey for a flash all the time and she'd give it too mostly and Melanie was mad laughing and copying her and I was skittin' laughing, but they looked really good too, Stacey's like, in fairness. Then later on she was sunbathing with no bra on so I had to wait til later again when we went to the bar to ask her again and when I did, she goes, You need a girlfriend is what you need. And after that she stopped giving me any flash.

Me and Melanie were mostly hanging around outside the bar then after that when Stacey was getting chatted up, and Melanie nearly got killed by a bus when she was only crossing the road to see a big blow-up unicorn and the bus had to stop fast then 'stead of knocking her down, like.

When I got there, the busman was screaming and roaring at the poor child in Spanish or German or something all gobblegobblegobble and another fella in a car was after crashing into the back of the bus too and he was screaming and roaring at the bus driver.

I kilt the busman over it, nearly knocking down a child like that, and later I kilt Melanie for it too and gave her a slap, cos you have to look at two sides to be fair. But she was all crying and fighting-mad and I give her a big hug then and took her to see the unicorn, but she forgot about it and gave me a kiss instead but her nose was all snotty and she was coughing and laughing after that, cos her snots was all over my cheek.

And she went missing an' all for ages another time, like, cos I was busy at the time and I forgot. And Stacey even couldn't find her and all the people in the hotel even couldn't find her in the hotel or down the beach or nowhere. After ages though she just walks in the front door of the hotel like nothing happened. She walks in like the Princess who owned the place. And all the manager and all the people working there are going like, Aahhhhh!

I'd say the manager knew he was lucky cos if the girl's mother was around he'd be in big trouble. Stacey'd say nothing to him though.

Most days, everyday, there'd be all lashers at the beach and Stacey goes to me one time, Go on and chat one of them up. And I walks over to this one and I was bright red the whole time and I goes, Hey, you want me to rub suncream on your chest?

And the fella next to her got up and chased me down the beach. I never even seen him there before that. I'd say he was around twenty five an' all and she was much younger than that, but still way-older than me. I like the big ones, see.

Stacey was laughing when I snuck back to them and she goes you can't be saying the wrong thing. Girls don't like it if you say the wrong thing unless you're loaded like, so don't be asking them for a flash or anything like that even if they're nice to you. Let them get the idea of it first, she said.

●

Another time after that I was standing by a shop and I tapped this one on the shoulder and she looked the wrong way and when she looked back I was on her other side and I laughed at her but she ran away. I didn't get lucky like my mother did on that holiday, I tell ya that for a fact.

Anyway, after a few more days Melanie's face was all red and her cough was getting worse and worse and after a while Stacey goes she probably needs to go to the hospital, but my mam got back before we went and she said Melanie'd be grand. It was time to be heading to the airport anyway cos she never told Stacey how many days we'd be there, like, even.

I asked my mam then where's her boyfriend and she goes, Paolo had to go. That's all she said. And me and Melanie and Stacey too even was saying it all the way to the airport: Paolo had to go! Paolo had to go! We had a laugh saying it over and over, when Melanie wasn't coughing non-stop, like. Paolo had to go! Ahahahahaah!

●

It would've been better if Tara and Cillian was there, like in fairness, cos I mainly minded Melanie on our holidays, and

Cillian'd be better at it than me, like, but it was my first time on holidays with Melanie too and she was pure gold the whole time.

Court Showdown

When we got back home, we were on the way to where Melanie was staying first and I goes, Can Melanie stay at home with us tonight? Cos she was on my lap fast-asleep and giving me a hug. But my mam goes no, she had a load to do and she's flaaed-out from her holidays. So Con dropped her home and then he took the rest of us home, but when we got there I asked Con where was Cillian and he goes he didn't know, he thought he went with us. And we were looking everywhere for him for days and where was he in the end? Who was he staying with? Bridie is who! Of all the people, after all that! Bridie imagine, and he wouldn't even come home neither when my mam was phoning him and telling him to all the time.

She had no choice after that 'cept to put in a claim with the government cos Bridie was molesting him too an' all! Stacey was knotted laughing at that when my mam said it to the social worker. She goes to me, Stacey like, when my mam was still on the phone saying it, Cillian got molested better than you at least. And I starts laughing too, but then I stopped cos I remembered it's not even funny. And I was never.

Then, the next day, or later that day like probably, they came round with a guard and a social worker and my mother told them all about it and they said they'd be taking Cillian off Bridie and bringing him back straight away. But when they went away they never came back a load more days and when I asked

Stacey, she goes Cillian didn't want to come home but our mother was fighting to get him off Bridie still – and Tara too.

As well as all that, my mother was in deep shit after we got back, and after the cops remembered to pick her up too, cos she skipped court, like. I was in deep shit too like, cos I never went neither for mine, but my case was put back a few months at least, but my mother was up first so she was making sure all of us was in the court with her to back her up: Stacey and Con and me and Melanie was there. And even Cillian was there too, but not Tara cos it wasn't Tara's visit time with her mother, so Bridie wouldn't let her. The lady who minded Melanie at that time at least was there with Melanie. And I saw Murder She Wrote there too in the audience cos she'd give me sangwitches still sometimes then. I was never back inside her house after I got the jewellery off her that time, up to then at least, but sure you couldn't blame her really. Least she never went on and on about it.

That was the first day I seen Cillian 'til then since the holidays. I goes to him, Are you mad or what Cillian, staying with that wan, does she have you locked in a cage like Tara too or what? And Cillian goes, Naw it's not like that at all Mickey, she's A-1, Bridie is!

I had a shock an' all at that.

After the judge come out anyway, they read out all the charges they had on my mother: not turning up to court, smashing a girl's face open, drunk and disorderly in a public place, shoplifting, disturbance of the peace, other shoplifting another time, possession, possession with intent to sell, another thing like "lood" something and some other thing too. Can't remember now. The judge goes, That's quite a list – and failure to turn up to court is demonstrably true and means there's prison-time due for that alone! But let's wait and see what else might be tossed in the pot...

He was all-posh of course. Seemed alright though in fairness.

Then there was a big long scene about the woman with the cut face, but she never showed up and the judge goes after a while they couldn't convict without witnesses and Con jumps up and gives out to the judge and goes, I hope you lock up that wan too for not even turning up! And Judge Nagle got a shock and tells Con to shut up and goes who are you. And it carries on like that for a while, but when Con is still shouting, the judge tells the guard remove him or he'd be going-down an' all. It was lucky Con stopped shouting then, I'd say, and marched out with the guard follying him. But he had a point when you think of it – Judge Nagle already said he'd be giving my mam jail time for not turning up and here's this wan who was spreading lies all the time and there'd be nothing done on her for not turning up neither!

They went through the different things anyway. One drugs charge wasn't proved and the judge said the other one was serious. Then onto the shoplifting. One shop had CCTV, but no proof. The judge goes we can't see what she put under her coat and the shop manager goes she had a list of things they took off my mother after she got outside the shop and after they got back into the office, but my mother goes they took other stuff off her too and the manager says a security guard from another store was waiting for her to come out cos she stole stuff off their shop too. Then the judge stopped her cos my mother wasn't up on charges about that other store and it's the first the judge heard of it and they took that stuff off my mother an' all at the time, but they had no rights on it, cos who says she stole that? And the manager goes the security guard for the other store is there to say she stole it and the judge goes it's the first he heard of that and it wasn't on his list.

So anyway Judge Nagle got all confused about it and how could my poor mother even understand all that if the judge couldn't? I hadn't a clue what was going on either, like.

The other shoplifting charge had the security guard witness who said she done it alright, but my mother explained she only put the fire extinguisher in her bag 'til she got to the till, but forgot it was there before leaving. She was intending to buy it, she says. Then the judge goes, But the fire extinguisher was in case of fire, it was not for sale. And my mother got a shock and was like, So I wasn't even able to buy it at all!? And she was laughing then cos she knew, How could I steal it so if it wasn't even for sale!?

I don't know if the judge was thinking the same thing, but I'd say he was.

One thing after another anyway, the charge of Disturbing the Peace comes up and there was sixty seven call-outs from the police to our house mainly cos of music being played. I could agree with that one myself cos I could barely sleep with it when I was at home all through the night. And the judge asks my mother why she had the speakers outside the house and she goes cos they were too loud inside and he goes why not turn it down and she goes the volume was broke.

And what's this I hear about drugs being sold from your premises? the judge goes and my mother gets a shock off of that an' all, and goes, That's outrageous! (all posh-like, I was laughing my ass off) Who says there was drugs being sold at my house, over-right my own children!? And she pointed at the lot of us (but not Tara like) who was all clean and our hair brushed and everything.

The judge asked her if these are her children and she goes yes, there's three of them here supporting her, except one of them couldn't make it due to circumstances. And then she named us and told all us, one after the other, say hello to the judge. And the judge said hello every time. Then he goes there's this lood charge but he didn't bother with it after a while. He goes there was plenty more to be getting on with. I don't know what's all that about, but posh people call pissing "going to the loo," see? I don't blame him, being honest, the judge. When you gotta go you gotta go, sure.

So after ages anyway, the judge goes I have no alternative but to send you down and asked my mam if she had anything to say and she goes she was very sorry, your honour. And he gives a big long speech and he doesn't even care if she's sorry or not and it's his job to send her down if she done any crimes and he was going on and on about all that. Then my mother made a speech an' all.

Your honour, it's like this you see, she goes, I try hard to provide for my four children, but I'm all alone, living in cramped conditions on a paltry allowance and I know they're running wild outside cos it's a terrible neighbourhood and I only want what's best for all my children, but I feel I can't cope with all the pressure and I'm seeing a psychiatrist for my mental health and I had severe backpain for two year that I'm only now recovering from and I didn't even get paid for it in the end.

And the judge is stopping her all the time, saying none of that is the point, but she's carrying on like Braveheart and I'm getting all sad an' all listening to her. And that bastard Nagle is only telling her shut up and making me mad-out.

And the only reason I couldn't turn up to court was because I had a holiday booked for my young 'uns and they never had a holiday before, but I couldn't let..

And he was still telling her shut up again and again all the time and he goes, Saying why doesn't matter! But my mam wasn't letting him off.

...their one holiday ever and yes I fucked up, sorry your honour I mean mess up now and again, but I couldn't deny my kids. What mother could? Just look at them!

But the judge refused to look at them. And Melanie was even roaring crying and I was nearly crying myself, but he wouldn't even look and he was getting ready to send her to prison and it was all fierce sad. Then my mother gave us a shock.

Your honour, on top of all that I'm pregnant, you see and I only wanted for them to..

You're pregnant!? he goes, shocked an' all, like the rest of us. And after that he goes, That's no reason _not_ to send you down, you know? And she goes, Of course not, I fully expect to be sent down with my baby, if you find me guilty. And I wasn't even going to mention it, but just now thought I should... But that was all the more reason I had to give my other children one bit of a break before I go...

And the judge was all silent for a bit, but my mother carried on, ..and especially in the cramped conditions. I've been trying to be re-housed, you see, and there's a place that the council are willing to pay for, but if I go down, your honour, my family will be all busted up and we'll have to go on living in that shithole, sorry in that hole, forever and it's a fierce burden on us to be there with all the loud music blaring everywhere, but the new house is detached and there'd be no one bothering us and it's big enough and the council was willing to put us there an' all, but now I'll have to be locked up and the new baby will be born in the prison and the house will be gone when I get out and we'll have to stay in that neighbourhood forever cos they're all mean to the lot of us – And my children...

And the judge again is telling her stop stop still, but she goes on and on and on and on 'til he bangs his hammer and bangs and bangs and finally she stopped when he got mad-out and there's all silence for ages.

And after a while he asks if it's true about a house and he's told there are ongoing discussions regarding an alternative housing arrangement for the family, but most of the family aren't living together – and again my mam butted-in and proved to the judge that she was telling the truth by asking all of us if we was living at home and we all said yes, one by one after our mother goes Tara wasn't allowed come cos there was another lady minding her at present, but she was due to return to her family shortly. And she handed up a letter saying that too. And then she asked Cillian if he was moving home and Cillian said he was looking forward to the new house and he'd be moving back home if we could all fit in the one house. And I said I was living at home and Melanie even said she was looking forward to 'sploding the new house. It was funny see, cos she meant to say exploring, but she said 'sploding. I was thrilled-out at all that an' all – all us living in a big mansion imagine!

And the judge asked if this house was available and if it belonged to the council and he was told the house was newly-vacated and the council was renting it from a private owner. And the judge wasn't having none of it cos he thought the person telling him was lying so he asks where's the owner of the house and is he here? And he was told the owner was here, so the judge said he'd have a word with him.

So next thing, Con was brought back in by the same guard who walked him out and the judge had a shock an' all when he seen him and goes, Do you own this house and are you willing to have it rented to this lady and her family?

And Con goes, True as God, your honour! That other lot only made shit of the place! And the judge goes and what is your relation to this lady? And Con goes, She's my sister, your honour!

And the judge couldn't understand it and he goes, So why were you shouting earlier, insisting on having a prosecution witness in the court?

And Con gets mad-out again and starts screaming at the judge for not having that other bitch locked up cos she wouldn't be bothered turning up although she stood there while his sister had nothing to defend herself with 'cept only a broken bottle!

And Judge Nagle had Con thrown out again while he was thinking. And he asked if it's true that the defendant is pregnant and he's told it is and he's shown pieces of paper for it an' all. And while he's thinking, he looks down at the lot of us: our mother's children ('cept Tara). And I said nothing, but when I looked around, Melanie was smiling at the judge and she had a big snotty nose again and I was scarlet embarrassed and wiped my arm off her face in case he'd think she's a traveller or something.

●

111

Well, she done it anyway, my mother. She got off and after that we moved into Winchester. Not long after that.

I was telling Con, outside the courtroom, about the bits he missed – how she got the judge to do it and he was delighted with his sister and he went over to give her a hug when she come out. And Cillian comes over and Stacey too. I asked Cillian if he knew our mother was boxed and he said no he never knew about no new baby. And Stacey goes, Paolo gotta come! and she went off, skittin' away to herself. You'd never know what's going on in that girl's head.

Then Cillian tells me again I should leave. Leave my own mother, like! Just cos he wanted to leave didn't mean I'd leave her too. And I told him, sure we're all going to be living together now in our new mansion and Cillian goes no – him and Tara are going to be living with Bridie after we get the new house, and that's the deal they all done so my mother could get the house. And I had a shock again and goes I might come too, with him like. And he had a think about it and he said he asked Bridie and Bridie said she'd love to take me too but my mother wouldn't let me go cos she loved me too much cos I was her favourite.

And I was thinking about it and knew it was true anyway. And I goes, Who else would mind her?

He had no answer for that one. And I said he should stay with me too and help mind her, but he says he was doing things for her the past year and he hated it all the time – mainly fighting with the other family that was in the house we was going to be moving into. Winchester it was called, he told me for the first time. He was making them move-out the whole time. Con was at it too, other times. He said it was his job smashing windows sometimes and other times he was breaking in, robbing stuff, but they had nothing good there so he had to do terrible things in there to mess it all up.

He started saying something about it and then he stopped. And I goes what's wrong with that if it's our house not theirs? I knew Con owned it, anyway like, and it belonged to us, so why couldn't Con tell them get out? And he said that the council was paying for it, see, so Con couldn't get them out with the law. And he goes there was kids there an' all and he saw them all the time when he'd be casing the place. Loads of them and they all went to school all the time and weren't doing trouble. And in the end, Cillian felt bad for it. One time, he told me then, he dragged a mattress outside their front door and burnt it and he hid around the corner, laughing away, but after a while the kids was screaming and roaring inside, like as if the house was burning down and he knew it wasn't, like, but they thought it was burning cos the front door was opened and they probably only saw burning outside and they was all panicking inside and Cillian felt fierce bad about that one and ran up to piss on it with his langer out and the dad there spotted him and chased after him and flung the empty bucket at his head and his head was split open an' all cos the bucket was metal, like. And I remembered his bleeding head now he said it, but I never knew that's how he got it.

And why didn't you get me to help ya, so? I goes. But he only shrugs and goes, Didn't want ta, like we wasn't even friends no more.

And I thought about it then and I knowed it, knew it like: *Like we wasn't even brothers no more*, more like! And did he even ask Bridie about me living with him too? I'd say not, an all. And I spat in his face and ran out of that place. *They're all full of shit the lot of them!* I goes to myself.

The Last Supper

I stayed out of home for a bit after that. I slept one night down by the river where me and Cillian cut up the fish with the dagger. Another night I called to Murder She Wrote and her husband answered the door and he goes Hello Mickey do you want something? And I goes nah. And he goes is there any chance you managed to hang onto that jewellery Mary had next to her dresser that you robbed off her that time? I had a think about it, but I was too tired to say anything, so I just goes, Nah, again, and walks on.

I went up by our house after that and there was a party going on, like, and I sat down on the footpath across the road for a bit watching the lights and the people shouting and roaring and laughing their heads off inside. Wasn't much music there. A bit maybe. I saw Con come out and he drove away up to get the gatt and he come back after a while and unpacked all the slabs out of the boot. He didn't spot me at all and I left him off.

I didn't want to go to the party or to talk to no one. I knew I'd be able to crash in Davie O'Brien's place, if I wanted to like, but I didn't want to talk to him even or to see him even neither. I didn't know anything. It was just things. Ended up in around town mostly, just looking for somewhere. After a while I found a spot, but I won't say where now cos the same spot is still there and it's a good one too, like, and I kipped there the next few hours til it got bright.

Next day I even got on a bus and walks for another bit after that and I was passing by Mr. Mulcahy's house and slowed down. That's the fella I used live with before that, for a year or more, who my mother said was a bender and called the cops on him. Far's I knew he was still alive then. I wasn't going there to see him or anything, but just for a spin on the bus and for a walk, like. And there was no one home anyway. I didn't knock on the door, like, but I looked through the window and could see all the books was gone and the place was empty. He had a big letterbox you could get your hand into and up to the latch to open it, that I told him about loads of times, but he never bothered getting it fixed.

I used it now, this time, and got the door opened and I went in. It was a shock seeing the floorboards and hearing the loud noise in there when you'd be listening. I don't know why, but I was sad alright, like. Without the books the place was like a totally different place. The sounds were different and the smell. Before, it used be like being up close to something, being inside that house, like. Now there was an echo off the place when I walked around and it was like being outside with nothing near.

And when I went upstairs and saw all the photos and painting stuff was gone that he used to have on the wall going-up, and the piles of books on every step was gone too, I was kind of thinking am I in the right house at all? And the landing at the top had no bookshelves where there used be a kind of a black cat like a tea cup with a load of biros in it. I never even thought of it, but now I was thinking it's not there. And there was no pile of clothes hanging over the bannister and there was no ironing board in the room where he used do his ironing and he'd do mine too sometimes or tell me do it, an' all. And I never even seen his bedroom before, but I had a look in now and there was no bed in it or nothing else.

And my own room. That was empty an' all, like. Floorboards was all. I used have posters all over the walls an' everything. He took me to an art gallery every now and again and he'd be asking me, Do ya like that one Mickey? or, What was your favourite thing? he'd ask on the way home. And I'd go the ice cream! Or the echo you'd get when you shout! (I'd be shouting "Evening Echo!" like I'm selling the paper when I'm in there, like.) And he'd buy me a poster every now and again. The best one was The Last Supper by Leonardo the Vinci. I took it off him and stuck it on the wall when he asked if I wanted to stick it in my bedroom, but I never said to him that was the best one. I stuck my own posters and shit on there too, like, but I was never really into anything, 'cept the stuff he gave me was all arty stuff, like, so I added other things like soccer or model women or fast cars. I never gave a shit about them things neither really, but had to have something proper there or it'd be nothing but artsy fartsy stuff instead. And Cillian or my mother'd be mocking me if they ever saw it, like.

I closed the door behind me now in my room and lied down on the ground where my bed used be. That's when I seen the Leeds United poster on the back of the door. I was never into Leeds United or any other team, me, but Leeds was Cillian's team and they was my team too cos of that. I was in the right place alright.

●

I was only starting to doze after a while when I heard a key in the front door and I jumped up on my feet. Are you sure you saw someone? I heard one fella saying. HELLO!? And the other fella goes yeah. And the first voice says, I'll have to fix-up that letterbox. Looks like there's no one here now. I'll take a look around anyway.

That's when I opened the window and climbed out, but I was making too much noise, cos I was going too fast and I dropped down and ran away over the back wall when yer man was shouting after me. Here you! he shouted. Scumbag! What are you doing there!? Don't you come back here no more! he screamed. He's dead anyway! he shouts out then. You hear me? He's dead so there's nothing here for you, OK SCUMBAG?

And I kept running across the field and across the next field, into a bog an' all and across it even, but I kept running and I didn't even know where I was going, but I was jumping around the bog for ages and I could barely see the next sod to jump onto cos there was all water in my eyes an' all cos it was so boggy it must've been coming up through me and out.

Then I got out the other side after ages and got onto a dual carriageway and started hitching a lift, but no one picked me up, probably cos one of my legs was full of mud, up past my knee, but the other one wasn't. So I kept walking and I didn't even care.

I didn't even know either if yer man was telling me the truth anyway. About Mr. Mulcahy, like. Well, I knew it I suppose like, cos it felt like it, like, but maybe he was telling it about someone else? But how did he know who I was anyway? Did he know me? Why'd he call me a scumbag if he never even knew me, like? Maybe he thought I was a different scumbag? Maybe Mr. Mulcahy told him I was a scumbag who used live there and smashed up his books? But what did it matter anyway? I wasn't living with Mr. Mulcahy no more if he was alive or even if he wasn't alive. He wasn't my carer, so why would he even care if he was alive? He'd be probably mad at me for trashing the place, the way I did, and my mother getting the guards on him an' all. He'd be better off alive and not with me than dead and not with me, I was thinking. So I knew not to go back there no more cos of it.

●

I was starving when I got back to town and I walked into McDonalds and asks them there do ye have any jobs? And yer man goes no sorry. There's a sign on the door saying ye're hiring, I tells him, cos he was getting saucy-out now. But he told me the last job was just gone. Seemed like a load of shite to me, but I was too starving to stand up for my rights, so I left him off.

One time, years ago like, I was in there with Cillian and the two of us was starving and we walks in and I stayed back, like, and Cillian goes up to the counter and goes, Do ye have any job?

And yer wan serving looks at him and then she looks at me and then she gave us a load of food, like. Works sometimes, ha.

Outside the door, who was standing there, stopped in the street? Murder She Wrote is who, an' she staring straight at me. Mickey love! she goes, with all teary eyes, Are ya alright? I thought that was you when I saw you go in!

And I only laughs and says 'course I am Mary girl, just got offered a job an' all, but I don't start til next week. Would ya like a bite to eat? she goes and I goes OK so, if you want, sure.

I'll go in and bring it out to you, she says, but I follied her in and sat down waiting.

After she brought it, she sat down across from me and gave me the bag and the drink and goes, Will we go outside on the bench altogether? she says. It's a lovely day outside!

But I looks out the window and it was all wet everywhere. It wasn't raining no more, but it was all wet. I never even knew it was raining but the ground was still soaking so I says nothing, only eats. And I was halfway through my food when the manager comes over – same fella I was talking with just a while ago, imagine, and he goes, sorry now ye'll have to leave. And I got mad-out and goes what do ya mean, didn't we pay for it? And Mary is looking at me like a sad nun. Don't Mickey, she's saying all soft-like and she stands up to go.

I'm not budging nowhere, me! I said, out loud like. And some people near me ran out and left their food after them on the table, as if I was going to attack them or something.

I wasn't, like, but seeing them run out like that made me mad. I was only there to eat a bit of food is all and I had to get all this!?

JESUS CHRIST! I screamed and sucked down my fizzy drink through the straw 'til I calmed down and the rest of the people in there bolted out the door. Still the manager stood there, looking at me. I didn't even know what it was. Fanta probably, but it could've been Seven Up or even Coca Cola for all I knew.

I'll have to call the police, the manager goes and I shouts at him, GO ON SO! I says. And Mary tries telling him not to and that we'll leave soon, but he just walks away with his phone, like he's shit-hot and I takes no notice of him.

119

When I finished my drink and my chips, Mary goes, Come on we go 'way now so Mickey. But I goes, nah I want to stay a while, and I goes over to the next table where they left two trays of food and I starts eating them an' all. Poor Mary didn't know what to do with herself. The manager thought she must be a scumbag an' all, in there with me, I'd say, buying me food. But I didn't give a shit, me. I paid for my food and I had a right to eat it.

I PAID FOR MY FOOD, I shouted at the restaurant, AND I HAVE A RIGHT TO EAT IT SAME AS ANYONE! I told them.

If others left their food after them, I was doing the place a favour even, keeping their bins clean. That's what the rats do isn't it? Keep the bins clean by eating the food? I'M NO RAT ANYWAY! I shouts out then to anyone listening.

Scumbag, I thinks, stuffing my face with chips. I'M A SCUMBAG ALRIGHT OK?! I let them know, BUT I'M NO RAT! HAHAA! I says that, laughing, but I wasn't laughing really. He couldn't throw me out just cos I was a scumbag, just cos there was a bit of mud on my pants. I had a right to eat my food if I paid for it, didn't I?

The whole place was like on a shutdown. Everyone working there was staring at me. Everyone not working there was after running out, 'cept me and Mary. I was clearing the food on my third table when the shade walks in and I knew him and he knew me. It was Garda Mick, like, who gave me a chase when I had that Honda.

You've been through the wars, Mickey! he goes when he seen me, Did you escape through a sewer?

Some people would say that and you'd be mad at them cos they'd be calling you names, but Garda Mick arrested me a few times and he was always fair enough with me, in fairness, so I just talked with him instead, same as he always talked with me. It was only a bog, I told him. My foot slipped and went into the mud.

It was more than your foot, Garda Mick said, And you probably don't realise, but it smells more than a bog, he says and puts his hand up to his nose to block it.

That's only when I had a look at my arms and they were all brown with muck. The good jacket my mother got me was destroyed an' all and I never knew it. My pants was soaking on both legs. One was worse than the other one alright, but they were both covered in mud and muck.

But when I put my arm out to smell it, I couldn't smell nothing still.

I looks at the manager and everyone working there and at Garda Mick and then at Mary. Is there a smell off me Mary? I goes. And she starts crying and puts her hand up to her nose and nods yes.

•

Garda Mick called a Paddywagon outside for me and when it got there he was talking to the other guard from the van for ages. And me and Mary was standing there looking at them. He wasn't holding onto me or nothing and I could of run away anytime. I'd say he was waiting for me to do that an' all, but I didn't have nowhere to run to even if I thought of it. The garda from the Paddywagon was shaking his head for ages and finally he got in the front seat without looking at me and shut the door. Then Garda Mick opened the back door and told me get in and they'll take me home. All that time I was thinking they'd take me to somewhere else. I wasn't even thinking where. I never even thought they'd take me home, like. That was the last place I wanted to go.

That's alright, I goes to him, I don't want to go home, but Garda Mick says, Mickey, you're covered in shit. You need a wash and a change of clothes and I need to speak with your mother.

I felt fierce sad, all of a sudden, like. I didn't know what it was. Just a load of stuff. I nearly started crying an' all, so I hops into the back of the Paddywagon before anyone saw it and Garda Mick shut the door fast. All the way back I was bawling my eyes out on my own in the back of the Paddywagon. I never told no one that before, but that's what I was doing. Say no more.

•

At home then, the Paddywagon stops. Outside like, but I just sat there ages, clearing my face. Waiting. After a while the back door opened and my mother was standing there with Garda Mick.

Christ the state of ya! she goes, You're not setting foot in that house covered in shit! I told her it's not shit it's muck, but she says it smells like shit. Come on get out, she says and I got out all slow, like.

A gang of people came around me to see what's up, kids mostly who I knew and some mams and dads too. I knew the lot of them, like, but they were only gawking at the state of me and I just wanted to go inside, but my mam wouldn't let me. She goes, Wait there now 'til I get the hose! And Garda Mick an' all goes to her why don't you let him run in and take a shower? And my mam laced-into him and tells him fuck off out of it. And he

122

looks at me and gave me a nod and then took off with the driver of the Paddywagon.

And my mam goes into the house and I tries going after her but she's screaming at me not to set foot inside the door and to wait outside 'til she gets the hose. And Stacey's standing near the door and puts a few things in my mouth. Tabs I suppose and I swallies them.

Next my mother walks out the door with the hose on already, full-blast and she starts hosing me down and everyone is screaming laughing. And I start getting into it after a while and opens my mouth to get a drink and I drinks a load to move on the tabs. And after my jacket is mostly clean, I throws it off and everyone gives a bit of a cheer when I thrun it in the air. And she carries on hosing down my T-shirt and when that's clean I tosses that and gets a big cheer. People are singing and kids are running in to get a splash and I'm laughing and clapping now too and my mother is hosing down my shoes and I whips them off and my socks are gone. And my pants was soaking and still all filthy like, but I didn't give a damn. I was dancing away by now, turning in circles, taking off my pants and everyone was clapping and laughing and I was laughing and my mam was having a great time an' all. And off came my pants and my old Y-fronts was mostly hanging off an' all already cos they were so heavy with the wet, so I whipped them off an' all and there was a big cheer and my mother gave me a proper wash all over by having her fingers over the top of the hose to get the best speed off it, like.

I was twirling in circles without a stitch, with my hands in the air to Jesus or to Our Lord himself for ages, 'til Stacey handed me a towel. Then I kind of woke up and saw my mother was gone inside with the hose and nobody else was around. 'Cept Stacey.

Winchester

I didn't even come out of my room 'til a few days after that. Just stayed there. I felt sick, like with the gawks, but I never gawked. My mother was telling me come out and she looked after me alright when I didn't. And Stacey brung me stuff too. Corn Flakes every now and again, like. And my mother came in and said I'm getting you a new bed, come on. So I follies her out the door. And Con is sitting in the car and he drives us away out the road to a big house out on its own, with a wall around it all the way. Still in the city, like, or thereabouts and there are other houses near enough, like, but this one is the biggest. It's a mansion even alright.

He drives in the gate an' all and parks there and I'm like, Is *this* the house!? Cos I couldn't believe it'd be this big. Cillian was after saying it was, but this was even better.

Downstairs there was like four or five big rooms at least and a toilet too. Upstairs I was able to pick out my own room and I picked the one where I could see Shandon out of. It was miles away, like, but it's the tallest building in Ireland, I'd say, so I wasn't surprised to see it there. Either that or the County Hall. I couldn't see the County Hall though, so probably Shandon was taller.

One time me and Cillian got in the door around the side of Shandon and snuck away up the stairs. There's a church downstairs, like, but upstairs there's stairs and stairs all the way up. An old fella working there seen us go up an' he starts screaming and waving at us come down, but we was gone up around the corner and up more steps before he could do nothing. Up at that level, just above, there was a load of ropes with numbers you could pull to play a song and me and Cillian played some shit, but he was hitting my hand all the time cos he said I wasn't pulling the right number rope and then we starts pulling all the ropes and you'd hear the big bells in the tower way up above making the bing bong noises outside.

Looking out the window there, we were already far up, I thought, but Cillian goes come on we go 'way up the top and he ran up the next stairs that was all stone all the way up and up and up. I'd say there was at least a thousand stairs.

Up above we was inside the clocks an' all that are halfway up the tower on the outside. Then you go up further and you're inside where you climb past the big bells. And we climbed in around all the bells an' all 'stead of going up the top and Cillian goes, Caught – you're on it!

And we jumped around the wood planks that were holding up the bells, playing chasing and it was a good laugh 'til one of the bells bongs and I nearly collapsed with the fright. Then there was another bong from another bell and a few more bongs from the one right next to me, like. And Cillian is shouting at me come on we go up to the top and I'm hanging onto the plank of wood cos the bell might ring again and blow me off it, but he's alright cos he's near the stairs, but I'm over the other side and can't get around the bells.

Took me ages, but I got back to the stairs then and up another thousand steps. I got out then to the walls like the walls around a castle and you could see everywhere in Cork, like, for miles and miles. The whole place. And you could walk all the way around the tower – four sides like – seeing everywhere everywhere. I'd see my bedroom in Winchester an' all if I was up there now, but I didn't know it then, like, cos I never lived there at the time.

Cillian hoiks a glugger then over the side but the wind turned it and it landed straight on my neck and we're both knotted laughing at the state of it when two older fellas come around the corner, up in the tower. How's it goin' Cillian, goes one of them, cos he knew Cillian, but didn't know me much, What brings you up here? he goes.

Cillian waits a while, checking what to do, but we were all the way around the tower so there was nowhere to go to, 'cept either through the two of them or over the wall behind us, that was the roof of where we come up into the tower. And we was hundreds of foot up in the sky already, so I wasn't going to be climbing no wall to escape.

Joe was his name, who was talking to Cillian, asking him questions. Joe Cotter, like. And his friend was Niall O'Shea. They lived around there, around Shandon, like, and they were probably up there all the time for all we knew. Both of them was a few years older than Cillian. I'm trying to think now, I'd say I was around seven or eight at that time, so they might have been around fifteen each. I knew them alright and I knew we was in trouble. They'd be alright sometimes, like in fairness, but other times they'd rob you too. You'd know when there's trouble though.

Just up to show my brother things, Cillian goes and none of the two of them even looks at me, but they go either side of my brother and locks onto him. Cillian gets mad then and starts shouting at them to leave him go, but they starts lifting him up

126

and I'm screaming and roaring at them to stop, but they put Cillian upside down and hangs him over the side and I'm bawling my eyes out screaming at them Stop!

Next thing, after ages, Niall looks around at me and goes to Joe, We'd better take him in cos yer man is having a canary.

And I'm bawling still like a real baby and they bring Cillian in. And they're all smiles together then, like friends or something. And Cillian is laughing, even, at the thrill off it. And I'm like calming down cos I was screaming so much before that and Cillian locks onto me then and goes, Do Mickey next! And I screams again and legs it around the corner, then down the line along the tower and around the next corner, then down the line and when I'm getting over by the stairs to go down, Niall hops over the roof of the stairs in front of me and I goes into a freeze, like. Like how could he climb over the roof when we're hundreds of foot up so high? He was like an acrobat or something, I'm thinking, but I'm still in a shock. Next who follies him over in front of me too? – My brother Cillian! And he has a mad smile on his face and he's staring straight at me. And Joe Cotter is straight behind me and I begs the lot of them not to do it please, but they lifts me up and hangs me over the side by my ankles and I shuts my eyes and I don't even know if I screams or faints, but when they takes me back in, Cillian holds my head to look at me and he's bursting laughing and saying that was some laugh wasn't it? And I bursts out laughing then too and goes ya! What a laugh it was!

That's why I picked that room in Winchester. I was never up in Shandon no more after that, but it was a great laugh. Being up there, like.

●

Cillian stayed with us in Winchester for a bit an' all when we moved in first. I was still odd with him from the court, but we got friends again then alright. For a bit. He pretended to be too posh though, even then. He had his own room and I had my own room and Tara and Melanie had a room together, cos they wasn't there much like. And Cillian wasn't there much either in the end, but least he was there more than them two. And My mam had her room and Stacey had her room an' all, mostly, when she wasn't living at home with Mrs. O'Connor. And there was another room downstairs at the back where Con stayed mostly an' all too when my mother'd let him. And other times there'd be loads of people all over the house from parties and shit and sometimes there'd be a few lodgers too. And people'd be calling always to do a bit of business and pay extra sometimes to stay there a bit after, but my mam mostly wouldn't let no one stay unless they were alright cos they'd be nothing but trouble. Cos the place belonged to Con now, see, and the council said they wouldn't pay for no damage no more, see, if someone damaged anything. Cute bastards when you think of it too.

And sometimes Stacey's new boyfriend would be living there 'til she got a new one. And there was Jordan SueAnne too after she got born, like, of course. But that was later on. I was up in Dublin and back an' all by then, I think.

But by now, I wasn't. I was staying in Winchester cos it was our new home and it was daycent-out. We all had beds an' all and everything.

•

I had a load of D10s off Moxie one day, about a week after we was living there, cos I was supposed to deliver them, cos Cillian wasn't doing that no more so I was, but I didn't do it yet, like, and that was the first time (supposed to be) and it was getting night time so I said I'd do it in the morning.

So, cos Cillian was around and he wasn't even having any sweets, I brought him the bag into his room and says, Look what I got off Moxie, do you want some? and he gets mad-out straight away and throws a raaby, What are you doing with all that!? he screams at me, Are ya selling now an' all!? (Like he never done,) He can't be giving ya all a'that!

What ya mean, boy? I goes to him, Sure I'm doing same as what you done always. I have to bring them to Farmer in Blarney. Cillian, though, is going ape-shit, Who's Farmer in Blarney? he goes to me and I told him that's the fella I need to bring them to, like. I told him where I was supposed to bring them that night at eight o'clock and he throws another raaby and goes it's already gone eight o'clock. And I'm like, What's wrong with ya at all? And he goes that it's a trap cos no way would Moxie be getting you to bring a big bag of D10s to that place out in Blarney, like that, at that hour anyway. And I says why not?

He says for one thing, after you get off the bus, you have to walk at least five miles til you get there and for another thing, why would he say what time to drop them? And for another thing, even, why would Moxie get _you_ to do it? He says "you" like there's something wrong with me, like.

And what's wrong with that? I goes to him. Is there a smell off me or what? It's OK for him to be giving _you_ jobs but not me?

Then he goes all quiet a while and has a big huff and goes, You know who Moxie's up against don't ya? The travellers! I tells him. Ya! he says, And who sells for the travellers? And I lists off all the fiends and the beors who we know, but he stops me again and goes, Ya but who do they all get their gear off of?

Con! I goes, I know that, but… but he stops me again and goes, It's not Con at all no more, you know even? It's our mother is who, ya fool! And she'd kill ya if she found ya delivering for Moxie. And Moxie will kill ya to get her back!

And then he goes on and on, calling me all the names like I'm an idiot who knows nothing, only him who knows it all. And on and on like a prick.

After a while he calms down anyway and I could talk. It's not like that at all, I tells him. Moxie's A-1. He says he has no bother with the travellers no more cos the place is big enough for everyone to make a bundle, 'cluding me too, he says an' all!

But Cillian isn't even listening to me. He's mad-out and takes all the tabs and tells me don't be going near Moxie no more. Then he runs off out with the lot of it and I put on the telly downstairs and starts watching Top Gun cos it was on and I likes that one and I needed to calm down for my nerves, cos Cillian made me right-mad and he run off with all the tabs and Moxie'd really kill me now, I was thinking, cos I didn't even have the bag no more. It's not my favourite movie though. I'd say Braveheart is my favourite one, like, but we had it on video a few days before that and Melanie broke it in the sink when she washed it cos it was all dirty and she washes everything all the time cos she's a real clean-freak, Melanie. Even now she'd be washing and cleaning everything all the time. And when I tried playing it in the video after that, it broke the video player an' all with sparks and shit. And it was only when my mam walks in and seen all the smoke, she got Cillian to pull out the wire and out the fire. But after he burnt his hand he used a cushion. Well it wasn't really a fire, but it was nearly. And she throws a raaby an' all about that and goes she couldn't have nothing with the lot of us and I goes it's not Melanie's fault at all, she was only cleaning. And my mam then goes she wasn't blaming Melanie, she was blaming me! Me, like! I don't know if there was any DVDs in them days, but we didn't have none anyway. It was ages 'til I seen Braveheart again too, an' all. So that's why I was watching Top Gun on RTE, like.

●

Next day Con brought a load of post from the old house and dumped it all on the table in the kitchen and an empty pint glass fell off and smashed on the floor, there was so much post. Mostly it was brown and white ones, but I seen a bright orange envelope in the middle and when I looked, it had my name on it an' all. Like, who'd be writing to me, 'cept the court? But even then it'd be to my mam, more like. Just had my name on it and our old address. I was just going to ask Stacey about it when my mam walks in and goes, Come on we have to visit Cillian, he's in the hospital, she says.

And I got a shock and drops the envelope and goes what happened him? And she says he got hopped and he has a broken leg, go get your coat, she said to me and Con. She's going through, looking at the post while she's talking. And she was opening the orange envelope an' all when I ran out to get my coat. When I got back I didn't see that letter no more. She was picking up a load of other letters and just crumpling them all up without opening them even and filling up the bin with them. A load of rubbish, the lot of it.

What was that orange letter about? I goes to her, The one with my name on it?

And she goes you're up in court again in three weeks ya stupid shit, get out that door now before I bate ya! And we're laughing about that, getting into the car.

●

At the hospital, Bridie was there with Cillian, before me and my mam got there (Con was parking the car. Stacey stayed at home to mind Melanie and Tara). When she seen us, Bridie starts talking with my mother, giving-out and shit, saying she's supposed to be taking Cillian and Tara already, but my mam laces into her and gives her some proper stink about who do she think she is and stuff.

While they were fighting, I goes to Cillian, Who done it? Was it Moxie? and Cillian goes yeah, but it's alright now, like. He had a fight with Barry, Moxie's man, like who was around forty I'd say and Barry broke Cillian's leg and gave him a cut under his eye and knocked out two of his teeth and his shoulder was all black and blue and probably broke his ribs too. But after that Moxie told him tell me (Mickey, like) stay away from him in future and I won't be getting no more jobs off him neither cos I'm a snake who'd rather be working with travellers, Cillian said and I told him it's nothing to do with me, but he goes Moxie's only mad at our mother so it makes no difference.

Then Con comes in and my mother turns round to Cillian, and Bridie shags off, and my mother goes, What were you up to? and Cillian told her he got mugged and my mother wouldn't believe him. She goes no muggers break your leg and

132

they were fighting about it til Cillian tells her Barry Murphy done it cos he thought he was someone else and it was an accident and he said sorry after, so it was all alright. But my mother goes we'll see about that and she looks at Con and he's smiling, but not really like. I'll get that fucker Barry-the-bastard! he goes, He went to school with me and he was never any good, that bastard! and my mam has a look in her face too, thinking like. His dad done the same to our dad too, remember years ago? she goes, but Con didn't remember.

Ya, she says, He robbed a car. Barney was his name. He got killed falling off a bridge, later. Years later. He robbed it cos they were doing a job up in Tipperary and they needed a fast getaway car. And Dada was only an innocent bystander and saw him drive off and he knew him too. Then later-on, didn't Barney Murphy spot him on the green and drove straight over him with the same car and broke two of his legs so he'd tell no one. Fuckin' bastard Barry! I goes. And Cillian goes, He was still driving the same car and used it to knock down Granda?

They're all the same, those Murphys, my mam goes, They're low-level scum who think they're in the mafia!

But, was this before or after they done the job in Tipperary? Cillian goes, but he was asking too much questions and the rest of us was mad-out by then. Con and me 'specially. We have to get him back for what he done to our father – or to my grandfather, like, Con's father. And for what his son done to my brother. They're all the same, them Murphys.

And Cillian then is begging the lot of us not to be doing nothing about it and he says he won't be doing nothing on it and he wants to leave us all and my mother needs to sign the papers to let him and Tara go like she promised, but she's only on and on about Barry and how she's going to get him back for what he done. And Cillian is giving out and wouldn't even leave us talk about Barry, so after a while we left him there and went home to make our plans.

On the way though, Con stopped off in the pub and we stayed there a few hours and we couldn't really talk about it there, cos there was too many around and I ended up walking home cos they got into a sing-song and everything. The most pints the barman would give me was two anyway and when he caught me having another one I was thrown out. I got fed up by then anyway too so I wouldn't be bothered.

●

The next day, around, I was outside and Stacey comes over and goes she'd give me a treat and I was after forgetting about her flashes by then so I got a shock and I follied her an' all. And she brung me to McDonald's and walks over to where Tina O'Mahoney was sitting and says, Here's Mickey now Tina, I told you he'd love to meet you after all these years. And I was scarlet and Tina was scarlet too, I knew it.

I knew Tina from school years ago, like, when we was in the same class for a bit and we used live near where she used to live and we all used play in the same gang on the road. But I never seen her for years and she was older now, but I still knew her, like. She had squinty eyes and big glasses then, but she was after an operation on her eye now and it was all bandaged up to make it not squinty no more and she had no glasses. Besides that she was alright. A bit of a lasher even, in fact. And she was looking at me and smiling, but scarlet too.

I didn't know what to say and Stacey goes, Well Mickey are you going to say hello to Tina? and I said hello Tina are you

134

getting your squinty eye straightened? And she goes ya, but Stacey says she's shy about it and talk about something else, to me like. So I goes, Do you want chicken nuggets? And Tina goes yeah, but I didn't have any money so I told Stacey and she gave me a fiver and I waved it at Tina and she laughs. I got chicken nuggets and chips and a Coke and told yer wan behind the counter keep the change an' all and I gave most of the stuff to Tina and she ate it and drunk it too and that was the start. We was going out together then.

I won't go on and on about all that cos it's soppy shit, mostly, but Tina and me was in proper love for ages. A load of weeks I'd say. She was staying with another family called the Murviews. There was around ten of them. And around five of them, including Tina, was fostered and they were alright mostly and they left me visit there too mostly, if we wasn't at Winchester. But I had to leave by nine o'clock, but I stayed most nights til around ten at least I'd say.

They was from England originally. Glasgow, Tina goes. Took me ages to understand the dad he spoke mad like. Didn't think he even said English words for ages til he was talking to Tina one time and she was talking to him too and I knew she knew what he was on about and when he went away I was like, How do you know what he's saying? and she was laughing at me only.

Anyway after a while I could understand him too like, mostly, just by listening. That's how I learnt to speak Scottish an' all, I'd say. His name was Seán and he was from Cork originally an' all imagine, he goes, but his mother went to Glasgow when he was a baby and he always wanted to move back to Cork since then and now he was back there with his big family and he had another wife in Glasgow who had seven more children, but Karen who he come to Cork with was his favourite wife and their family together was his favourite family and they didn't see the other family no more hardly, 'cept one time he went to visit his oldest son who was in prison, but he's out now and his other son died in the army in Iraq or someplace years ago. He "absconded" after his son died, he goes. Ahahahahaah! I thought that was funny when he said it. Absconded. The way he said it was funny. It's a funny word. Well, he laughed, so it must of been.

I walked home mostly at night-time after the Murview's house. Took me around two hours like and I had to walk all through town an' all on my way, but I didn't care like, cos Tina was alright and we done nearly no drugs most of the time or nothing. She didn't like to be doing them and I was fed up with them anyway an' all.

•

One time – I tell ya this funny one what happened me one time when I was on my way home, walking through town. I met Con, just out of the blue like, staggering out of a pub an' I passing. He was langers. I seen him loads around then of course, cos we lived in the same house mostly. And he starts talking like I was with him all night as if we were both on the batter together all the time. He goes, We need do a job, and I didn't even know if he knew who I was cos he was fairly legless, so I goes, Hi Con it's me! And he goes, We need do a job, come on folly me I'll show ya.

And I follied him, but he didn't say much and he stopped for a slash twice and he asked me for a fag but I didn't have none and I tried asking him where we was going, but we turned the corner and he went into a shop that was still opened. A sweet shop, like mostly. Sold fags too. And I stayed outside cos I knew. And I saw him inside talking to the Indian fella behind the counter and I didn't hear it, but the fella grabbed a bat and Con hopped straight on top of all the sweets, but didn't make it over. And he grabbed the bat and twirled it while he was grabbing it off yer man and it hit him on the head and he went down, an' Con still up on top of all the stuff on the counter. He couldn't get off cos his foot was stuck between the end of the sweet shelf and the till. And he fell off on the outside, but his foot was still stuck in the air. And there was others in the shop and they all run out and I was thinking what to do. And all sudden like, there was sirens and lights everywhere and I legged it too, fast as I could. That was some funny shit. I seen Con a couple of days later at home and he only looks at me like he was going to ask me something, but he never said nothing about it and I didn't neither, cos he'd be only giving out to me for leaving him there, like.

HAPPY FAMILIES

I was going out with Tina about a week or two when my mam was giving out. You're living in the lap of luxury, she goes when she walks into the kitchen one day and saw me and Tina and Stacey in there, And you're paying nothing for it! I suppose you're giving that whore presents every day an' all?

She says this over-right Tina, like. I goes, Mam you can't be saying that about me oul doll! And Tina goes, Hey who you calling your oul doll!? And Stacey goes, Oh you don't like him saying oul doll, but you don't mind being called a whore?

And my mam goes, Her mother was a whore all her life. (She says that to me, like, cos she never even talked to Tina all the time I was going out with her.)

And I'm like, Mam! Don't be talking like that!

And Tina goes, I'm not no whore, no! And neither is my mother, no! Who's she calling a whore?

And I'm telling Tina no don't, cos she's getting stuck on my mam and I know my mam will get her back if she don't be nice to her. Then Stacey goes, Maybe ye should go away out for a walk, Mickey, and call back later?

And I goes OK. And when we was going, my mam goes, Don't be wasting your money on that thing and remember you need to be back here by six o'clock!

The reason I wasn't giving my mam no presents wasn't cos I was giving them to Tina, but cos me and Tina was at her house all the time the last week, and on my way home I wasn't bothered about doing nothing else, 'cept go home to bed, cos it was nice and cosy in my new bed, like, and I never even thought about it. But on the way to her house, Tina was asking why did I need to be back home by six and I said we had to do a job tonight at Mrs. Savey's house. And she goes, Who's Mrs. Savey? and I had to tell her then all about what happened Cillian, getting beaten up and shit, and how we was getting Barry back for it. But who's Mrs. Savey? she goes again and I remembered then that's what we was talking about cos I got mixed up and forgot and I goes Barry's not around, see, and neither is Moxie even (but by then we weren't even thinking of Moxie, it was Barry, see) so we was getting Mrs. Savey instead, see? But Tina didn't see cos she still didn't know who Mrs. Savey was and I had to tell her, but I couldn't even remember cos I was all confused cos this shit gets confusing, like. And Tina goes, Are you going to attack Mrs. Savey or what? and I got a kind of a shock then cos it's like she was asking if I'd attack her an' all. I never thought of it even til she said it. And she didn't even say it, but that's what it seemed like to me at least, cos she got all shy and quiet when she asked it and looked at me with her one eye and I was like all shy or something too all of a sudden, like.

I don't know! I goes and it was the truth too, cos I didn't even think of it 'til then. I suppose I thought I'd have to smash her window and I told Tina that. And she goes, But why? and I was telling her again what Barry's dad done to my dad or to someone and she's asking again what has Mrs. Savey got to do with all of that and I don't even know, but I know she has something to do with it so I tells her, Tina like, stop with all the questions will ya, you're as bad as Cillian, I goes. And she left it off then at least.

But later-on when we was at her house, we were all in the front room having a laugh, a lot of the Murviews, like and the telly was on. And Tina goes to Karen, can Mickey have his tea here? And Seán straight away goes, Curse he can, love! The mur the murrier at the Murviews!

And I bursts my arse laughing cos he always had something funny to say and he'd always be laughing, him in fairness. He was stone-mad, I tell ya.

So I had my tea there and it was only after that again when I remembered I was supposed to be at home by six, but it was like half-seven by then. And Tina goes don't bother going home yet and we was sitting together up tight on the settee cos there was three other Murviews on the other end of the seat (one was a smallie on Tina's half-sister's lap). And Tina had her whole head turned towards me when she was talking to me cos she couldn't see out of the eye that was closest, so she had to turn fully around all the time. And she was smiling straight at me with her full face and sometimes when she'd be turning I'd get a rub off her tit too on my arm, like, and I knew I couldn't get up anyway for ages cos I had a massive horn on me, like, and they was all around in the room having a laugh and watching telly and there was me on the end of the settee, scarlet and dreaming away to myself.

When I got home there was no one around so I just went to bed. Wasn't even twelve o'clock and I went to bed. Next day my mother barges in and she's screaming and roaring at me. Where were you last night? she was saying.

You know you had a job to do! Didn't I tell ya be home by six! You need to be doing more jobs now you're old enough

140

and Cillian's after fucking off and I need you (me, like, she meant) to be doing more of the stuff that has to be done.

Cillian left the day before that, like. Or the day before that. Bridie came and took him and Tara too. From then on, mostly they were living at Bridie's. And I knew there was no one else to help her, my mam like, but I didn't even care cos I had a good time at Tina's. They were like a real family like you'd see on the telly. I thought they only made that shit up. We're living in this big house now, she was still saying to me, and you need to be blah blah blah.

But I knew she'd kill me if I didn't be doing more jobs and getting things for her, so that night I done three jobs. Three houses, like. And in one of them I got a load of rings and I always knows the ones my mam likes best but there was none of them ones, so I gave them to Tina next day and she was mad about them. I wasn't expecting that cos my mam would of said they were shit, but Tina was all over me, rubbing hard up against me an everything with her chest like and I got a shock and a thrill off it too. You didn't do anything bad for these Mickey did ya, she goes. And I goes what of it. And she gave me a shift and said I wasn't to be taking any risks cos she loved me even if I didn't ever give her no presents.

Then when I got home later on, my mam goes, Were you out last night and where's my presents. And I goes no I forgot. And there was another big fight til I found a load of CDs and gave her them, but she wasn't happy and she was calling Tina all names again, like it was her fault.

•

141

A few days later on, my mam shoved in the door in my room. I was in there with Tina, like, at the time. I wasn't after doing anymore houses or stuff after the first one the week before, cos Tina didn't want me to, like, but my mam was giving out and giving out the whole time. So I done another few houses the night before this and I was after throwing a load of the stuff up on the bed when Tina called round. And after that we were having it off, like, and my mam shoves in the door and knocks over the cabinet I was after moving over to block it an' all and she gets mad-out, screaming and roaring when she seen the both of us. We wasn't under the blankets or nothing, but I was on top of Tina alright.

JESUS CHRIST I KNEW IT! she screams, A WHORE LIKE HER MOTHER!

And we hopped off the bed and started getting dressed and my mother is screaming and roaring the whole time, looking at all the jewellery and going, Did she have all that stuck up her fanny? She probably shits diamonds an' all, she's such a tight-arse! Butter wouldn't melt in her mouth!

All that kind of stuff from my mother, she'd scare the life out of anyone, mine would. She stopped talking to me for days after that, then. Wouldn't let me out of the house if I was already in. And she wouldn't let me in if I was out neither.

And then my court case comes up.

●

Only me and my mother and the judge and my social worker and different guards and lawyers and stuff was allowed in. No one else. Outside, Tina was hugging me and crying and I was telling her I'd be grand, but my mother goes, Time to give it up, Mickey. That wan's no good for you. She'll only get you in trouble every time.

And I told her fuck off then, my mother like, and she stares at me like I spat in her eye. I never told her fuck off before, but she was really pissing me off now and I got no peace off her.

She just walks away then, all sad-like to my social worker, who was standing there looking at me. And I was sorry-out straight away but I went back to shifting Tina and that's all I was bothered with really at the time.

•

They starts by reading out all the charges. Joyriding and drugs found in the car (wasn't me, it was them older fellas – Shane O'Brien, like); Filling Station Theft (I stole nothing, was only buying fags but there was no one on the counter when I got attacked by the manager in an ambush); Attempted Burglary (I wasn't even in the house 'til the shade who owned it chased me in!); Vandalism and Anti-social behaviour (I admitted to those ones alright cos I couldn't really remember what they were). Then there was not turning up to court. I had to admit that one an' all.

When all that was done, the judge had a long think about it and he looks up then and gives out to me like mad. About all of it. He tells me I can't be going around like a thug and a thief and I told him I was very sorry your honour. And I was too, cos Tina'd be sad and I'd be sad-out too if I had to go down now, just when me and her was probably going to get married or something.

And then he goes, And what about the parents? And my mother stands up, all sad-eyes and worried-looking. And he tells her she can sit down and she's saying I'm very sorry your honour, I'm trying my best, but he's out of control and I can't get him to do nothing. And the judge goes to her why didn't she ensure I made my court appearance and was it true she took me on holidays instead? And she had a think about that one and looks at me and I'm smiling at her, 'til she goes the holiday was booked in advance and she didn't want to disappoint the other children, but she told Mickey he couldn't miss his court appearance and he was upset about that and the other children were all upset and there was no one at home left to look after him if they all went away and she was trapped into bringing him and she tried calling his social worker to leave her know, but she couldn't be reached at the time.

Then the judge had another long think. And he asks my social worker why isn't she doing her job looking out for young Michael, making sure I done the right things and not the wrong things? And was she out of contact when Mrs. Collins tried calling her before the court case?

Her name was Elaine Something and she was alright, but she was only around for like the last three months and she didn't know me much and I didn't know her too, but she had my files at least. And she goes she had no record of a missed call and it's the first she heard of it. And my mother starts on then, mad-out like, but the judge told her shut up and I had a laugh.

Mickey's actually behaving very well lately, Elaine told him, and hasn't been in much trouble for the past month around. The family are living in a new home in a respectable area and Mickey is home every night in good time and he has a girlfriend now, he tells me, who seems to be a good influence on him and he has been drug-free and submitting to regular urine samples. And on and on, she done a good job convincing the judge in fairness. Can't fault her at that.

And the judge has another long think about it and my mother tries talking a few times but he tells her stop talking a while cos he has to think about it. And he's moving his papers around and my mother is going, He's out of control your honour... And the judge is telling her stop, he's thinking.

Then he looks up and starts talking. He's saying he was wondering if a custodial sentence was appropriate and my mother goes it was and he tells her shut up again and starts saying he's thinking maybe Mickey's too young at fifteen to be going into the system and it might be better for all if he was able to prove he was on the right track for a bit longer and maybe we should all meet again in a few months to make sure progress is being made.

And then my mam slams her hand on the table and stands up and gets mad at the judge. She tells him straight-out that Mickey is out of control. He won't do a thing she asks him. Whenever she tells him don't go out, he won't stay in. When she tells him go do a job, he won't go out. He disobeys her all the time, wandering the streets at all hours, hanging out with known criminals. He never goes to school, they haven't seen him there for over a year!

And I shouts out that she's lying cos I was there a month ago! And the judge tells me shut up or he'd have to send me down.

He's having underage sex with prostitutes, she goes. And I jumps up and goes, WHAT!? and I tells him my mother's lying. And the judge tells me shut up again and my mother goes, See your honour! He won't let me speak and won't listen to a word I say! I'm at the end of my tether now with him! Social workers is one thing, but only a mother knows what goes on under her own roof – or outside of it! …And he's spending all his time with this other family. From what I can tell the place is a brothel being run by degenerates from Scotland! Seanie O'Brien's his name. He's from the O'Briens originally. Their lot were run out of Cork nearly fifty years ago for drugs and prostitution imagine – you can check the court records. My father knew them well and often spoke of that fella's father and how ruthless he was. Goes by a posh-Scottish name now. Murview of all things! But they're back and claiming turf!

The judge gets her to stop then and goes, These are very serious allegations you're making here Mrs. Collins, but they have nothing at all to do with… And my mother interrupts him again with more of it, but the judge carries on… I know nothing about what you're saying and the matter has not been brought to my attention heretofore. I appreciate you're upset and you need to take any information on all this to the Gardaí, if you haven't already, but you can't go disparaging others in this manner without any proof.

My mother carries on like he said nothing, …And he robs houses all the time, my darling son. she goes, And gives the proceeds of his crimes to Seanie O'Brien's whore in exchange for sex.

And the judge is telling her stop, she made enough accusations, he says.

He pays this whore for sex, your honour – I caught them in the act in my own home in fact and found this lot that he was using to pay for it.

146

Next, she opens her bag and poured out all the jewellery she took off us when she caught us at it a few days before.

I was shocked your honour! I find it outrageous that he has taken to carrying on in this manner in my own home! He's very hard to teach a lesson, especially with me expecting and being the sole adult in the house, she carries on.

I can't be bringing a baby into that! And she's older than him too, this wan. Taking advantage of his special needs and everything. I really do feel that a custodial sentence is needed now to set him on the right path. I wouldn't suggest it only I don't know what else...

And I'm like in shock that she kept all the rings and things and throws them out now here in front of the judge and I barely heard what she said.

And the judge is thinking again while she's talking and looking at me and reading all the papers and notes in front of him. And we all got a shock, I'd say. And finally he goes, Irrespective of allegations on the behaviour of this other family and regardless of Michael's special needs...

And I hears that for the first time and jumps up and starts screaming at him. SPECIAL NEEDS! I'm shouting, SPECIAL NEEDS? WHO ARE YOU CALLING SPECIAL NEEDS!?

And the officers there had to hold me back cos he was mocking me an' all and I knew then it was all a stitch up, cos now they're making out I got special needs or something. And the judge starts talking about Tina and he's saying that she might be taking a vantage off me and I'm screaming at him again and he won't listen to it and my mother is asking for me to be sent down for a few months so I can learn a lesson. And, to make a long story short, the judge goes he won't send me down for a few months but he will send me down for a week and see if I can learn a lesson off it. And we'll all be back here in three weeks and he'll, Want to see an improvement in your behaviour, young man!

And I'm in shock again and my mother is thanking the judge and smiling at me and says, Now Mickey, I hope you'll learn always to be listening to your mother cos mother knows best! And stay away from whores and prostitutes.

The Big Smoke

On the road up to Dublin (on the way to where they were locking me up, like) I'm looking at the shade sitting across from me in the car and he looks over at me and next he looks away fast. He says nothing, like, but I know he's laughing at me being called special needs. I'm saying nothing either but I'm getting madder and madder looking at him cos I know he's dying to say it and it's not fair on me, like, cos they probably had a big laugh about that over a cup of tea and a biscuit, all them guards bursting their arses at me and what they're calling me now.

And I'm thinking too about that fella, the judge like, saying Special Needs. Like, who do people like that think they are? talking like that? And I half-remember then that it was my mam was the one who said it first. She must of got him thinking of it. It's one thing my mother saying it, but he have no right to be saying something like that. Like, what a prick! All of them even! I'd be better off in that place I'm going to, I was thinking, well-away from the lot of them. I was wrong about that one in the end though. Well-wrong when you think of it.

But in the meantime I have this bollox looking over at me every now and again like he's picking up shit and I know the only thing to do is to give him a lesson, then leg-it. But I'd say they knew it an' all, cos when they stopped for food, the driver-shade (who was alright, like) took me to the jacks and stayed talking with me. And the prick-shade stayed back a bit, saying nothing. And he kept out of the way, like.

Are you alright Mickey? the driver-shade asked me when the prick-shade went up to pay. You seem agitated, he goes – *agitated* like! *Me*, like! And I told him that other guard won't stop looking at me and I knew he was laughing at me, inside like he was laughing. And he asked me what the other guard was laughing at and I told him what the judge said and he started laughing then an' all. And I got a shock at that, cos he seemed alright. But before I could hit him, he goes, Believe me, Mickey, special needs is nothing. A cute-hoor Corkman like yourself'll be the most intelligent fucker in the place where you're going, I guarantee ya that! And I laughed at that then too cos I knew it was true and when yer man came back after paying, he goes what are ye laughing at and I goes, You wouldn't have a clue, you're from Sligo! And me and the alright-guard starts laughing again, but the prick-guard (who was alright again then too, like) goes, I am not! he goes, I'm from Cavan, me!

And the two of us bursts our arses laughing at him again for that. First time I got a good laugh with a shade, I'd say. That Cavan guard drove us the rest of the way up and me and the other guard sat in the back and one of us every now and again would go, I'm from Cavan, me! the same way he said it. Some laugh we had.

●

Up above, I was in a cell with four other fellas. One of them was alright, but the other three were either bolloxes or a prick. They all had bunk beds, but I got the mattress on the floor cos I was the last one in, see?

When I got put in there first, like, they all stops talking and one fella with a load of freckles on his face goes, Your bed there, lah! pointing at the floor. And I thought to myself, he's a prick anyway. His hair was standing up on the top of his head like he got out of bed that way. You know how some people's hair is always tossed? Well his was always tossed like that. He was lying on his bed, looking at me, still pointing at the floor like he's ordering me lie down there, but I wasn't doing nothing and all the others was saying nothing too. Only one of them was looking at me though, waiting to see what I'd do. The other two were playing cards mostly, on the top bunk like, over the freckle-fella.

What's your name? the other fella who was looking at me goes and I told him my name was Mickey and they all starts laughing and calling me Mickey Mouse, like I never heard it before. Then the fella who asked me my name hops up and goes, That's alright Clicky, I'll take the floor! and he hopped down on the mattress straight away, straight-out like. And all the others starts laughing again, calling me Clicky instead.

He seemed alright, that fella on the floor though. He told me his own name was Brendan. Then the freckle fella, who was after telling me lie on the floor goes, Say nothing t' that fella!

His voice was all hoarse. I'd say he was sucking the spraypaint too long. I thought he was telling Brendan not to talk to me, but when I looked over, I knew he was warning me say nothing to Brendan. Nothin' 'tall 'fyou know what's good for ya! he goes, like a threat.

That's Clarksy, says Brendan. And the other three laughed, including Clarksy too an' all. Clarksy! said one of the

151

card players without even looking up from his game. Then Clarksy stomped his foot up in the air to the top-bunk above him, where they were playing and goes, I'll give ya Clarksy ya faggot!

His foot messed up the cards and the betting and the two lads starts screaming and roaring at Clarksy. And Clarksy shouts back and it all goes on a while like that, but they were only messing with each other, like mostly.

When they stops with all that though, Clarksy goes to Brendan all-quiet like, Some dopey prick you are, Browndawn Amadawn! but he was only laughing at him too an' all. Then he turned away to face the wall and said nothing else.

He was all talk after that then, Brendan, and he told me again lie down on his bed. When I lied down then he was asking What's your second name, click? Where ya from, click? What part of Cork, click? He kept saying click after everything. Who'd ya know, click? Were you ever in here before, click? All that kind of stuff. And I told him everything and said it to the whole cell too cos I thought it didn't matter. But it did.

When I got to that place first like with the two shades, the screws were taking my details and signing me in and telling me stuff. And they told me I could have one phonecall a day and I had to give them two numbers for me to pick from. Obviously I wasn't going to be calling my mother, but since hers and Tina's were the only numbers I had, I gave them those two anyway. But when I asked if I could call then, they put me in the cell first anyway.

So the guard comes back now when I'm done giving Brendan the answers, and said through the door that I could make my phonecall.

Tell *them* fuck-all an' all! says Clarksy when yer man was opening the door.

I want to call my girlfriend, I told the guard when I was walking out and all the fellas in the cell goes Ooooooooooh, he wants to call his girlfriend Ooo Wooo! The card-players even stopped their game to mock me over it. I didn't care though, cos I said it on purpose so least they wouldn't think I was a bender, like.

He rang Tina anyway for me, the screw downstairs, and put her on when she answered. She was all tears though. Nothing but crying. Bawling crying she was. I only had a few minutes so I had to keep telling her stop cos I could hear nothing and she couldn't either. I said I'd be out in a week and there was no way I'd be living at home with my mother after this and I'd find my own place and would she move in with me too, like, and we'd have our own spot, away from everyone else. And she goes I can't be going out with you no more if you'd be going to jail and stuff all the time. And I told her all that stuff I was in for was before I met her and it wouldn't have got me time, only my mother screwed me over and blamed her too, Tina like, for it. And I asked her again if she'd help me get away like Cillian got out of it and we'd get a place together when I got back to Cork. And Tina goes I miss ya already Mickey, but I don't know if we'd be allowed move in together since I'm only sixteen and you're only fifteen (me, Mickey like). She turned sixteen a couple of weeks before we started going out.

They mightn't give us a house at our age, she goes. She was smart-out, Tina. She'd think of things like that.

Anyway, before we finished, I told her I'd call her again tomorrow. On the way back then, I got to the top of the stairs and there was a fella walking towards me with a guard behind him. I wasn't really looking at them, but when we got up close yer man fell over and kind of got me straight in the gut with his elbow or something while he was falling. I could barely breathe from it and I doubled over, winded-like. SORRY 'BOUT THAT! yer man shouts out, I FELL! – IT WAS AN ACCIDENT!

I was on my knees and the same fella was picking me up and the two screws around us were only standing there. That's alright, I goes, I'm alright! even though I could barely talk. And while he's pulling on my arm he goes, Tell your mother Terry Twomey says hi!

And I looks at him to see if I know him, but I don't. Alright, yeah, I goes and nods at him cos I'm surprised that the fella who fell on me knows who I am and who my mother is and whether she's my mother an' all, up in Dublin, like. And I feel nearly good about that until I think about it again. Did he know who I was only when he was picking me up, so? What odds would Mr. Mulcahy of given me on that one? And I'm just going in the door of my cell when I know what happened – yer man falling on me wasn't an accident at all, like! He did it on purpose, like! He knew me and wanted to give me a message for my mother! Did Terry Twomey get that fella to do it or was *he* Terry Twomey, could be? And the door was closed behind me before I know what to do with myself cos I'm still bent with the pain, holding my stomach and my head is kinda like spinning now an' all. And everyone is in their own bunk now. The two card players are back on their own ones – two top bunks. And Clarksy is in

154

his. And Brendan is lying down on mine, saying, Are ya alright Clicky? Did ya fall?

I was in a shock cos I didn't know what to do or to say, like and I just turned around and sat on my bed. But Brendan was going on and on.

Did someone do something to ya? he goes, You need to watch out for yourself in this place, Click. By the way, you're sitting on my bed, there Click!

And I look behind me, at him and tell him get up cos I need to lie down, but he gets a shock an' all then and goes, Get up!? This is my bed, Clicky! Yours is on the floor, clam!

And there's all noise and laughing in the room when I look at the mattress on the floor, state of it, filthy and full of wet-spots.

I think Mahoney and Co-Brien spat on it too when they were done with their cards, says Brendan, You'd better watch out for them fellas, Clicky!

And they all starts laughing again, but one of them goes, Hey! Nothing to do with me!

Instead of doing anything about it, I fell down on the mattress and just kept in by the wall and I'm wondering how did yer man even know who I was or how I was in here even? Did everyone in this place know who was coming in before they got there?

What's your girlfriend's name, Click?

And I was thinking then, the only one I said it to was Brendan – and everyone else in my cell, I remembered. But how could they even have had time to say it to anyone else? Or been *able* to say it to anyone else, even? Or what was the chances someone else would want to say hi to my mother straight away like that? Or to hit me cos of it, like? I never even seen that fella before – how did he know I was the one he was supposed to give a dig to?

Tina! I goes, cos he asked, but I still hadn't a clue what was going on. And I fell asleep then, when they were mocking me over it, soon after, while I was trying to work it all out, I'd say, even when they were all screaming and laughing and mocking me the whole time. And spitting on me too I think. But I didn't look around or say nothing.

●

Next day was bad, like. I don't even want to be going on about it. I was woke up by splashes and noise from piss hitting the pot next to my shoulder. Clarksy was up first and was having a slash next to where I was lying down. YA LANGER CLARKSY! I shouts out when I looked around. There was pots in the cell, see, kept under the bunks mostly, and Clarksy was after putting it down next to me to piss into.

YEAH CLARKSY! goes one of the others, laughing away. Clarksy said nothing but finished up and before he lied down again, he turned to Brendan and gave him a hard dig, That's your fault ya dozy cunt! he goes to him. I didn't know why, like, but I know why now.

During that day I got two other batings at least from fellas. It's a bit hard sometimes to know if it's deliberate or just an accident, like, that would happen anyway.

One fella, Asher, saw me give my eggs to a fella who asked me for it at breakfast. I don't like eggs, me. And scrambled eggs is the worst eggs of all of them. So I scraped mine over to yer man, cos it was wetting my toast. And this massive fat twenty year old fella, Asher, hopped across the room and bate the shit out of me until the pigs called him off. They didn't even drag him away or nothing – just told him get back to his food. They left me get a hankie alright to stop the bleeding on my ear. My eye too was all black and blue and half my face was swollen after him.

After breakfast everyone was hanging around the yard and the corridors and I didn't know what to do or who might attack me next, cos I was getting all stares and calls about Cork or about my mother and I didn't know whether they were saying it cos they knew my mother or cos they were joking like: "I had your mother." I think it was some of that, like, but some of it too was they knew something about my mother or my mother done something to someone they knew. Whatever it was anyway, I was bricking it by then.

And then I seen a fella up there that bate up Cillian before. Shane Something was his name. He was looking over at me like he was trying to work out who I was. That fella was selling stuff near our house a few year before that and Cillian said what's your name and he wouldn't tell him anything so the two of us just walks off, like, and come back a few minutes later with Con and when he seen Con and Cillian get out of the car, he legged it. They chased him like, but he got away. A few days later anyway we were in town. In the middle of Patricks Street, like, and this fella Shane and around four other fellas jumps on Cillian and bate the shit out of him. Just there by the Savoy, like. Around two o'clock in the daytime and they all hopped-on!

There was nothing I could do, but we knew who it was at least. Far's I know, Cillian and Con got him back later for it.

Now he was up here looking over at me. So I went back to my cell, fast as I could without looking like I was running, like, cos I kind of knew I could keep my back against the wall there at least a bit. When I got in, Clarksy was the only one there lying on his bed already. I wanted to leg-it out again straight away, but there was nowhere else to go. Any of the rest of them, I thought would be better than him, but I went in and turned over my mat and sat down on it.

Next Clarksy stood up and goes, Lie down, he goes, pointing at his bed. And I got a shock cos I thought he was a bender looking to rape me. He lies down on Brendan's bed then and only laughed at me and goes, I'm not lookin' to ride ya – g'on. I'm staying here, now on.

So anyway I was in a shock again, but he left me take his bunkbed and he stayed on the other one. And when the others come back he told Brendan take the floor cos Brendan was after telling me I could take his bed and he squelt on me too. He was around two years older than me I'd say. All of them were older than me, but he was probably the biggest. Not the oldest, I'd say, but the other two was messing all the time, but not looking to fight, like. Just to annoy mostly. Annoy *me* mostly, like.

"Clarksy" was cranky most of the time, like, and didn't speak much and I don't know if he'd of been able to bate Brendan in a fight. Brendan was a bit wilder, like, but he took the mat on the floor the next few days after that and said nothing to me about it. He couldn't anyway, cos I was in Clarksy's bed, not his.

His name wasn't Clarksy neither. He told me that himself before the others come back that day. His name was Stephen Lark, he told me, so people in this place called him Larkser mostly. Only Brendan couldn't speak proper, like, so he called him Clarksy. Now I knew it. He was alright too, Larkser.

For the rest of my time up there, I kept getting baten-up or thumped or spat-at. My mother kept being brought into it too and mostly it was my real mother too – not a "mother joke", like. But people know people and my mother was someone people knew everywhere. Up there even. And they all wanted to get her back. That was obvious by the end of the first day even.

Yer man Shane Something caught me later that second day. I thought he'd be on about Cillian, but it was my mam again he was looking to talk about.

Hey Mickey! he goes, like he knows me, when he comes up to me in the corridor. He had a friend with him and I tried to leg-it straight away, but yer man grabbed me and dragged me back. There were guards around, like, but they couldn't care less. I'm not going to hurt ya, he goes, I just want a word.

I starts off then shouting at him for beating up Cillian on Patrick's Street. I called him a scumbag and said he could only do it cos he had four other fellas with him and the only reason they were able to catch him too was cos he wasn't looking. But I seen while I was giving out to him, he never even remembered that one and when I was talking about it he remembers and he smiles like Con smiled, 'cept he doesn't have the same bad tooth Con had that stuck out.

I never knew you were Cillian's brother! he goes then, like he's thick stupid. He knew sure we had the same mother, so what does that make us so!? We have the same father too even and you can ask anyone that!

How's Cillian doing? he asks me then, Me and Cillian go way back! he says. And I told him then that Cillian won't be around no more cos he got adopted and he breaks his hole laughing at me.

Anyway, after all that he gets serious and says my mother thinks she's shit-hot and she was spotted in Mahon the other day without a care in the world and she won't get out of there with her legs if she's seen there again, he goes. And I goes you can do what you like with the bitch for all I care and Shane starts laughing again and I'm sorry already I said it, like.

And he starts walking away and then comes back and gives me a thump into my gut again and when I doubles-over, he kneed me in my face.

That's for Cillian! he goes, If I don't see him, you'll have to do! and he tried to stomp on my head then, but got my shoulder mostly cos I turned around. But the pigs ran over and pushed him away and picked me up and asked if I was alright. But I only pushed them off too and went back to my room.

Later on I wanted to talk to Tina, but it was annoying me too, like, what Shane said, but I only could make one phonecall and I was asking the screw if I could have two this one time and there was no way he'd do it like, the pig. And I goes I want to ring my girlfriend and when he was dialling it, I goes no I want to ring my mother instead. And he rang her instead.

Hello Mickey, is that you love? she goes and I starts crying straight away. I didn't even mean it or know why or nothing, but it was my mam, like, and when I heard her I starts bawling like a baby.

Are ya ok Mickey? she goes, I'm going mad you're locked up, love, I really am! and I'm trying to talk to her, but I can't even say nothing and she's all like that.

Remember when we went down to Redbarn, all of us, and stayed in the hotel? she's saying and talking about all the fun we had before, like. And it's like all far away now and I'm wondering if it happened really or was it like in a movie or something, but I can't even think anyway cos I'm still bawling my eyes out and I can't stop. And she keeps talking about all lovely things like that and the good laughs we had and snuggles and things and the prick pig says time up and I tries talking again but my mother's only saying goodbye and I'll see ya soon and it's only for a few more days and we'll have a party an' all when you come back and Con is getting you a present for your return. And the line goes dead and I'm in shock cos I didn't even get to say nothing. And I slams down the phone and screams CUNT! and the screw gives out to me then like *I* done something wrong.

•

All the next day then I'm wondering who'll I call. I want to talk with Tina-only, but I never got to talk with my mam really and she could be in danger, like, and she's my mam when all's said and done, like. I didn't want to call too early neither cos then my call would be gone for the day. And anyway my mam would be probably in bed if I called too early too.

And all the fellas are screaming at me and bating me and calling me all the names. And all's I want to do is think about who to call, but I can't get away from no one. Even in my cell,

Brendan is like a train in my head that won't stop. If he's not asking me questions, he's going on and on about his horse at home and I tells him I had a pony too. And when he asked me his name I just shut my eyes tight and turned in by the wall and Brendan carries on and on and on like train-tracks forever and ever and ever. And ever.

●

Anyway, when the time came again, I said I'd better ring my mother, cos I seen Shane just before that again and he was looking over at me with a warning face and I knew she'd be a goner cos she'd never keep away from nothing.

So I goes to the screw I want to ring my mother and he dialled it and put her on and she goes, Mickey love! again and I tells her shut the fuck up this time and listen to me, ok? And I tells her about what Shane said about her being in Mahon and she was spotted down there and she needs to stay away cos they'll kill her the next time.

And when I'm finished, she waits for more and then starts laughing and I have to say what's so funny (cos she always waits for me to say what's so funny, she'll never tell me herself what's funny, no, always has to wait for me to say it!) And she goes, Is that all there is?

And I goes yeah and she goes, I was down there at the doctors is why I was down there, only! and I goes yeah, why were you at the doctors so? Are ya sick or what? And she goes yeah I got a lump in my belly. And I goes WHAT!? in a shock, like. And she goes, Yeah, don't ya remember I'm pregnant? and then it was my turn to start laughing, cos I was after forgetting all about that

162

and here's me thinking she got the Cancer or something when she said it, like.

And what did the doctor say so? I asks her and we were mad talking about the baby then, only. And what room he or she would take in the house and what colour the room should be – all that kind of stuff. And the screw goes time up and my mother is saying bye and we're best friends again and I want to be there to mind her and the baby, like, and I'm sad again that I can't be and I has a shock then at the end and goes, But you can't be going down to Mahon no more! I goes and she starts laughing again, but she's gone before we can talk about it, like.

I swear to God my head was spinning again by the time I got back to my cell. I didn't know by now if I was coming or going or what day of the week it was or how long I was locked up already for. Felt like forever. I just wanted to get the-fuck out. Out of there. Out of everywhere. Everything was so all over the place, like, and complicated. I couldn't even think of nothing without everything mixing up. And always there was pricks everywhere annoying me and messing with me and poking at me and beating me up and stuff. And there was eggs all over everywhere. Every dinner there was eggs. For breakfast there was eggs. Eggs, eggs fuckin eggs! Doing my head in the whole time!

Even next day I was… I never felt so bad before then, I'd say. At that time, like. It was like the whole world had it in for me and I could do nothing about it.

I kept away from people, or tried not to get bothered by their crap at least. But I was like half-closing my eyes the whole time, hiding away. Away from everything and every *body* too, like. I was just waiting to make my phonecall so I could talk to Tina and it'd be all alright then, like, for a while at least. But I didn't want to do it too quick either cos I wanted to look forward to it, like.

So I was back in my room at some stage that day and Larkser was there with a bit of tinfoil and a lighter and he was lighting underneath and smoking the top off it, like. I never seen it before, believe it or not, but I knew it was heroin straight away. I got a bit of a thrill when I seen it and goes, Are ya allowed smoke that here!?

I couldn't believe it – he was smoking heroin, sitting down on his bed, like!

But Larkser only leaned back and put out his arms with the gear and I got a shock. He was offering it to me, like. 'Course I was going to take it! Why wouldn't I? I stuck my head out the door first to make sure no screw or no one was coming (they wasn't) and then I grabbed the gear off him and sat down. Took me a few goes to get it cooking, like, and get a proper drag, but when I did…

man it

was like nothing

like who invented the world?
besides God I mean

I know it was God, like

                                        but if it was

a person who

                    who would it of been?

            like there's only so much space in space, like, ya
                                    know?

and all the   space

            and all the escape you can make

in that space, like, ya know?

            all of it is inside that first hit of heroin. The very
                                    first one.

Purest, beautifulest, heavenest

                    piece of   faaar-away you
can get

for ever.

Amen.

        When I was in school first, first day my mother said,
there was big tall windows in the classroom, like. I don't
remember them, but my mother told me about it a load of times.
And Cillian used be mocking me over it too, like. The windows
were very long and tall and only opened up, up at the top, like.
She had a long stick, the teacher, to open and close the top of the
window, it was up so high. But she looked around one time for
me and couldn't find me, but when she looked up at the window,
she just saw my legs sticking out, into the classroom. And my
head was out the other side. You should hear my mam tell the
story, cos she tells it better than me, like, saying my arse was
dangling and my legs were flaking around and the teacher was
screaming and dancing, trying to jump up and lock-onto my
feet. But I kept going and I tumbled out the outside and smashed
my face off the floor outside and kept going, like. Cos when they
ran out to get me, I was sitting on the swing across the yard with
blood pouring down my face and my arm was in a sling for ages

after it, an' all. But I didn't care cos all's I wanted was to get to the swing I seen through the window.

There's a photograph an' all of that time, if you don't believe me. Someone's birthday party and I have my arm in a sling and half my face is swollen up, like it was now up in this place. They never knew how I got to the top of the window and out of it. I didn't neither, like, cos I don't remember it anyway, but it was a funny one definitely.

Anyway, same thing happened now up there, more or less. There was a basketball court, see? And I kind of woke up (although I was awake already like), hearing all fellas shouting at me. Pigs an' all screaming and roaring, they were. I'm sitting in the basket without a care in the world. I see them below and I don't remember getting up there, but now they're all shouting at me get down and nobody seen me get up there either. And I'm only looking at them and leaving them off. And someone throws a ball and other shit up at me but I couldn't care less. Eventually the screws get them to stop, but they can't get me down. Someone got a long stick an' all, like the one the teacher had to close the windows. And he shoved it up my arse and tries poking me up and out of the basket, but he never got me out. I robbed the pole off him too and used it to push anyone away who came near me again.

I ended up staying there the whole night. They locked the door an' all. I only came down next day for breakfast. I was walking funny for ages after it too cos it felt like the ring was still around my arse. I have a ring outside me hole and a ring inside it too! I goes. I made it up myself and when I told it to the others they all starts laughing every time and they'd be asking me how I did it an' all after that. And fellas'd be trying to climb up the pole all the time and get over the board and into the basket, but no one could.

Mucky Dan alright got up there and nearly made it over the board too an' all, but one of the screws pushed him off with the pole and he fell down. After that they got a ladder and put grease on up high on the two poles so nobody'd be able do it again. But that was the one laugh in the place, in fairness.

Chasing The Dragon

I missed my phonecall the night before and was mad-out about that one. And the screws wouldn't let me have two calls next day neither. The one good thing was most fellas left me alone after that or even smiled and nodded at me when they seen me coming. Mostly. I was like famous there for a bit.

Coming up to my call with Tina, alright, Shane comes up and gave me a thump on my arm. It was a hard thump and was sore, like, but he pretended he was saying well done.

Fair fucks to ya! he goes when he digs me, Your arse scored a two-pointer! I only looks at him, like.

Didya tell your mother what I said? he goes then and I told him I did ya and she was only going to the doctor cos she was pregnant and he goes, Doesn't matter, sham, if she's spotted again in Mahon they'll cut the bastard out!

I'd be rattled enough when someone says something like that, like. And I knew the people Shane was on about and chances are they'd do it an' all. But it was around three or four days now at least since I was talking to Tina and I told her I'd call the next day and I didn't. And I couldn't ring the both of them. So while I was having a think about it, I goes up to Larkser and asked if he had anymore of that stuff, like, and he laughs and goes, Chasin' the dragon! with his raspy voice. That's the first time I heard that one, like.

You'll be chasin' it a long time, he says. And I didn't have a clue what he was on about and didn't care neither and I thought he meant I'd have to pay him, like. I hadn't a bob on me, but I goes, How much so? and he only laughs again and goes he got none and I nearly chokes him, but Brendan was near and goes, Whatcha lookin' for clam? Chase the dragon clam? I'll get it for ya! Cost ya, like!

And I said I'd pay it, whatever, only get it. And he ran out and I nearly ate my fingernails off waiting for him to get back. I just wanted a hit 'til I knew who to call next, like. My mother's one thing, but what if they cut out my little baby brother or sister, like? If it was a boy I'd be like Cillian, showing him things and how to do things, like. And if it was a girl, I'd be like her dad, like. I'd look after her proper, like and make sure she'd have everything, like. Like what I done for Melanie on our holidays, like.

But I wanted to talk to Tina too, like. I needed to talk to Tina nearly more than another hit off heroin, like, but like I just needed a bit first so I'd know who to call, like. I'd only take a half-drag this time. Just a taster so I wouldn't totally zonk-out.

And next, Brendan comes back and he's half-laughing at me and saying there's none in the whole place cos the pigs caught a bag coming over the wall today and only one other one got through, but there was a scatter for it and it went to Johnny Chester out of Galway, who claimed it was his anyway, but he got hopped for it, like by the Dublin lads. From Galway like! He was a mean fucker alright, but there was never no way a fella from Galway'd be allowed keep a bag of heroin that come in over the wall like that. They got it off him anyway and used the lot of it and sold a bit of it to junkies who used it too like. And Chester was mad-out now and blah blah blah, like I give a shit.

I said I'd find some myself and pushed Brendan away, useless cunt, and went around asking everyone if they had any.

And who'd I find an' all who had some, only Shane himself. He's laughing at me and says yeah he could get his hands on some, but why should he get it for me and what am I going to do for him, like? And I says I'll give my mam the message, but he's only laughing at that. I said I'd pay him then and he said show me your money so, cos he knew I got none.

Anyway, he looks at me and goes, Wait here! and he went off to his cell and I got all excited waiting for him. One of the screws was looking at me an' all, kinda hopping up and down, like, and I nodded at him and smiled and gave him a bit of a wave, but he said nothing.

Then Shane came back with a note in his hand. He goes I want you to deliver this to Asher. I looks at the piece of paper that was all folded and goes, Asher!? he was the fella who bate me up the other day cos I gave my eggs away. He's mad, like. Yeah, goes Shane, Give him that and I'll give you the heroin.

I never really thought about it at the time, but if I was thinking now I'd be going *why don't you give it to him yourself?* Or asking him to show me the heroin first, like.

His gang were all around now, Shane's friends like, looking on and laughing. And Shane was telling me go on. And I was laughing too, like, and I probably thought it was a trap alright, but I was thinking even if it was, I'd get bate up, but at least I'd get the heroin off Shane after and it'd be free too, like. What's it say? I goes and starts opening it, but Shane told me I couldn't look and he wouldn't pay me if I did.

171

So anyway, next thing, I'm walking up to Asher and he's sitting in the TV room, like, looking at The Tellytubbies and looking at me walking straight up to him. And he's scary-out, with a massive spot on his nose and another one on his forehead and bad, lumpy skin all over on his face. He's looking at the telly, but his eyes are looking straight up at me and his mouth is open and I can see his teeth.

I was told give you this, I goes when I got up to him. He took it and opened it and there was a few lines of writing on it and he barely read it when he hops up and screams at me and lifts me off my feet, into the air. And next he thrun me against the wall and bate the shite out of me. And after that, when I was being carried to the hospital, like, I passed Shane and his gang and they're all breaking their arses laughing and pointing at me and I tried laughing too with them an all and I put up my hand to give them the thumbs up, like, and I seen then it was all covered in blood and I forgot to keep laughing and that made them laugh more.

I didn't know what the note said or what happened with Asher, but I never seen him again. He wasn't around when I got out of the hospital. It was next day, like, cos I was given painkillers and left sleep in there for myself in a grand comfy bed. I was well battered. I only lied in bed in my cell all day that next day too and couldn't barely talk or move. I was thinking I was too sore and tired to even want heroin straight away, like, but I'd say I was thinking it only cos I knew I had none. But on my way to my phonecall I passed Shane alright and I goes, Do you have that for me so? and he starts laughing again then and calls me a dumb shit. Then he goes when I get out call down to Mahon to collect it. Tell Johnno I said you were to have it!

172

I just kept walking on, me. Didn't have the energy to be arguing with him. I will, I goes. I met Johnno later on alright, but I never said it to him.

I got the screw to ring Tina and when she come on she's all crying again and I tells her it's alright, I'll be getting out tomorrow or the next day (I didn't know what day it was) and it'll all be alright. And then she goes she's moving away and I'm never to call her again, like, cos my mother was around causing trouble and she got the dad, Sean Murview into a fight with another fella and both of them got arrested. And Karen, his wife like, the mother, blamed Tina for it all and told her she's getting Tina out of there today and never coming back and to tell you an all (me like) never come back here neither cos ye're nothing but trouble the lot of ye Collinses. And I was trying to talk to her, to Tina like, but she's shouting all these things at me and saying my mother will burn the house down and she was being sent up to Limerick, Tina like, cos of my mother and then she hangs up before I got a chance even.

And I'm bawling my eyes out down there by the phones for ages cos I knew I was on my own again now. I knew that straight away, like. But even when I was thinking it like, I was still half-thinking I got a new friend now anyway, so fuck 'em all. And that was true too. I'd be chasing the dragon a long time. I knew that straight away, like, too. I'd have one place to go always to never be alone – or feel like I felt alone, if you know what I mean? I mean when I don't want to be alone, it's my friend, cos I can get it. But, like, when I use, it takes me away from everything else too, like, and I can be alone, like that. I know that and kind of knew all that even when I was still bothered crying. And by the time I was going back to my cell I stopped crying an' all and didn't give a shit no more. I passed Shane an' all on the way and he was teasing me and I only gave him a look and he stopped laughing and saying anything.

●

What I know now, like, but what I didn't know when I was young then, like, was that every hit of heroin was like a tiny bit smaller than the last one. The first one was – man – it was like Heaven, that's as true as God. It was like, if God showed you what the Universe was like and how far away you could go before you'd meet anyone – and even then you wouldn't meet no one and you'd have zero problems ever in all the world and you'd feel great. That's what the first hit was like. Other hits was nearly as great and nearly as great. Then they'd be like, nearly as good, nearly as good, only. Then you'd need more of it. And sometimes you'd hit a one that's better than that, but mostly they'd only get you to the moon at most – or not even. Instead of deep into space, like. And usually, after a while it wouldn't barely get you into the sky.

In the way it feels, like I mean. It's not like heroin *really* brings you into outer space and stuff. I'm not saying that much, like it was Star Wars or something. But it really feels like it does. To me at least, anyway. Sometimes. Used to, like. Now it's not like outer space at all, but you'd need it anyway cos it's like the only way to remember the <u>feel</u> off it, like. D'ya know?

I was talking to another fella lately about it and he goes she's a cruel lover. And I goes, Ya, that's what she is alright! I knew exactly what he meant straight away, like. A cruel lover.

And I love her and I need her, but she's not as good as she used be.

174

THE RISE AND FALL OF MICKEY COLLINS

Mickey 2

So I gets out the next day anyway, or the day after, and I was supposed to get a lift back to Cork off the cops again, but instead I got a shock when I was standing in the office and Mr. Mullins walks over to me and goes, You're walking, sonny.

I thought he was telling me I'd be walking all the way to Cork, like, and I starts shouting-mad at him, calling him names and stuff, like. But he's only laughing. He goes he was told there's someone outside to pick me up instead and I shut up then, like, and was wondering who it was but he wouldn't tell me.

I was thinking it must be Tina, definitely, come up so we'd be well-away from Cork and we could run off together or something. We could head to England and I'd be a brick-layer. Or a plumber, more like, I suppose seeing as all my experience.

I comes out the big door then and sees Con there standing in his brown suit, leaning on his blue car, smiling at me with his mad tooth sticking out. And when I walks up to him, I gave him a tight hug cos I'm so happy get away from that place. It was like a year since I been in, but it was only a week. And he's like pushing me off first, but then he kind of hugs me back too a bit, like, and it kind of hurt a bit too cos I'm black and blue all over and I nearly starts crying again then cos I'm out of that shithole.

But, *"This is Mickey 2!"* I was thinking to myself – *"this is Mickey 2!"* The new Mickey, like. I never said that or nothing to no one, but I was thinking there was Rocky and then Rocky 2. I

177

was Mickey 2 now. Only Rocky 2 is shit and Rocky 3 is the best of them when he'd be fighting Clubber Lang and Hulk Hogan an' all. I says I wasn't going to be crying no more since then. And I didn't neither, most part. Mickey 2.

●

And we're on the road down and Con is driving and going on about all stuff. And he's smiling at how he's going to get back at the travellers cos my mother caught them selling into Kerry and it was us, see, who was after doing a deal with Shamie in Tralee about that. Not the travellers. Con was saying, first we need to find the prick they were selling to, before he got too big, like. And then we'd take on the boys at the halting-site after that. And I got a bit of a thrill off that an' all, but when I thought of it then I was a scared too like straight away, cos he never told me things before like that, only afterward, like, but this was before. And I was thinking I'd probably get killed doing it. Serious shit, like. Usually he'd just tell me do something and I might probably do it. But it was never, like planned-out. But now he was telling me what we'd be working on and I didn't want to know all about that. And I was thinking I'd never do that stuff and how would I get out of it, like?

But I said nothing and left it off. The sun was shining in the window all the way down and that felt good an' all. And we stopped and got our breakfast and two boxes of fags (Con smoked Major and I smokes John Player Blue mainly, like) and it was much better than sharing a ride off some shades who'd probably be pricks about it.

●

We were down nearly at Mallow and we weren't saying nothing, but Con still had a smile or something. His tooth was sticking out anyway and I was looking at it. And he looks over and back and over and back, and goes, What're ya lookin' at? and I goes, How come nobody never knocked out that tooth before?

And he laughs and goes on and on then about it and says no fuckers'd get close enough, he says. Then he lists all the different times different fellas nearly got close enough, 'cluding shades with their boots (Always fast with their steel-capped boots, them fuckers! he says) and different fights with travellers. And there was that time Kieran Ballister slammed a baseball bat straight into his face and knocked out half a dozen tooths (he says tooths, like), but that front tooth stayed there. He gets technical, like all dentist-talk then and goes on about his face collapsing after that and all his times at the hospital. Con could have been a doctor or a dentist an' all himself I'd say, he was so smart about all things. You could listen to him and listen to him and you'd learn a lot just from that.

And the front tooth, he was telling me, like shifted and stuck out more, he says, 'til he got reconstruction done on his jawbone. And it was all news to me, but I didn't want to hear it anyway cos it was 'scusting, like! I'd never be a dentist myself. I tell ya that now, looking in people's mouths all day. Like, who'd do that!?

And he got Ballister back later-on too when he found out he was drinking in the lounge in The Mirror Bar where nobody'd find him, like. Sounds like a posh place, but the lounge was in the second door and it was open early for the roofers going to work and the bouncers coming off shift and it was always full of people who didn't want to be found too, y'know?

And Con found him there, standing at the counter, taking a swig out of his pint and he walks up beside him and has a crowbar in his hand and he smashes the pint and the crowbar through yer man's face til he was like a clown, Con says, with a massive red smiling scar across his mouth on both sides after that.

He's bursting laughing while he's driving the car, like and he looks over and seen me kind of cringy then, Con, cos he knew I always didn't like things that'd be too 'scusting. And he gives me a bit of a thump then to toughen me up and goes, I'd of thought you'd learn how to take it, he goes, Inside.

Well I never neither.

After a while then again, we were past Mallow an' all and he goes back to it: Jumped off Patricks Bridge, he did a few year later, Con says, Ballister like.

And I looks at him and he looks sad, even.

Killed himself. Out of his tree, probably, cos he always was, he goes. Then he says, I miss him too, an all, I'd say, he goes, Wasn't the worst of them!

And I swear he's serious about it and I was going to ask him how could he miss someone who'd do things like that, like. But I didn't bother. And I know how now anyway, too like.

•

I was made do things for a bit when I got back alright. My mother didn't say nothing much to me, but she let Con take me around. But then I stopped like after a while cos I was no good at all that, but my mother starts at me about it then again, so I stayed away for around a week or five days. I'll tell you about all that in a minute, but after being in that place, up above, I kind of lost a bit of a thrill off it, to tell the truth. I don't know if it was that place what done it, but I'd say I was never really good at it to be honest, y'know? I knew I didn't like all the real violence and stuff (not the way Con'd be doing it anyway). The messin' we always done alright – busted arm, broken nose now and again, at most. All that's fine, like. Solk a few bob and things, I'd say, y'know? But after I got out they were like looking for bigger things off me and I just wanted to chill, like. Mickey 2 was more chilled. Mickey 2 had a new friend who definitely helped me with all that. I could escape escape escape, cos that's all I wanted to do an' all, man. And it worked for me too, like. I got out of joining the gang on all their raids and shit.

I remember one time, weeks and weeks later, I was after getting back home at that time and I was a lot better and my mam was after getting back from holidays an' all, but I was still keeping out of the way, like. I'd say nothing and they left me off mostly. But I was walking into the kitchen this day anyway and I heard her saying to Con, my mother like, and there were a few other fellas there too, like, she goes, …Leave him off, I don't want him bottling it. He'd only get in the way.

And I stopped by the door then and went into the front room til they left, cos I knew they were on about me, like, and I was thrilled out, me. I wouldn't mind like giving someone a fright for a laugh or something, but this was more serious stuff, like, they were on about. It's like, you could get actually killed doing that stuff. That was like Scarface stuff they were on about. Not me at all, like!

•

Johnny Silver got killed on one of them raids too, an' all, so it's not like I'm talking shite neither. A load of travellers or maybe the Kerry lads bate the shit out of him and cracked his skull and kept bating. His mother couldn't even have an open coffin at his funeral neither, cos there was cracks and holes all over his face an' all, Con goes, And his hair was like scalped with the top of his head flapping-off.

And I was trying to tell Con stop, but he was going on and on about it at the party we were on. I think it was for Melanie, who was back at the time. A birthday or communion probably. He was saying about the different things he seen on Johnny Silver's body and I was running out of the kitchen cos he wouldn't shut up about it.

And he had a massive langer on him an' all! Con goes then, and everyone starts laughing, so I stayed there then cos it was funny. He stopped for a piss out the back, see! he was telling us after, Con, And the others goes in the front door to teach them a lesson.

We were only going there to rough them up a bit, Con goes, It's not like we were gonna kill 'um or anything! ...And Johnny Silver and Kanturk was supposed to watch the back, but Johnny Silver had a slash instead. And when the boys run out they were carrying machetes and bats and stuff, so Kanturk legged it straight away and the lads then lashed-into Johnny Silver. So his langer was still out an' all when his face was smashed opened and Con and the others found him.

I swear it was like a hose-pipe! Con goes, He had that in his pants the whole time, the dirty bastard!

And my mother then goes, If he had it in his pants he wouldn't have got himself killed, would he? and I laughed out loud at that one, cos my mother's always the funniest, like. But then I seen the others was smiling only, but not laughing. So I shut up.

It was only at his funeral that I heard his real name was Jonathan Sylvester and I was knotted at that an' all cos it was so posh. Sylvester, like! Jonathan even! And I seen others laughing too, cos they never knew neither. Like where would ya get a name like that?

And at the party then like, at the funeral everyone was telling all stories about him. And I didn't really know him that well, but going by the stories I wished I did, an' all like, cos he was a great laugh. Con and himself were in school together an' all. I never knew that even.

I asked my mother, at one part, when we were all sitting around having pints, How come he was called Johnny Silver? I always thought it was cos of the silver line of grey hair on his head, but was it cos his name was Johnny Sylvester so?

And she goes, Naw, that wasn't it. And she looks around and everyone at the table shuts up for her to tell it.

He was called Johnny Silver since he was in school, she says. Con and himself used to play The Lone Ranger all the time, didn't ye Con? and Con nods yes, Con was The Lone Ranger, she goes, And Johnny was the horse he rode in on!

And everyone thought that was the funniest thing ever. The whole place was bursting their arse laughing, like. Me too, but I didn't get it. Con too was only smiling and nodding cos it was true. But then Timmy McGrath goes, I suppose that's why he had the massive langer so!

And everyone breaks out laughing again, but all of a sudden, Con got madder than I ever seen him before. It was like his head turned bright red and exploded straight away. He grabbed the whole table full of drinks and flung it across the room like it was nothing. Without even looking even! Then he jumped straight on Timmy and bate him nearly dead. He hit a load of people with the table too and with glasses and everything. I got drink all over me an' all! My mam was after getting me a new suit to wear and everything and it got soaking-wet when Con done that. But he just was screaming mad, Con. And when he stopped hitting Timmy, he marched straight out the door of the place. No one went near him, but Johnny's uncle had to be taken away in an ambulance too cos the table nearly killed him, I heard. He never squelt on Con though, in fairness. And my mother had to get my suit cleaned in the cleaners too, after.

•

Before that funeral though, after I got back from Dublin and stopped doing stuff for Con and my mother, and when they knew I was serious-like, she said no one was to give me or sell me nothing never, like, cos she knew I just wanted to chill. She said I needed to get my head straight and step-up. Whatever that was supposed to mean, like. So I had to find somewhere else to get it, like, and I stayed away a few nights too, like I said. Around five or six I think at the time. Nights out, I'd say around. The place I got the stuff, like, was off the lads in Mahon and they weren't bothered who I was either like, or neither. Cos I knew this fella, but I said I was talking to Shane and it was alright. I never told them Johnno owed me some, cos I'd have to tell them why and I couldn't be bothered getting into it about being beaten up by Asher an' all that. Anyway I had a load of money after a few days when I was on the streets cos Con was after getting me a brand new computer for school and I got back in home the night before and got it back and got a hundred notes for it next day. And I won twenty five in the bookies (*was twenty-two-fifty actually*). And I met Cillian around then too and he got me a milkshake and gave me fifty notes an' all, imagine!

Anyway, after I got it this day, I was walking around, trying to hold off using for a while so I'd enjoy it more, like. It's not like I was a junkie or nothing at the time, I'd say, but it's just – heroin wasn't really around Cork back then, but I was after getting this bit anyway so wanted to make it last, like. But it's something else, y'know?

Next thing, a load of fellas jumps out of a van and starts bating me and bating me. And I thought it was the Mahon lads cos I never seen them before. And while they were hitting me and bating me and kicking me in the face, I was trying to tell them it's alright, like, cos Johnno owed me stuff anyway and I was after paying for it too, like. But they wouldn't listen or I couldn't even speak enough to say it to them. And when they were done they never took nothing off me even or checked my pockets even, 'cept one of them goes, That's for Paddy Murphy ya shit scumbag!

And I can't even move for ages after they leaves. I can't even *try* to move for ages, even. So I'm lying there thinking, Who the fuck is Paddy Murphy!?

It feels like parts of my face are falling off my face when I turn my face even and I can't turn my body cos my ribs are like swords sticking into my side. And my knee doesn't work when I get up after a while. And my other pants leg is torn all the way up, like. And a woman got out of a van then, like and she looks at me and I put out my arm so she could help me, but she steps away and then spits at me in the face and gets back in the van. And the spit makes it feel a bit better cos it landed in the middle of a big lump on my cheek that was like throbbing hot, but that made it cooler. A bit anyway, like. Then I seen the van when it was getting away and it was the same one the lads got out of, I think, so she must of been with them too. I never seen any of them before and I never seen the van and I still don't have a clue at that time who Paddy Murphy is neither, like, so I'm thinking it must be whatever my mother done. So that's a good reason to head home and at least she can look after me for all the trouble she done on me.

Around that time too, around a bit before I'd say, or something like that, my friend Davie O'Brien got done for a job he done weeks earlier. He broke into this house, out in Turner's Cross in the middle of the night, see? When I was locked up, up in Dublin, see, he done it. He thought the place was empty, like, and he was going through the presses and stuff when this old fella walks in on top of him, like, in his pyjamas. Davie was just inside the door when yer man lit the light and screams at him. And Davie got a fright and hopped up and give him a dig straight into his gut and then legged it out of there, fast.

It was in the papers and on the news and there was a big hunt for who done it after, like, cos the old fella died two days later. It was an accident, like. Anyone who'd know Davie would know that. He wouldn't harm nobody, Davie. He'd be windier even than me, I'd say. I mean, I wouldn't say I was windy, like, but I wouldn't be bating someone up if I could help it and Davie was never nothing like that neither. More than me even!

Anyway, when my mam seen me back at home, she screams, JESUS! LOOK AT THE CUT OF YA! and she was mad-out straight away, like, like it was my own fault or something. I tells her what happened, anyway, and she hasn't a clue what it's all about neither, but she puts me up to bed straight away, like to lie down and brings me tea and toast and everything, but I can't have nothing and don't want nothing, but I'd like the heroin in my pocket alright, like, but I can't say that to her cos she'd be asking who I got it off, like, and she'd kill me over it.

Then when Stacey comes home, my mam sends her up to look at the state of me and she's like, JEEESUSS! when she seen the state of me and she asks me if I took anything for it, the pain like. And I told her my mam gave me some things but I didn't know what they were, but they were no good though.

And I gives Stacey the nod then and told her look in my pocket and give it to me. And when she looks she says Jesus again and, I never knew you took that shit! she goes. And I told her cook it up for me, but she wouldn't and put it back in my pocket. And we were talking a bit and when I told her Paddy Murphy she goes, I'm sure that's the name of that fella Davie O'Brien killed by accident! They must have beaten you up thinking you were Davie!

Then I knew it. Made sense to me, like, and I nearly starts laughing, but it's too sore and I tells Stacey again give me the stuff wouldya? But she tells me get a bit of sleep and goes off downstairs for herself. Poor Davie, I'm thinking. Poor me, I'm thinking then! I don't blame him though, cos I wasn't around and we was kind of hanging around together before then an' all. He's about my height alright, Davie like, I was thinking. I wouldn't say he looked like me, like, but someone must of seen us together sometime.

He got a few year for that an' all even later on, but he was under-age, see. And it took a while for the trial to come up, so by then he was eighteen. The only thing that stopped them throwing the book at him, I'd say, was that he turned himself in too, around a week after he done it. All the News was done with it an' all, but he still handed himself in. He just walks into the Bridewell himself and says he done it. He would of got away with it an' all if he said nothing, but he shopped himself over it. Cunt was never the same.

Around a week or two after that then, the lads in the van done the job on me. And in between was Johnny Silver's funeral, like I said.

I think I got some sleep, but I was dying with the pain mostly and it was all dark then later on when Stacey comes back and gets the stuff from my pocket when I asked her again.

Did ya start on that in Dublin? she asks me while she's cooking it up. I got a great hit off it anyway and I think she got the rest, but I was well happy with myself after that one. I tell ya now if I was to give a greatest hits of all my hits, definitely the first time I done the heroin would be top of it, but this one when I'm in bits in bed would be my second one, probably, cos I was nearly out of it already an' all, cos my mam was after coming up just before Stacey and gave me a rake of D10s. But I said nothing to Stacey about that in case she'd only stop. And the pain kind of made it better too an' all, cos one second I was still sore everywhere and then it was like I was floating on top of all the pain and I could feel the echo off it, like, behind me only, but not the pain, see?

•

But what are you going to do about all that, too, y'know? A bit of it is needed, isn't it like, when you look at it? Violence I mean. Some people can hack it. Others wouldn't be bothered. It's a dog-eat-dog world. My mother says that sometimes. And you have to eat a dog too, like I know in fairness, if you want to get on. 'Cept I wouldn't eat no dog, me. Mickey 2, like.

Mickey 1 was fighting and got a bating every now and again, like. And Mickey 2'd be getting a bating too, like, but like Mickey 2 would be still doing it his way and wouldn't be eating no dog, no matter what, see? That's the difference!

Back To School

A nd my mother calls the guards to the house an' all next day imagine to take a statement off me. In fairness she'd look after you alright when you need her to, like, my mam would.

I told them what happened, but nothing happened about that of course. No way. They'd never find people who'd do something like that. Oh no! But what did happen cos of that was my social worker (who was still Elaine) got wind of it and she came to see me too and goes you need to go back to school Mickey. And I'm like, I can barely move here ya daft bint! and she gets all huffy about it, like they do, and fucked off and I never seen her again for a week.

By then my mam was gone on holidays and Stacey was minding me mostly, when there wasn't a party on, like. My mother was still pregnant, see, so she couldn't be dealing with all that up and down the stairs stuff all the time. She needed a break too in fairness.

She wouldn't get any heroin for me though, Stacey like, while I was getting better. Not that I wanted it really, but I'd be telling her get it anyway. It was good to wait in-between though, like. I knew that too. She said I needed to build up my strength and she brung me food from the chipper all the time in fairness and no drugs, only pain killers. And hash.

Con came in a few times and if I had a bit of hash then I'd have to out it straight away or he'd get mad. He wanted to find out off me who the lads were that bate me up – and the woman. He wouldn't believe me, like that I didn't have a clue who they were. What am I going to do? Protect them, like!? The fellas I barely seen anyway, like I told Con, but the woman alright stared straight at me and I seen her face like an angel, I thought first, cos I thought she was saving me. But then she gobbed-up like it was in slow-motion. And I can still see it now even, if I think about it, with her small nose and slitty eyes and her lips building-up a big one.

But she only spat at me like, when you think of it. And she could be that fella's daughter, an all, for all I know. Paddy Murphy's like. Did ya ever think of that, Con? I goes to him. But he wouldn't think of something like that at all, Con. All's he knew is someone bate up a Collins and someone had to pay. I didn't give a shit about it, me. What do I care, sure? If it wasn't fellas like that it was another gang or someone else. If I had to get Con to get back at everyone who gave me a batin' his knuckles'd be red raw. He'd probably enjoy it too like, but – life is too short I say. That's what I always say: Life is too short. Who said that? Jesus probably said it first, when you think about it. Fair fucks to him.

Anyway, I got back home for it, didn't I? And the bed was lovely and there was loads of room at home an' all now. Things were looking up, far as I'm concerned. Then, next thing Elaine comes back and tells me I have to start going to school again.

●

And I gave out mad, like, but later on I was thinking about it and I talked with Cillian an' all on the phone, like, and I

191

says I might as well give it a try. School, like. Sure why not? I mean do it proper, like and get my Leaving Cert and be posh like Cillian (he was getting posh even by now and it wasn't funny no more, but he was like good with it). He was doing his Leaving an' all at the time too, imagine. He was eighteen, like or over, but when he give me that fifty notes a few days before or a week before, like, he was telling me then about it and he says he might be going to college an' all if he gets it. I bursts my arse laughing at him at the time, but later on when I was thinking about it I was kind of glad he was doing it too, like. And I know I couldn't do it with him, but maybe if I done my Leaving too, I was thinking, we'd get a job together in the same office, later on like, and we'd be like at home together again then too. We'd probably make enough to buy Winchester off Con then, I was thinking, and make a granny flat out the back for our mother, all posh-like. And Tara and Melanie and the baby (who I didn't know was Jordan SueAnne yet then) could live with us an' all – and even Bridie could move in an' all if she wanted cos Tara would be thinking about her only otherwise.

So when I starts back, I was thinking *Yeah I'll get my Leaving and see what happens*, y'know? It's not like I wanted to do bad at school. That's just the way it turned out.

•

And it wasn't too bad for the first bit either I'd say. School, like. I'd go in and I'd do stuff and Mr. Sullivan was there and he was alright mostly. And Brenda was the name of the woman who was in there with me too. She was like looking after me in there with the rest of the class. And she was nice too like.

But they'd all be at me too, like, and be too serious all the time. And if I didn't have a pencil and got one off the desk next to me or something, they'd be like, Oh you can't do that now!

Or the girl next to me used be crying in my ear the whole time like she was in babyland or something. She'd be saying things like, Stop Mickey! all the time, when I'd be doing nothing really, only messing. But she'd be saying it out loud for everyone to hear all the time and she could never take a joke. And they'd be giving out to me then for that, so I wouldn't come back for a week or more, until Elaine come and got me again and made sure I went.

And they moved yer wan away who was sitting next to me and put a big fella, Keith, sitting there. And Keith wouldn't let me have nothing on to him and he'd hit me an' all sometimes if I went near him and the teacher'd only give out to me then after that. Not Keith at all, like!

And one time, I remember, Mr. Sullivan was telling us read a book out loud now to the class and all of us had to stand up, one by one, and read a bit like to the class. But he got to me and he skipped me instead and told Keith read next. And I never wanted to read anyway, but I got odd with him then like for missing me out and I wouldn't speak with him or to no one there for ages. About a month I'd say at least, when I went there like.

And Brenda'd be like all very nice and saying things like, If Joe left Cork on the train at 9 o'clock, Mickey, and the train went a hundred miles an hour…

And when she'd stop saying the question then I'd be like, Who's Joe? and I'd get them all laughing, like. And we'd all be having a bit of craic with it and Mr. Sullivan then butts in like he's the boss and tells me I'm interrupting the class. And he'd be alright one minute and then the next thing, he thinks he's in charge of everything. And I know – I knew even then, like – he can't be holding up everything just cos one person, but like at the same time he only wanted to make a fool of me too like. I knew that much. And Brenda was the same. She'd be like, in front of everyone, Do you know the answer, Mickey? and she'd put me on the spot then an' all, cos they'd be all waiting to hear what I'd say. And they all needed a laugh too, the other students there like, cos it was a bit much all the time, in fairness. I made them all laugh mostly with my stupid answers. And I got on alright with most of them too mostly.

But there was a lot of shit too like. One fella had a phone one day that was like a super duper phone that no one else had and he was showing off all the time with it. And like a load of people didn't even have a phone at that time, like, and there was no need for one either. And he was all like, Oh look at me and don't I got a marvellous phone! (he spoke like that too!) An Apple it was. An Apple phone, like. Probably the first one. An Apple 1.

And the bell went and everyone was heading out to the yard, like, and yer man had his phone in his hand already and was waving it and I grabbed the pencil case on Keith's desk and thrun it from one end of the class across everyone getting up an' all and smashed it out of yer man's hand straight away. And I was like, OH WOW! DID YOU SEE THAT! and Keith dug me into my face and didn't even see the shot I made. And the other fella is screaming and roaring over by the door and Brenda, who saw nothing, is looking at me now, giving out to me even when I'm trying to get up off the floor. And Mr. Sullivan then is coming over to me like it's all my fault! And I was trying to tell them the joke of it, like, but they wouldn't even listen to me, none of them. They were taking the posh fella's side in it and

Keith's side too. I wouldn't be bothered with none of them after that. Bastards the lot of them. Always the same.

And the joke was loads an' all! Like, number one he wasn't allowed even to have no phone, but he had it anyway, like, so I caught him at that! The second one was the way I thrun it. It went behind one fella who just walked past me, like, when I was throwing it. And another fella was just after moving backwards in his desk and it flung in front of his face after he moved it back and the last wan, over by the door was just pulling her bag up off the floor and the pencil case bounced off her back and hit the phone I was aiming for the whole time! It was like a game of pool the way it bounced off her, like, and straight in the pocket! And the other joke was him too anyway – the fella who's phone it was. His name was Oliver, like he was posh. But he wasn't posh at all, like, but he thought he was. And his mother brought the phone for him too, but he probably robbed it, I knew, cos I knew where he lived, like, and they thought they were great with two cars and a dog like the Queen of England!

But the other thing was the real joke! I left that out, like! The real joke was, I was thinking I was throwing an apple, the whole time! What I *meant* to be throwing was an apple. That's what was in my head when I done it, see? An apple for an apple, y'know? That's the funny part that you have to remember!

But they was all screaming and roaring in my ear, knocking me to the ground and giving out and crying about it and sending me to the principal. And I knew by then I didn't throw an apple so I wouldn't be bothered telling them the joke then, cos she wouldn't understand either. I knew that much. Not worth the bother in it anyway.

And anyway, by then I was already sixteen and had enough of the place.

Daylight Robbery

If Con was called for a song – at a sing-song like, he'd always get up to sing a song and then you'd think he's going to sing, but instead goes on instead about the average age of the Vietnam soldier. And he'd end it with Nineteen – na na na na na Nineteen! And we'd all be skitting, like, but we wouldn't know if he'd be joking, cos he'd be serious with it too like. And then he'd sing The Red Rose Café and everyone'd join in. You'd be afraid to ask him what's that all about Con? And no one did, but by the time he sings Red Rose Café anyway we'd all be after forgetting it.

Just remembered that now about him, while I'm on it, like, cos I was thinking what I was up to when I was around nineteen and I felt like an old man by the time I was nineteen and that's no word of a lie. I was probably in my twenties before I knew anything at all, looking back now. And by then, even, I knew nothing I'd say, no way like. You can believe that if anything.

•

Jordan SueAnne was born and grew up in Winchester. She was always my favourite and I spoilt her rotten. We all did. Getting her things all the time and looking after her. Melanie and Tara, when they'd be back would be all over her, but they were more like aunties who were visiting, I'd say. Cillian would be all over her too, bringing her big fancy presents like on her birthday. But mostly Stacey or me'd be looking after her like all the time cos my mam (and Con too like)'d be busy with things most of the time. I was never told nothing 'bout all that and I didn't want to know neither. But definitely for the next few years, after sixteen around, I was looking after Jordan SueAnne. Mostly, like. Looking after her, and stuff. And if she got in a fight (like she did too sometimes, cos she'd be a little terror when she wants to be, like) I'd be there to back her up and look after her too that way. I was her big brother, me. Still am, like, probably.

Stacey'd be there too and I'd take her out sometimes, Jordan SueAnne like, mostly and we'd go for a spin in the pram around town or up to the park or wherever. And I'd have a few bags with me like cos people'd need stuff like. But I never sold nothing proper like when I'd be with Jordan SueAnne. Just a bit of hash, is all I'd have. Mainly like. Jordan SueAnne would be happy-out and some others'd be bringing their kids too, like. And the kids would be on the swings and it was no big deal or nothing. Just I'd give the mam or the dad or the uncle a little bag and they'd give me a little cash and we'd all be grand and happy and what's wrong with that, sure? It's not like a big drug-deal and shit. It was a walk in the park. And me and Jordan SueAnne'd have a grand afternoon. 'Cept she'd be stinking by the time we'd get home usually. I couldn't be changing nappies like cos I'm allergic to it. Ask anyone that.

I tried changing it one time, but it was like toxic when I took it off. I was less than nineteen at the time.

Around eighteen I'd say or under. My mam was giving out to me all the time cos I never changed a nappy, she was saying, so I said I'd try it that day. And what a mess was made of that one, cos I got sick into the nappy an all before I run away from it. Had to come back to grab the baby, like, then ran away again. I left the pram there an' all beside the bandstand cos there was no way I was going back again. That shit was lethal, man. But I left Jordan SueAnne crawl around on the grass a few hours after that and I dunked her then in the river below by the Shaky Bridge after and she was delighted, splashing in the water. Mostly the grass scrope it off, like, so it was only the harder bits that was still stuck on by then.

When we got back to the bandstand her pram was gone an' all, but an old woman come over waving at me and I thought she was telling me get out of the park, but she was calling me about the pram, see? She goes was that your pram what was there by the bandstand? She seen two young people, a fiend and a beor like, running out the gate of the park a while ago and the beor was pushing the fiend in it. And I goes, Just now is it? and she goes, Around twenty minutes ago. So I had to follow her out by the gate then to look. And I was carrying Jordan SueAnne, like in my arms, and we all looks down the road and we could see the two of them straight away, way-down the Mardyke, like, and I'm not sure what to do cos they were nearly down as far as the traffic lights. I couldn't be running all the way after them with a baby in my arms. The nosey wan was there though looking at me and looking down the Mardyke and saying, Go on – why aren't you going down after your pram?

But I'm trying to figure out what to be doing, like cos it's not as simple as everything at all, y'know?

You couldn't see who they were from where we were, but I knew who they were straight away when I seen them – and I knew even before I seen them too, cos I was after selling the two of them a bit of hash about an hour earlier. Yer wan was a scrawny yolk and she was still the one pushing the pram, but she was barely moving by now cos she was flaaed-out after going about nearly a mile down the road. I'd say she couldn't push a ball down a hill, in fairness.

She was half cooked an' all even before I sold them anything. I knew that, like, and I was after leaving them off, taking only twenty quid for it. And then she even dropped another tenner on the ground an' all at the time and I only told her about it and said hang on to that, love. I mean they were out of it even then, like, the two of them and I never seen them before, but she had an accent like Northern Ireland, y'know? So you'd never know what you'd be getting there, like. So I stayed well-wide at the time. I'd say they were celebrating a job or something, but I had the baby there with me (on the grass like, at the time) and they were definitely IRA, I was thinking cos why else would they have accents like that down in Cork, sure? So cos of that, I wasn't mad to be running after the pram – and I was right about that too in the end, the more you think about it. But the old wagon standing there next to me is nagging at me now go get them. So I starts down the Mardyke after them anyway then.

And it was yer man was in the pram, definitely. The more I walked down the more I could see him cos when she'd turn a small bit I could see his two legs was sticking way out in front and his arms were out the sides and his head was up nearly as high as yer wan's too when she'd pull back his head. And she was trying to push the pram away down the road, but she was nearly falling over the hangle of it too sometimes, barely able to push it like. He was skinny too, like an' all, but fierce big and totally out of it.

I still don't know either was it just the drink they had before I seen them first, like, but I'd say they had something stronger too after that (not the hash I mean), like cos they were in bad shape in fairness when I seen them both earlier, but much worse now. Whatever though, they were after robbing our pram now and I had to carry on after them, cos the old wan was still standing there at the gate behind me anytime I looks back at her.

I didn't have to go too fast, though, but all the way down I was calling yer wan. The wan on the pram, like, but she took no notice, only kept walking on like she done nothing or couldn't hear nothing too.

Here! I was shouting at her, Sorry like!?

Then when I got a bit closer I was shouting things like, Here, that's my pram, where ya goin' with it, like? or, Sorry there Girl! but she still never even looked back.

Next I caught up with her when we were all nearly at the gate of the hospital and I grabbed the hangle and goes, What are ya doing, like? That's my pram! and she spun her head around and starts laughing when she seen me and goes, Blow for twenty? and her teeth were like too big for her face and she was dipping her head down to look up at me and I only wanted the pram back and I was rocking it off her, but she forgot about that when she seen the baby and she gets a shock then when she looks at Jordan SueAnne and she looks like she hates the look off her, then she looks like she loves seeing the baby, then she looks like she's in a shock again then and doesn't know what to say, with her teeth sticking all out again. The ones she still has, like.

And when she seen me trying to rock yer man out of the pram, she remembers then and goes, Whataboutya there Jackie? to me like, in her Northern Ireland accent.

Fachnad's not well, man! Whatya doin' there? and I told her she's robbing my mother's pram, my sister's like, and I'm taking it back, but she's giving out to me and pushing me and I only have one hand and I'm trying to rock yer man out of the pram and he's totally out of it, zonked-like. And yer wan goes, I got to get Fachnad to a doctor! He's not right I tell ye! and we were nearly outside the gate of the Erinville, where Jordan SueAnne was born, like only a year or two earlier, so I goes, There's a hospital there, like, so gimme back my pram now!

Next thing, there was a fella standing by the gate that I wasn't after seeing, smoking by the gate like, and he goes, This is a maternity hospital.

He was cool-out like, yer man, tapping on his fag while he says it. And I looks at Fachnad in the pram and he looks like he's after ODing, but this smoking fella's calm-out.

Do you work here? I goes to him, Are you a doctor?

He looks at me, blowing smoke out and goes, I do. I'm not.

And I haven't a clue what he's on about and I'm trying to empty Fachnad out of the pram so I can take it home, like, and yer man then goes, He can't come in here! This is a maternity hospital only – no junkies unless they're having a baby!

And I goes, How could *he* be having a baby!? cos the idiot hasn't a clue, like. And yer wan is screaming in my other ear, yer man Fachnad unconscious in the pram, this smart-arse fiend giving me stick an' all now and to top it all, Jordan SueAnne starts screaming and roaring too, trying to wiggle out of my arm, like, cos she seen her own pram an' all now and wants it back too. She was good as gold up to now, but now she's getting mad-out and who could blame her too, like?

202

Next thing, a squad car pulls up and two shades who I know hops out of it.

What're ya up to now, Mikey? Garda Piggy goes. He's a right prick this fella.

It's not me at all, Garda Piggy! I tells him, It's these two robbed my pram!

And I'm rocking it forwards when Garda Piggy turns round to yer wan and looks at her and I'd say he can even see she's out of it and she turns round to him then and starts giving him grief an' all 'bout harassing her and won't help Fachnad and shit. And Garda Fitzgerald (who I know less, but who's alright, like) goes, Is he alright, there? and the fella who was smoking starts laughing and says, Nothing twenty-four hours in a drug-tank won't cure.

And Garda Piggy is going to tell yer man get lost when Fachnad finally kind of shifted in the pram and tumbled out onto the ground like. But when I turn the pram back the right way, a bag of heroin falls out too on top of him too, like and Garda Piggy is delighted with that one. You could see his eyes light up at the sight of it when he looks at me. And I gets a shock and goes, It's not me at all!

And yer wan from Northern Ireland don't know what's going on still, but all hell breaks loose then and next thing we know, I'm back in the Bridewell trying to tell them what happened.

That was one of the first times an' all that Jordan SueAnne was taken off us, like. We never got her back for ages. Around four days or five at least, like. My mam was killing me over it for ages too an' all, like it was all my fault, cos she had to come up early over it from a party down in West Cork to collect

203

the baby or they wouldn't give her back at all for another week at least, they said. So she had to come all the way back two days after that (or three days maybe) to collect her, but she wasn't allowed collect her then again for another two or three days after that. And she was mad-out over it and gave out stink over it too.

But it wasn't my fault neither! Most I done was sell them hash, like, but I'd say they didn't even remember that, yer wan and yer man Fachnad, like. And it was only cos the cops knew me and the bag of heroin was on the pram like that they decided to get me involved in it. That was a right pain in the hole for ages, that one, cos after they searched me and got the bit of hash I still had, they searched the bag under the pram then too and finds a bit of heroin there too like an' all. Inside a jar of baby-food, like. All's I was doing mostly was looking after Jordan SueAnne the whole time like, but the two who robbed the pram and done the drugs and shit got off it all. And Garda Piggy and Detective Long made me to blame for all of it. I'd say they were afraid they were in the IRA an' all cos they're both shitty bastards when it comes to it. And that old biddy too who made me go chasing after the two IRA junkies down the Mardyke gets me mad when I thinks of her an' all. Some people'd be like too much business going on for them to be keeping out of!

Give It Up, Mickey!

When we got back to the Bridewell I had to ring home to let my mother know where they got me, and about Jordan SueAnne, too like. But it was Stacey there, only, and she told me we won't say nothing to my mother about it yet, in case we didn't have to bother with that, like. I didn't know she was gone down to West Cork, see. She goes Jordan SueAnne'd be grand to be minded for one night, Stacey like.

So they done their questioning when we got back and I told them all about it, but halfway through they're checking out what else is in the bag from the pram, see, and they found the other heroin in the baby jar then. And with the bit of hash they got off me too they goes they'd be keeping me in for the night at least, see what happens next day, like.

I didn't know nothing about the stuff in the jar, like. I swore that to them an' all, but they wouldn't believe it. And the other heroin must of belonged to Fachnad or whatever his name was. And yer wan. Sure you'd never be getting heroin in Cork around that time. They never thought of that one! I couldn't find it nowhere even for ages around that time and here there was two loads of it in the pram I'm shoving 'round selling hash with! If I knew that, sure, I'd've been taken care of better than Jordan SueAnne even!

But Detective Long was interviewing me and he's as bad as Garda Piggy, so the two of them decided to pin it all on me instead. And he asks me, Do you want to phone anybody to let them know you'll be our guest for the evening?

And I goes, Naw, leave 'em off! then he said I should go and chew on it overnight cos I'll be in a lot of bother next day if I don't tell them where I got it, Pronto! like he goes, Detective Long.

It was while he was standing up to be heading out of the interview, that he said Pronto and Garda Piggy is grabbing my arm just after that, to pull me up off my seat and he goes to me, ...And he's not talking about the Lone Ranger's horse either!

That rings a bell with me, like, but I takes no notice what he's on about, still. I have enough to be getting on with. My Legal Aid is leaving an' all, lot of use he was, and next thing, Detective Long is standing by the door and looks back at Garda Piggy and shakes his head and he goes, You're thinking of Tonto – not Pronto! Tonto was his buddy – not his horse!

And we're walking out of the room and Garda Piggy asks him, So what's the name of his horse so? And Detective Long looks back and shakes his head again and goes, It's Silver, ya dumb schmuck – the horse's name was Silver!

Next thing I broke my arse out bursting laughing at that and Garda Piggy starts shaking me and shaking me and telling me shut up while he's dragging me down to my cell. I couldn't help it like. I couldn't even tell him I wasn't laughing at him at all, being called a schmuck, but I just remembered my mam's joke at Johnny Silver's funeral and I know then why Con bate Timmy McGrath nearly to death an' all. I got the joke!

Like, how many years was it since Johnny Silver died? I'd say two at least. Or three at least. And I never even thought about it since then neither. And I never even knew I didn't know the joke of it til that time neither! But now when I thought about

Con riding Silver into school I couldn't stop the laughing. I'm glad I didn't laugh as much back then, like, cos Con might of bate me up too, like he got Timmy McGrath. But instead I got it off Garda Piggy instead. Must be something about that joke makes people want to bate the shit out of someone. Garda Piggy done it better than Con at least. No blood. They're always careful that way. No blood, no marks. I think it can be even sorer that way too, y'know? But I wouldn't give a shit anyhow. And he knew that too. I wouldn't say nothing about it, mainly cos the same as what Foxy Bill told me that time – nobody'd believe me. And if they did, nobody'd care. And he was dead-right on that one too.

He enjoyed himself anyway, Garda Piggy did, and I left him off cos I was still only laughing. And around halfway through him bating me, what he didn't know was I stopped laughing at the Lone Ranger and then I was laughing at him for real. Really like! He'd be a long time getting that joke too, Dumb Schmuck that he was.

And he moved me after that too to the shittiest cell an' all, a'course, deliberate like.

I learnt a good trick off a fella one time I was in there with after getting done for a house job. He was in before me like, but he spent most of the time talking and talking. To himself mostly, but sometimes I joined in too. And while he was talking he was pulling off bits off his pants. Threads like first, then bigger bits, and dropping them down the drain. The drain was a hole in the floor, like, for piss and for a shit too, like if you had to. It was a kind of a sideways hole in the ground that went down and the water'd be running through it and took any of it down the hole, see. So this fella, Jez I think was his name or Jezzy or something like that, was talking and I wasn't taking no notice of him tossing bits of his pants into the drain. But after ages he was after stopping talking and he takes a dump into the bog, see when I'm not looking cos I was asleep by that time. Next thing there's a smell in the room and I wakes up cos it's 'scusting, like. And next thing, the drain is all blocked up and still blocking up more like and we had to bang on the door to be left out or moved to somewhere else before the whole place filled with water and shit and we'd be drowned in it. Or my feet'd get wet at least, like, cos it wasn't me what done it at all. The smell was totally 'scusting and I'd say the whole crap from everybody in the Bridewell was inside there it was so bad. It was funny too, like, cos when they got us out Jez was wearing a short pants and when he went in there he was wearing a long pants.

Well anyway, the cell Garda Piggy landed me in that night was like that an' all. There was no one else in there, but the drain was blocked up and I was wondering was Jez back ahead of me. I didn't take no notice of it first, like, cos there was the same bleach smell in there like always, like, but when you'd be in there an hour you start
getting the shitty smell too like on top of it and it'd crawl into your nose and down into your belly and make you sick an' all it's so bad. And it was bad like that all night long and they wouldn't let me out neither.

●

Next morning then, after Detective Long woke up from his warm bed, likely, and probably got a bit of hanky-panky in the bed, like, and got his big breakfast cooked for him an' all and dropped his children to school on his way to work and stopped off then for a bit more on the side an' all probably, cos they're all dying for it, them coppers like, he slides in to have a chat with me eventually around eleven, when it suits him to get me out of my shit-soaked cell. And I'm mad-out by this time and rearing to go. My legal aid was back for it too and so was Garda Piggy. He took me to the interview room too a'course and told me I didn't need to be getting no more grief like I got last night if I'd be good, like. And I'm fuming-mad. But quiet-like.

So we starts off anyway and I had to go through it all again with them what went on yesterday and all about the nosey wan who sent me down the Mardyke after the two who was after robbing my baby sister's pram. I never got that wan's name and it's all her fault too when you think about it, I tells them. Like, without her I'd of been the one who was robbed and had stuff stolen off, like. They were forgetting that too! I was the one who's pram was robbed in all this!

And where's them other two? I goes, Fuckwad and Fuckhead-with-the-missing-tooths?

I know it's teeth, like, but I forgot at the time how to say it right and I said tooths like the way Con would say it, like. I was missing a few teeth an' all myself even by then. Some were after falling out, some knocked out and I was waiting on an appointment at the dentist. Garda Piggy knocked none out to be fair, I'll give him that.

And they wouldn't even answer me that though, like that pram robbery was nothing to them.

And what about my sister? I goes, I'm apposed to be lookin' after my sister, like! Where's she?

And Garda Piggy starts up then, What will your mam do to ya when she finds out Mikey? he goes, That you lost your sister Sue, and she was taken off ya? Will she be mad at you Mikey?

And I gets mad then at that and starts shouting at him, Her name's Jordan SueAnne, not Sue alright? Ya dumb schmuck! I goes to him.

And it takes ages then before everyone is chill. And I'm willing to carry on only after I get that fucker thrown out an' all and another garda comes in instead of him, who was Garda Fitzgerald, who was alright like, but I don't know how he'd even stick that other fella himself.

Then after all that, when it's all quiet like, Detective Long asks me how's my mother. And I'm in shock like for a while cos I'm trying to work out how he means it. And I says nothing, but he probably seen me thinking about it, shocked like, cos he goes, I don't mean it in a rude way, you understand? and it's only then I thinks what rude way he might be on about, that I know he's a randy bastard who'd get up on anything anyway and I want to hit him – if I felt like it, like. And he goes, Will she be mad at you? Will she make out like it's all your fault, Michael? he goes. And I'm still thinking about it, Or will she be happy you succeeded in recovering your sister's pram, perhaps? and I'm still thinking.

Or will she be concerned that all these drugs were discovered in the vicinity of your innocent baby sister? Will she be afraid for her baby and wonder where these illicit substances came from and blame you?

I still had nothing cos I'm still thinking what would she be doing next and I'd never know what my mother'd do or what she'd kill me for doing, but I'm starting to worry now alright what she'd do, while he's saying it, like, and I know it's my fault alright and I'll be the one blamed for it.

Or maybe, he goes, She'll be mad at you because you lead the police to the heroin that *she* left in her own baby's food jar?

And then, I tell ya, I got the fright of my life, cos I never thought of that one. And it was true too, probably, I'm thinking. All the time, I'm only mad at the smell in the cell or the bating I got or at the junkies or at the cops for getting it all wrong, blaming me the whole time, like for everything. And I never had no time to think about that one. Like no way did them two put heroin in the jar in the baby bag, like surely? So if it wasn't them, like, who was it?

And now Detective Long had me stuck and I knew it too. If I said it was me, I'm in trouble. If I said it must have been my mam, I'd be in bigger trouble. Much bigger trouble, in fact, when you think about it.

Did your mother put heroin in your baby sister's food jar, Michael? he goes to me, all quiet like. And I'm like in a shock and I goes, How would I know? and he goes Did she keep it there in case anyone wanted something stronger than a bit of hash, maybe? So you could do them a favour that way, perhaps? he says.

No it's not like that at all! I says, cos he hasn't a clue what he's on about, So how is it, Michael? he goes, softly.

Tell me, who do _you_ think _could_ have put the heroin in the baby jar?

And what else could I say? Who would *you* say if you were me, like? I had to say someone! Who could it of been, like?

Who else had access to the baby bag before you left the house yesterday morning, Michael? he was asking me now after

211

that. And there was only one person it could have been when I thought of it. Like, that stuff could have been in there for a week when you think about it, but still it's all the one. I didn't want to say it, like, but there was no other choice when you think about it. And it's not like I was saying it <u>was</u> her, but only that it <u>could</u> of been her, like. I tried thinking of everything, but I couldn't think of nothing else.

There was me like, I goes, But I know it wasn't me! and he waited there a bit for me and he left me have a think about it. And looking back now, my legal aid must of gone to sleep cos he said nothing an' all. If I was in there now I'd know alright how not to say nothing, but I was younger then and I knew nothing, like I'm saying. Admitting to nothing, like.

Stacey, I goes.

I said it to him alright, Stacey alright, I said. It was me who said it. And I tried telling him then that it wasn't her at all neither, but he wouldn't listen to me, Stacey who? he goes, What's her second name?

And it's like an echo all around me when I heard him say it and it's like an echo when I said it too:

Stacey O'Connor, I goes.

Bull

By the time I got home then, later on like, there was no one there. The house was empty and nobody would answer the door when I rung it. No sign of Stacey anywhere so I could warn her like, if I thought it was a good idea. Con was on a job or in the pub somewhere maybe. I still didn't know was my mam in West Cork or where was she. None of my sisters or my brother was living there mostly and I knew Jordan SueAnne was taken away too. And no Stacey.

So I waited around by there a while, see who came home, but then I had to break in through the small window in the bathroom that was already smashed, so I only broke the bit of wood behind it this time. I'd of never gotten in otherwise, cos the whole place was locked up. And I'm inside around half an hour and the phone rings and rings when I'm watching telly, only. There was nothing on, but I was just after sitting down and I wasn't after going through all the channels yet, see what's on. And then later on it rings back again and I had to answer it this time. And when I do, it's my mam and she's wondering where's everybody and she knows nothing neither about none of what happened and she's telling me she's looking for Stacey and I lets-on nothing and says I haven't a clue where she is – cos I didn't either, like when you think about it. And, Is she gone out with Jordan SueAnne so? she goes. And I goes, Eh, no I don't think so! And I'm trying not to answer her, but she's better than any cop and gets it out of me after that with her questions, all of it mostly. About the wan who made me chase after the two what robbed the pram and how I got done by the cops then cos yer wan at least was from Northern Ireland and my mam knows Garda Piggy is a shitty bastard and yer man in the pram couldn't even talk and they only blamed me for it, then like, the shades, and locked me up and took away Jordan SueAnne too and Stacey was supposed to talk to you about it (my mam like), but she probably said nothing and I don't know where she is now, Stacey like. Or Jordan SueAnne neither since she got took.

And she goes what were you locked up for? And I tried saying cos you know they don't like me, but then I'm saying cos I still had a bit of hash, but then she doesn't believe that neither and I said yer man had a bag of heroin on him and it fell out of the pram when he fell out. And she kind of leaves me off with that much and I says nothing about the stuff in the jar. Whether she knew now about that or whether she didn't, I couldn't tell you, to be fair, but she's getting madder and madder while she's asking me all the questions and she's screaming at me by the end cos I'm not telling her fast enough 'til she asks. And by the end of all that she's going, You spoiled my buzz now! Why didn't you tell me all of that at the start? – Or better still, she goes, Why didn't you let on you know nothing so I wouldn't have had to bother? You're only good at that when it's true! And it's true all the time, isn't it? And I says nothing and she goes, Isn't it? And I goes yeah and she goes, What's true? And I goes what? And she says, WHAT'S TRUE? And I don't have a clue what's true and she's calling me all the names cos I'm so dumb all the time and she never had an abortion, but she should of when she was having me. An' all that kind of stuff mam's'd be saying when they're mad, like. Blah blah blah!

214

And when she's finished, I told her I had the number too for her to ring about Jordan SueAnne, like if she wants to, but she didn't have a biro on her and she told me tell Stacey ring them and pretend she's her (my mam like) and tell them we'll collect Jordan SueAnne on Monday. Or Tuesday at the latest, at least.

This was on a Wednesday, see, and Stacey wasn't back til later-on when it was darker, like. And she didn't want to be talking then and I didn't neither. So she only nodded when she come in and I nods too like cos I was watching whatever was on. And then she went up to bed and I didn't see her til around three o'clock next day in the kitchen.

I was after getting a new bike down the road and I took off the wheels and was washing them in the sink to get the mud off and make them all shiny and shit when she come in, Stacey like. She gets the kettle and stands next to me with it and when I looks at her she only smiled a small bit and then filled the kettle when I moved out of the way, like, and she still said nothing. But she wasn't odd with me at least, if she knew anything to be odd about like, so I found the number for her and I told her my mam said ring that and pretend she's her so we can collect Jordan SueAnne next week, like.

So when the kettle was boiling, Stacey takes the phone into the front room and dials it and she's gone ages and my wheels are perfect an' all after a while, but there's no sign of Stacey to show her. So next I makes her a cup of tea and brings it in and I can hear my mam shouting at her on the phone and Stacey is nearly crying cos she knows it's all her fault that my mam has to come up now from West Cork by tomorrow cos Stacey never called for Jordan SueAnne and now they're saying if we don't collect her back on Friday they're going to be looking to have her taken away and kept off us. Probably forever.

And when my mother hung up on her, I put out the cup for Stacey and she only looks at me with teary eyes for ages and then she gives me a big hug and starts crying while she's hugging me and I'm like, What are ya doing? Like, you're spilling all the tea! and she don't care, she's only crying and hugging me and after a while I dropped the cup on the settee and hugged her back too. Not like in a sexy way, now, (but her chest was straight up against me, like alright, and she only had a T-shirt on), but in a sad way.

She was sad alright and made me all sad then too, cos Stacey's alright, like, mostly. At that time anyway she was. And the two of us was all-sad for ages and she was crying and didn't say nothing. And I didn't know what to do and I didn't ask about it neither. She probably spilt it on purpose though anyway cos I can't make tea for shit my mother always said.

●

Next day after that, on Friday like, my mother gets back around two o'clock cos she had to come all the way back from West Cork. And she looks wrecked and she's mad as anything. And she's shouting and roaring at the lot of us, the two of us like, saying she can't go nowhere and have a break without the whole place falling apart and us two making a mess of everything and treating this place like a hotel. And Tony is with her, her new boyfriend like who was driving. And he gets a can off the slab on the table when she's giving-out and he goes upstairs for a lie-down for himself without saying nothing.

And my mam has to have a lie down an' all after all the aggro and she couldn't go out to get Jordan SueAnne then til around four and she was gone ages, like. And when she got back she was like a bear then too cos they told her she can't have Jordan SueAnne now 'til Monday cos they said she got there too late and the plan was made. And she kilt us again then cos she said she didn't need to come back up at all and we all wasted all her time, so herself and Tony had to go again then til Monday for her nerves.

And next day Stacey was gone an' all too the whole day, more or less, and didn't come back til nearly night time, so I had the place to myself, but I was saying I'd give up the drugs, like Cillian, so I went out for a long cycle on my new bike. Keep fit, like. And I was gone ages, up by the Blackstone Bridge mostly, up on the Northside, see, or near enough and I was looking for thorneels there like we used do long 'go. And next thing I seen a load of cows in a field and I tore off after them, for the laugh like, like me and Cillian used be doing out in Blarney when we used be staying at Madge's house.

And the farmer was standing by the gate looking at me when I was halfway into the field and he shouts out at me to stop, so I ran away off the other way and into another field, but the farmer keeps running after me and screaming. And I'm halfway into that field when I seen the bull that was looking straight at me and I froze on the spot. Next thing, the farmer got to the part where I ran in and he goes, What are ya doing there? You need to get out of that field or that bull'll kill ya!

When I looks again, the bull is there, la, rubbing his foot off the floor like you'd see in a movie or something an' he looking straight at me still. And I checks my clothes for red straight away, cos they gets mad at red, like, cos I know that. And

217

there's a red badge on my jacket so I took it off and rolled it up, but my T-shirt has a bit of red in it too, bigger than the badge was, so I took that off too and had to pick up my jacket after I dropped it. And I'm looking at the bull all the time and he's still mad-out at me and getting ready to stampede on me. Next the farmer goes, He's fierce mad if you wear jeans! and I looks at my pants and they're jeans an' all, so I whipped them off fast and had to get my shoes off first, like, but my socks were white with a red stripe at the top, so they had to go too. And my underpants was purple, but the farmer goes, Purple is the worst colour for bulls for Jaysus sake get them off fast! and I didn't bother taking them off, but I thrun all my clothes in the air to make the bull chase them instead and legged it out of the field like a rocket, up over the ditch and through it too, full of nettles and thorns an' all. I don't know how I got out, but the bull couldn't follow me, even though he was chasing me alright by then cos I never took off my purple jocks.

And I'm cut all over and full of nettles all day after. And I have to pass loads of houses and people and traffic and shops all the way back home, but I wouldn't be bothered about them cos I had an idea after a while. I pretended to be a jogger, out training, see. And I jogged home all the way. Or mostly, much as I could anyway.

At home then my legs and my arms and my belly and my back even were all stinging me and bleeding too and I searches all over for tablets or something to take the pain away. I even searches Stacey's room an all, and my mam's room an' all too after I picked the lock, but she kept all the stuff hidden and not in the house in case I'd find it, like. I filled a big bath with loads of suds too at one stage, to get into like, but it kept stinging my foot so there was no way I'd be getting in with the rest of me, like. There was nothing at all there to help me and I only had a bit of hash to chill with for ages, til Stacey got back.

And I'm hoping she has something when she comes home cos I need it now like to fix me up after all that. And for my nerves too, cos that bull would've definitely killed me alright.

I heard her come in and I called her but she was on her way upstairs straight away, but I made her come into the front room and asked her if she got stuff and she only shakes her head and starts walking away before I told her about the bull and the thorns and the nettles and the mad farmer and I showed her my legs and my arms and she knew I was serious then and she kind of smiled and came back in and pulled a full supply out of her pocket, the good stuff, heroin like. She doesn't even look at me and says nothing, just takes out her bong and her lighter. And when she's getting it ready, like, I mocks her and says, You were keeping all that for yourself an' all! I goes, All that much would kill ya, I'd say! but she only holds out the stuff and gave me first go and then I had a brainwave and remembered my bike – my new, good bike, out by the Blackstone bridge and I left it out there and I knew straight away some knacker'd be after taking it on me by now an' all, cos you can keep nothing round here. So that's another reason why it was the wrong day to go cold turkey.

So I got my hit and zonked out and I knew Stacey got hers then, cos I was out of it and enjoying myself for a long time, away and away from all that and everything. And when I come back, still not able to move, barely, and enjoying it, still too like, Stacey was already sitting up having more and lying back down on the settee then for a rest. And after a while I was able to move and I was looking at it and there was still a load there and I knew

Stacey wouldn't mind, so I got another hit and off I went again then. What a night that was.

Mickey's Birthday

I wasn't going to be saying nothing about this now, cos my mother said tell no one, but I'm going to say it anyhow. Sometimes, like around then, I started sitting down on the bridge, Patricks Bridge usually, or the North Gate Bridge sometimes, if that other fella wouldn't be there who'd chase me away, like. And when people'd be passing I'd go, Big Issue! and most people wouldn't even be bothered, but some would look for the magazine then and they might see I don't have it, but I'd be laughing, see, so some of them would laugh back and if they said, You're not selling the Big Issue! I could charge them for laughing. Ahahahahaah! Fifty pence a laugh! I'd tell them. And then sometimes they'd say, It's cents now, not pence! and I'd go something like, No! I got no sense, me! and then they'd laugh again at that one and I'd go, Oh that's a euro you owe me now! Ahahahahaah! I got them on that one every time. Mostly.

It was my mother cut me off, see, around then cos she said I was too thick and I wasn't getting her no presents for ages, cos I dunno why, but I didn't want to be. Didn't feel like it, like, for a while at least around then. She wouldn't even let Con let me do nothing and make a few bob. He was busy too anyway, mostly, cos the feud with them travellers was after starting up again. Dirty bastards was always pulling fast ones and didn't like it then if my mother'd be getting stuff off somewhere else too, as well as off them, like. I wasn't allowed in on any of that (not that I wanted, like), but I sussed out what was going on cos Stacey

221

told me one time when we were whispering about it in the kitchen. She didn't used be saying nothing, but she was telling me things around then alright. Someone to chat to, I suppose there's that. She was alright again, Stacey, like, around then. She was saying Tony was my mam's best friend now and she was only looking after Jordan SueAnne mainly, is the only reason she was still around, she goes, but she didn't mind cos Jordan SueAnne was the best child ever. And my mother wasn't being nice to her most of the time no more, to Stacey like. I could see that myself, like an' all. She'd be giving out and giving out to her all the time about nothing mostly. And to me too, in fairness. One time Stacey was trying to have a fag, cos she was going easy on the gonge, and Jordan SueAnne was on her laps, trying to grab the fag, laughing like, but Stacey was holding it up too high in case she'd burn herself or if she took a drag. Then my mam comes in and stares at her – at Stacey, like, and goes, Are you alright there? The kitchen's like a fuckin' tip! and Stacey says nothing to her, til my mother leaves. Then she says, It's tough at the top! and carries on playing with the baby.

Begging is what Garda Piggy called it, what I was doing getting money on the bridges. I didn't think about it til then, but after he hopped out of a squad car and locked onto me, he goes, I have ya this time Mikey – begging on the street now! when he said it straight away it was like a brainwave for me. I'm not, no! I goes, This is a bridge, not a street! but inside I'm thinking, separate like: *Why didn't I think of that?* It would've been easier for me to just beg for it, I was thinking, instead of having a laugh, making a joke of it, doing all the hard-work for the same thing, like.

Straight away I wanted to go down to the North Gate bridge so I could use that idea, but yer man was arresting me an' all for it, then. Another fella would tell you move on, but Garda Piggy didn't like me more than anybody. Mikey Mikey! he goes when he put me in the car and got in himself. That's what he called me: Mikey. Sometimes he'd call me Mikey the Pikey, just to annoy me, get me going like, cos why would he want to say something like that that's not true? Call me other things like other people, but number one: nobody calls me Mikey and number two: I'm no pikey. Mikey, Mikey! that day he goes, Where did it all go wrong? an' he laughing when he says it. He was a proper pig, that Garda Piggy, I'm telling ya, Lord have mercy, like. He was a pig cos he was a cop and he acted like a pig too and he looked like a pig with his big fat belly on him. And his name was Piggy, too. So all that altogether made him a real pig an' all!

Inside the Bridewell anyway, he stuck me in an interview room and made me wait there for over an hour I'd say. Like what did he want to do that for? Was I out robbing banks or something? No. Was I selling drugs, even? Or hash even? No and no! Just having a laugh I was doing and he had me in here for no reason.

And after all the waiting, it wasn't him at all who walks in for a chat, but instead it was Detective Long and another fella I never seen before. Serious looking special branch fella. I can't even remember his name right now, but he was like Samuel Jackson from the movies, 'cept he wasn't black, like. Do your mother know you're out begging on Patrick's Bridge, Michael? detective Long goes when he gets going, like, and I'm telling him I wasn't begging I was having a laugh, And are ya selling much drugs these days? he goes. And I told him I never sold drugs. The other fella's saying nothing all the time.

Have ya ever been to West Cork? he asks me then, Detective Long, like. Down around Glengarriffe direction? It's beautiful down that way isn't it? and I remembered the time we all went around Ireland with Con driving in the car and I told him I was all around everywhere, me: up in Dublin and in Limerick and Tralee and Killarney and in Galway too even. My cousins live up there, I was telling him, My mam's cousins like. But I never been to Sligo.

But how about West Cork, Michael? he goes and I asked him what way was west and he tells me you go out past the County Hall and keep going. I said I been out that way loads of times and the other fella, the cop, Samuel Jackson like, leans in and goes, Where were ya? he goes.

I got a shock at that, when he said something like and I had to think about it, Ballincollig like! I goes, That's out past the County Hall, Ballincollig. I had to go out to there on the bus with my mother one day cos she wanted a big chair they were selling in Aldi that gives you a massage when you sit on it. For her back, like. But it was sold out when we got there and we got a taxi home after that. I told that to the cops an' all, but Detective Long wasn't interested.

How about further west, Michael? he goes, Out past Ballincollig? Past Macroom, down west – Clonakilty direction? As far as Skibbereen or Schull even maybe? Have ya ever been to those places? There's some lovely spots down that direction aren't there? Did your mother ever take you to the beach down there, like to Inchydoney or Owenahincha or Tragumna or to Barley Cove even, maybe, hm? There's some fierce beaches down that way aren't there?

I had a think about it, but I never heard of them places and they all sounded stupid to me with stupid names, I don't think so, I goes, We mostly go to Youghal. Or to Crosshaven, like.

Samuel Jackson was annoyed at me now and got all barky, like, When was the last time you were in Youghal and who were you with? he goes, all cross like and I had a think and then I had another think and I said I think it was around five or ten year ago, probably with Stacey and one or two of my baby sisters. Or with my brother Cillian too maybe.

And how about your mother? Do she like the beach? detective Long asks me and I said, no, not in Ireland. She likes Spain mostly. And Samuel Jackson is all annoyed and stands up and sits down again and I swear he's going to start shouting "Mother fucker" now like the black Samuel Jackson would go in some movie and I starts laughing then at that and he asks me what am I laughing for and I goes nothing and he goes, You think all this is funny do ya? and I do but I tells him no.

Anyway they carries on like that for ages and I got annoyed after that and goes where's my lawyer, like. I should have a solicitor there with me, shouldn't I? And Detective Long goes, sure we're just chatting aren't we? What do ya want a solicitor for? And I goes, Well ye arrested me didn't ye? and he's all shocked and goes Arrested? No no no! We were only passing by and I spotted you waiting in here and came in to have a chat, is all! Sure we're old friends, aren't we Michael? You're up in court soon aren't you? he goes and I said I am, at the end of the month, far's I know and he goes, Maybe I could help you with something? and I was in a shock then at that cos I thought he was offering me drugs and I could do with them an' all, after all that. And I sussed them out for a while, but they were only

225

looking for dirt, like on my mam or Con and I'm no rat, me, ask anyone. And I told them that an' all.

Anyway they left me go and I got out of there and I told them nothing, I was sure of it, but I never told my mother or Stacey or Con, just in case like and I forgot about it for a few days. But that next weekend then my mother got arrested and Con too and a load of others including Tony Harrington (who was my mam's boyfriend) and Scanny and Kanturk and Timmy McGrath even.

And I was trying to think what did I say straight away when the house was raided. First thing in the morning they came on Saturday, like usual, and we were all still in bed and Jordan SueAnne was bawling an' all the whole time and they didn't care a damn about it, just ransacking the whole place. Sure I could of told them they'd find nothing cos I could never find nothing in that place myself and I looked often enough. I was full sure I said something though. Something to give the game away to them two that day, but I couldn't think what it was. So I said nothing when it was only me and the baby and Stacey left in the house after they all went away. And Stacey didn't ask me nothing about that either, so I went back to bed.

●

It was a few days after, before they were all back out and sitting in the kitchen, having a party. About a week I'd say, cos it was the weekend after. But there was no one singing or listening to music. Just all of them who was arrested and Stacey and Jordan SueAnne was there when I walks in. My mother was giving me jobs again and I was just back from a delivery, Was there a car across the road when you came in? she goes to me. I didn't see nothing, but I went out again to have a look so she wouldn't be shouting and good news: there was no one there. But when I come back in, Con was saying, Sure he don't know anything anyway do he? How could it be him, sure?

I got a shock at that and shouts out, Who? What are ye talking about, like? and they all stops and looks at me and Stacey goes, Your mother knows who shopped them.

And I got a bigger shock and goes, Who like? It wasn't me anyway, Ahahahahaah! and my mother then goes, I know it wasn't you, you definitely know fuck-all. If I can depend on you for one thing it's knowing fuck-all anyway! and they all had a big laugh about that and I had a good mind to shove it up their holes by saying it was me, but I might be a fool but I'm definitely not an idiot!

Who so? I goes and she says, You wouldn't remember him. my mother like, He used be around years ago before he fucked off. He went to Texas, of all places around fifteen years ago. Texas! I didn't see or hear from him 'til a couple of weeks ago when he turned up asking me if there's any work. I wouldn't mind, but he stole money off me when he went an' all! she goes, It's him alright. Has to be.

But how would he know anything? Con goes again. How would he know all the names even or what they was up to? Tony, even! He wasn't around back then, sure!

Tony went all red like when Con said that and my mam said nothing too and everyone waited and my mam said then Tony met him a few weeks ago and he was at the party down in West Cork.

And then I pieced it all together when she says West Cork and I remembered that that's what Detective Long and the other fella were saying about with me all the time when they were questioning me, like! So, obvious it was that fella alright who done it. I still kept my mouth shut though.

Anyway, they were talking about him for a while and trying to work out a plan what to do when my mam told me she had a job for me early in the morning so I should go to bed and they all waited for me to leave before they said anything after that.

●

Next day of course there was no sign of my mother first thing or second thing neither and I had to go to town around half-one on the dot, cos I was meeting my brother Cillian, see, by the Opera House, cos it was my birthday and he knew it and said he was taking me to dinner. I was laughing when he told me that and I goes he can just give me the money for it instead, like, but he goes he'd give me the money anyway as a present too an' all, so I knew straight away I'd have a twenty-spot off him anyway for that. It was just like him an' all to say we'll go to lunch, cos he's the poshest one in the family nowadays like. You'd never think it neither, but he's posher than Tara or Melanie even. I don't know how posh is Jordan SueAnne lately, but she's not posher than Cillian I'd say anyway, wherever she is. He'd be wearing a shirt and tie an' all most days even when it'd be boiling hot out. He's like a multi-millionaire, him, Cillian, with his own house and a mortgage and everything!

Back at this time though, he was still in college, like, but he was still all posh. You'd know the posh ones by their shiny shoes. The proper posh ones wouldn't have a thing wrong with their shoes, they'd be like brand new, without a speck on them every time you'd see them. But they'd give you nothing those ones, mostly. The next ones would have all fancy brands all the time, with the right colour stripes in the right places. But most of them ones would give you nothing too. The next ones would be like wearing brands and some of them would be wearing shoes maybe a year old and they'd be the ones who'd give you the most, usually. Except mostly it's people with terrible shoes would stop and talk to you and end up giving up a present of big money an' all – big money to them, like. I have no idea what's going on there, like, cos sometimes I'd be like going to give them my money and they turn around and give me money instead! I'd take it anyway, like of course, Ahahahahaah! Chalk it down!

But Cillian, if I saw him just by his shoes, true as God I'd say he's the poshest and wouldn't give me nothing. But in fairness he always still gives me a present every time it's my birthday, Cillian. My brother, Cillian, that is.

When we were walking further into town, we passed two fellas I know who were hanging around like, Colin and Scrawny. And Colin seen the two of us walking along and he don't know who's the posh fella with me, like, and he goes, Where're you off to Mickey? sussing us out, like. And I only laughs and goes, We're going to a restaurant for my dinner – that's my older brother Cillian there, lah! He's taking me to dinner for my birthday! and Scrawny looks up and takes a look off Cillian and goes, Him? He's a faggot that fella! You'd want to watch out for that fella Mickey! He'd pull the mickey off ya! Ha ha! and the two of them had a great laugh at that, stupid bolloxes the both of them. Scrawny Seanie. He never says nothing without making you all sad, the prick. And Cillian said hello to him and Scrawnie goes, Don't be saying hello to me at all, ha ha! Say hello to that fella there, lah instead! he goes, shoving Colin at Cillian, He'd do anything for a tenner only! and the two of them are pushing at each other, messing like, when we got past them. And I was sad then they were talking like that with my brother, but I was thinking I might drop back there later on, see what's going down, like, if anything's up.

We went around the corner then and we're in the middle of Patrick's Street and Cillian asks me where I wanted to go, what restaurant like and I goes McDonalds straight away cos I likes the nuggets mostly and the milk shake, if it's ever working. But that day I got a Big Mac and we sat down by the window looking out at all the people walking up and down the street with things to be doing. And I'm thinking about it for a while, but I says nothing 'til Cillian asks me what's wrong and I didn't want to be saying it, but I asks him then if he's gay now or what? And he only laughs at me and that makes it worse, cos he won't answer me, like. But then he goes, No I'm not gay! and then that's alright, I knew that Scrawnie's full of shite the whole time! I tells him then so he won't feel bad about it, like.

We're talking after that, having a great laugh, in fairness and I told him about things, like the time the heroin fell out of the pram and that wan who made me chase after the pram. And about our old times, up on the roofs and stuff, and all that. And I goes, Remember Fuckface, the pony, like! and I was bursting laughing, but Cillian remembered him alright and stopped laughing straight away and I stopped then too, cos I remembered him.

And he was asking me about everyone else, cos he'd talk to them alright, but only sometimes like, so I was filling him in on everyone and all about the raid last week too. And he's like, What's the name of the fella who squelt on them so? and I told him it was Harry the Jinnet and Cillian nearly has a heart attack then and I don't know why, but he fills me in on it and I remembers what happened when he said it, like, about when Tara was a baby and she found a roll of money under my mam's pillow and Cillian got Anthony down the road to buy us a bag of cans out of it, but Harry the Jinnet was my mam's boyfriend at the time (and I'm sure he was Melanie's dad too maybe, like) and he was in trouble with the law and skipped town, left Cork an' all like and my mother blamed him for robbing the money, so we got away with it, like. And I'm laughing, but Cillian's deadly serious and all worried about it 'til I tells him don't worry and tell me other things instead, like. And then he tells me a load of things about what we done years ago and I remembers it when he says it, like, cos I was after forgetting all about that and he told me about the first time we met Con, with the piss, and I remembers that and about the fire in the quarry an' all and everything else. It was some laugh in fairness we had, growing up.

We were in there around five hours I'd say at least, in McDonalds, like, the two of us talking, talking, talking non-stop, bursting our arses laughing the whole time. Definitely the best birthday party I ever had, I'd say. Just me and my brother, Cillian, like. We always had the best parties and never needed no one other. And at the end of it an' all he gives me a twenty-spot, like I knew he would in fairness. And he says I'll meet you again next week and I'll give you another twenty for your birthday, but that'll be it then til next year! And I goes off to find Colin and

Scrawnie then to put them straight about all that, so they'd know, like, that my brother's not gay at all.

●

Anyway, the way it turned out, like, there was no bother with Harry the Jinnet after. He was out mountain climbing and he fell into a big hole, my mother told me, but I'd say she gave him a fright and sent him running off back to Texas.

The Courier

Next thing I know, before I know it like, the judge is giving me three months. Three months imagine, for doing nothing! Besides anything else, there was one other thing made it that long I'd say. That was the thing with Florrie alright. But that wasn't even me and shouldn't of made it three whole months!

He was passing the bridge one day, Florrie see, and he seen me and he knew me cos he used be Davie Gonad's cousin. I don't know what Davie Gonad was up to around then, but he was always a dryballs anyway, even though he had one ball only, like. But his cousin Florrie was alright. He was a courier driver, now like, Florrie, and he stopped that day anyway and we had a laugh for a while about the old days and shit. And then he told me he got a load of iPads that got robbed out of his lorry, like and he needed someone to make a few bob on them. Someone like my mother, who might know how to shift them, Cos it's like a big job – big job! he kept saying it like that: Big job – big job! he'd say. And he'd split the money, like, with my mother for them, long as he wasn't the one to sell them. And I'd get my cut out of them too.

I told him there'd be no bother cos I know exactly how to get the best price for that type of thing, But you'll say it to your mother about it, won't you? he goes, Cos it's a big job – big job, this! Or do you deal with that kind of stuff yourself now? and I goes, Say no more Florrie boy! The less you know, the better! and I give him a big thumbs up.

A few days' later then, anyway, when I knew there'd be no one at home, I told him drop them round to Winchester and it'll be all taken care of. And he did too, but he was looking for my mother again, Cos Mrs. Collins was always alright, he told me, She'd always give us money or cans of drink for bringing stuff to her, like, he goes. And I laughs and knew it was true. And I told him then she had to go out cos she had to look after the warehouse down Little Island. And he goes, Where is it? cos he was going to drop them down there instead. And I had to think fast and goes, Nah it's alright – she told me get you to drop them here cos the warehouse is all full up this week, like.

So he did, an' all.

Thirty-six iPads or iPhones there was there, like. They weren't phones, I knew that. I could see that, but they were shaped the same as them, like. And black and they all came in plain white boxes each. They were like computers or some shit like that anyway at least. And they were all brand new too. I took one out after he went away, just to have a look, but hadn't a clue what to do with it. They were heavy enough an' all. You'd only lift around four or five of them at a time I'd say. I thought I might as well keep one of them anyway for myself, like, for the baby when she got older. She might need it for school. These things were well worth like at least a grand each, I'd say, I was thinking like.

So next day anyway I borrowed a wheelbarrow off a house over the road. Yer man wouldn't mind, like I knew that. He's A-1 that fella in fairness. He told me one day his wife was having it off with his friend, like, and I got a great laugh off it.

234

He told me the whole thing, how he caught them an' all at it in the middle of the day, down Jurys. The same fella, his friend like, was after telling him a load of times he had it off with wans and brought them down there and he knew the room number an' all, like, cos he always used the same one. So when he knew they were having it off, he went down to catch them at it. And they were an' all! In there and at it like rabbits, I'd say, Ahahahahaah!

Anyway, I knew like he wouldn't be bothered now if I borrowed his wheelbarrow for an hour, cos he'd be more bothered about his wife getting shagged by his friend, like I'd say, and I got the iPads out my window onto it, so nobody'd see me taking them out the front door, see? Most of them made it on it too (or in it) and the boxes weren't even dented mostly when I fit them all on. And I had my blanket an' all with me from my room, like, cos I was after thinking about it all night, what to do, like and how to do it. And I put that over the wheelbarrow and walked in to town with it, so nobody'd know about them, to this place I knew who'd take all that kind of shit and pay ya for them too. I was going to give Florrie half an' all at least or give him a couple of hundred anyway, probably I'd say, I was thinking, depending how it'd go. And I'd show my mother an' all how useful I could be if she wanted to give me something like. A job or something. Put me in charge of things, like, sometimes. And she could have the lot for this job, all I care, just to prove it, like. We might get a holiday out of it, I'm thinking while I'm pushing the wheelbarrow along. Blow the lot on a big party for everyone! That would be massive, like, in fairness. Probably rent out a big hall someplace and have strippers and coke the whole night. Man, that would be some party!

I walks in the door of this place anyway, with the wheelbarrow in front of me like and the blanket. And I seen the two fellas behind the counter lamping me straight-out and they're wondering what's under the blanket. And I puts down the wheelbarrow and goes to the older fella, You buy computers don't ya? iPads like?

And he's looking at me and at the blanket too still and he goes, Ya? What have ya got? and I goes, iPads. Thirty-five of them like, if you like. How much would you give me for them each like?

And yer man goes, Wait a while now, I'll come out and take a look, and he tells the other fella stay back, cos he knows straight away there's a bit of business to be done here.

So I lifts the blanket off anyway when he come out and he gets a shock and has a whistle and goes, Where did you get all them? and I was smiling, cos he was impressed, but I wasn't expecting that question, so I ignored it and goes, Have a look. These things are worth a thousand each or more! How much for the lot of them, like? There's thirty-five grand's worth here at least! and he's walking around the wheelbarrow first and taking his time and then he goes, Do ya mind if I shut up the shop? We don't want people walking in off the street when we're in the middle of it, do we? and he's smiling at me and I knew he was serious then and that we'd do a deal. So I told him do, cos I wanted to make sure I'd get the best price and these things were brand new, so if he didn't think about it proper, he might try to give me a second hand price for them. And we didn't want nobody getting wind of it neither.

So he puts down the shutters then and tells yer man at the counter go on away out the back. And he goes out the door behind the counter, like, that fella. And then it's just me and the manager and he's asking me questions again and he picks up one box and asks is it alright if he takes it out and I say it is and he takes it out and he has a look and goes, I thought iPads have a screen on them, don't they? and I goes I don't have a clue what they are, but they're computers anyway, Like mini computers like an iPad, I tells him. Then he asks if I can turn it on for him. And I says there's a button there somewhere, like, You just turn it on and it's on then.

I don't know really if it's on or not, but it's on alright now, I tells him and I'm starting to get a bit nervous alright, cos he's asking me things I don't know the answer of and I don't know why he's asking me it neither.

How many did you say there were? he's asking me again. And I'm telling him again there's thirty-five, And I have one more at home if you want that too! I tells him. Then I'm saying count them all if you don't believe me. So he loads all the boxes out, one by one and he counts them two or three times, I'd say. And I'm asking him how much and he's laughing and making a joke of it and saying Come on, tell me where you got them, Mickey? cos I told him my name was Mickey, like, by now, They're off the back of a lorry, like, I goes to him, cos he seemed alright, like. And I tapped my nose.

Say nothing, I told him, Know what I mean, like sham? Ahahahahaah! and he's laughing along like that, so I thought he knew what to do about it, how to handle it, like. So I asks him again how much for the lot and then, while he's thinking, to hurry him on like (cos I want to get out of here fast now, like) I says, Just give me a grand for the lot of them and you can have them all!

And he's picking them up and putting them down and turning it all around and pointing at the dents in the boxes and all this shit. And finally I goes, Alright, just two hundred for the lot of them. Give it to me fast, like, and I'll get out of your hair, and he's laughing at that one and saying he don't have much hair no more and we're having a laugh about all that. And then he goes it's too much. The price is too high, like. He's not sure if he'd be able to sell them all. And I goes come on, like they're worth that, easy.

And I'll throw in the wheelbarrow an all! I goes to him, But I want my blanket back! That's my own blanket!

And he's shaking his head and saying, I'll see what I have in the till, and it's first thing in the morning like, so I know he won't have it in the till, so I'm thinking what would I do if I had to load them all up again, one by one, and take them away? And would I have to cart them back here again later on or what? So I says, OK so, just give me what you have in the till. I'll take that, whatever! and he carries on walking over by the counter and goes through and locks the door and comes up behind the plastic glass like and opens the till. But he's very slow all the time and I'm all nervous to see what he has in there. And I goes, How much have you got? and he reaches in and pull out a twenty euro note and I goes, Christ! Is that all you have? and he's telling me it's only first thing in the morning and he never keeps money in the till like that. And after a while I'm having a think about it, cos I suppose twenty quid's better than a kick in the teeth at least, but Florrie's getting nothing out of it, 'less he's happy with two bob, cos it's me taking all the risks when you think about it. And I'm just saying alright so, when the door opens by the counter and who's standing there in front of me, 'cept that prick Garda Piggy and around three or four other fellas, all shades like. They caught me easy enough after that.

That was all before the time he took me in for begging (what *he* called begging) and before the thing in the Mardyke even when they found stuff in the pram and he bate the shit out of me. I'd say it was around a year before that. Or before that even. I was still a juvenile then, I think, but I wasn't now like. He had me in for a few other things too, in between. And other shades too, like. They'd all be trying to catch me always, making it impossible all the time to do anything. You couldn't even smash a window by that time, accidental like, and they'd catch ya – catch me anyway. Other's'd get away with everything but I got away with nothing the whole time. And if all that's not doing nothing, what is? That's what I'd like to know!

And the judge called up "Garda Piggott" an' all, to read the charges, like. Cos that's his posh name for the court: Garda Piggott. Ahahahahaah! That's a good one. Piggott. It's like Pick it! And there was a few more cops said some more things about me that weren't true neither, to the judge like, so could you blame him in the end for sending me down after all that? Anyway, Garda Piggy (or Piggott, like), as part of his charges, he reads out that I tried to sell thirty-six laptop batteries and I screams out straight away, I DID NOT, NO! THAT'S A LIE, YOUR HONOUR! cos my mother always told me, if you're in court, always be proper respectful to the judge and he might leave you off with it. They was iPads, not batteries at all! I says, And they were brand new too!

That garda Piggy was thinking he'd have them for himself, I was thinking, but I wasn't leaving him off with that one.

But the judge tells me leave it off a while and we'll hear the rest of it first, ...Thirty-six laptop batteries, Piggy goes, Valued at €2,875.95.

And I was impressed with that one. I knew they were worth at least that much. So I turned my head over to look at my mother, who was looking straight at me in the audience and I nods and smiles at her and I could tell she was impressed too when she heard they were that much, but she only throws her eyes in the air, the way she do, and shakes her head at me.

At the end of it all, then anyway, the judge gives me three months for all that, even though I didn't rob nothing. (No batteries or iPads, like at least. There was one or two small things, but nothing to be doing three months over, like). And I was only selling them first cos I found them on the street, but by the time I told them all about Florrie, he was after skipping the country and going back to London, where he lived for years before that. And yer man in the shop I brought them to an' all wasn't even charged with them either. So it was only me they pinned the whole thing on! Me only, like.

A Miracle Behind Bars

Straight away when I went in there, into prison like, I was put into a cell with three other fellas I didn't like at all. Not one of them was from Cork and none of them I'd hang out with if I had a chance. One fella's farts would gas the whole place for hours. One fart, like, and you'd breathe nothing else for the next two hours at least I'd say, but he'd have around fifty farts in one hour and you'd be dizzy when you come out for a walk around and that's no word of a lie. I tell ya it was 'scusting in there locked up with him. Fat fucker with a beard and if he turned over to scratch himself you'd smell it even if you weren't looking at him. He didn't speak much but he said it all through his arse. Spoke enough through there alright. I tell ya, I met plenty of people who spoke through their hole all the time, but this fella, Mushy was his name, spoke a whole language through his hole the whole time and you could hear it and smell it and even see it like a cloud hanging over him and that's no lie.

I'm lucky I wasn't in the bunk above Mushy, I'd say. That was the one fella in the place who didn't seem too bothered by the smell, above Mushy. Least he never gave out to him about it. Peter used read all the time and not be bothered. He'd be reading a book or the paper if he got it or a magazine or the back of his toothpaste if nothing else. He'd read anything, that fella. I'd never trust no one who reads like that all the time, me. For one thing, he always thinks he'd be better than you – than everyone else, or something, with his books. You'd ask him, Peter like,

241

something like, you'd say something to him, and he'd only shrug and not even turn 'round to look at ya. I'd say he don't even know what I look like and he locked up with me in the same cell long enough! Well, it was only a few days in the end, or a week or two like, but that's long enough anyway when you think about it!

The other one then was the loudest and the crankiest too. A small fella called Cracker who'd scream and roar the whole place down every time Mushy would let out a ripper. Mushy'd go "Brrrp" through his arse, he would like, and Cracker would scream, Jesus Christ would ya leave it off! and sometimes then I'd go, That's what he done – leave off, he left off like, Mushy, Ahahahahaah! to make a laugh at it like, cos it'd be 'scusting alright, but it'd be funny too like even when you'd be choking on it sometimes. But Cracker never laughed one bit. You couldn't have a laugh with that fella, with Cracker like. I'd say he'd of slit Mushy's throat if Mushy wasn't built like a brick-shitter.

One time we were eating our dinner (cos we had to eat in there an' all, in our cell, like, with all that smell) and Mushy farted and Cracker thrun his own food on the floor and starts screaming and roaring at Mushy, calling him all the names, Ya fat cunt ya! How are you farting so much when you're eating the same shit as us day-in, day-out? Are you sure you're not sucking on a sewer pipe on the quiet? he was hopping up and roaring at him like that non-stop for ages cos of that one fart and then he sat down on his bed and he kept it up, calling him names and calling him names. And then he lied down and he's still going on and on about Mushy and his farting.

Next thing Mushy finished his dinner, stood up and sat on him. On Cracker like. And Cracker was screaming under him and waving his one arm all over, cos Mushy was sitting on the other one and on his legs too mostly. So Mushy then lies down on top of him and traps Cracker's two hands. Both of them, even. And we could hardly hear Cracker no more even underneath him, like. And I was bursting my arse at that an' all, cos Cracker's screaming was nearly worse than Mushy's farting. And I'm laughing and saying, Good one Mushy! quiet like, I said it, so Cracker wouldn't hear it cos he'd attack me an' all if he heard me like, when he'd get up. And I was looking over at Peter when I said it but he only takes one look and smiles and goes back to his book like he's the lord of the manor. I didn't like that fella at all, Peter. I found out later he was in there for murder. Out of all of us, in there at the time, he was the only one who murdered, but he'd still be looking down from his bunk the whole time like he's better than us.

And by the time I'm finished my dinner like, my burger, Cracker's after stopping screaming mostly and Mushy's just lying there on top of him still. And I stood up and looks at him and goes, Come on Mushy, you'd better leave him off now, but Mushy didn't budge. And Cracker's underneath and he was saying things like he can't breathe all the time before that, but now he sounds for real alright and it's only every few seconds you'd hear a bit of a sound from him, like he's trying to shout, but can't talk or breathe, but it's stopped now an' all mostly and I'm trying to tell Mushy to leave him off, without joking about it like, cos now it's like he's already after killing him an' all, for all I know. And I'm nearly crying from it saying, Come on please Mushy, like! an' all, but Mushy don't even say nothing the whole time. Just lies there.

Then Peter goes – to Mushy like, without even looking over: Put it this way, he goes, If you love this place so much you'd like to stay here another ten years, don't bother getting up.

And Mushy has a think while he's lying there a bit more and then he gets off him. And when he's getting up, his arse is stuck into the bunk, near enough to Cracker's head, who isn't moving. And Mushy let out the biggest ripper known to man, right in his face while he's getting up. I'd say he was building it up the whole time while he was lying there, for Cracker like.

At the same time, then or just before, like, Cracker makes the biggest gasp for air, like he was already drowning and after jumping out of the water after ages down below. And he breathed-in only the massive blast of air that was all of Mushy's fart.

Took him half an hour to get over it at least, Cracker like. Or an hour, more like. He didn't even bother going out to the hall for fresh air like he usually done and give out to everyone while he's out there. He was a quiet boy for the rest of the day that day, I tell ya that much. And it was at least a week, I'd say, before he told Mushy stop farting no more again too after it, like. He was back screaming at him again after that. But all that stuff was a few days in, after I got there like.

The first day I got there, I was out in the hall only a few minutes to have a look around, and I was coming in again, back to my cell like, when this fella come up to me, who I knew from Cork (I kind of half-knew him sometimes, but not really – Knew him to see like, put it that way) and he goes, Keefa wants to talk to you.

And I goes, Who's Keefa? but he was gone again straight away and I carries on back to my cell cos I was nearly there anyway and it was time to go back so I got no option.

Next day then, when we was coming back up with our breakfast, another fella who I never knew was walking in front of me and he turns around and goes, Keefa's out for your ass!

and he was gone again before I could ask him who's this Keefa fella I keep hearing about. And none of the lads in my cell knew who Keefa was neither. Never heard of him when I asked them. Least that's what they all told me anyway. Well Cracker said he never. Mushy let out a kind of a sad bit of wind for his answer and Peter kind of just turned in to the wall. I tell ya, the only bit of gas in that place was all Mushy's.

Next thing then, after breakfast like we could go out to the hall for a game of cards or whatever for an hour like, so I goes out for a walk around, see what's happening, like, and I spots Moxie, who used do a bit of business with my mother and who me and Cillian used do jobs for and who got Cillian bate up that time by Barry, who was dead now. Killed in a car crash, like, out by the Viaduct on Bandon Road, I heard. He tried running a cement truck off the road, like a dope and the truck smashed his car up instead, I heard. Anyway, he's over playing cards over by the wall, Moxie, and looking at me and nodding at me to come over, like. And I'm frozen on the spot, thinking if he's going to kill me or if we're alright, cos I can't remember, like. And I looks over the other way and seen a load of travellers over that side and I know a few of them an' all and they're definitely not happy to see me. One of them looks like he's going to rip my head off too, whatever I done to him. Then I looks back at Moxie and he seems calm enough and not even mad at me. And he's still calling me over, like too. So I said I might as well go over that way anyway. He might know who this Keefa fella is, if nothing else.

How Moxie, boy! I goes to him, like that, when I goes over, I never knew you was in here! and he's smiling away to me when I sit down at the table across from him.

245

You didn't? he goes, That's a surprise to me now, since it's cos of your mother that I'm in here, the cunt! and straight away I gets a shock and I know it was a mistake like to sit down like that. And I'm trapped now and can't get away fast. The game is stopped now an' all and they're all looking at me, all the fellas playing cards with Moxie, like, and around him looking on. And I'm looking around and I see most of them are from Cork too, but I don't know what to say and after a while I goes, What are ye playing anyway? Don is it? and the fella next to Moxie, over the way, goes Yeah. I says then I never played it myself, never had the time, like. And Moxie goes, You need a brain to play don, and they all breaks their holes laughing like it was funny or something and he's going to say something else, Moxie like, but I goes, You don't know this fella Keefa I'm supposed to see, do ya?

And there's all quiet for a while and then some of the other fellas starts laughing at me cos I don't know Keefa. And then Moxie bursts out laughing too and I laugh an' all, like. And he goes then to the fella over near me, who was the first fella who told me about Keefa (now I see him), he goes, I told you he was special, but you have to laugh.

And the other fella who gave me the message is only nodding and smiling at me and they're all having a great laugh, all them others.

So I smiles back at him and at Moxie too like. And I asks him then how long are you in for, Mox? But he don't answer. Instead he says, What do you think I should do with you, Mickey, since it's your mother's fault I'm in here? and he's playing his card when it's his turn and looking at me like sometimes, waiting for the answer. So I has a think and goes, Did

246

she tell the shades on you so? and I know she didn't do that, but I don't know what she did do. He says nothing, only plays a card. And I goes, No she did not! Did she write a letter to the judge and tell him what you done? No she did not!

And it's his turn now, but he's waiting for me to shut up so I keeps talking like, in case. And I goes, Did she get you baten up and leave you for the cops to find or something? No she – and next thing, Moxie jumps up and cards go flying and he grabs me across the table and thumps me in the face and there's all roaring going on and I'm on the ground covered in cards and my cheek is probably bleeding for all I know. But he only left me off then. And when the screws was running over he walks away.

It's nothing to do with me neither! I shouts at him by the time the pigs are standing over me and everyone else is gone or walking away, …What she done. Whatever like!

Are ya right there Mickey? says one of the screws next to me then who I never seen before that. The older fella. Mr. O'Ryan was his name, Were ya caught out binooing were ya? HuhHuh! he thought that was fierce funny, They don't like binooing in Don, they don't! HuhHuh!

And he walks away laughing at his joke, Or maybe it's that you crossed the Big Don? he carries-on talking to himself, to me like, while he's walking away, Mr. O'Ryan.

That would upset a Corkman an' all, crossing the Big Don. Here! We're a more-civilised bunch up here in Limerick compared to our Southern brethren. There's no crossing or binooing going on up here I tell ya that much! HuhHuh!

Later on then I'm on the phone to Stacey cos my mam had to go out. And Stacey goes Con is fierce sad I was sent down and he had to go to the pub an' all cos of it. And I believe it too. I know Con from all his stories about this place and other places. He never wanted to be going back to here himself and he always said how he'd be praying that none of us never goes to prison cos it's a hell to be living through. I knowed it the way Stacey said it that Con would be gone for a week at least. He was never into any drugs. Hash even no way for Con. The only thing he'd have would be a drink. He might drink forty pints easy, him. Or fifty. Murphys mostly. And he'd do a job then that night no bother. But when he'd be sad or need a break like, he'd be on the ran-tan for who-knows-how-long, til my mother'd probably catch up with him, like, get him do something.

I was talking with Stacey anyway and she put on Jordan SueAnne then too and I was telling her how I'd bring back a lovely dolly for her from my holidays when I get home (cos I couldn't tell the child I was in a prison like). And my sister Jordan SueAnne was all happy-out when I said it and she goes, Do they have dollies in prison? and I'm in a shock and goes, Who told you I was in prison? I'm not in prison at all!

Tanya! she goes, cos she called her own mother, my mother like, Tanya all the time instead of mam or mamma like we done.

And then I heard our mother come in and she got on the phone and I told her about Moxie and about the travellers who was in here too like and they all look like they want to kill me cos of her. And she only tells me they're all full of shit and this is my last chance to toughen-up now cos they <u>will</u> kill me if I don't. And she goes she done nothing to put Moxie where he was too. He was only dreaming all that and probably looking for a fight for the hell of it. She said I should get a knife and stab him straight away through the heart or into his eyeball before he gets me first. And the travellers would respect me an' all for that too and they'd all back off then.

Simple as that! she goes, You should do what your mother tells you for once in your life!

She thinks of all the angles, in fairness, my mother.

•

I was feeling so bad that night especially, I tell ya, I didn't know what. I don't know was that the first night or the second night or a whole load of nights now when I'm thinking of it, but I got no sleep hardly most nights like that. Just listening to all the noises inside, in the prison like. Or inside inside, from Mushy or Cracker. Or inside my own head even too, like.

I'd say I always had noises in my head, like same as anyone, but inside the inside here now I had more noises inside, like in my head, than ever anywhere else, like. All night long there'd be loud bangs or fellas screaming all of a sudden or screws walking or running up and down or someone shouting something out to someone else or Mushy farting in his sleep or snoring and Cracker screaming out like he's right next to your ear – you name it. All the noises and it was hard to know what was real or only like a dream or a nightmare or something.

In the morning then, next morning, I was just kind of about to doze – or I'd say I got asleep for around 5 minutes at the most and next thing you hear all the doors being opened with the keys and the screws walking down the corridors to open them for anyone who wants a breakfast. Same fella then opens my door as yesterday in the hall, Mr. O'Ryan like. He pushes the door open a bit and sees my face and goes, Rise and shine Mickey, it's a beautiful morning! The sun is shining and the birds are twittering in the big open sky. It's all happening out there in the real world!

And he's moving on to the next cell even when he's saying all that back at me, laughing away to himself the whole time.

After a while then, the others all went down to get their breakfast, but I'm only sitting on the side of the bed, trying to wake up proper, when a fella walks in and I looks up and it's Davie O'Brien, my old friend! Only he looks wrecked. More than me even. He's like a skeleton, number one. And his eyes are all red like he was crying for months, secondly like, second thing. And the third thing is his head is shaved and if he was a colour I'd say it'd be green. He don't look good. At all, I mean. And he goes, Hello Mickey it's me, Davie.

But he's not even looking at me, hardly. I goes, Davie! Man It's good to see ya! I never knew you were in here! How ya getting' on? but I can see, not good is how. Davie was a few years older than me. Like, more around Cillian's age really, I think. But he was quiet too. Like me like. Not like Cillian. So we'd be hanging around together. And a few others too, but Cillian'd be doing his own things too, mostly like, when we was younger.

He sits down next to me anyway on the bed, Cracker's bed like, cos it's only two of us in the cell. And it looks like he's going to cry, but he doesn't, but he's trying to talk and he can't say nothing. So I says, It's alright Davie, I'm here too. I'll look after things and we can look out for each other, man, alright? We might be able move into the same cell, even, if you want to! I could ask the guard, like, and we'll have a laugh at least like before, like. If you don't do my head in, in the meantime, like, Ahahahahaah!! cos I'm making a laugh of it, cheer him up, like, but he'd do my head in alright if he was like that the whole time.

And he's looking down the ground all the time now and kind of nodding and shaking and shivering like. And I goes are you cold or wha? And I put out my hand, like that, to feel if he's cold and he jumps back and stands up and lashes me with something sharp like a screwdriver straight away and cuts me too a bit on my hand an' all with it. And I'm looking at that and I'm looking at him too and he has the screwdriver out in front of him and I don't know what's happening, like. I starts screaming at him then, but he's like, It's not me at all Mickey! I'm sorry, like! Keefa made me do it. I have to do it, and I goes do what? Why'd he make you do it? I don't even know Keefa, like, I tells him. And Davie goes, Moxie, like. It's Moxie's Keefa! That's what he's called in here, like. Keefa! He said your mother's no good and I told him you're not like that at all, but it's no odds. He said he has to send her a message.

And I asks him what message do he have to send her? What do ya have to do, like? I goes to Davie, Just cut me like this or what? And I showed him the bit of blood off my hand. And he shakes his head, but won't even look at me.

Naw boy, he says, He said I need to make a hole in your stomach at least. Hand or a leg won't do, he says, or he'll murder the two of us. Stomach or chest at least, he said. I'm sorry Mickey, like!

So I'm standing there thinking about it and he's wondering what to do next too, like. And I lifts up my top to leave him do it an' all, take his best shot, like. But he's too sad for it and I stalled a while, like that, and then I bursts out laughing and I run out the door and pulled it behind me an' all, so he couldn't catch me fast. And I'm walking fast down the corridor towards the restaurant place where they're giving away the breakfasts and I seen Moxie and his gang over the way looking at me. So I put up my hand to show him the cut on the side of my hand, at the back, like, so he'd know I got cut alright. But the way I showed him, I had my two baby fingers closed a bit and it looked like I was sticking my two big fingers up at him and his eyes got wide-out and he got mad-out and he points and shouts over at me that I'm a fucking dead man. And I goes, No Moxie, Keefa like! It's not like that at all, like! I was showing ya my cut, not sticking my fingers up at ya at all, like!

But it's no good cos he starts chasing me with his gang and I ran proper now down to the restaurant and the screws there all see me and one of them starts shouting at me then and I gets in line for the breakfast and Moxie/ Keefa's a bit behind only but they leaves it off after a while cos I think they already got theirs, like, so they stall-on back there a bit and I'm looking back the whole time when I'm queueing up with my tray.

Then the fella in front of me goes, Alright or wha? he goes, Want me to carry that for ya or something? cos I knocked him with the tray too, by accident like, cos I got all nerves. And I goes, Alright so, thanks like! and I hands it to him, like that. And he takes it off me an' all and walks along and I put a bun on it and a drink of milk and he's still holding it for me and I'm still looking back for Moxie and it looks like they're after pissing off too.

Then when we're walking back to our cells, me and that fella who's holding my stuff, he goes, Y'know I wasn't asking ya f'rit!

He says that when he's handing it back to me. I wasn't supposed to give it to him when he said it, like. He was only being funny. But he's alright about it too, like. Kind of a funny accent, like a bit.

252

Oh right, thanks! I goes, Sorry like! I got stabbed see, and I showed him my wound, but he wasn't bothered.

You can tell some people though. I knew he was alright, like. Better than Moxie at least I'd say, but he was sound-out in fairness, keeping hold of my stuff when I give it to him. He looked like I knew him or something too, when I seen him first. Like Cillian even, my brother like I was thinking. He reminded me of him straight away I think, so that's why I trusted him with it.

He was older than me too, yer man. About a year or two older than Cillian even. I'd say, anyway. Bigger too. He had muscles on him, even, so I stuck by him all the way back, most of the way 'til he went one way, down to his cell and I legged it back the other way then to the others in my cell, like.

After a while then, after breakfast like we were allowed out to the hall or whatever, but I stayed around the cell and Peter stayed too, reading his book, but I didn't bother talking with him mostly cos I wouldn't be bothered. And I was up walking around in the cell all the time, but I didn't want to go out cos of Moxie, like, so I was walking up and down and I went out for a look around outside and back in a few times then cos I seen fellas from Moxie's gang down further, down by the hall, so I knew they were waiting for me like, so it drove me mad like, but I had to stay there. Then after our dinner we had a chance to get out again so I hopped out that time straight away or I'd go off my head, and there was no sign of Moxie or that lot, cos their cells weren't unlocked yet, see. But down in the hall instead I seen that same fella from breakfast over in one part, so I goes over by him to have a chat like, see what's happening.

Alright boy! I goes to him when I went over and he nods at me, wondering what I wanted to say. He seemed friendly enough though still. And he still reminded me of Cillian too, an' all. You'd look at him one minute and he wouldn't look like him at all, but then he'd turn to the side or something and he'd look like him straight away when he'd do that. I told him that an' all then.

You look like my brother Cillian! I goes, We're from Cork, him and me. Both of us, like.

I could tell, he goes, and starts laughing, You can always tell when there's a Corkman in the room! he goes, then says, Like! – Ho ho ho! like he's Santy or something. He says room longer than the normal way you'd say it, too. He says it like you'd say mushroom. Longer even than that, I'd say, with more rumbles and more os on it too, like. Rrrooomm! Funny like, but I wasn't laughing at all.

Are y'mocking me or wha? I goes to him cos I don't know if he is, but he seems alright, like.

No mun, like, he goes, Where are you from so? I asks him straight out and I'm still wondering if I need to get stuck on him or what. He don't sound Irish neither and he sounds different.

I'm from Swansea, like, he says. He still might be mocking me, but I'm not sure, but it don't matter anyway cos he's laughing with it, like.

Wales, mun! he says. And I says, No shit? My old man's from Wales too! and he smiles mad at me and says No shit? he goes, Well that's a coincidence because my oul man's from Cork!

And we both starts laughing straight away, cos I'm from Cork and my dad is from Wales and he's from Wales and his dad is from Cork!

And we're talking mad like that for ages and he don't know what part of Cork his dad's from and I don't know what part of Wales my dad's from. My dad had to leave, see, when I was only a baby, I was telling him that. I don't know much about him, like. Or anything really. But he was a sailor, I know that much. My mam said it, and he had to leave too when Cillian was only a baby, but he come back for me and had to leave again then.

He's a captain now, I told him, Sailing all over the world, my mam said. Got a promotion like, so had to go.

He didn't even think about it, this fella, but straight away he goes, Don't be acting twip, mun, he goes, She's takin' the piss a'ya!

Then he starts laughing at me again. It was funny though like the way he said it, Yeah probably, I goes and starts laughing too, cos it's like he knew my mother an' all and like that's what she'd do: Take the piss out of ya and there'd be nothing you could do about it neither.

Dylan Carver was his name, this fella. And he was in here for the same as me – nothing! He said it was a load of things but nothing really. The biggest thing in the end, he goes, was pissing in the street, imagine.

You can't even take a piss in this country! he tells me. There's no public toilets nowhere! You can have a shit on the street alright, but don't let those bastards catch you having a piss! Oh no!

I was laughing at the way he'd be talking. Oh no! he said it funny like: Oh-uh know-uh! and I goes, Ain't that the truth!

He came to Ireland a few year ago, he was telling me, with a gang of lads for a stag party, like, and he lost his ticket for the ferry back. He goes he thought one of the lads was having a laugh on him and took it off him. But he couldn't find it anyway when it was time to go back to Wales, like, so they all went home without him and left him there on his tod.

And what'd ya do, so? I goes to him and he told me a big long story about all the things he done. His friends wanted to go to Dublin for the stag, but after they went back to Wales, he went to Cork cos that's where his dad's from. Walked to Cork, imagine, from Dublin. Must've taken him weeks I'd say. Or months probably. He said he stopped in Fermoy for a bit when he got there, cos that's in Cork too, like, and he lived there for a bit. A few weeks, like, 'til a gang chased him out one night for no reason and he carried on to the city, then like.

And when he got there, he didn't know no one there either and I was telling him if he knew the different places to go to, to kip like, and he didn't know most of them, so I told him the good ones and said he had to keep it a secret or they'd all be there. And I was telling him things and he was telling me stuff and before we knew, it was time to go back to the cells. So we walks back, still talking all the way, and only then I seen Moxie and his gang were around and looking over at me the whole time, but they left me alone as long as Dylan was around, cos he's bigger like and tougher probably.

And when I was nearly back I asked the screw if I could ring my brother Cillian, cos I was after handing in his mobile number too like. And he said I could on my next break. So that's what I done then after my tea.

Are ya alright, Mickey? Cillian goes when he answered, How are ya getting on in the prison? and I told him all about

Moxie and he's called Keefa now and how Davie O'Brien tried to kill me, dirty bastard. And I got a chase off Moxie then too, But I met this fella who's alright and Moxie is staying away so far cos I'm sticking near him, I goes to him.

And he was asking me about Dylan and I told him he's sound-out and does things like we'd be doing things even though he's from Wales and not Cork at all, like. And he walked all the way from Dublin to Cork too, imagine, cos he's from Cork – his dad is like – and the fellas in his gang went back to Wales without him cos that's where he's from and he's like you too (him like, I was saying – Cillian too). Looks like him even, I said. And Cillian told me be careful who I meet in that place and I told him I am a' course.

Next morning when Mr. O'Ryan come in to wake me up, I made sure I left straight away with the others, but I seen Davie O'Brien when I going downstairs fast, cos I passed his open door. And he's sitting on his bed, looking out at me an' I passing and he goes, It's not like that at all Mickey! but I kept moving and goes, Up your hole Davie! I goes, Ahahahahaah!

And he's there calling me and going, I'm sorry Mickey! and the whole place starts mocking him then an' all, Oooh! I'm sorry Mickey! someone shouts out, all like a woman. And they're all laughing and whistling and mocking him still and it's fierce funny.

Suck my mickey! I shouts after him and that gets everyone cheering and whistling too an' all.

There was no sign of Moxie that time neither and Dylan Carver was getting to the restaurant around the same time as me, over on the other queue like, so I salutes him, over, and he nods back. And then, back a bit, I hears a fella saying, Look at them two faggots, lah, and I looks back and it's a fella in Moxie's gang talking about me and Dylan. And Moxie's there too, but he's only looking at me, saying nothing.

Anyway, after I got back to my cell with my dinner that time too I didn't bother staying back out again til later on, afterwards like cos it was too much bother to be putting up with all them.

When I met him next time in the hall then, Dylan like, he was with another fella and when I comes along the other fella laughs and goes, Here comes your brother! and Dylan looks up and goes, No, mun, that's me butt! and I gets a shock an goes, I'm not no! Ya bender! I'm not a butt, no! standing up for myself, like. And the two of them are still only laughing at me, like, when I looks over and Moxie's passing by, so I stayed around, but it looks now like he's one of them alright, Dylan like. So I need to get away again, but I can't right now.

I got a girlfriend, ya know! I says to the two of them, Dylan and his friend like and the two of them are still laughing-mad only. His friend's foreign an' all too, wherever he's from himself.

Next, another fella comes along then before I could get away and he goes to Dylan, What about ye? so I know he's from Ireland at least straight away, even if it's a long way from Cork he's from, but least it's not too bad there now with four of us, like. And he looks at me an' all and back at Dylan and goes, Is that yer brother right there?

He was talking about me too, like. He thought we were brothers together in prison too. Everyone was saying it now. Like, I didn't think Dylan looked like me, like, but he looked like Cillian alright I thought.

No mun, Dylan goes to him, This twp's using me to hide on that mung over there and his cronies, like! and he nods over at Moxie and carries on saying An' he's calling me names too all the way, even so!

And I goes, Naw boy! It's not like that at all! but the fella, who's from Northern Ireland goes, Nevermind that Keefa, he goes to me, He's nothing more than a little trout, him. Doesn't know he's swimming in deeper waters now with the big fish.

His name was Gerry Gerrity, the fella who said that and he was from Northern Ireland, but wasn't with the Ra or nothing, he told me later-on. He was alright too an' all in fairness, like.

Anyway, to make a long story shorter, I was talking with Dylan over the next few days and we were saying we might be able to get me moved into their cell, cos it was only himself and Gerry Gerrity in their place so far and neither one was a bender, they told me an' all. And Moxie and the other Cork fellas left me alone while they were around at least.

Meantime like, I was on with Cillian and with our mother too and with Stacey too on different days. And I was getting bits of news off them (only in bits) when I was asking about our father, me and Cillian's like. Well anyway, one thing Cillian knew as much as me and wasn't bothered anyway either an' all, cos he knew he was a piece of shit, like, our father like. I wasn't bothered either, me, but I was telling him more about Dylan and how everyone's calling the two of us brothers and we're moving into the same cell. And his dad's from Cork and my dad's from Wales, so they can't be the same. And I was asking my mother about him, the father like, and what's his name even another time and she said he's a lowlife scum, not worth shit. And she wouldn't tell me nothing else and I'm a bad son who doesn't even love his own mother for asking about someone who fucked off from her a load of times. And my brother ran away too. And does that mean so I'm going to run away too an' all or what? And I goes, Course not, like!

And I had to tell her then over-right all the fellas around who was listening to me, like, that I love her and she kept annoying me more to say what I used say to her when I was a baby, but I kept saying I can't say that cos everyone's listening, like. But she was crying and saying I was all mean to her and she had no one only me. And I said she have Jordan SueAnne and Melanie sometimes and the other two sometimes too. And Stacey like an' all. And she had Tony too, her boyfriend. And Con even!

But she was fierce sad missing me like. Only I was the one looking-out for her always, she said. And I knew it was true alright. So I was looking at all the other lads on their phonecalls and fellas behind me too, waiting. And they all shut up and the screw was listening to me too. And I tried to say it quiet, like. *Titty milk me,* I said, quiet like, like that, like. And she said, What? I can't hear it! and I said it a small bit louder and she said, Say mamma! and I said mamma. And she said, No! Say it all and say it out fucking loud or you don't love me at all! and I got mad then and goes, TITTY MILK ME MAMMA! and then I slammed down the phone when they're all cheering out loud and laughin'-mad. And I shouted, CUNT! and fucks off back to my cell, mad-out.

But I got Stacey then another time to tell me finally, after ages. I told her Dylan's dad's name was Frank Dillon and Dylan was named after him, but his mother's name was Carver so he was named after her too. And when I said Frank Dillon I heard

260

Stacey got a shock and I goes, Is that the same fella so!? cos I knew by now he was an' all, cos I knew it, just knew Dylan was, like. I knew it the way we'd be talking with each other and how he was looking out for me the whole time an' all, like Cillian, like, and not a bender at all.

And he was too, Stacey told me. The father like. Frank Dillon from the Well Road area (not Wales). And my mam and him were going out for years and then his mam and dad sent him away, to get away from her like. But he was the love of her life, Stacey goes, and he come back a few years later and then she had Cillian and he went away again, cos he used be having it off with loads of other women and my mother threw him out. And later-on then he come back cos they were in love again then, like.

I didn't want to be hearing all about that at all, but Stacey was going on and on about it, like. But Dylan was like Cillian now to me, far's I'm concerned. From then on.

And I knew it too – we all knew it anyway. He was my brother alright, imagine! And I met him there in the prison.

It's like Gerry said later on, Gerry Gerrity, like: The Lord works in mysterious ways.

And that's no word of a lie, right there! All of it dead-on fact!

The Three Little Pigs

One thing on top of another on another on another, in fairness, there'd always be something up and something up and something up. And after a while, it all, all falls down like. Probably. Like it's always the same. Same ole' shit.

I didn't bother saying it, like up to now, cos it wasn't part of what I was telling, but now it's here alright now in fairness, this part I suppose. But anyway, sometimes alright there'd be like all noises all over, or something. Straight in front of me. Blocking me and stopping me. And *in* me too, like an' all. And it don't go away.

It happened before a few times, before like and Cillian mainly'd take care of it, look after things like 'til I got better. A few weeks probably. He'd get a doctor like, and get our mother to get me taken-in too, cos I know I'd be gone a bit – y'know... Crazy like is one way of putting it. Fuckin' tapped is another way, Ahahahahaah! Looking back on it, thinking of it that time, and the crazy things like I'd be saying sometimes, like that. And mostly it'd be someone out to get me or I'd be worrying about shit with no reason, like I would be, realistically.

But mostly I wouldn't give a shit in normality times like, but then sometimes I would too, like. Like that. And my nails'd be gone. All gone like cos I'd be biting them mad and wouldn't be able to scratch my head then even and I'd have to tear my hair out instead to get the same. Same as others, like. Ahahahahaah!

But anyway, sometimes it'd be getting worse than others and, sure I wouldn't know anyway, when you think of it, if it was happening, like, but I'd know later-on alright. And this time, it was. Like.

He was my brother, see? And he tried do his best with it, I know that much. Must of, when you think about it. But he wasn't Cillian neither cos he didn't, like, grow up with it. With me like. So he wouldn't know how it goes. How I goes, like, sometimes, without knowing it.

But after I moved into the same cell we had a grand few days with no problems or nothing and we were all the best of buds – or butts, he'd say, my brother like. Dylan would say best of butts. And Gerry Gerrity was there too. The three of us was happy-out like a pig in shit. That's what Mr. O'Ryan said when he seen us one day: Here come the three little piggies! he said, Ye're like pigs in shit! an' he laughing away to himself when he says it.

Then Dylan woke me up at night time that night, one night first, cos he said I was shouting. I wasn't asleep at all, like, cos I couldn't. But I wasn't awake either. But he woke me anyway, alright like.

Y'alright there mun? he goes. And I thought he was a monster standing at my bed or the Devil, like maybe. And I screamed out and lashed him, like. I didn't know what was going on, see? Anyway, we got over it and moved on, but I got no more sleep and next day I know I was hearing him and Gerry less and hearing my head-noises a bit more, like. People. All the noises and all the noises.

And all the *real* noises and people were getting away, further away. And all the shit I *thought* then was the real noises (like the voices that'd be whispering usually like), all got louder all the time and after a while they'd be screaming at me everywhere, the voices like, and I wouldn't be able to hear nothing else, even.

They wouldn't be saying nothing like. Not real words. Just mocking me or screaming at me or shouting shit for no reason and not shut up at all.

Then there was a bit when Dylan was running away from me for days, like. Wouldn't even talk to me or nothing cos I'd be off my head, he'd be saying. And he wouldn't be wrong about it neither, I know. He'd be telling me shut up and shouting at me too, like to shut it. And Gerry'd be saying, Ah leave the wee lad alone there, and he'd turn around to me then, who'd be probably moaning away or something and he'd go Houl yer whisht there, young Mickey! and he'd be saying prayers with me and getting me to say them too with him, like. There was the Our Father and the Hail Mary. I knew them ones alright like, mostly, but he knew a load more and he said them too on me, like, but Dylan wouldn't be bothered with it.

He finally got the screws to believe me and call someone about it too when Mr. O'Ryan come in and saw him shouting, Dylan shouting at me like. And me and Gerry saying our prayers. Before that, they said it to a few of them alright, Dylan and Gerry did, but they all thought we were all messin' only.

Little Piggy tales to get out of here! Mr. O'Ryan said the day before, Here! he goes, Not by the hair of my chinny-chin-chin you won't!

264

Now though, he believed us alright and got me put into the hospital. And when I was leaving, Gerry said nice things and give me his rosary beads. Then Dylan goes, – I thought he was going to shout at me again, first like, but he turns around and looks at me and stares at me, like for a while and then goes: Ah, give us a cwtch!

And he gave me a big hug, my brother Dylan. I drove him mad for a week I'd say before that, around, but I was still his brother like, an all. I never seen him again no more, since. I keep waiting to see him in Cork, like, but I'd be looking in the spots I told him about sometimes, but he never.

Foxy Bill At The Scapa Flow

The doctor's'd be asking you all the questions and writing it all down in case they'd catch you out about something then after, like. And one would be there one day and another one might turn up the next day then and ask you the same old shit and you'd give them the same old answers 'til around 5 o'clock and there'd be no doctor, hardly, cos they'd all be gone home and for the weekend and leave ya with all them other nuts in the mad house, like, til we got better on our own. Cos there'd be fuck all they'd do about it an' all, when you think about it.

In fairness, like, they wouldn't all be all like that at all. Like me, I mean. Some'd be screaming all the time alright and you'd be shitty of them ones, but others'd be like alright and not even a bit mad, like y'know? I was given my tabs one day by Mary, inside there like. In Cork, this was, back in Cork. My home by the Lee, as they say! Ahahahahaah! It was up the top of Blarney Street still at the time, but I'd be in the Mercy now since, if I needed it, like, sometimes. She was the nurse, like – Mary. She was alright too. She was working in the mad-house all her life, she was telling me and she seen plenty of nuts in her day. I got a good laugh out of that one and made them all laugh when I said she'd seen all the nuts and she'd be talking to the nuts an' all. Ahahahahaah!

I goes, when I put out my hand for the medicine, like, I goes, Are you working here long, yourself Mary? (I was nearly better by then, like. I was in there around three week. Nearly a month, even, close enough.) And she goes, All my life, Mickey boy, for my sins, I'm working here all my life!

I mean, you'd want to be something special for that, wouldn't you say? I would anyway.

I bet you seen some nuts an' all? I goes to her, looking around at all the other lads in the room, like, Ahahahahaah! to get a laugh, like. They were all quiet, mostly before that, afraid to say a word. But they were all laughing then like when I said that.

And she goes, I've seen 'em all me, Mickey, every kind of nut there is! and I goes, Sure if you're talking to nuts you must be nuts too an' all, cos who'd be talking to nuts, isn't that right? Ahahahahaah!

It's funny though when you think of it. Must be true. And she was laughing with it and agreed with me. And Cian in the next bed over, starts listing different nuts: You got your walnuts and your chestnuts… and another fella called Peter (who wasn't the same as the Peter who was in the cell with me, who'd be reading all the time, like) says, Chocolate nuts!

And Thomas was standing next to Mary, cos he'd be follying her around mostly. He drops his pyjamas then and he had a massive horn on him and he goes, Have ya seen my nuts, Mary!? and we all laughs at that one cos yer man Thomas was doing that all the time. Fierce posh, this fella was now, Thomas. You'd think he'd be working in the bank, but he's there in the madhouse with me and all the others too, like, and he flashing at everyone fifty times a day, around at least!

Mary didn't even look at him. Not at his knob like, anyway. She just goes, Yes Thomas I've seen your nuts. Now put them away or I'll have to call someone else to look at them! and it was like Thomas was all shocked, like the way he'd be, like. And he pulled up his pyjama pants fast and legged it straight into the jacks. We were all bursting laughing again at that one like, cos he was all posh too on top of it, poor bastard!

It'd be a good laugh in fairness, sometimes in there like, but mostly the place would drive you nuts in there an' all, like, you ask me. Ahahahahaah!

It took a while, anyway, for things to calm down, like that time, cos we were all bursting our arses. Even Paddy, who was ancient and barely knew what was happening was kind of hopping up and down in his bed like he was laughing too an' all, it was so funny like. Peter was still listing nuts too and making us all laugh with the names of the different ones when he'd think of um: Brazil nuts! but he was running out now and it was getting boring, so I took my tabs and next thing, Cian across the way seen me do it.

TIME AND TABS! he tells me, pointing like at me, Cian was, with his other hand pointing up to the sky with his middle finger, to heaven like, probably. And I goes, What? and he goes again, Time and tabs! That's what works – and if it doesn't, it's not enough time or it's not enough tabs!

And he had a big massive mad smile on his face an' he saying it like Jesus, pointing at me with massive mad eyes on him too. His eyes would make you shitty. And he did scare me too, like. Or something.

Or made me think about it at least, I'd say. Time and tabs. Time and tabs. I was going around in circles then like on a merry-go-round and couldn't jump off, Time and Tabs, was going round and around in my head, like non-stop. I'd be trying to jump off in between the "and" and the "tabs". And they'd go round and around a load more times and I'd keep missing the right spot and couldn't do it. And then I'd try do it right after the "Time", but I couldn't make it then either.

Time and tabs, time and tabs, time and tabs… and I'd say I was like that a long time and probably like that a lot since then, cos when you think about it really like, it's all true too, y'know?

Cian was that fella's name, I'm fairly sure who said it like, but it could have been Billy Joe for all I know too or Diddy Dydo. If I was thinking of him though like, saying what he said: Time and Tabs, like, I'd think his name was Cian. But when I says it to some people like sometimes, I gets stuck again and can't stop.

One time I says it to Con an' we sitting at the counter in a pub in town and I kept saying it and kept saying it (I can't say it now or I'd start again like), but I couldn't stop and it was getting faster and faster. And Con was looking at me, I know, and he didn't know what to do cos we were only halfway through our pints at the most. So he hit me. Like what else could he do in fairness? Knocked me straight off the stool, down to the floor. Some dig he give me too, like, Con. He has some dock on him when he wants. Or had at least. Yer man behind the counter starts screaming at him then anyway, like, and he thrun the both of us out, but Con was only fixing me when you think of it. Worked too an' all. He knocked me off the merry-go-round, Ahahahahaah!

We were outside anyway and the barman an' all was calmed down by then, cos he seen I was alright, like, and he goes, That's alright, but you can't go knocking someone off their chair, like that! and Con was telling him why he done it all the time and the barman then goes, Sure come back again another time!

He was sound-out in fairness about it and we walked on then cos the other fella inside, the owner like, wasn't sound at all. He was a langer and I know that for a fact cos I seen him another day too when I was on the bridge and he never even looked at me but spit down on top of me an' he passing. He was getting ready too, to call the cops an' all next, knowing him, I'd say. That's all we needed. Con was only taking me out to celebrate getting out, like. Last thing we needed was to be locked up again, either of us. 'Specially cos his own case was coming up in two weeks around – Con's, like.

That's the time, now I think of it, I met Foxy Bill again, too. I wasn't after seeing him in years by then. Ten year I'd say since I was locked up with him, in his place, like. I used go to school an' all for a while from his house, imagine! Well, I don't know was it his house or his work, but either one. It's all the one!

He was sitting at the bar when we went in this place. We were all the way down by the train station. Past it, like, cos they wouldn't let us in anywhere else. I was never in this place before. Closed down since. Funny name on it. And we were standing at the counter a while with our drinks before I seen Foxy Bill at the end of the bar, sitting on his stool with his legs crossed and a big smile on his face, the way he'd be, like he heard a joke all the time and it was him only who heard it. He'd be smiling, but to himself like, without looking at no one.

I goes over to him anyway and goes, Bill! Remember me, Mickey! I'm Mickey! and he looks at me and not really looking too, like and goes, I do! and he nods and looks back at his pint, still smiling. And I said, I'll buy ya a drink so! and he was going, No no I'm alright! but I was saying, Go on I'll pay for it an' all. And I called for it and when it was put up, Con paid it and for another two pints for the two of us too. Bill was drinking Beamish and Con stuck with the Murphys and I'd say I had a Fosters at the time. I'd say I didn't have a bob on me anyway though cos Con was taking me out, like but I knew he'd pay for Bill's pint an' all no bother, cos he'd be sound-out in fairness, Con like was.

I miss him too, Con, but Bill was listening away to me all the time nodding and smiling an' I telling him things about what happened me since I seen him last, like. An' he nodding all the time. And I told him I been in prison an' all by then and says I never even done nothing for it. And he goes to me then, Ain't that the truth!

And when he said that then, I don't know. I felt funny like or something – Good, I'd say maybe, cos this was Bill and I knew him straight away again and it felt – you forget what a fella's like, like, but when you meet him then again you know straight away too and you remember, y'know?

Bill, like. I never – when you think of it: Dylan's dad was my dad an' all. And Cillian's dad too like. But I never think of him, that fella, cos he's not like my real dad cos of what he done to my mother. But Foxy Bill when he goes, Ain't that the truth, then like that, was that, like that. ...To me at least.

And Con didn't even hear the way Bill goes, Ain't that the truth? it made me nearly cry, I'd say, but not in a bad way. But Con starts telling him then about the horses and the Eurovision and God-knows-what, like either of them give a shit about it, although Con knew loads alright. And Bill was smiling and nodding and drinking his Beamish all the time when Con'd be buying it, cos he wouldn't let Bill put his hand in his pocket after I told him he used mind me in his house long 'go.

We stayed there all night in that place and it was a grand night and there was no trouble or fellas getting stuck in us or nothing. Bill called the last one an' all, in fairness. Happy times.

And I was fierce sad saying goodbye to him an' all that night, to Bill like. I mixed him up with Mr. Mulcahy too though, I'd say, who I never thought of no more at the time. In my head, like, I mixed them up. I forgot it was Foxy Bill and not Mr. Mulcahy for a while and I was talking to two of them. And when I was saying goodbye then, Con was pulling me off him an' all, saying, What the fuck ya doing? cos I was hugging onto Bill like he was my brother. Ahahahahaah! Like he was Dylan like, with his cwtch, he'd say it an' all, like that like, Dylan.

I don't think Foxy Bill even know'd me really though, I'd say that night. I was thinking of it later on when I was telling Cillian, like on the phone. I was telling him all about meeting him and Cillian goes, sure that fella didn't have a clue who you were! and I goes, no he did, cos he was alright, Bill like, but Cillian kept telling me he hadn't a clue, cos Cillian met him too like first time, so he knew him too. And I kept telling Cillian he hadn't a clue and Bill knew me well. But later on again then when I was thinking, I'd say he didn't know me alright. Bill like.

But in the bar that night he was still smiling when I was hugging him and he was telling the barman leave us off when Con was dragging me out of the place. Mr. Mulcahy'd of known me no bother and he'd of hugged me big time and not in no queer way neither. And my brother Dylan'd of hugged me too, the way he did that day, no bother neither. Not that I'd be looking for a cwtch like that or anything, but you know what I mean, like anyway. And Cillian'd have no problem neither too, cos Cillian's my brother even more than anyone, like.

And it makes no odds on me if my mother says he's scum and he's a rat and he's the devil and Cillian'd be better off dead. He's still my brother like, an' all, no matter what she'd be saying.

Comeuppance/ E Me One More Time

Con was due up in, like, two or three weeks, but first my mother was up, mainly cos of around that time the cops raided the place. They got everyone on the same thing: Kanturk, Timmy, Scanny were all up already before that, and Timmy and Scanny got only a fine and community service each. But Kanturk had too many other things too, so he got six months.

Cops were waiting in this place, see, where a boat was coming in, like. And my mother and all the gang were only at a party and went for a walk then down the road. And they come across this fella who was after taking his boat in to the beach, first like, with a bit of coke. Cocaine like. But first there was a load of travellers there to meet him too, cos they thought that my mother was bringing in a load of stuff, so they wanted to rob them and shit first, see?

And my mother and her gang got a shock when they come across all that going on, cos they weren't expecting that at all! So they were fighting against them travellers, trying to help the fellas only who was being beaten-up, like, when all the whole place got surrounded by cops all over!

Sounds mad if you ask me, like, but I wasn't there at all. I know nothing about it, me. I only knew it much later. About a week I'd say, if that. The whole navy was there an' all, like, to catch the big boat, see, and they did too, catch it. And there was a rake of cocaine on it. And it was on the news an' all. But they only caught the fellas on the boat, proper like, and just one or two of the travellers only. But our gang was only passing by, see, when it was going down, like, so they done nothing wrong when you think about it.

That's when then, after that – a day or two later, like, the cops raided all the houses (including our one) and they still tried charging all the whole gang on it all too, like.

And who was the main cop in charge of the whole thing who was in the witness-box against my mother for longer than anyone else? Samuel L. Jackson! The same one who looks like him, only white, who I was talking with that day in the cell with Detective Long.

And he was up there all the whole of one day and then the next day he was up there and the next day again he was up there an' all, the whole time, an' he saying things – loads of things like about my mother and the whole gang and what they got them all doing on camera and recordings and stuff. And they played that crap too, but I couldn't understand half it, but some of it was funny alright.

But anyway, it was a great laugh in the court all the time, but at the end of it, the judge was giving out to him an' all a load, saying he didn't have nothing on my mother and he had no right to be doing her like this. And yer man's name was Burns, I remember now, the Detective like. He was getting redder and redder. And all this was after a load of days after giving the judge a load of news about the dirt they had. But the travellers messed it up, see, cos they got there first and then the cops panicked and

275

raided the houses then after. But they got nothing there on my mother. Not really, like.

And anyway, yer man Detective Burns (or Samuel L. Jackson, like still, you ask me) was getting down off the box, like and he had a big red face on him from being pure scarlet, from the judge. And he looks up fast, like that, and he seen me. And I got a shock off it, like, cos it wasn't me at all and I didn't say nothing to him, so I looked around then to see who was he seeing, like, and who was behind me only that wan, Stacey! She was around four rows back and she had big wide eyes on her, like someone rammed a stick up her ass and kept going!

And I knew it then what she done, straight away. The bitch shopped my mother and the whole gang! She done it alright, Stacey like! Knew it straight away, I did, don't ask me how. Just by the look off her. And she had the cheek too to be sitting with Jordan SueAnne in the court the whole time, holding her hand!

I felt dizzy after it, I tell ya that now. And when I turned back, slow like, to look at Detective Burns, he was after moving-on. And then I seen my mother instead and she was sitting there staring straight across at me, saying nothing like, only staring mad. Then I looked back at Stacey again and looked at my mother and she looked at Stacey then too and Stacey looked at my mother and I was in-between them all and I said nothing, 'cept I was only shaking my head, cos it wasn't me at all. And my mother's eyes got even wider an' she looking at Stacey and I knew then she knew it too it wasn't me, like.

Then Stacey left with my sister and I didn't know what to do, cos the judge was going on and on about things and everyone else was gone quiet in the courtroom, about my mother and shit.

But my mother was only staring, staring mad at the door where Stacey left, the whole time. And she was red-out too at it, an' all.

But anyway the judge was mainly saying they got nothing on her, far as I could make out, but he still give her six months an' all, after all that! I couldn't believe that one neither. She done nothing, but here's six months? Work that one out!

●

Outside in the hall, then, outside the courtroom, like, in the courthouse, still, Con and some of the others was talking and I looks around and seen Stacey down the way a bit, with Jordan SueAnne. And she was looking at me, Stacey like, and calling me over.

And I wasn't after saying nothing to no one, but I left Con and the lads give out with themselves about it and I walks over to Stacey, who was bawling crying.

I didn't mean it Mickey! she was going, handing me Jordan SueAnne, who was old enough by then, but they were holding hands still since the court. And Jordan SueAnne didn't have a clue what was going on. And I didn't neither, more or less anyway, you could say. And I goes, So you shopped my mam so did ya Stacey? It was you done it after all that! and she was still bawling, but I only took Jordan SueAnne's hand, but didn't even look at my sister cos I could only look at Stacey crying and I didn't know what else to do. Then Stacey give me her handbag, that she had in her hand and goes, Look after yourself Mickey love. I loves ya! and she kissed me then in the hall in the courthouse and walks on.

That was the last time I seen her really, unless that oul wan in the Mercy was her that Cillian said it was a few year later. A few months ago, like. I still can't believe that was her though, cos she was off her head, that wan that time, but you never know too though.

First, I was standing there for ages with my sister, and then Con and the lads come over and we all went out then for our lunch to the pub down the road. And I was on my second pint when I seen Tony Harrington looking at the bag next to me on the seat, like. And I looked at him then to catch him out and I goes, That's Stacey's, alright? I'm minding it for Stacey! and he goes, Alright, no bother there, fiend! he goes, laughing at me only, cos he always calls me fiend like as if I'd be calling all the fellas *"fiend"* all the time, but I don't even!

And it was only then that I remembered it an' all and I goes I have to take Jordan SueAnne home cos she got no dinner or nothing. And on the way then I had a look inside the handbag and what was in it, only mostly a load of tabs and hash and even a bit of coke too. You name it, it was in this bag from Stacey, like, the whole time! It was like a party in a handbag – and she give it to me, just like that! No questions asked or nothing, Stacey like, in fairness.

When I got home I went up straight to my room and emptied out the bag out on the bed. There was like hundreds of tabs – all different ones that I put into different bundles, and hash and a bit of coke, like I said. No heroin, though, but I didn't care about that at the time. And her girl-stuff was all there, a small hair brush and lipstick and shit. And her bundle of paper things (no money though) and her phone an' all. The amount of stuff she had inside that sparkly bag! It was small enough too, I tell ya, but had a load in it. Where would Stacey be going without all a' that, like? It was my first time having a phone too, proper-like of my own. It was an iphone too, top-of-the-line job. Paul Pot offered me thirty euro for it and I laughed at him, but then I got it wet after that (when I dropped it by accident) and it was no more good.

One Eye Higher

A few days later, then, I was waking up and Con was screaming at me again where's Stacey, like. I remembered him saying it a few times, last few days, but I was out of it, man, and he knew it, so I couldn't even think. But now he knew he had me cos I was out and he was after taking the last of it off me, what's left like, last night. And I was just waking up. And he drags me into the shower, screaming at me say where's Stacey and I was screaming at him I don't know, an' all. And Tony Harrington was shouting at me too and Con told him fuck off downstairs a while and he wouldn't go 'til Con made sure of it. And he went then and left me alone. But I got sick a load first and then had to crap too, but I couldn't and Con was outside the door all the time waiting for me, like and I didn't know what to tell him cos I couldn't remember what I might of known about it.

Anyway, I come out and after a while, Con went out too, looking for Stacey again. And left Tony there with me and Tony goes, Come on now, ya little shit, and tell me what you know! and I tells him I'll squeal to my mother on him if he don't leave me alone and he goes, This one's from your mother! and he knocks me hard to the floor and I swear it was like my face got a smack off an iron bar. I never knew he could hit so hard, but he could in fairness. Well, maybe it was cos he hit me where Con got me too, like, so it was already sore. Must be it. Y'know when your jaw is kind of lumpy and soft and you press it but you don't feel nothing 'cept it feels like a spongy carpet or something? Well it was like that after Con, but somehow Tony got the feeling back to it, cos it hurt mad after he digged me hard, too. And that's fair-going I'd say, after that. And when I was on the floor he kicked me in the stomach and goes, And that one's from me! She told me you were a grass all your life to save your skin, he goes, And if there's one thing I hate, it's grasses! and I goes, I hate grasses too an' all! I'm not no grass and I don't know where she is!

Next thing, in the middle of it, like, there's a knock on the doorbell and both of us is frozen listening for it. And I was thinking then it was Stacey come home and I'd say Tony was thinking the same thing an' all, cos both of us ran to the front door at the same time. And when we opened it, there was two women standing there who I never seen before and two shades with them an' all, behind like.

And the first woman says a big long thing like a poem or something and I didn't know what she was on about. And then she hands out a big page of writing and I'm like, What? and she's looking at me, funny-like, probably cos I'm bleeding on my face and my jaw is nearly busted and I have a black-eye, probably. And Tony goes, She's here to take Jordan SueAnne away! and I couldn't understand it and starts shouting at her about it then, but she goes our mother said she could. And she showed me my mother's signing for it too then, but that didn't fool me, cos my mother told me about the way they'd make her sign it or else they'd take them fully. And when I'm still giving out to her then, Tony is coming back down the stairs, cos he was gone up and he goes, Where is she? and I knew he was talking about my sister then and I got a shock, cos I didn't see her in days. And today the only thing I seen is people batin' me up. And I starts shouting out her name JORDAN SUEANNE! JORDAN SUEANNE! I'm shouting, while I'm running all around the place, but there's no answer. And when I come downstairs and get to the kitchen, there she is an' all! Just finished her breakfast what she made herself and she had a big fright on her face then when she seen me, cos I'd say she knew straight away they were taking her away. It would break your heart, I tell ya, when the bastards'd take her away like that from her own home.

●

After that I stayed out of the house for ages cos I didn't want to be going back there no more. There was all parties there all the time, an' all. And I'd be outside sometimes, to look in, like. It was Tony mostly and all the lads and a few of their oul dolls, but I was trying to see if I could spot Tony shifting any of them, but he never did. When I was there at least. Con might be around sometimes, but mostly he'd be in the pub instead of at the party. Or out working, like. And I'd be with him too sometimes, cos Con'd be alright, but you'd never know with Tony.

That was around the chicken-supper time for that fella, Ironside, in the wheelchair, too. Around then I think, when yer man's wife was shouting at Con go 'way, for no reason. And he went too. That court case coming up and Stacey squealing like that had him rattled alright, I'd say. A bit like. He'd be saying the same things over and over sometimes. He'd forget, like, he said it. And he'd say it again then. And then a few minutes later, he'd say it again. Like that, like. It was only all the nerves.

When my mam wasn't there though, mostly I didn't bother going home. Left it off. For the first load of days, weeks-like, I was around town and thinking I might see Dylan. Done the odd job where I could, like, got a few bob on the bridges during the day and a bit of a laugh in someone's house or somewhere you'd get into overnight or something. Or sometimes there'd be a bonna going on and you'd have a party 'round the fire like for the night, bit of a laugh or something. Other times you'd just forget about it and kip down for the night or whatever.

And then, who'd I run into one day? Only Murder She Wrote – that Mary, like! I didn't see her in ages. She didn't see me first and I didn't even know her when I said, Big Issue, cos she looked old-like, but when she ran-on then, like some of them do, I was looking back and ran up to her and I goes, Mary girl! I didn't see you in years! It's me – It's Mickey like! Remember me?

And she stops then to have a look off me and she's already like crying nearly and she goes, Oh Mickey, how're you doing, love? It's lovely to meet you, do you need some money? and I goes, Nah Mary, you're alright girl, I seen ya there and I said I'd say hello cos I didn't see ya in ages and I remember you were always minding me an' everything growing up, And my brother Cillian too. He's gone to college too an' all now, imagine! And he's finished it too now an' all and has a grand job out of it even, Cillian! and she was well-impressed by that and we had a quick chat, like that like and then I goes, I said I'd say thanks anyway, like for all your efforts, y'know?

And I give her a bit of a wave and I was walking on, leaving her off, like, cos I knew she was afraid of me or something, for no reason, cos I didn't mean it like that at all. But I know they do be sometimes. I only meant I was, like, fond to see her, like. And she goes, Wait! Can I get you something Mickey? she goes, Will you go for a bite to eat with me?

And she looked sad and I don't know why she'd want to be seen around with me, like, but I was thinking I was hungry alright, now I thought of it, like, and I goes Are you sure? Where would you want to go to? cos I wouldn't like them posh places, me, but I didn't tell her that in case she'd say one of them, but she goes, I'd love to go to McDonalds, wouldn't you? and I goes, Nah! C'mon we go down to John Grace's for a change, like, if you like.

Cos we been in McDonald's last time I seen her, I remembered.

Then we had a grand time down there and I ate nearly a whole snack box and she ate nearly none of hers, I'd say, cos she wasn't even hungry. And it was like meeting Cillian on my birthday, every birthday like, cos she was telling me things that I never remembered, like what I said here earlier about stuff growing up. How she wrote all stuff down and got in trouble with my mother, like, that time. And I remembered it then when she telling me and it was very funny hearing it all. And I told her we used call her Murder She Wrote after that and we was both skittin' laughin'. Even Mary too, a bit. We was wild alright, the two of us, me and Cillian like, growing up.

Those were the days, Mary girl! I goes. And she kind of smiles.

And I was telling her too about stuff I been up to since the last time I was talking with her when we went for a meal and I was covered in muck (not shit at all). And we were laughing at a load of that too. Well, I was mainly, I'd say. And she was shocked when she heard I met my brother in the prison an' all and she wanted to hear all about him, not like my mother at all. She wouldn't let me even talk about him, my mother. So I told Mary and she couldn't believe it.

Then when it was time to go, like, she goes to me, Would you like to stay in my place – just for a night or two, I mean? and I was – well, I don't know what I was – surprised! Shocked even, I suppose. I could barely talk a while, I'd say. And then I goes, But how about your husband? I'd say he probably wouldn't like it if – , but before I could even finish what I was saying, she tells me he died. Last year. It was the Cancer, like, that got him, So, you know, you'd be a bit of company for me, I suppose, she goes, But no drugs! I won't have any drugs in my house, Mickey! You know that! and I explained it all to her then how I was off the drugs now. Stopped doing any since my mother's friend, Stacey like, ran away and got my mam sent to prison. That wasn't fully true, but I had to let her know or she wouldn't believe me, like. And I was after deciding already only that day I wasn't going to be taking anything else ever again anyway though, so this was like a sign now – Mary coming along, out of the blue like that for me. A sign, like from someone who's dead like an angel or someone, not to be doing no more drugs and things. And I meant it too.

And we had a load of days in her house, most of the time, with no bother at all even. And she cooked all lovely food all the time. Proper meals and shit. And we went out on walks and she brought me all new clothes an' all, Mary in fairness. And then I had to meet Con about something and he goes, Your mother wants you to visit her. Next Sunday. You're to call up to her then. I'll bring ya.

And I was brickin' it like straight away, but I said I would so, cos I knew he'd never leave me off if I didn't. But next Saturday night then there was a party, like in Mary's house, cos Mary said I could bring my friend over for an hour only. And she didn't mind when there was two of them turned up, cos we were quiet-out in the kitchen. And the others wasn't even with me, like, when they came along later-on. I never met them before, most of them. It was lucky, like, that Mary was gone to bed though cos they wrecked the gaff that night and probably solked a few things out of it too, knowing them. I didn't get nothing out of it, me like, 'cept a bit of a laugh, like, at the time.

But I was wrecked then next day and I couldn't go to Limerick. And by the time I got up, Mary was after cleaning nearly all of it up and I was watching the telly when I heard her coming in to give out to me, so I stood up again to leave the gaff, cos I was full-sure she'd make me do that, like, but instead she made me breakfast and brought it into me on a tray while I'd be sitting in front of the telly, like!

She shocked me a load of times like that, in fairness, ole' Mary. Another time we were in a shop and I got a load of Mars bars off the counter when yer man turned around to get the fags Mary was buying for me. She seen me do it and said nothing, 'cept when yer man was cashing it in, she goes, And five Mars bars too, wasn't it Mickey? and he looks at me, yer man, and I put my hand in my jacket pocket to count them and I goes, Yeah, five – or four, like.

286

Then I had to say which and it was five alright, so he put in five and Mary paid for all of them. I don't even like Mars bars, but she paid for them anyway.

And the next week and the next too I couldn't make it up to Limerick neither cos different things like. And in the end, Con took me home, back to Winchester like, on Saturday and kept me there til Sunday, or else he'd bate the head off me, like. And took me to Limerick then next day an' all to see my mother. And that was that, then.

●

Y'know the way you'd hate to be doing something that you know full-well'd be awful and there's no way it could be anyway else, like – and then you do it – and IT'S NOT AWFUL AT ALL!? Well, somehow anyway, that's how it was like that day when I went to see her, my mother like. It's like I _knew_ she'd be killing me, but she wasn't then when I went. Not one-bit even!

When I seen her first, she was looking at me with big teary eyes, like she misses me. And I got all tears then too straight away. And she goes, I missed ya Mickey. You're the only one left! My only child! and she starts bawling crying to me. My mam, like! She done it quiet, but with mad-tears flopping down non-stop. And two of us are crying like that for ages, cos I'm sorry-out I couldn't mind her from this, but I was thinking then I'd get Stacey back for what she done instead. And I goes, We looked all over for that bitch Stacey.

And my mam is shaking her head and she goes, Don't say her name! and I goes, I searched everywhere, but I couldn't find her – that wan! and she shook her head again and said it doesn't matter. She knew exactly where she was. And I goes where and she told me she's in Birmingham with her mam's cousin and she's gone mad as a hat and they're trying to ship her back to the madhouse in Cork, like, but they can't do it yet, but my mother'd be ready when they do!

And she was getting mad-out again then when she was telling me about "that wan", so I was asking her about being inside, like, instead and she was telling me a bit, like it wasn't too bad. Boring shit mostly. She said one or two of them tried it on alright, thought they were the hardshaws, like, but my mother proved them she's the hardest. That's my mother alright for ya!

And when we was laughing at how she dared yer wan get her back, after she smashed her food-tray, I goes to her, for the laugh like, And did you meet your sister yet? I said. And she didn't have a clue what I was on about, like. She goes, Wha? and I goes, Y'know, like I met my brother when I went to prison! and she got mad at me then, a bit, cos she didn't like me saying Dylan was my brother.

I told you don't mention him to me! she goes, And he's not my son so he's not your brother neither! and that made sense to me too, then, when she said that, come to think of it, so then I knew it.

And there was all quiet, 'til after a while, she goes to me, Was one of his eyes higher than the other? and I didn't know, but when I thought of it too then, thought of Dylan like, I goes, Ya, it was! How did you know!? and she didn't tell me, but she went quiet again on it and a bit mad. And she goes, Don't you let me see that piece of shit 'round Cork, I'm warning ya now! and that was the end of that one.

●

By the time I got back home then anyway, to Mary's house like, her son Jeremy was around. He's older than me, like. I didn't know him that much, but he was ok. He answered the door when I rang it and he opened it a bit, only. And I got a shock and goes, How Jeremy! It's me, Mickey Collins! Remember? I didn't see you in years, how you getting on? and he goes, I'm alright Mickey how are you? and I goes, Not too bad I suppose. Is your mother around? and he goes, Nah. She's gone out a while. But the thing is I'm living here now, Mickey, and I'll need my room back.

And I knew what was going on, like straight away, but that's OK. I knew there was another bedroom there too, like, but it's all the one really. He had a bag ready for me an' all. So I said goodbye to Jeremy and told him I said thanks to his mother for all the help – And sorry too, like! I goes, cos, y'know.

Love And Affection

Did ya ever hear that song, Joan Armatrading? It's like, Feeeee-eeeelll Lovvvve! That one! Well, you mightn't believe me now, but that's my mother's favourite song. She always had that CD like and she'd be singing it all the time, sometimes, over and over. To herself, like, or to me, when I was a kid. It'd be on the CD, I remember. She'd be singing it to Cillian, long 'go, and smiling and she'd turn around to me then and be singing it to me in the middle, along to the music. She had the CD an' all with the black wan on the cover who's the singer of it, Sing it! sing it! sing it! Once more!.., like that, like. We all loved that one and my mother the most.

Well anyway, I was going through the records in this posh house up in Sunday's Well one night. There was all guitars and books and shit, but I like to take my time sometimes, see what's there in case there'd be good ones, like. Things. And imagine living in a place like this? With all the things, all the things! I'd say I'd never go to another house in my life if I lived here, in this posh house or one like it, like.

And I was going through – these were records, now remember! Proper big albums like. Not CDs at all! I was going through them all, flicking 'um one by one, past all the hundred records or more. And next I seen that one straight away when I got to it, and I was like, JOAN ARMATRADING! THAT'S MY MOTHER'S FAVOURITE

SONG! there was no one else with me, like, but I says it out loud like that cos I got a shock when I seen it. And then I had to wait ages til I knew no one was coming, but no one did. So I knew then, like, I had to get that one for her cos she was getting out next week and it'd be a special present for her to hear it too!

I was happy-out with that and didn't even get nothing else there. Left the whole place cos they were sound-out having that one, I was thinking. But when I got home and showed Tony next day, and told him all about my mother's song, he goes, And what are ya going to play it on? There's no record player here!

But that was alright cos I knew where there was one anyway, so I went back to that place that night again, same place, cos I knew there'd be no problem cos they wouldn't even of known I was there, like, cos I was quiet-out an' I leaving the place an' all. The record player was a massive yoke though. I'd say it was ancient. Like 1980 at least by the looks of it, with the record player on the top of it and all the lights on it an' everything.

Then next day I showed Tony and he goes, Where are the speakers for it ya dumb schmuck!? You need speakers to be able to hear it!

Like how am I supposed to know that in fairness? I tells him that an' all. And after he told me what they look like, I told him I know where to get them too and he goes, You're wasting a lot of time on this record! Are you sure there's no cash in the house? She loves a bit of cash, she do, your mother! an' he laughing away at me, mocking me like again, the way he do, rubbing his tit like he had money on it.

And when I went back again that night I seen the key they usually left under the pot wasn't there and it wasn't under

291

the mat and I searched around the bushes and even over the door-frame, an' everything but they never left it out this time. And I searched around the whole outside windows and doors and was looking up at the upstairs an' all, but there was no way in.

I don't like to be breaking windows to get in to a place, unless they're the thin ones like, cos mostly there'd be an easy-enough way in or you could go next door. But I had to get into this one place now, only, or that record player'd be no good to me without the speakers. And the speakers'd be no good to them people neither when you think of it.

And that's when I got my idea! There was a garage out the road a bit, like and I walked out there and got a box of fags and asked them if they have a loan of a biro, but he charged me for it an' all, but I said it'd be worth it, so I paid the money for it on top of the cigarettes and he give me a receipt, so I used that too. I wrote a note, see on the back and said: SORRY GOT RECORD PLAYER HERE LAST NIGHT. FORGOT SPEAKERS. IF YOU DON'T NEED THEM NO MORE, COULD YOU LEAVE THEM OUTSIDE TOMORROW PLEASE + I'LL PICK THEM UP + WON'T NEVER BOTHER YOU NO MORE GUARANTEED. SORRY.

Worth a bash anyway, I thought. And next day when I got up, Tony was up already and he asked me and I told him what happened about the speakers and he was knotted laughing at me, calling me all the dumb names and he was saying, Did ya sign it too? and I got mad at him then and goes, I DID NOT, NO! and he was laughing at me and mocking me again til I was leaving. And then he goes, Come on I'll drive ya – I gotta see this! and when we got there, what do you think, but the speakers was outside the gate, out on the road like! Four of them, even, not two at all, like! Plus the wires too, that I didn't even know about! And Tony was shocked and I was mocking him then for ages, getting my own back on him. And he still couldn't believe it and I was bursting my arse laughing at him the whole time. And he stayed there when I went down the road to collect them, in fairness, cos he wouldn't get any closer, in case.

And on the way home then I was 'splaining it all to him, see, cos the speakers'd be no use to them no more so they'd be glad to get rid of them, like, and they knew too I wouldn't be breaking any windows, cos I'm good that way. And I said please and sorry too! So everyone's a winner!

•

I was in bed when Tony went up to collect my mother and bring her back home. And when they got back, I was just after coming down the stairs and I ran out the door and give her a big hug and she give me a big cwtch too back. It was great to have my mam home after all this time. She was happy-out too to be back too an' all, out of that place.

Con was after spending about a week at least on hard work before that, in fairness, doing-up the whole house and painting it and driving an open-top truck he got a loan of, around everywhere so we could dump all the shit we had to clear out of the house before his sister got back, or she'd of kilt the lot of us stone dead, the state of the place. First, we'd all load it up (Tony too) and then Con'd drive it around and mostly I'd be sitting in the back til we got to a dark spot and I'd be able to throw it out while we were going along, like. Took a few nights too, see, cos that place was full of paint pots and boxes and chipper wrappers and empties and stuff after all them months.

Some kip it was. That's when it started, I'd say, when my mother was away that time. All downhill after that, more or less, the more you think of it. Being a kip, I mean.

Before that, I remember when the place was spotless all the time and the smallest mark you'd get a batin' over. But, no matter anyway, we had it all lovely and shiny for her, true as God, when she got home that day. It was like a brand new home, outside and inside too. And she was well-impressed even. All smiling and happy to be home.

And when she was going in the door, I told her Mam! Wait there now and close your eyes! and I ran into the front room and grabbed the record and brought it out and told her open her eyes. And she done that and then she goes, What's that? and I goes, Joan Armatrading! Don't you remember? – That's your favourite song! Remember you singing that to us all the time?

But she was only laughing and mocking me over it. Then we went inside and had a big party anyway and I put on the record one time, but it was all slower than I remembered and wasn't the same, and we didn't really listen to much anyway 'til Scanny brought over his boom box and we were all dancing mad to that one for ages and ages, my mam too like, jumping up and down all over the shop. Some laugh!

●

And the party was over, more or less, and I was in the kitchen half-asleep talking to Con and a few of the others, or listening to them mostly, when I heard music going on again inside the front room. It wasn't our type of music, like we'd be listening to, but soft shit, one song after another. Nothing fast. Boring stuff, like.

I didn't know what it was and didn't care either, but I wasn't listening and Con was going on about his case that was after getting delayed again and wondering if they could prove it. And he'd have no bother doing any time, he was saying, if they thought they could bother him, like and stuff. And he was saying all that again and again. And Kanturk then was on about stories from his prison time again too, cos he got out two weeks before my mother, like and he already told us all about that, all the time, but he was telling us again now. And I could hear the same song going on a few times in the front room, but I took no notice again.

And after a while I had to go to the jacks, but someone was after gawking-up inside there and it was 'scusting, so I went upstairs. And when I was on my way up, I seen my mam standing in the middle of the front room, listening and swinging around to it, like. Tony and Timmy and some other fella and a few of the beors were inside there, mostly asleep or zonked, like, but my mother was enjoying it, moving to the music. And it was only when I was pissing upstairs and could hear it clear, I heard: Sing it! Sing it! Sing it! – like that. And I heard then it was our song alright – Joan Armatrading, like! Once more with affection!

And when I got down, the saxophone bit was on and it was nearly over and I was going mad I missed it, but I could see my mam was enjoying it still with her eyes closed and the fag in her mouth, wiggling-around, quiet-like: Once more with the feeling!...

And when it ended then, the next song was coming on, but she went over and lifted the needle on the record player and put the same song back on again from the start and picked up her fag again and turned around to the room. And the sound too from those speakers all over the room was something else. I got Tony to set them up for me, cos he does nothing anyway, that fella, but he done a good enough job on them in the end, fair dues. Worth a few bob too, them speakers I'd say. But no one else now was even listening, or watching my mother either. 'Cept me. And it started off and she knew all the words too.

She sung it soft, like, with her eyes closed,... I am not in love, but I'm open to persuasion.. and she was smiling away to herself and rocking, side to side and laughing like to the music too, like she was making a joke an' she singing it, on and on...

I could really laugh really laugh! – then she turned her head and opened her eyes and seen me standing there. And she had a big teary laugh on her face and goes, Thank youuuu! – to me, like soft, with her arms out and she thrun her head back and closed her eyes again. I can still think of it all, like in slow motion. And it was part of the song too, the thank you bit. But she was singing it to me too only, I knew it, saying thank you and smiling like that and looking at me only! And I was frozen on the spot looking at her – my mother! She was – *is* like – *something*! Always was. She's, like beautiful too, like of course, my mother like. You'd have to give her that. But at that time, even, she was gone a bit fat too, like, but she was moving now like she wasn't even a bit fat. You'd do anything for her and she could do anything too. And now she was singing this song perfect cos that's what she wanted to be doing. She could be a singer an' all on the stage if she wanted, like. And she'd do it better even than the wan singing it too.

…With a lover I could really move, really move, I could really dance, really dance, really dance, really move…

And while she's singing it, the music's getting louder and a bit faster and she has her hands open and spread out in front of her, with the fag in her mouth while she's singing. And her knees are bent and she swinging away to the music, Really dance, really dance, I could really move, really move…

Next she puts her arms down and stands up tall for the next bit, and sings, Now if I can feee-eeel the sun in my eyes and the rain on my face, why can't I feeeee-eeeeeeel…

I swear to God there was a tear flopping down her face an' all an' she singing it out loud. Then this is the time Tony Harrington was just after waking up, and he dances into her open arms (when her eyes are still closed) and he grabs her to swing her around all-happy and laughing, like, to cheer her up. And he joins in for the laugh, just when she's singing, LO-VVVVE!

And the song carries on singing, but my mother hit the roof. She gave Tony some thump. I'd say it nearly knocked him out. And when he's down the ground, she thumped him then again too. Hard, like.

JEE-SUS FUCK-IN CHR-IIST! she screams, mad as hell. Madder even than I ever seen her. I'M SURROUNDED BY FUCKING IDIOT PRICKS THE WHOLE TIME! THE LOT OF YE!

And the song is going, Love Love Love Love Love! that part! And my mother sticks her foot down into the whole record player and smashes it all first go. Her foot goes straight into it and she pulls it out again and it stops playing straight away, but she keeps smashing and kicking it. For ages. And she gets the record on top of it too with her foot by the time it's stopped going around. Smashed the whole thing to bits, no bother.

IDIOT MEN! THE FUCKING LOT OF YE! she's shouting and screaming. Then she storms out of the room and up to bed. And Con is there and Tony's only half-getting up off the floor. And when she's marching up the stairs I'm wondering about it, so I have to ask before it's too late: Me too mam? I goes, cos I thought we were all-good between the two of us at least, but she screams back, YES YOU *FUCKING* TOO! and then pointing at one person after another, after another, who was there looking at her AND YOU AND YOU AND *FUCKING* YOU TOO! She goes to Con too an' all and to the other women who were there too an' all too. NOW YE CAN ALL FUCK OFF AND KEEP FUCKING OFF WHEN YE GET THERE! she screams back even after she slammed her bedroom door and thrashing the place inside.

She'd do that sometimes, like. Or something like that anyway. Throw a raaby, like. But that was a big enough one, that day.

Cob Stable

The more Con got close to his courtcase, the kind of nuttier he got, you ask me. I didn't know it first, but looking back I knew it. My mam says to me one day, a few days before the court, Where's Con gone? she goes. He was on the batter for around a week or more before that. He'd be home some nights like, but other times he wouldn't bother, probably. Either way, he'd be down the early morning places then next day too anyway, like. But he was after coming back yesterday (the day before, like) and now he was missing again. Not in his room and he didn't take the van he had at the time. And he wasn't around the house anywhere I could see when she said it.

We thought no more about it though, til later-on Tony comes in and says Con's outside in the car in his underpants. He was sitting at the side of the road, cool as a breeze, an' he passing by. I burst my arse laughing straight away and we all ran out to have a look off him. There he was alright, sitting in the front seat with no brown suit on him. I never seen him in his underpants and vest before that. He looked different. I'd barely know him I'd say. Like a fella – did you ever see a fella with glasses all the time, and then you see him without his glasses and his face looks all totally different, like smooshed or something? Well that was like Con without his suit too, that time. Even when we went on our holidays before that, he mostly slept in his clothes cos he'd be in late and up early next day, like.

I couldn't stop laughing when I spotted him and my mother was skitting too first. For ages before that, Con'd be talking about only the courtcase coming up, so when my mother seen him, she goes to Tony, Take a photo of him there, lah, on your phone so we'll show the judge and he might get off with it! so he took the photo and my mother told him, No take it over there! so he took one over there and then she told him take one from over here, with the two of them in it, her and Con, like. She was standing up next to him, holding his hand and rubbing on top of it. And Con was staring into space like a spacer or something, with only his vest and his underpants. That was the funniest one and she knew where the best spot was to take the best photos too, see? Cos his belly was sticking out and it looks like she was holding onto her pet monkey or something.

Then she got me to put Con's arm over my shoulder and get him out of the car, but the two of us only falls down the ground, even though Con's awake an' all, but not saying nothing much. And she photographs that too with her own phone, with me and Con on the ground. She got a good laugh off that one later on too, but I didn't think that was a funny one at all, like.

I couldn't get him up and neither could Tony, but my mam gives out mad to Con then, cursing him and saying he was a pervert to be walking around like that and what would people think of him. But Con was only mumbling mostly. Then my mother goes leave him there and she sent me to the shop cos there was no milk for a cup of tea, but the shop is miles away from there. And when I come back it was all over. Con was gone to bed or somewhere.

On the table in the kitchen though there was a letter and it was from Con and it said something like, I hereby declare that

I give my house, known as Winchester to my only sister, Tanya Collins.

And he signed it too, Con like in fairness, before he went to bed. And underneath that, Tony was after signing it, cos he seen him write the letter. And my mam got me to sign it too an' all then. And when I did, she goes we owned it now and might sell it too if we wanted. And we could get a nice house in Spain out of it and have cash left over an' all. And I goes, would Con be living with us still and she goes course he would, if he liked, but she says forget about it now and say nothing to no one or to Con too even in case he runs around in his underpants anymore. And we could surprise him with a nice holiday in the new house when he gets out of prison. Cos we all knew he was going down this time, alright, in fairness.

See, that time down in West Cork when the cops busted them, bating up the travellers, Con was the best at it. Bating them up I mean. He was on his third one when all the cops landed on him and he picked up a machete belonging to one of the travellers, that he got off them, like, and sliced a cop with it too an' all. It wasn't even his weapon, ask anyone. And it took twenty of them to bate the shit out of him after and into the Paddy Wagon. So they were all dying to get him sent down too. So when they raided the house then next, they planted a load of stuff on him, in his room like, so they got him on weapons and drugs and everything stashed all around his room. That's what they said anyway.

So, his case took the longest to come up cos they had the most on him and it kept getting put back and they were adding a load of stuff on it the whole time – even things that happened in the past, a long time ago that they said they found proof of in his room. They'd be coming back and saying things like they found a load of sweets buried inside the washing machine in his bedroom, in Con's like, but Con never even touched any sweets ever. Ask anyone. And then they comes back another time and goes, That's the same painting stolen off that job in 1999 what we found behind the picture in your room! like, as if there was a famous painting worth a load of money behind the photograph of his own father that my mother give to Con when we moved into the house! And just cos stuff was stashed out of the way in Con's room too and the house belonged to him an' all, didn't mean that stuff belonged to him, did it? It was the council paying him for it too, you have to remember that much! And my mother was only renting it off the council at the time!

Naw boy, when they want to see you go down, cops have their ways alright. And they wanted to see Con go down that time, for slicing the cop on the belly, if nothing else, put it that way. And meantime, he was going off his game the more things went on the list, but they couldn't care less about that. It was fierce sad to see him all upset the whole time.

Six year he got in the end, imagine. And when the judge give it to him there was screaming and roaring in the court. I thought Con was going to trash the whole place to bits. He nearly did too before the judge cleared the room and they dragged him down the steps. About forty of them I'd say it took, Con was some fighter.

Later on, in the pub, my mother goes, The wild Cob smashed up the stables alright! and I goes, Are you laughing at your own brother or something? and she only throws her eyes in the air and got Tony buy us one last drink before she told me fuck off.

302

After that then, weeks and weeks later, she had a load of papers and told me, Sign that one there! and Sign that there too! and I signed them and asked her what's all that about and she goes, That's for the house.

Made sense to me and I forgot about it then.

But then after around a year after Con went down, I knew he wasn't well, like, in fairness and he was in the hospital too. I wasn't up to see him, but my mam was and she said he don't know what planet he's on, that fella. And we had another look at them loopy photos of him in his underpants and had a good laugh off them. Then, next day she brought me to see this other fella in an office down the South Mall. And she told me before we went in, Just say yes to everything he asks you – that's all you need to do now and we'll have the house and a load of money then!

So I was grand and happy with that one and I said OK and give her the thumbs up, like that. It was good when you'd be in on something with my mother, like. But when we got in there then, yer man starts talking about child abuse and all these things and asks me all about it and I goes, What? and he showed me a big load of pages what he said I wrote and signed and I goes I did not. And he showed me that picture with Con in his underpants on top of me and I can't believe it. And all the time, my mother is giving out to me and saying, Sorry sorry! to yer man behind the desk, He's all embarrassed about it, see? but I wasn't embarrassed about it at all cos it wasn't true and my mother takes me out and kills me over it then outside in the pub. And she says I need to tell the man Con was abusive to me all my life cos he's mad now and has no senses no more, so if we don't get the house off him the government will take it away. Then she gave me a couple of sweets and brought me a pint to wash them down.

But then, while I was having a drink, I remembered the letter she got me to sign on the house and told her it's all the one, cos the house is ours anyway, I thought, so we don't need me to be in on it too. But she only starts shouting at me then inside the pub, giving out, saying they wouldn't believe her with that one, even though he signed it himself an' all, Con like, before he went down. The government want the house for themselves, she goes, and this was the only way to get it back off them bunch of gangsters. She said they probably drilled a hole in Con's brain an' all, those bastards. And Con would want us to have the house too, when you think about it, not the government at all. If he had any senses on him anymore, like. But they definitely turned him nuts too the way they did with that other wan who used live with us. I knew straight away she was talking about Stacey there, like, but I didn't say her name cos it could've been a trap.

Anyway, after lunch she brought me back into yer man in the South Mall and goes, Now Mickey, tell the man what Con did to you.

And I was sitting there chilled-out and looking at her and looking at yer man. And she goes, Didn't you tell me he stuck his finger up your bum when you were six? and I kind of laughed at that, cos by this time I couldn't care less and I thought it was funny like the way she said it, but I didn't know she was still waiting for an answer, Tell the truth now Mickey! she goes. And she was all serious about it, in front of yer man like, but I knew alright what she was looking for, When I was six, yeah, I goes, but I was only messing. Then she says, And didn't he make you suck him off a load of times since then?

My mother. I'm telling you now. She'd say things and do things and even _I'd_ find it hard to go along with it, like, but she'd always have a plan so you'd say alright mostly like. Some things though are too much, no matter how much sweets you'd have. There was no way I'd be going along with all that. No way. It took me a while to get out the words though and she was already explaining all the things she said Con done on me. And the man was listening to her and taking notes, but I'm like, That's not true at all! and she told me shut up, but the man was like blah blah blah. Whatever. And then I went from laughing at it to crying. And I was sitting there crying at his desk saying Con never touched me and neither did Mr. Mulcahy or no one else neither. And my mother was only saying sorry to yer man and saying I was traumatised by it all, over the years.

Anyway, that plan didn't work to get the house back off the government and neither did the first plan where Con even _gave_ it to us. And my mother wouldn't talk to me anymore for ages after that and I had to sleep somewhere else mostly for about a year at least, I'd say.

Gram Not Gone

And I found God around that time too, soon after, when Con was still locked-up, thanks be to Our Lord and Saviour, Jesus Christ. And without Him, true as fuck, I don't think I'd of gotten through everything else that happened after. And that's a fact.

It started, probably, when I met my old friend Davie O'Brien. I met him on the street one day and I goes, How Davie boy, I never knew you got out! he was all calm-looking, like he was after taking some sweets and he smiled at me and nodded his head and goes, Peace be with you Mickey. It's great to see you and I must apologise for my behaviour when we met last time. I was in a low point in my life, but with the help of our Lord and Saviour, Jesus Christ, I managed to turn my life around. *He* is the answer, I'm telling you Mickey. And if you were interested, I would like to show you the way, too.

Thinking of it now, as I'm saying it like, that must of been when I started being one with Jesus alright, around then. I couldn't even remember what he was saying sorry about, but he was all happy so I says, Ya, I'd be on for that alright, like! Chalk it down!

Why not? I say. Try anything once at least, me. So he says I'll meet ya back here Wednesday at seven o'clock so and we'll walk the righteous path together, for a change, with the light of the Lord guiding our passage, God willing. And I said, Amen!

Ahahahahaah! and give him a clap, cos what he said sounded like a prayer and it was funny, like. I couldn't help it, laughing when he said it and I thought he'd be giving out to me for mocking him like, but he only smiles and says Amen back to me then, with an even bigger smile on him. Next he blesses me while he's walking away and I goes, You don't have a loan of a fiver til then do ya Davie?

I was only messin' like, see what he'd do and he comes back with his hand in his pocket and goes, What I have is yours brother! and he slapped a load of change into my hand without even looking at it and closed my hand on top of it and looks into my eyes for ages like he's looking to get a shift off me. But he didn't do anything else. Weirdest shit ever, you ask me, but he was happy walking away at least. And I goes, Hey Davie can I borrow your pants 'til Wednesday night? and he walks back to me an' all with his hands on his belt and I waves him away, mocking him again. I says, That's alright ya steamer! I was only checking! I'd rather you kept them cos they're too holy for me anyway – full of holes they are an' all! Ahahahahaah! Probably full of holes cos they're holy, like yourself Davie boy! and that one made him laugh an' all while he's walking away again and I was laughing too ages after it. And when I looked at how much he give me there was nearly three euro there. And that was all he had too, I knew that.

I was thinking about him for ages too after that. Ole Davie, like, my buddy. We went back a long way, in fairness and he's not the worst of them. He was sound-out really, like, mostly always. 'Cept when he murdered that old man in his own home, of course. And that time I got the batin' over it too! And then when he was going to stab me too in the prison that time! *That's* when I remembered what he was saying sorry for, Dirty Bastard!

I was after forgetting about all that. And now I remembered it! And the next few days then, when I'd be thinking about him, like, I'd be getting mad-out at him all the time and I'd smash a car window or something thinking of it. And one time I got caught by the cops cos I smashed a load of them on one road and that was Davie's fault too, so I chalked that one down to him too while I was adding them all up, like. And I was looking forward now to Wednesday and seeing him again, cos every time I was thinking about him since I seen him that day, I'd be getting mad-out again, what I'd do to him when I catch him, like. Imagine he tried buying me off for all that with a bit of change from his pocket. Made sure he had no notes in it too I'd say, the bollox. And I forgot about him then, 'til I met him again a few days later and he goes, before I seen him, Mickey! Where were you that Wednesday? I was waiting for you by the North Gate Bridge and you never showed up! and I forgot about being mad at him when I seen him and I goes, What time were you there? like, cos I didn't let on I wasn't there or didn't know it was Wednesday already. And he said he has been there every Wednesday since then at seven o'clock and I said, Ah that's why so, cos I'm always there at half-six, like, to be on-time, but you were never there so I had a bit of business on, like. Couldn't be waiting around, like.

And he goes, There's a meeting on now in my prayer group if you'd like to come with me? and I said, Now? I thought it was only on Wednesdays? cos I was full-sure it was Monday now, only. And he goes it's on Friday nights too sometimes, come on I'd love to introduce you to my friend Jesus. And we were walking off then and I goes, Here, did he used play on the wing for Brazil? Ahahahahaah! Jesus, like! Himself and Pelé I'd say! and Davie again was only laughing along with it, like, cos it was funny alright in fairness, even though I thought he'd kill me over it again, but he didn't.

So anyway, he brought me into this place and there was a load of people there already and Davie was smiling and blessing all his friends and they were blessing him and saying, Who's your friend, Davie? and they'd be smiling at me too and shaking my hand, like, and giving me a big hug too, one by one, an' all, saying something like Welcome Mickey, I hope you can find peace in the light of the Lord! and shit like that, like. And I'd be like, I do too, brother! cos they were all saying brother and sister like that too, like. And after a while then, I was waiting for the priest, but it was one of the fellas who I was talking with already and I never knew it. He just stands up and starts speaking all bible stuff to everybody like he knew the whole thing off by heart, cover to cover. And I knew then what he was saying was all true, too, alright straight away. Had to be, like, cos it was written in the book, The Bible, like what he had in his hands and he never had to look at it one time when he was telling it. Then someone would shout out, Amen! when they felt like it and I'd be skittin' at that. Next thing a fella across the way would stand up when the first fella'd be speaking and he'd carry on talking about the Lord and how he got on over the last few days with Jesus by his side, like he was really there standing next to him in the supermarket when he was looking at the potatoes. And I goes to Davie, Is that fella a priest too? and Davie says anyone can take the floor and tell everyone about your encounter with Jesus at any time. And then another fella starts saying how many sins he sinned and how Jesus helped him through it, but they were all only baby ones I never even knew were sins like bad language or thinking bad thoughts or smoking even too, he said! Cos he was destroying the lungs God give him! I never thought of that one.

And Davie then got up, too an' all, and says he found Jesus and lost him again and he kept going back to where he last found him and tonight, finally he found him again. And I'm thrilled-out for him and give him a clap an' all. Then he says, When I look at this man here – this friend I've known all my life, I see Jesus.

And I'm like, Me Davie!? and he carries on and tells them all about we used be breaking into people's houses together and smoking and drinking and selling and doing drugs all over. And when he's telling everyone, I'm looking around to spot the cops, cos this is like a confession and we'd be locked up again, the two of us for it an' all, I'm thinking. And I'm trying to get him to stop, but they're all cheering him on.

Then he got to the prison and they all already knew why he was in there, like, so he jumps to the bit when he met me in there and how Satan told him stab me. Before that, I always thought it was Moxie done it, but I suppose he was off his game even then, Davie like. I know what it's like with voices, in fairness, but I never had the Devil himself telling me, least he never told me he was, anyway.

That's some scary shit, the more you think of it. But Jesus raised him up, Davie goes. Raised him up, from that lowest point and now, God willing, Jesus will raise Mickey up too, cos Jesus is in him now.

And they're all screaming, AMEN BROTHER! and I'm jumping up and down and giving him a big clap an' all, cos it was the best speech I ever heard in all my life, I'd say. Pure Braveheart stuff!

310

And then someone'd be saying things like about Jesus again and they'd all stand up whenever they'd feel like it or all at the same time even and do a funny dance or shout out something like, AAAAMEEENNNN! like that and wiggle their arms around. And I broke my hole laughing a load of times and I was doing it too, but I was only messing with them, copying them doing it, like. But they were all looking at me now like I was famous and they were nodding and smiling at me and trying to do it like me then too an' all, some of them, like they thought I was Jesus or something.

And I'd say they knew too I was only messing, but they couldn't give a shit neither, an' all. They were all laughing and enjoying themselves like they thought it was funny too when I done it. Cos I'd say they never saw someone doing the things the way I'd be doing them, cos I was probably doing it the wrong way anyway, like, knowing me. But they got a laugh off it anyway, same as me. And we finished it then on a sing-song at the end and I was clapping along and we were all singing at the top of our voices to the music: Come Follow Me Through the Barleycorn – that one. And, There's No Sinner Who Sins No More, But I Try! I like that one too, like.

•

Some laugh it was there, in fairness and I went again the next time and the next time. And when I met my mam one day when I called to the house, I knocks at the door and she opened it and goes, I heard you found Christ? (cos you can't get nothing past that wan). And I goes, Peace be with you, mother, I just wanted to tell ya that I am travelling in the light of our saviour,

Lord Jesus Christ, who has saved me and I'd like to... then she slammed the door in my face.

I didn't bother going back to my Jesus friends that night. I was thinking I'd have a chat with my mother and she might come too, like, cos it was a good laugh and all the people there'd be helping you too. She'd get help there alright. But I knew straight away then she wouldn't, like.

I was after taking just one sweet to calm me down before I called to the house, see, just in case like. But now, while I was walking along, I put my hand in my pocket to take one more, but when I looked there was around ten or fifteen of them there, what I got off yer man Froggy the day before. And I looks at them then for a bit and they looked like a party, like, so I says why not, like. For a buzz, yknow? How bad?

●

Next thing I know, I'm waking up in the hospital and I feel like shit. Like my throat was exploded and I got the gawk out my eyeballs. I could barely see or talk or I couldn't lie there or get up. But when the tears (not real tears now, like, but water-tears blocking my eyes, y'know?) When the tears started clearing off my eyeballs and it was all-bright in my eyes and then it went away, the first thing I seen was Davie O'Brien and Brother Jude standing there looking at me, saying, Praise the Lord! How do you feel, brother Mickey? and I tried telling them I feel shit, but the way it went from very-bright to normal-bright in my head, like at the same time, was like Jesus appearing, I thought straight away, but I was only goo-gooing at them and spit falling out of my mouth for ages, so what I said after a while sounded like "Shit Jesus," but I didn't mean it like that at all and they were standing there trying to hear me say it and say it. Jesus! I was saying (badly like) and they were nodding and then I'd say, Shit! but I was answering their question and I'd forget and I wanted to tell them then too I saw Jesus when I opened my eyes and saw them, so I was saying them two words over and over. And my two brothers didn't know what to do. In the end, anyway, I got my two hands to go together and I held them in the air, holding onto each other and they knew then I meant it like praying, like, and they were grand then after that.

They was my brothers, every bit as much as Dylan to me alright, I'd say at the time, and probably even nearly as much as Cillian too. I'd say a bit less than Cillian and a small bit more than Dylan – but not much, like. They had a special meeting about me with all the gang when they took me out of the hospital that day. There was Davie and Jude and Brother August and John and Mary Elizabeth and Mary Sylvester and Brother Raymond and Sister Olive-Vera and Ormondo and Derek and around six or more others too. They had a talk about me and what to do, like, 'til I got better and they were all going to box-in to pay for me to stay in a hotel an' all, the lot of them like, but they asked me if I'd like that or if I'd be able to stay in the prayer room? Only, if I went out at night time, the door would slam behind me and I wouldn't be able to get back in. But I was welcome to live there a few nights if I thought I could do with it. I says yeah straight away to that one, cos if I was in a hotel I'd only fuck it up, I says. And they all laughed at that. What I meant was – well, I don't know what I meant really, but I didn't want to be around all posh people in a hotel all the time, like that, like.

They took turns calling in to visit me with breakfast in the mornings an' all, in fairness. And we were having our prayer meetings and I knew then I was off the drugs for good, like, and I told them all that too, every time. And I had a few turns telling the whole room about where I saw Jesus and it was Jude and Davie coming to save me. Not one at all, but it was _two_ Jesuses, like! And it was true too at the time, an' all, all a' that, like.

I ended up staying there a load of the time and I was the caretaker an' all in there. Sometimes there'd be a delivery in the morningtime and yer man would tell me, Sign there! (_me_ like!) And I did that an' all every time, and I'd open the package and put out all the books on the chairs for the brothers and the sisters for our next meeting. And I'd tidy-up the place too a load of times when they'd all be gone. Just me and Jude or me and Ormondo, putting stuff away, like.

And one time I was out on Patrick's Street with Ormondo and Mary Sylvester and Brother Raymond and another fella and I had a laugh, telling people about Jesus and things like that. And I'd be messing with them too, like, saying, Big Issue! sometimes, cos I'd be handing out a Jesus book, like. And when they'd stop then I'd go, naw, I'm only messing with you, I want to tell you that Jesus loves you! Ahahahahaah! See?

After that, Brother Raymond wouldn't let me talk with people no more about Jesus. I wouldn't blame him neither, in fairness like. I went door-to-door too with Jude a few times and with one of the Marys, or the other one – either one, like. I wouldn't say a word, me, only hold the books mainly. A few times people would leave the door wide open when they'd go in to get their purse or they'd invite us in for a cup of tea or something to discuss the Lord and I'd be in a bit of a shock over it. Like, they'd never know who they'd be letting in, like, but the

Lord opened doors for me anyway, put it that way. And I didn't rob nothing from no houses neither at the time, I didn't.

One time alright, we were up around Sunday's Well, myself and brother Jude, like. And we were right in front of that house where I got the stereo out of, for my mother that time, and Joan Armatrading like, before I knew it. And I walked-on past it and Jude goes, Why do you pass this house, Brother? and I told him I don't know. And Jude says we need to be open to anyone who opens their house or their heart to the Good News. Like, it wasn't cos I was in there before, cos I was in most of these houses too. But that place, I kind of wrote a note that I'd keep away from it, so I suppose that's what it was, if anything.

Knocked on the door anyway, we did. And waited a bit. Next, an old sort of fella comes out with all college-type hair and Jude starts talking with him and he's listening and looking at me and half-answering Jude, but looking at me like. I think he was anyway, all the time, 'til his dog ran out and he's all over me, the dog like, and I'm rubbing him mad and he's a lovely fella, all friendly-like. I'm great with dogs, me, always. I love them. And I goes, Oh what's your dog's name? Can I take him for a walk? and he tells me her name is Gertrude, but he doesn't say anything about a walk. And Jude is going on about Jesus and I have to chase Gertrude down the path to make sure she don't go out on the road a few times and yer man who's house it was is laughing and calling Gertrude and saying, Close the gate! and I'm laughing and calling Gertrude too. And Gertrude is running all over the shop and she runs out the gate an' all after a while, so I had to run out after her and down the road. But then she came back and I chased her back in the gate and I'm bursting laughing, cos it was a good laugh and I asks him again can I take Gertrude

315

for a walk? And he's like, We were out for a walk earlier – maybe some other time.

When we're walking away then, Jude is smiling, but he's saying, We shouldn't allow ourselves get too distracted from the Word of the Lord! with a smile on his face, like. And I goes OK so, but I didn't bother mocking him, cos he was alright, him, Jude mostly. It's Brother Raymond would be the main one giving out to me, but Jude mostly would be only smiling when he's giving out, like that. But he'd annoy ya too, like. They all would after a while cos they're like too good all the time and you'd be exhausted trying to keep up with them, y'know? Like the song goes though: But I tried!

After I was living there in the prayer room for about a week, or a few days at least, word got around to others I know that I was staying there and I had a fight a few times when I got back during the night, if I went out and left a prayer-book stuck in the door. I'd be trying to sneak in without them seeing me, like, but I seen a fella I know one night when I was walking in. And he was with two other fellas, down the road, like. And I had to shout at him so he'd know he wasn't allowed in there at night-time, only me, like.

Don't you be trying to get in here now! I goes. Then I had to wait for him to walk up the road and he's like, Hey Mickey, leave us in there, will ya? and I goes, No fuck off boy! and I'd be kicking them back off the door. I was trying to be nice, then like alright to let them know, but you couldn't be nice to some people.

Then, when they all got to know how I'd keep the door opened, I got back one night and a few of them were there saying prayers inside the prayer room, reading the books, like, cos there was no altar. And two fellas I know were having a party with a few cans an' all. Mostly, people wouldn't be bothered robbing chairs, like, cos that's all there was in the place really. A few of the books were all over the place alright that night, but there was nothing worth robbing there really, I knew that much. Anyway I got mad-out at them all and told them get out, but none of them moved and after a while a fella called Freddie give me the ucks of his can. We were talking before that, and I was telling them about this place and about Jesus, how he died for our sins and stuff, but they knew all that already and mostly they all left after that, cos one fella said this place was the work of Satan and I goes, No it's not like that at all! but he wouldn't even listen and he was shouting about pentagons and I didn't have a clue what he was on about, but he was saying I was being tricked cos they were all Devil Worshippers in this place and they were only pretending, like. And then I started thinking maybe he's telling the truth, cos he was saying a pentagon is a star inside a circle and that's how them Devil Worshippers do it. And I was thinking I seen that alright before, but I couldn't think where, like and he was telling me look out for them, cos that's how I'd know it. And I starts looking all over for them, in the books and on the walls and on the ceiling and under the chairs and stuff. I was getting all-rattled, like. That's when Freddie give me the ucks, to settle my nerves a bit, like, after yer man went away and most of them left.

Anyway, a couple of them stayed. Freddie stayed and this wan called Kelly stayed and another fella was asleep in the corner. I never even seen him til next day and he left then after Brother Raymond showed up. She was alright though, Kelly like. Funny one was, I'll tell ya in a minute, but Kelly and Jude ran away together in the end. They told me that later-on themselves.

317

They got married an' all, or something and they're living down West Cork now, last I heard.

Anyway, next day, Brother Raymond woke me up and goes, What has happened here, Brother Mickey? and I had to tell him then all about it, cos there was a bit of a mess still alright, cos I was searching the place for pentagons, but found none yet. And Kelly and Freddie and that other fella were still there, but saying nothing, like. I didn't bother telling him about the fella who said about The Devil and the pentagons, cos I didn't want to, like, but Brother Raymond was all mad-looking when I was telling him the rest. And his face was red-out too an' all. This was all about a week after I was staying there, or a few nights. Anyway, Brother Raymond went out to make a phonecall and the others left and I was clearing up things when Brother Raymond comes back in and he seemed a bit calmer at least and he goes, Mickey, we're going to have a meeting this evening, I trust you will attend.

And I told him I will, but I wasn't going to, like, 'til Davie found me later on, on his way to the meeting and he brought me along with him. I was telling him all about it and why I couldn't go, but he said, You owe it to Jesus, Mickey! That's all he'd say.

Anyway, long-story short, as they say, Brother Raymond made a speech and he said he met Jesus today and he was reintroduced to Him by our newest member. He said when he came in this morning he was raging to see our prayer room all messed up, but when he had a chance to calm down about it, he knew it was the Lord sending us a message.

We have an empty room here most of the time, he goes, Why are we not using it to help Our Lord's children?

So anyway, after that, I was put in charge of minding it at night-time and I was let leave people in who I liked and I was let leave others out who I didn't. And if some of them wanted to come to our prayer meetings, they could. And if some of them didn't, then they didn't have to neither.

Mostly people didn't bother coming at night time though, cos they knew there was nothing worth taking and most of them said it was a Devil Worshipping place only. But I still didn't find any pentagons, so I was telling them all they were all full of shit, on that one. We had a few loony ones around a few times alright, shouting and roaring about it, but I proved it to them with no pentagons. And then one fella goes, Gram not gone! and I got mad-out at him and I goes, No, they're all gone and there's no drugs around here! so I kicked him out anyway, straight away, that fella.

Kelly was staying there regular, like, and after a while she was coming to the prayer meetings too. And Freddie stayed there most of the time too, but he wouldn't go to none of the meetings. There were others too mostly. And mostly there was nothing broken or robbed out of the place and we all kept the place all tidy all the time, in fairness. I took the odd thing alright like sometimes, sweets or a drink I mean, if I had a bit of money or something, a few times alright, but Kelly'd be giving out to me and clean things up after, before the others would get there, like. Then I'd be out with Jude and the others different days, different places, like that.

What else, now? I ended up never going back to yer man with the dog, Gertrude, after. I was too windy about it, I'd say. I know, see, if I said it to one of the others, they'd only make me confess to him I took his Joan Armatrading and his stereo. He probably wouldn't be bothered about the speakers, like, cos I done him a favour there alright, but he seemed alright-enough for a posh fella, like, and I was all formed with the Lord, far's I knew, mostly by then too, see? So why be dragging things up?

Coming Home

A few things happened, then, co-together one day. First thing was, I wouldn't normally be around the prayer room daytimes, like mostly, but on this day a lot of the gang were out doing a collection in town, Patrick's Street like, and Brother Raymond told me stay at the prayer room while that's going on cos a few times he told me stay away and I met them on Patricks Street then, cos I forgot they were there and I had a bit of a laugh with them all telling everyone about Jesus and I joined in too, since I was around like. But Brother Raymond didn't want me doing it, see, so this time he said he needed me to look after the room while they were in town, just in case like.

And it's a good job he done that too, cos I was in there on my own like, doing a big jigsaw Mary Sylvester brought me, that I had to get done before they got back, when someone was pushing on it from the outside, on the front door like, shaking it like mad to get in. When I went to look then, who was there, give a guess? Tony! Tony Harrington, like! I goes, How Tony, boy! Jesus says hi, like! I got mixed up and forgot what to say, cos I got bit of a shock when I seen him. And he goes to me, your mother said if you give up all this holy shit she'll let ya come home to live for good. And he come in an' all, having a look around while he's saying it. He's laughing then when he seen my jigsaw, but there was nothing funny about it – just a Jesus one, is why I had to finish it.

I told him I'd probably stay with the brothers and the sisters, cos they were looking after me alright and they needed my help too to look after things, night times like. Then he starts mocking them all and calling them names, saying they're only fooling me and taking a vantage off me cos they're all Devil Worshippers really.

Everyone knows it! he goes. And I goes, That's not true at all cos there's no pentagons cos I looked everywhere for one! I knows all about them too, like! he hadn't a clue what I was on about though cos he's a dumb shit. Always was, but I was being nice as I could so I didn't bother telling him.

So he rang my mother anyway and I wouldn't talk with her, so he smashed my jigsaw and put her on. And she was all sad, saying she missed me mad-out all the time and would I come home to live there. And I told her no I'm alright here, like, where I was. Then she was on about Jordan SueAnne. My baby sister was back home for a bit and she missed her big brother too. And she put on Jordan SueAnne to me then too and I was talking to her for ages, asking her things and we had a great laugh, the two of us. And when my mother come back on the phone again then, she was saying if I wanted to see my sister I had to come home.

And I told her Jordan SueAnne could stay with me here, but she told me it couldn't work like that and she started screaming and roaring then too about Devil Worshippers. The whole world was on about Devil Worshipping, seemed like! And I had to explain it all, all-over again then about the pentagons, cos nobody'd believe me they're not there – anywhere like.

Then she was on about, did I know my uncle Con'd be getting out soon enough and he was asking for me all the time, but he's all crazy still and doesn't know anything about all this Jesus Devil Worshipping stuff. And we had a big fight on the phone and Tony trashed the place, best he could after that, but I still wouldn't leave with him, so he was leaving then and he goes, We have a holiday booked in four days' time, so you need to be home to mind your sister or it'll be your fault if something happens her!

But she was nearly ten, around, by now anyway, so she'd of been old enough. I told him that too and he said our mother wanted me there cos they'd be gone for two weeks and she might burn the place down and there's no insurance.

So anyway, I was thinking about all that when I was fixing the place up after he went away. And I was still thinking of it when Ormondo came to the door looking for Brother Raymond. I told him he's not back yet and then he goes he got the money in the van and could he leave it here 'til brother Raymond got back and I goes sure thing brother! So I helped him lift the collection boxes into the prayer room. There was around ten of them and there was a bit of weight in them all, in fairness.

After we got them in, we were looking at them and I goes, Are you sure you're supposed to leave them here? I goes, cos like, Ormondo was black and not from Ireland at all, like. And he didn't really know me either, what I might do, like. Not that I'd be like that no more then, like, but Ormondo didn't know anyway. And he goes yes, brother Raymond was coming to collect them. Then he left. Like that, like! And here's me straight away going off my game looking at all them boxes the whole time and thinking of Jordan SueAnne too at home, like! I was running around the room a few times to think of something else, first like, and then I checked was Brother Raymond here yet, but I seen Ormondo was after taking off already, so I ran back in and started piling all the money into one or two boxes that would be light enough to carry still, like. And I got all the notes out of them too, separate like and I got it all down to three boxes and two of them was very heavy. The other one was just heavy-only, but not very.

•

Next day anyway, morning time like probably, I'm at home and still in bed, cos I had a bit of a party the night before, like, and the doorbell rings. Then it rings again and it rings again a few more times. Then I hear my mother getting mad and going down to see who it is and I remember who it probably is, so I ducked down to the top of the stairs to look out. Sure enough it was Brother Raymond, Brother Jude and Brother Davie there, alright.

Hello Mrs. Collins, says Davie, Peace be with you, in the light of our Saviour, Lord Jesus Christ.

What the fuck you do want at this hour? my mother says to them before he barely had time to say more.

We're looking for Mickey, says Brother Davie. The other two were keeping quiet, still.

And my mother starts shouting and roaring at them, who they think they are, calling here at this time of the morning and all that stuff. Then Brother Raymond goes, We'd like a word with your son Michael! and my mother keeps giving him abuse too.

Then he goes, We have reason to believe he has money belonging to our group.

She shut up then alright. What money? she goes, How much? and Brother Jude 'splained how he was going home yesterday with Ormondo driving and he told Ormondo drop the money with Brother Raymond, but he meant to his home, but instead he dropped them to the prayer room where Mickey was. And they only found out about it this morning cos of the mix-up.

And my mother goes how much was it. And Brother Raymond goes there was possibly two thousand euro there and likely more. And I give a whistle, where I was, cos I forgot where I was and I never knew it was that much and next thing, Davie starts shouting, Mickey? It's alright Mickey, the Lord forgives you! then Jude goes, We're all brothers, Mickey! We can get through it! and Brother Raymond goes, Just give us back the money please Mickey because we need those funds! We have nothing to pay the rent on the premises this month and our insurance is a lot higher now we have overnight lodgers. And that's why we needed... but my mother stopped them shouting in case they wake up the child. She told them she'd have a word with her own son to see if he knows anything about it and she'll give them a call if she can get it. And brother Raymond says it'd be best if he could have a word with Mickey and my mother goes, Sure as Christ, if he has it, he'll hand it over to me! then she slammed the door on them when Jude was saying it was probably all a misunderstanding, and she ran up the stairs to where I was.

●

Tony trashes the whole place anyway, my room like, looking for all the collection money and my mother is giving out and giving out to me about it, saying I was paying no rent all the time I wasn't there and I owe her for that at least, like. But I still wouldn't tell them nothing. He had the mattress on the floor and the bed upside down and tossed all the mess everywhere, but he couldn't find nothing. He was checking all the floorboards and banging on all the walls an' all and I goes, Who says it's in the house anyway? and my mother goes, Check outside! cos she knew I went out there after I come back yesterday in the taxi. And I went straight up to my room, see, a few times. I was sorting the shit-money out in the garden, is what I was doing, see. Bring up the good stuff. Ten cents and up. I'd get the rest later, but I was able to take my time, going up slow a few times with my pockets full and back down then again too. So Tony ran out in the garden and I ran out too and went over to where the boxes and the shit-money was, in case he'd find it, like, but he found it then and when he did, he starts shouting at me again then until my mother come out to see and she said, Naw, it's in his room alright! so we all went back up again, see if they could find it.

Anyway, they searched all my room a load of times and in the bathroom too, next to my room, he pulled off the mirror off the wall and thrun the basket out the door, cos there was nothing in it and then he searched the whole of the upstairs, all the bedrooms and toilets and hall. And found nothing cos he's a dumb-shit, like I said.

My mother did all the things mothers'd be doing to get you to do something, but they didn't work this time and then she said she didn't want to be doing this to me, but it's for the best that she let me know. And I goes, What? What is it, mam? and she goes, Wait there now! And she went off downstairs. I tried follying her, but Tony wouldn't let me.

She told ya wait there! he goes to me. And after a good while, she come back up and hands me the prayer book what Tony brought to her the day before. I goes, Yeah, what of it? and she tells me look hard and see if I can spot anything in it. So I looks at all the pages and sees nothing, but she goes, Don't you see it there!? and she opens it on page four. And there, where she's pointing, there's a pentagon! That was one alright at the end of the sentence, written in black, up above a photo of Sister Mary Elizabeth planting something in a garden. I got a bit of a fright off it, first like, when I seen it, but then I goes, You're only codding me! You done that yourself! and she goes she did not and then she proved it.

She told Tony get his lighter and light it and hold it up close to the back of all the pages. And on the first page, inside, when he holds up his lighter, all-invisible before that, but all visible once he done it: A Pentagon! It just appeared on the sheet, all big. It was hidden all the time, behind or on top of the writing, but only my mother knew how to find it.

I blessed myself straight away and dropped the book and says, Jesus Christ, our Lord and our Saviour, help me follow the path you have chosen for me! then my mam picked up the book and opened the next page and made me look at that one when Tony held up the lighter there too. And there it was again: Another Pentagon, clear as day! And I said it again, Jesus Christ, our Lord and our Saviour, help me follow the path you have chosen for me!

On all the pages there was an invisible pentagon, same as them other ones. And she told me then, when I was still in a shock on it, Do you want to be helping those fellas keep up that

Devil Worshipping or what? and I goes No! And she goes, Or do you want to help Jesus get them to stop? and I told her, Help Jesus! I want to help Jesus stop the Devil, I do! and she goes, Of course Jesus wants your mother to help you crush those Devil worshippers! Sure that's what I'm here for, isn't it? and I goes, It is! and it was, alright like.

So I went into the bathroom that's part of my room and d'ya know the shower in there? The bottom of it, like, where you stand? It's plastic and it's on two sides. And, not at the frontside now, but around the side, after you take out the clothes basket (like Tony done, but never checked). In there, underneath, you can open it a big bit and that's where I used hide things, mostly like, inside, under the shower. I still had some stuff in there for years, but mostly it was nothing. Junk. 'Stead I just got all the one euro coins and the twos and the fifty centses and the twenties and tens and I stuffed them all in there. And when Tony got the plastic bit opened, it all spilled out like a buried treasure and I got a bit of a thrill off it, seeing it fall out like that, alright.

It took him a while, see, scooping it out, but he got fed up then when he seen it was only all coins. And the two of them gets mad again then when they seen the jars of sweets too I had in there too, cos they knew I got those with the rest of it. With the paper money, like. I spent all a' that on the sweets, last night, before that, see? There was still a good bit left, like, but they took all the twos and the ones and wouldn't be bothered with the fifties-down, see. She goes, Tax! (my mother, like), but she was only smiling-mad when she says it. I'd say she thought it was a good hiding-spot alright.

Kinsale Pub-Crawl

Cillian was finished college an' all by now and got a good job too an' all out of it. Guess what doing? Social working for young fellas, like mostly! He's fully qualified helping drug addicts and winos get off the drugs and the drink and not be doing the wrong thing all the time. If that's not funny, I don't know what is. So I calls him on the telephone when our mother and Tony was gone on their holidays, see if he wanted to stay at home for a while, like. And he did too. It was me and Cillian and Jordan SueAnne and Melanie living there a few days on our own, together. But Tara wouldn't be bothered coming. She was busy with her job too, like. Melanie had a job an' all by this time too. I won't say where she's working, in case she gets in trouble for it, cos she's still working there like and we got a load of stuff out of that place for years and years. Jocks and socks 'specially. But it's a funny one too that she's working there now an' all when you think of it. Cillian brought us all a big feast from the chipper the first night we were all at home and I told him tell us about the first time when Con brought us in there and he loaded all the things into the pram on top of Melanie. Cillian goes it wasn't Melanie at all, it was Tara, but he was wrong there, it was Melanie alright. We were all knotted-laughing though at that one and Melanie too, but she was all embarrassed then thinking of it and it's where she's working now, but she never even gets nothing out of the place now either. I won't say what shop it is. Rhymes with Benneys though.

He told me we can't be having no drink or drugs in the house while we're all staying there, Cillian like. And I told him he's as bad as my Jesus buddies, but I was only teasing him, like. By then I didn't know what to think of them. I know they were all Devil Worshippers really, like alright, but I was thinking maybe they didn't even know about them pentagons neither, most of them. I told Cillian all about it and he said my mother tricked me somehow on it, he'd say. And I'd say she did too, thinking of it, like.

Later on anyway I went down by the prayer-room for a look, show them there's no hard feelings, like. But the place was shut. I went back again then Wednesday (next night after that, like) and it still wasn't opened then either, even though that's the night for all the meetings. I never met all the gang again. I met Davie alright one other time around a year or two later, just before I got locked up last time. I'll tell ya about that one now in a minute.

But anyway, we weren't drinking or anything else in the house when we were staying there together, but Melanie alright got odd on the second night or the night after, like, and said she's going to the pub. (She was around twenty, or nearly, by then anyway, imagine, so she was well-old enough to do what she wants.) The rest of us played cards a bit and I still had the shit money, most of it, by then, so we played for that. Then we were watching movies or whatever. Telling stories and shit about old days and our mother and stuff. Some laugh!

Anyway, day three or more, who walks in the door when we're all there in the kitchen, 'cept Con. Remember him? Our uncle, like. I never even knew he was coming out and neither did Cillian or any of us. And my mother was after telling me all the time he's loony-out like a balm-pot and doesn't even know his own name. But here he is walking in on top of us in his own house and, sure as shit stinks, he knows us all straight away, cos he's laughing-mad to see us.

AHHH HA HAHAA! he goes, All the clan! (*He forgot about Tara, I'd say*), 'Tis great to see ye, although not one of ye'd come see ye're own uncle in the hospital.

Hospital? Jordan SueAnne goes straight away too, I thought you were in prison!

Prison!? Con goes… and we had to pretend he wasn't in prison then all the time, like none of us knew. And when Melanie asked him what was he in the hospital for so, he goes the bastards tried to take him down with a tazer and they switched off every cell in his body. He was in a coma for the past three and a half year and only woke up last week. Imagine that? and I swear I believed him too, looking at him and listening to him, cos you'd believe anything he'd say. But when I asked Cillian later-on if he was in hospital or prison, Cillian set me straight. It was definitely prison alright. And I asked him was he in a coma? And Cillian goes no, but he might have been in the hospital a while for going nuts or something like that.

And Con was delighted to see Cillian too an' all, cos he hardly ever seen him now cos our mother can't stand him by then, Cillian like. And Con tells me then run down to the off-licence, get a slab. And I'm going an' all, 'til Cillian tells him there's no off-licence 'round here. So Con has a quick chat before he goes off in the car by himself. Tony's car, like, cos they left that there when they went to the airport. Con's van was after been taken away. He said he'd be back straight away and we'd have a party. And soon as he's gone, I'm jumping up and down for a party, but dryballs-Cillian goes he can't stick around for no party and I got odd with him then and gave out to him for trying to leave. Then Cillian goes alright so we'll have a bet. He'll wait one hour, he goes, but if Con isn't back til then he's leaving. So I goes alright so, cos Con was coming back straight away, but in the end Con didn't come back 'til next day, so Cillian won that one alright.

He took Melanie home too in a taxi, Cillian like, to where she had her own house out in Bishopstown. She was living with an old wan called Joan for years, but Joan got the cancer around a year or two before that and died of it, so Melanie has her own place now with a lodger an' all paying her rent, but I was never there. Our mother isn't even supposed to know where Melanie's house is, but she knows alright. She got me to follow her home one time, but I lost her when she got off the bus and I was upstairs looking out the window when I seen her strolling away toward Wilton. By the time I told my mam about it she already knew where the house was, though. She knows everything, our mother.

My sister, Jordan SueAnne's other family wasn't around for another few days more, so she had to stick around, but there'd be nothing happen her meantime anyway. Our mother wasn't coming back for ages yet, but she was grand there anyway with her real family and her own big brother at least to look after her. (Me, like). And Con'd be around too now.

•

Anytime I said anything about our mother to Con over the next few days, when we'd be talking, like, he'd be kind of snapping only, like a bark, like he was a dog snarling-mad the whole time. I'd say he'd of laced-into her if she was there. He was odd with her over something alright, but he wouldn't tell me nothing about it, whatever it was.

Then one day, a few days after all that, Jordan SueAnne says to Con would ya pick up our mother at the airport at seven o'clock tonight cos the flight is coming in. She was after ringing Jordan SueAnne about it, see, our mother. And I thought Con would hit the roof and smash a window or something, cos it was the only thing to get him mad the last few days – talking about our mother, like. But instead he just goes, What time is it now? and my sister goes, It's just gone half past one.

So he goes he might as well head up along to the airport and have a pint in the bar while he's waiting. He always liked a pint in the bar at the airport, Con did. And he never got thrun out of there neither.

And I went with him too, in case I could talk him out of doing anything, just in case, and so he'd have a bit of company too along the way. Con was always good for pints too. He'd keep buying me them anyway no bother. Before, long 'go like, he'd get something off you, do a job or whatever, to make up for the free gatt, but by now he'd just buy the drink if you were there with him and not bother with anything else.

So we had a few pints up there. Two I'd say at the most, but it wasn't the right bar cos there was a new airport out there now an' all since last time we was there. Wasn't as good as it used be and the price was cat-out too, so Con goes come on we go 'way somewhere else and we'll come back at half seven for them other two. He knew a good place in Ballinhassig, see, so we went to there for a pint and the barman was a young fella and there was no bother, but the owner knew Con and didn't like him for no reason, so when I went back up to call next, the young fella goes, Sorry ye had enough now.

And I got mad-out at him, telling him our rights and all that, but Con only looks over at the owner who come in, down the end of the counter and nods at him and tells me come on.

We drove down then all the way to Kingsale. It was years since I was down that way and it was a grand spot an' all, down by the sea. I remembered I was there one time with my mam and Stacey and Cillian and probably Tara and we spent the day there, jumping off the pier into the water, but they wouldn't let the three of us into the pub after, where my mam and Stacey were, cos we were soaking wet. And they had to find another pub cos the manager told them they had to leave with us, even though my mother told him we didn't even want a drink (the kids like). I don't remember what happened next, that time, but I just remembered all 'a that when I got to Kingsale with Con and seen the pier an' all for the first time, must be in at least twenty year, I'd say.

We only stayed for one in any bar that day, mostly. Bit of a crawl, like. I was saying to Con a few times, about my mother, like, I goes, You won't be fighting with your sister now when you see her will ya, Con? and first time I said it, he was mad still at her, but next time he wasn't as mad and later on again then, when I said it, he was nearly crying, saying my mother was some piece of work and I goes, YEAH THAT'S WHAT I SAY TOO! and she was too. Is, like. You got to give her that much. Then he goes, But she's my sister and of course I'm only here to look after all 'a ye! and he starts getting nearly tears again and I never seen him all nearly so sad before. Not Con. 'Least he wasn't mad at her no more then, though.

Then I goes, What time is it anyway? and we found out off the barman it was nearly twelve o'clock and closing time and we knew then we must of missed the other two at the airport, but

334

Con said they're probably up in the bar waiting for us, so we'd better see if we can find them.

All the rest is kind of only like a tunnel, but by the time we got back to the car I was langers. Must've been before that too, I say, but I only remember dark, like, with a bit of light in the middle where Con was driving and talking with me. And I think I fell asleep a bit. Then I woke up with Con screaming in my ear to hold the wheel. I goes, What? and he goes, Hold the wheel there will ya? There's two bends coming up and you need to steer when I hop out.

And I only laughs, but I'm still waking up and getting ready to lock-onto the wheel. Con turned the first corner anyway, going fierce fast, then back around the next corner and he opens the door and throws himself out in the middle of it. It was only then I seen the blue flashing lights behind and the noise off the siren and here's me holding onto the steering wheel from the passenger seat. And I wouldn't mind, but I can't even drive! Well, I could if I wanted, like, but anytime I'd be in a car, someone else always wanted a go, like, so I'd leave them off.

The next bit of road was straight and the car was slowing down, but didn't stop for ages til I steered it up onto the ditch, by accident, like, and it kept going upside-down and I was lying on the roof inside the car when the shades come along, pulling me out like it wasn't even their fault. Who was driving the vehicle? one of them was shouting at me, but I couldn't even think where I am or what happened. I told them nothing anyway, of course. That was one of the things they hung on me too around a year later when I was back in court an' all.

But anyway, I was in the hospital for a bit and had a kip in the Bridewell after and then I had to go through all the questions for ages 'til they left me go. And the sergeant at the front door goes, Is there anyone you want to call to pick you up, Mickey? and I tells him I'll chance my mother, cos my pants leg was torn and I was missing a shoe and I had a bit of a bandage 'round my head, but I was feeling grand, like.

My mother anyway answered after ages, when the guard rang her and passed me the phone. She goes, Yeah who's this? and I tells her it's me, Mickey. And she starts screaming in my ear then for waking her and they only got in last night and had to get a lift back themselves from the airport and no sign of me or Con, who was supposed to be picking them up. And I goes, Can ya shut-up there a minute. I need a lift home, like. I'm in the Bridewell, and she goes, And what do you want me to pick you up in? A suitcase? Where's Tony's car?

I forgot about that one, like, but said nothing. Then she was ranting on and on, saying that's where I belong too, in the Bridewell. And her dozy, dumb brother, an' all, for not picking her up. And she hopes there's nothing wrong with the car, whatever was done with it. On and on she was shouting in my ear. And then she hung up.

The sergeant was looking at me when I put the phone down and I tells him I'll wait for her outside, she'll be along in a while. I went out then anyway and walked a bit, but another guard I didn't see in ages comes out the door and calls me and he goes, Come on Mickey, I'll give you a lift.

And it was Garda Mick, who I knew a good few year ago. And we had a grand chat on the way home, catching up. I thought he was gone from Cork, I was telling him, cos I didn't see him for ages. And he says naw he was only posted out to

Macroom for a bit, but he prefers the city. He says, They're fierce clicky out the country.

And I thought of that fella, Brendan then, who I was in juvenile prison with, like that time a good few year ago, when he said that, cos he used always say click and clicky, like that, after everything. And I knew what he meant then. They'd be talking funny in some places. Sure who'd want to be out of Cork, like anyway?

•

At home then, my mam and Tony was shouting and roaring at me the whole time. The shades were onto Tony in the meantime, she goes, wondering who was driving the car that I was caught driving and to get it towed away. And my mother got him to say the car was robbed while they were on their holidays and they probably kidnapped her only son too (cos she don't count Cillian no more). And straight away when she says that, I goes, WHY DIDN'T I THINK OF THAT ONE? and she goes, Cos you're a dumb shit is why!

She's always bang-on-the-button, my mam. You got to give her that much. Not that she's right, like, cos I'm not dumb and I'm not a shit, so there's that. But she'd be right no matter what she says, in fairness.

And next day then, around ten in the morning, my mother got a call that Con is down the early-morning pub, Donkeys Ears or one of them ones, cos she put out the word she was looking for him and the three of us went down – her, me and Tony, like, see what's happening. I was only going so I'd see what she'd do, like, and what Con'd do then too. We got a taxi down and he was in there alright, Con. And he got a shock when he seen my mam.

What'd you do to his car? she goes to her brother, pointing at Tony. Con let-on nothing and goes he don't know nothing about it and then my mother laced-into him, calling him all the names and saying he nearly killed her son when he jumped out of the car. And Con took it all off her. Long 'go he'd of never done that. He only said there was no way he'd go back to prison. Not after only getting out. She was shouting and roaring at him over-right everyone, giving him all kinds of abuse and she didn't care who'd hear it neither. In fairness though, most of them ran away over the other side of the bar or out the door by now. And all the while Con was like someone who got smaller and smaller the more she gave out to him. And by the end, I'd say he was smaller than the pint glass he was hiding behind. She told him, in future if he was planning on coming into her house, he'd have to come in quietly through the backdoor and keep out of her way.

After that, another way too she got him to stay in his own room over by the backdoor, is she got photos done of all the photos they took when Con was off his game that time. There was around five of them, or six, including the one I'm in too where the two of us is fallen on the ground. And including the one where my mother is there holding Con's hand, leading him. She got them all printed with frames, big as she could and hung them on all the walls downstairs, so he'd see them and anyone who come in to the house would see them too. They were all after seeing them anyway, anyone who'd call, cos we were all already after getting a good laugh off them, everyone, so it was all the one. But a bit of a laugh at least.

338

And after that, Con barely said no more to no one. If my mother'd tell him, Drive over there and bate that fella up, he might drive over there, but he'd come back next day, after forgetting to bate him up. Or if he was with her, he'd barely thump someone (I heard off other fellas). Con was off the boil alright and we all knew it too. After a while, my mother even stopped getting him to do nothing and he just stayed at home or the pub sometimes. They even left him back into a load of the pubs he was barred out of for years.

The saddest thing, one day though, was when I seen Con sitting down in the front room watching telly and Tony comes in and goes to him, I'm sitting there, come on get up! and straight away Con got up and went off to his room. I tell ya, my jaw could of hit off the floor when I seen it. Con like! He'd take that off Tony Harrington! And for *what*, like? When he was going too, he had half a can of Carling in his hand and I goes, Can I have that, Con, if you're not finishing it, like? and he give it to me then an' all. Nice one! Ahahahahaah!

The Lord Has Ways And Means

You could say I was back inside soon after that, more or less. Locked up, like, for no reason. There was a few small things, alright like come up, like what I was talking about before, with the car Con jumped out of and a few things here and there, like. Nothing major. And the cops sent a case to the Deep Heapy too about the money that was gone from the prayer group. My mother told me that the group weren't going to say nothing about it, like, but they got sued then and they were passing the blame on after that. *Why are they always passing things like that onto me?* is what I want to know. I suppose they're thinking someone's got to pay for it. Might as well be Mickey. But that wasn't even the reason I was locked-up, cos they were all pending, as they say, and wasn't even up yet proper.

Talking about the group though, before being inside, alright, I met Davie O'Brien one day. This was around a year or six months at least anyway, after I last seen him before that. He was off his tree, you ask me. I was on Oliver Plunkett Street, I think it was, around one of them ones by the Market there, like, when he was walking along. I had a blanket 'round me and was lying in the door of this place. I was inside a cardboard box too, like. That's even better than a blanket when you're outside, but I had a blanket too anyway, cos it was getting a bit cold, alright, and I was out of the house. My mother was driving me mental. She went pure nuts around then, ask anyone. First she got Con afraid of her, then she got madder and madder. I'd say all of Cork was afraid of her and what she'd do by that time. I was fast-asleep on the floor in the front room one night when she come in and my hand was out and she stuck her high heel into it, in my hand like. I'm not saying it now to be getting her into trouble or anything like that! That kind of thing is alright, like. But she'd do it for a laugh usually, but now this time she meant it like. I woke up screaming and she starts shouting louder at me for making a mess and look at me sleeping on the floor and what am I doing there? And I told her she cut my hand, cos she got me good with the corner of the pointy-bit, but she's not even listening to that. Only shouting. That's one thing, but there'd be more and more things like that the whole time, all the time, like, more than before.

Still, she was only like that cos she had no decent help, I'd say. I knew that more after a while. Thinking about it, lately like, I'd say Cillian would be best at helping her, alright, but he wouldn't be helping her. She'd kill him for different reasons than she'd kill us. Still you'd only want to be helping her, like, but no matter what, she'd give out cos you'd make a mess of it. She'd be killing Tony even an' all, all the time. I'd say I even felt sorry for him, a bit, sometimes too, cos he never done it right either. Anything, like. Might be making tea or how to do a job or where to get the best things all the time, my mother knew it the best and we all knew that was true. But no one else did, was the main problem. She just needed a bit of help off us. Off me like. A bit! To do it her way and it'd all be all grand then.

But none of us could do it her way, the right way like, cos I suppose she was right about that one too – we're all dumb shits, there's no denying. If I was any good at something I'd still be a plumber now, I'd say. Or working on the skips, probably. I'll tell ya about that one in a minute.

Anyway, there was no reason, particularly, that time I was out of the house, only I couldn't stick it there no more. For a bit anyway. I had to get away before she kill me or do my head in at least. All small things all the time, all the time. I just didn't bother going home for one night. And then it was one night and one night. And after a while I had a tent to myself up the Mardyke, but the other people in tents up there got odd with me cos I had a party there one night and there was one fella there who jumped into the river and got drowned. It was an accident, like, but caused a bit of trouble with the neighbours and with the cops too. I didn't even know his name or where he's from. I didn't know him before that, like, but he come along when I was sitting outside my tent with two other fellas and we had a few cans that night and someone had a few sweets and we were all sharing, like. And this fella goes, Gis' one of them will ya? and someone give him one and he went off his tree after that, starting to jump all over the place and dancing on the fire and everything. And we were all like, calm down there boy will ya? But then he got a shock when he saw his shoe was on fire and he thrun himself in the river and starts screaming he can't swim. And the rest of us are like, Is he for real or what, that fella? but he was for real alright. One fella from the tent next door starts running down along the river after him, but the rest of us didn't have a clue what to do. Couldn't swim, like, none of us. We found out later-on that he drowned after. Cops come 'round next day asking questions and everything and the whole place got busted-up cos of it. That was the end of my tent.

Anyway I was under the blanket in this doorway when Davie walks past without even seeing me and I'd say he wasn't seeing anything at the time. I looks up and shouts, How Davie boy! before I thought about if I'd be in trouble for it. He stops and turns back towards me and looks down then to where I was, with a kind of a dopey smile on his face, before he says anything. (I mean his smile made him look dopey. Just, it seemed like a weird kind-of-mad smile.)

Peace be with you brother, he goes, Hasn't the Lord given us a glorious evening? and I goes, I think it's a bit cold myself, that's why I have this blanket, y'know? Ahahahahaah!

He only smiles and says it's a beautiful blanket and the Lord is so good to provide it. I told him it wasn't the Lord at all, a fella from Simon was around earlier and tried to get me to stay down there, down the quay like, for the night, but I wouldn't be bothered, so he give me the blanket. And Davie says, The Lord has ways and means. Whatever that means.

And he stands there, only smiling then, for a while and he's a bit even more freaky than before. I goes, How ya doing yourself anyway Davie? Getting on alright?

I didn't want to be talking about the prayer group or any of them, like, but he wasn't saying nothing and I wasn't even sure he knew who I was, like, so I had to get him going. He goes, Oh I feel so blissful and at peace, thank you for asking. I am at one with everything.

You're at one with everything? I goes, Are you at one with me, like, or with my blanket? and he goes he's at one with me, my blanket and with everything everywhere cos we have all been made by the same glorious Being and to Him we are all one and we are all His glorious creation.

There is not a thing *He* doesn't know nor doesn't wish to happen! he says. And I goes, So do God want me here in this doorway so, under the blanket and the cardboard? and Davie says, God has a plan for us all. It is not for us to question the Lord. I have no doubt that the Lord would stop a falling aeroplane from hitting the ground, if it was not His wish that every one of those passengers join him at his Home that evening. And in the same way, I have no doubt, if I walked off a cliff and if it was not the Lord's wish for me to join Him at that time, I would keep walking into thin air and never fall. Because the Lord has made everything and we are all a part of that everything. And everything is there for a reason, whether it's to pull us up or knock us down.

So you'd be flying so? I goes to him, did he think he could walk off a cliff and nothing would happen 'cept he'd be flying in the air?

If it was the Lord's wish for me to fly, he says, There is no doubt I would fly.

Go on so! I tells him, Fly so! Go on! but he says it's not for us to tempt the Lord to show his powers and he even says some stuff like it's from the Bible word-for-word and everything. He didn't used to know all the quotes like that, but now he did. That one at least. And I left him off then cos I couldn't take any more of it and I needed a kip, like. Some fellas'd piss on you while you're sleeping in a doorway, some just give you shit. So he walks away then after a while. That was Davie anyway, last time I seen him.

I was at his funeral I'd say a week later. Two at the most. Cillian told me he died, so I went along, like, when he picked me up. Show a respect. And people there was saying how nutty he was after getting alright, Davie like. And Timmy McGrath's cousin, Lloyd, was related to Davie. I think it was Lloyd's sister was married to Davie's sister's brother-in-law or something like that. But he met Davie one day, after that (after I met him, like), down by Shandon, Lloyd was saying, before Cillian brought two of us a pint at the funeral. And Davie was after been up to Shandon an' all just before he met Lloyd and says the same thing to him about if he stepped out in the air he'd keep walking and not fall at all. But by that time, they were after putting a big cage around the outside on the tower up in Shandon, so Davie probably thought the Lord put it there to stop him.

In fairness, you wouldn't think he'd do it really, but he hitched it down to Kingsale one day, after that and went for a walk all around the place. And he got to the big cliffs down at the Old Head of Kingsale and thrun himself off. Looks like the Lord didn't want him flying. That day anyway, Ahahaah. I'd say I'll miss him alright, like, Davie. In fairness.

And you know who else I met at Davie's funeral? Kelly was there. Sister Kelly, like. She was alright, Kelly. She give me a big wave and come over all smiling and then sad about Davie. And then, when we were talking, she calls over another fella with long hair, who I didn't know first, but who was he, only Jude. Brother Jude, like, with long hair! Before, it was all-tight and nearly bald mostly. Now it was all long and nearly bald a bit too.

First he's looking at me all-serious, like it was my fault the prayer group got busted-up, but Kelly's telling me how they moved down to Clonakilty together, down West Cork, to Jude's mam and dad's place. And they're growing vegetables and shit down there and "living off the land," like. And next year they're going to be selling in farmers' markets and stuff an' all. And

Kelly goes then, And it's all thanks to you Mickey! and I got a shock off that then and goes, ME!?

She says, Yeah, if you hadn't taken the collection money we'd have never made the move! and I didn't know if I was supposed to admit it or say no problem or tell them it wasn't me, but that's the one time ever someone said it was my fault and it was good news anyway, tell ya that much, Ahahahahaah! Next thing, Jude kind of smiles and goes, The Lord has ways and means, I suppose.

And I got another shock when I heard that and goes, That's exactly what Davie told me too, last time I seen him! and we were all in a shock after that one, so that's proof right there, if anyone needed it, like.

•

Inside then, – well, I better say why I got in, first. That was nothing too, an' all. Just stuff, like. They picked me up a good few times, cos I was on the streets. Like that time when the fella jumped in the river. It wasn't my fault at all, like, but no one listens to me. But that one went on a while before they left me alone over it. Then they found a few sweets on me a few other times. And just a small bit of hash, only, too. More trouble. They'd leave ya off soon enough with it, but they'd add it all up alright. It's all added up, see. Then I was down at the Atlantic Pond one day and they said I was shouting and roaring, but I wasn't shouting and roaring at all down there. That was just the posh wans walking their buggies thought I was upsetting the ducks. Of course the shades'd take their word for it 'stead of me like, every time. Guaranteed a' that.

It was a few days after the funeral, that was. Davie's like. About a week later, I'd say. I met an old fella I knew called Mr. Lynch and I was telling him about Davie, cos he never knew it. I goes, D'y'know Davie O'Brien and what happened him? and he was going like he never even knew him, but he knew him alright. And then after I told him, he gave me a few sups from his bottle. Port, like. I don't be drinking at all during the day, mostly like, me. 'Specially something like that or like shorts, like. You couldn't be wide-enough later-on then when the lights go down, y'know? And you'd need to stay doggie-wide on the streets, too like, I tell ya that much. But this was just once. One time, like. And after a while, we were chatting mad and next thing, he's picking a fight on me, Mr. Lynch like, and I had to run away on him and I was down by the Pond before I knew I never give him back his bottle and it was all gone anyway. Then someone calls the cops.

And that's all it took, really. The judge said I couldn't be trusted on the streets. Me, like! Nothing 'bout Davie dying. And nothing about the langers who'd be staggering home from their discos and who'd set the cardboard on fire for a laugh, if you'd be sleeping in it. Nothing about the fellas who'd be opening their shop next morning and who'd throw a bucket of bleach or something on top of you if you were still sleeping there, like. Nothing about fellas who'd beat you up or stamp on you or piss on you when you're lying there. Nothing about people who wouldn't even look at you, cos now you're not even a real person no more and everyone knows it. Me too, like. I know it too, y'know? And if you'd say something to someone, like, or look at them only, even if you meant it nice they'd run away, cos they think you'd only want to be robbing them, like. And after that you'd forget if there's a nice way to say hello or a good way to smile even, cos you'd have no smile and no hello. Only screaming, cos the screaming in your head'd be louder than anything and you'd want it to shut up, but it wouldn't, most of the time. And I was locked up then in Cork prison on remand for six weeks.

And that's when things started going downhill then. After that.

The Bomb Squad

I shared a cell in Cork Prison, when I went in first, with two and a half of the stinkiest prisoners in the place and that's no lie. I wouldn't say smelliest and that's why I say stink. Some people'd be smelly without breaking wind all the time or anything else. These ones weren't smelly, I say, mostly in fairness, but their farts had some stink off them and their shits too (sorry now) were like stink bombs. I'm not joking, I thought I'd wake up dead most days from being gassed, like. It just wasn't – there's no way you could breathe in there, mostly like.

Frank Frank was one of them. His first name was Frank and his second name was Frank too. He was nearly twice the size of me, I'd say. Felt like it anyway when you'd be standing next to him. In tallness I mean, he was very tall. You'd get a sore neck looking up. He was inside, cos he owed money to the bank. I asked him how much and he told me, Less than three grand! like it wasn't much. When I told him I might get time too for taking around that much, he said the difference is I done it deliberate, like, but he only done it cos he didn't have enough to pay it back. I suppose that's true alright.

A fella called Bunny was the next one. Where he got a name like Bunny is beyond me, but that's his name anyway and no one even mocked him over it cos you'd get no joy out of it. He'd only sit there like you were telling him the weather. He was fat, Bunny. Frank Frank wasn't fat at all. Bunny was. He was inside cos his wife got married to someone else and he broke in a few times, to her house, like, to live there, even though her new husband was there an' all. He was alright like, Bunny, but not all there if you ask me. I'd say his wife and her new husband didn't have to even see him in the house, though, to know he was there. He'd be talking away and next you'd get a stale, burn kind of smell and it'd be there ten minutes at least and you'd go green from it and just when it's clearing, Frank Frank would let a ripper and that one'd be even worse. Frank Frank's were like choking most of the time – like someone was squeezing your neck. I swear to God I was banging on that cell door a load of times to let me out so I could breathe, but no one answered and I'd always stop cos I wouldn't be strong enough to carry on cos the air was so bad I'd nearly faint. I'm sure I did faint too, even in there, I'd say, cos who'd know the difference? We were locked up there most of the day every day and it was like a torture. Your eyes would water-up from the smell and that's no word of a lie.

Then there was Badger. He was from up the country someplace and I don't even know what he was in for, but probably nothing, like myself. He wasn't as bad as them other two, in fairness, but one time he stunk the place up the longest and the worst. For that reason, I give him a half, Badger. The other two were puky stinky a lot, so they're both one each, but Badger had the one most smelly "other thing" just one time and that was enough to get him a half anyway at least. I mean it stayed in the air for days, that one, cos he made a mess of the bomb he made off it.

All the three of them made massive bombs most days, all the time, like. See, we had to slop-out our own buckets. Piss and shit. We all had our own to empty all the time and we had to keep them in our cell 'til we could, like. But you couldn't be in the same room as one of them stinky shites all the time –

'specially on top of them farts too – and 'specially even the stink of piss was bad enough too on its own, even. And you'd have to eat your food inside the cell an' all too, remember!

So if there was a smelly lump, there was only one thing to do – make a bomb of it: You'd wrap it up in paper, newspaper like, and fuck it out the hole in the wall. The vent, like. And you'd hear it land down below in the yard then after, mostly, like a bomb. That was the only way to get a bit of fresh air after that. But what happened with Badger's bomb, that one time, was he didn't have enough paper and it was all a big soggy one and when he swung it out the vent, it burst open in the vent – inside the vent itself, like. And it stuck there for days and probably weeks and no one could do nothing about it. All that, now, on top of the smell from them others, remember like!

Sure, who could take that? Bad enough being in prison, locked-up all the time like, but even if you blocked your nose, your mouth would smell it and your eyeballs too even could smell it an' all, I'd say.

After about a week, when Badger's shit was after been in the vent for around two days, I got a brainwave. I applied for a new job in there and got it too – Bomb Squad! I couldn't take it anymore, like, any longer. And I knew I'd get a better cell downstairs if I got the job. So that's what I done. I thought, *least I'd be outdoors when I'd be smelling it, at least, like.*

It was the Bomb Squad's job to clean up all the bombs in the yard, see? No one could go out for exercise or anything 'til the Bomb Squad cleared all the bombs. It was a bit of a laugh, in fairness, sometimes, but a bit worse than that too though. We'd get a donkey jacket and a wheelbarrow each and there'd be gloves and a mask and a helmet an' all, if you wanted it and I knew most of the other lads in the Bomb Squad from around the streets. They were alright an' all. A bit crazy like, most of them, you ask me, but alright to talk to like. You'd get no shit in the Bomb Squad. 'Cept off the bombs, like, Ahahahahaah!

My cell downstairs only had one other person in it. Terry Something. He never said his second name or I never asked him. I know him too from around, like. Terry's sound-out. He speaks all soft like a priest or a doctor, 'cept he looks like a wino cos that's what he is too, mostly, outside. But he's very neat all the time. He'd only get odd with me if I didn't make my bed properly in the morning. Everything else, all the tidying and shit, he'd do himself whether he made the mess or if it was me, like. Mostly it'd be me alright, in fairness, but if I got a few crumbs on the floor or on my bed, Terry'd be over straight away brushing it and putting it away in one place til he could clean it out of the cell, like.

Anyway, one day the two of us were outside in the yard clearing the bombs with our big shovels, me and Terry like. And another fella had a hose. He had a mask and helmet too, that other fella, but me and Terry got none. Next, we heard <bomb!>, cos someone just dropped a bomb from one of the vents above. They'd do that, like, try to hit ya if you were in the bomb squad, but it was at least ten foot away I'd say from the two of us. And I looked up to where it come from and goes, Ahahahahaah! You missed! and while I was looking, I seen this big package come right down all the way and landed straight on top of Terry's head! It 'sploded all over. Like, Terry has massive mad hair on him and it got all in his hair and the newspaper was around his neck and burst open. And I only found out after that, that it hit me too, the bomb like, cos I was in a shock looking at Terry. And it was too funny to even laugh, I tell ya that much. I laughed later-on alright, that night like or maybe a few days later, but at the time I was definitely in shock, I'd say. I cried later on a bit alright, but after that, I laughed too. You'd have to laugh, sure, sometime. Terry just stood there at the time without turning around. He was in a shock too an' all I'd say. And I was too. Next thing, the other fella with the hose just hosed Terry all down and hosed me down too then when he told me I'm covered in shit an' all too. And I remembered that time, when he was doing it like, when I ran across the field in all the mud to escape Mr. Mulcahy's house, like, and I had my dinner in McDonalds and my mam hosed me down after that, out on the road, like. I just stood there now and pretended I had a sweet in my mouth, like what Stacey gimme that day when I was getting hosed, before she ratted on my mother. And there was all whistling and laughing and singing and screaming and roaring coming from all the windows in the whole place when we were standing there and getting undressed then when he was still hosing. And then we ran inside. We left our dirty clothes out there in the yard. We didn't give a shit about them. After that, though, we wore our helmets and our masks too.

I think it was two days after that when I had a visitor. My mother like. I'd say I was in there a few weeks before she came to see me, even though I'm in the same city. She had her own troubles too at the time, see, and I wasn't even there to help, cos I couldn't be.

She was sitting there anyway, waiting for me when I come in, all big red eyes on her. I didn't even have the chance to sit down and she starts screaming at me, WHAT'S THIS I HEAR ABOUT YOU IN THE FUCKING BOMB SQUAD? IS THAT

TRUE? DID YOU SIGN UP FOR THE BOMB SQUAD? WHAT KIND OF... I ALWAYS KNEW YOU WERE RETARDED, BUT I'D NEVER THINK EVEN YOU WERE STUPID ENOUGH TO SIGN UP FOR THAT!

And the screws are getting her to shut up all the time, cos she's shouting too loud and then they start taking the two of us out and she calms down then enough to let them leave us there. But she's still mad at me, only she's giving out quieter now.

What kind of show are you making of me at all? she's going. How *dare* you do that to me! Your own mother! and I'm like, What did I do to you, so? Why can't I do it, like, if I wanted? and she's like fuming so much I thought her head would blow up. Anyway, there was a load of that/ load of that/ load of that. On and on. And finally I agreed I'd quit straight away and she was going complaining too to the warden and to everyone. And how dare they do that to her own son who has special needs. And there she was, going on about that again like it's something real, like, and I had to get odd with her then 'til she'd drop it, like.

After the two of us calmed down enough she told me after ages that Con got the two of them locked out of the house. Her and Tony, like. They went away for a few days, a couple of weeks ago and when they got back, the locks were changed in the house and there was a note on the front door saying they weren't allowed in anymore, cos the council stopped paying her rent and Con got a barring-order against her. *Con*, like! And I got a bit of a thrill off that an' all, when I heard it like, cos in fairness I thought Con'd never do nothing to her again. But his solicitor was always like a buddy of his and I'd say he got him to do it too. And I was – what would ya call it? *Proud*, I'd say. I was proud of my uncle for standing up to her and locking her out. But I couldn't tell her that, cos she was raging about it. Her own brother in there, like, watching the telly and he wouldn't let them into their own house!

And I goes, Where're ye sleeping now so? and y'know where they went to? They got a tent after a few days and brought it up the Mardyke, she tells me, but they were after been moved on from there now. So my own mam was on the streets an' all now, imagine! And she was mad-raging about it and only came up to tell me about it when she heard I joined the bomb squad. She said she thought she sunk as low as she could go, til she heard what I was after doing to her.

I'd say if I was out, Con might've listened to me about it and let them in, but I wasn't, like. That would've solved it all and nothing would've happened after, like. But they had me locked up in this place and I wasn't due to get out for another three weeks I'd say. Or something like that. What could *I* do, like?

Con Is Dead

I gave up the Bomb Squad after that alright. Had to, like. No choice. But they left me stay in the same cell with Terry, cos I got another job straight away. On the bins, this time. It was my job to go around with the wheelie bin and fill it up from all the bins around the place, every day, and dump it then in the big skip outside. One day I say I'll get a job doing that for good. I'll be working on the skip lorry then, on the outside, like cos of my experience, going 'round door-to-door and that'll be my job. I'll get a mortgage too around that time an' all and I'll be set. Retired, like. That's the plan anyway. See what happens, like.

So next few days I was going around collecting the bins anyway and you'd meet all the lads, like, and have a bit of a laugh mostly. And one morning I was just starting on my job and two screws come up to me and goes, Follow us, Mickey, and I goes what's up and they said nothing else an' we going along. They brung me down to the visitor rooms and I goes, Am I getting a visitor or what? Ahahahahaah! cos it wasn't even visiting hours. And they still said nothing, but they opens the door, one of them, like, and I walks in and there was two Gardaí in there – Detective Long, who I said before, and I didn't know the other fella, like, but I knew him to see alright. Saw him around a few times, I think. I'm sure he used be in Mayfield Garda Station before, but I definitely seen him another time in Togher Garda Station. Him anyway. He was with Detective Long an' the two of them looking at me when I walks in.

I goes, What's up, like? cos I hadn't a clue, like, me. And Detective Long is looking all sad and he's sucking in his lips to say it.

I have some news for you, Michael, he says, About your Uncle.

And I'm waiting there for him to say something and he's waiting for me, but I'm saying nothing.

Con that is. Your Uncle Con.

And I'm looking at the two of them, one to one to the other and trying to get him to hurry on, like, cos he's saying nothing again.

Ya? I goes to speed him up, What is it, like? What are you here to tell me about Con? and I have tears already and I don't even know why, but I'm getting mad too and want to smash things like. Anything.

He starts calming me down then and after a while I calms down and he tells me Con is dead. And I starts asking him a load of questions and he tells me he was attacked in his own home. Someone broke in and killed him. And I asks him was he on his own in the house? And he tells me that's what they're trying to find out, cos they're looking for my mother and they can't find her and do I know where she'd be?

And I tells him she wasn't at home at all, cos she was gone out of the place weeks. And it's a pity she was now, cos whoever done it'd never of done it if she was there. No way would anyone break into the place if my mother was there or she'd of killed them no bother first. Not even for a minute, I'd say, would they be living if they broke into our place, to Winchester, like. She'd get them before they got to the stairs even.

357

Is he dead? I goes to him, Are you sure he's dead, like and not gone kind of dozy? Cos he done that before…

But the other Garda with Detective Long says he's dead alright, but they're trying to find my mother and her boyfriend. And I copped-on to it then, like, what they were trying. And I says no way they done it.

Is that what you're planning on now? I tells them, You pin it on my own mother, like? No way. They'd of never done that to Con. No way, like!

And the two of them are there saying they don't know who done it and they're only trying to find her to say it to her like, that her brother is dead. And, Who knows, detective Long goes, Maybe her own life is in danger? and I got a shock at that and goes how d'ya mean? And he goes whoever done Con might be after my mother too. Maybe she was the real target?

And I knew then he might've been onto something alright, like, cos it didn't make sense, like, when you think of it, if my mother killed Con, sure. And the shades knew it too. He'd of left her back in anyway alright. And sure, he's no bother, himself, Con like. Was no bother there now, by then, like. By that time. He'd be quiet-out, doing his own thing, watching telly mostly. Judge Judy was his favourite and he'd have a bag of cans while he's watching her. And off-out he might go sometimes in the afternoon for a walk and he'd come home an' all later that night, mostly. Sure Con wouldn't – I mean, like, why would anyone want to hurt Con, like? 'Specially now he was no bother to no one!

They were trying to get it out of me, where's my mam like all the time then. They goes, they know she was up to see me a few days ago and what did she say and did she tell me anything

358

about Con or where she was living now. And I told them what I knew – just in case they were out to get her too, like, whoever done Con. She was living in a tent up the Mardyke, like, around there, but she moved on from there. And I couldn't get it straight in my head then, that my mam… – my own mother, like, was living in *a tent?* I never thought of it before, but now when I said it, it all sounded all, like *wrong* and I was thinking that must be wrong. I couldn't understand it, like.

And they were pushing me again where was she now and I tried to think what she said next, but all I could think was Con. Poor Con. My Uncle. I remembered the time there was a load of them pigs holding him down and a big fat Sergeant Pig walks in cool-as-a-cucumber with his long truncheon and give him a load of whacks hard down on his head and then they carried him out to the Paddy Wagon like he was a lump of dirt. That's what they thought of him the whole time, them pigs.

And anyway, I smashed up what I could and hit whoever I got to, but I didn't get to much of them before they got to me and bate me up too and locked me up and I stayed there the rest of the day in a cell on my own, thinking of Con and seeing him get smashed on the head with a Sergeant's truncheon. And I knew – like *I knew* – it had to of been a cop what done it, cos them bastards always had it in for Con all the time. It was definitely one of them, I was thinking alright. And I spent the whole time working it out.

Next the bastards, later on, came into my cell, like, and injected me with an injection, cos they knew I knew they done it and they wouldn't let me prove it. They goes it's for my own good and they're always saying things like that. One minute it's for my own good, the next minute I'm waking up and it's days later (or something) and I'm out of my tree. Off my head an' all,

I'd say, but how much of it was the drugs they give me? That's why, I'm thinking! Huh?

There was horror days before when everything'd be like rats and skeletons looking at me with loud, loud voices shouting and laughing at me in parties and things like that. But these next days were the worst for things like that. And everyone in the whole world went by to laugh at me and look at me, down, sleeping on the road. And only all the people I knew, like Cillian and my mam and Con and Tony even and all a load of others'd look at me and say something and they'd be all laughing at me too. And the skeletons and the rats'd be laughing at me and trying to bite my toes. But other people'd be walking along too and not even look at me and I'd be screaming at them to save me from them others biting me, but they'd just be walking-on like there was nothing happening. Like *I* didn't matter, cos I knew I didn't, even. And they knew it too. And I knew it too an' all.

And mostly it all made no sense and it was dark and green. All green, I'd say. Like a dark, dark green all the time.

And by the end of all that, mostly, I was only bawling crying the whole time. And there was doctors and women doctors too coming to talk to me, but I couldn't even tell them nothing, cos I didn't know myself what's up. It wasn't even about Con, cos I forgot about him dying then at that time. I didn't even know it, like, he was dead.

And Cillian came to see me too around then – real Cillian, like. Not like in my nightmares, but the real one. My brother. And he was talking to me and I was talking with him, but don't ask me what I was telling him or what we were talking about, cos I have no idea. I was mad loopy by then, still. But I knew he was there alright, like. I knew it at the time and I'd say

I was giving out to him about things, but I didn't mean it, thinking back, whatever I said to him. He knew that though anyway, I say. Cillian's sound-out, in fairness, my brother, like.

And I got a call then, later on, like. A phonecall, like. I was still what you'd call nutty, you ask me, but my mother called me like, on the phone and they brought the phone into me, like so I could talk to my own mother. And I'm like, Hello? cos the phone is up to my ear, but I forgets how to use it like and I'm wondering who I'm talking to or where they are. And then my mother starts talking like I'm already listening but I only hears the end of the first bit what she's saying, and it's something about the guards questioning her. And I goes, What are they questioning you about? and she's telling me, they're not questioning her now, but they were before. Yesterday like and the day before, but they left her out now, but it looks like they're going to charge Tony, her friend, like.

That fella I know, she says.

Tony? I goes, What did Tony do? and she says they think Tony done it. And I goes done what? And I had to ask her a load of times Done what? Done what? What did Tony do? But every time she's only giving out about everything and it's like she don't even know who Tony is, nevermind what he done. Then she goes, Done Con! and I starts screaming at her if she done it, but she's only screaming back saying, Shut up ya dumb fuck I never done it. I wasn't even there, she was telling me. And she tried to get me calm down cos she had something to tell me, I remember her saying that, but I wouldn't let her tell me cos I was told enough. And I'm telling her it was the cops done it, same as before with the truncheon over, onto the top of his head, like, cos I saw it happening. And she's like, That's probably what happened, but they didn't do it with a truncheon.

And then, when I asked her a load, she told me Con was stabbed inside the door, the front door like. It might have been the cops or it might have been someone breaking-in, she was saying, cos Con was gone all-soft and everyone knew it, like, so they'd of wanted to get him back for something he done before.

And that made sense to me too, like, but I couldn't talk and there was too much going on, crowded like inside my head. All full up, sorry now mother, Mickey's gotta lie down here, like!

Michael Collins

Next thing, I'm in the Mercy hospital and prison-time is over, far's I know. And Cillian is coming to see me a load of times, in fairness, most days. That's when we seen the mad wan with the pink night-gown who Cillian thinks was Stacey. Talking away to herself in the corridor, she was. It'd be funny if she *was* Stacey, I say. Probably was too an' all, sure, but I don't think she looked like Stacey at all though, so I doubt it. Madder than me even if she was, Ahahahahaah!

But by then I was nearly better anyway, but I got a phonecall then next day. The next day after that, like. I was called up to the desk for it, cos I had no phone myself, like. And it was my mother again. I goes, How'd you find me here? and she goes, Of course I know where my own son was, ya dumb fuck! and I had a laugh off that then, cos it was my mother, like. And I goes how come you never came to see me so? And she tells me then that they're after charging her on top of that other fella, Tony, so she's being held and can't get out. They're saying now she done it too, trying to frame her on it, like. And that got me mad then, cos them bastards'd try anything, but my mother calmed me down and got me to shut up about it. She goes I'll never get out of the hospital if I don't calm down and she's asking if my prison sentence is still on or if I can sign myself out. And I'm telling her, no I can't sign myself out (cos I didn't think I could), but the nurse, Angela is her name, is passing by when I said it and she goes, You can sign-out any time you like, Mickey, there's no one holding you here against your will at all!

She's from up around Montenotte herself, Angela. Grand big posh house I'd say she have, up there! And she walks-on then, the nurse like, Angela. And I'm like, Can I? and my mother heard it too and she's like saying how great I am for doing my time and for getting out and well done and all that. And I was always very good at taking whatever they thrun at me, those bastards, she goes. And I'm smiling-mad, cos it's all true an' all. They'd never knock me down! And I was telling her then about the time I was up on top of the basketball net and no one else could get up there and no one could get me down. And she's laughing at that. She never heard it before. And we're chatting away for ages, saying what will I do now when I get out? And I'm telling her I'm going to get a job on the skip lorry and she's asking me about that a while and we're talking like, having a bit of a laugh. Like normal people, even.

And before we go then she says, Remember ages ago, what Michael Collins' got for my grandfather? Don't say it now, cos it was a surprise present, remember I told you? and I knew straight away what it was. It was the knife me and Cillian took off her and left it in the quarry, that time. And I goes, Ya! Ya I do, like!

Well I think that fella, Tony, had it all the time! she goes, But I want you to have it. Not him! and I goes, Did he get it back? How'd he get it back? but she wasn't listening to me.

Cos you're named after him, like I told you, remember? and I goes, I do ya, thanks Mam! For that, like!

And she carries-on, saying, If I had to guess where it is, she goes, I'd say it's where the holy money goes. You know where that is. All your holy money? Tony thought that was a grand spot!

IS IT IN THERE!? I goes, HOW'D HE GET IT?

And she tells me shut up again about it. Say nothing, she tells me. Then she says, But I *think* that's the same one anyway. If that's not that one – check it carefully now, Mickey! she says, You remember what the other one looked like – long enough, with a long handle? Take a good look at this other one now – and if that's not the same present Michael Collins gave to my grandfather, I want you to make sure you put it somewhere Tony'd never find it, cos we don't want him getting it, do we? and I'm like, No we do not!

Say nothing to no one now! she's telling me, Get your brother, Cillian, to leave the hospital with you. You'll be let out if he's there with you – but make sure you don't tell him either! Tell him nothing too!

It was the first time she said his name in years, I'd say, so I was thinking then maybe they'd get friends again and make up. Wouldn't that be a good one? And I told her I'd do all o' that no bother. Leave it with me! I nodded and winked to her with a big thumbs-up, like.

•

This one's a big job. I knew that much. First time in a long time she got me do anything for her. She knew it was only me what could help her, like. And I'm not a complete idiot either, cos after Cillian come to get me it was after three o'clock, around I'd say, and he was all questions about how I'm feeling and where am I going to stay and I had to tell him I'm staying in

Davie's house. And he's like, Davie O'Brien? Sure he's dead, Mickey! and I'm like, No, not Davie O'Brien at all – another Davie, like, who you don't know at all!

And he was saying I could stay in his place with him for a little while, but I'm like, Naw, I got to stay with Davie, like, cos Davie needs my help! and it took me ages to get him to shut up about it, but I got him to drop me in the taxi out the road, near Winchester, but not near enough that he'd know where I was going really, like. So when I seen him go away in the car, then like, I turns back the other way towards Winchester and I was thinking about the whole thing and that's when I worked it out, what happened, like: See, it was Tony alright, I'd say, who done Con. Killed him like, I'd say. I'm only guessing now, cos I wasn't there myself, like remember, so it definitely wasn't me! But I'd say my mother found out too it was Tony, after like (cos she'd of definitely stopped him if she knew before!) And he buried the knife in my hiding spot, under the shower, that bastard. I worked all that much out when I was walking home, like.

And I was thinking, if it was *that* knife he used, our family knife, like, my mother wouldn't want the cops getting it again, so I had to rescue it, like, and hold onto it. I *had* to. No choice! But if it was another one – a different knife, like, I'd have to throw it in the river or get rid of it. Cos if they found it in my hiding spot, they might even think I done it, or something, like. So my mother was looking out for me too, that way, in fairness.

I knew all of that alright before I got there. Then I got there and I seen Winchester all boarded-up, with police-tape too all over the place. And it looked sad like it was on Scooby Doo or something. But I got in anyway alright, cos the board on the front door was a bit loose when I pulled it hard and I ducked-down and the door inside was broken anyway too, the front door, like, so I got in that way.

It was getting a bit dark by now, but it was alright like. I could still see inside there, so I didn't bother turning the light on, just in case, like. And I went upstairs to my room and into the bathroom. But when I was bending down to check under the shower, it was too dark and I had no light, so I tried the light in the room then and it was working still.

So I opens the hole and it was empty mostly, when I looked. And I put my hand inside and I found some things and pulled them out, but it was all rubbish only. Old rubbish things, plastic bags and shit. So I stuck my hand in again and this time I found a watch! I got that years ago on a job, I remember, out by Ballyvolane. I was looking for that for ages and it was in there the whole time! If I only knew it, like! Worth a few bob too, I'd say, so I put it on and had another dip inside, but grabbed nothing this time.

Next I tried opening the hole a bit more by pulling on it, but I couldn't rip it any more, like, so I put my back against the wall and used my legs and shoes on it, to push hard and to get the tray to rise up.

Then I had to break off the part up on top of it first, the part with the glass, like. I broke off all the panel off the wall and then I tried it again down below, to pull the tray up, hard as I could and I was smashing it with my shoes and everything. Plumbing. And I got it too, then! It all ripped up off the floor. Half it at least. Or three quarters even. And the first thing I seen was a shiny handbag. Stacey's old one, like. I knew that straight away when I seen it. I kept it in there, what she give me that time when she left. So I was picking that up when I spotted the knife.

It was thrun back into the far-corner, so I had to reach under still to get to it.

I knew straight away it wasn't Michael Collins' scian. No way. This was a smaller knife. Much newer. I'd say it was brand new. Black hangle and kind of like a triangle. It was nothing at all like the old one Michael Collins had. And that was the proof too, when you think of it, that my mother never saw it neither, cos she'd of known straight away it wasn't his knife, like, no bother. And I knew it straight away, even, too an' all!

It was a nice knife, in fairness and I nearly thought I might hold onto it or sell it, but I knew my mother'd kill me, so I said I'd better get it out of here and hide it someplace, get rid of it, like.

But when I'm getting ready to get up, I seen Stacey's bag again and I had a look inside, see if there's anything. And there was too! A letter, like an orange envelope. An orange envelope was in there the whole the time, but I only ever got the good stuff out of it, didn't bother looking at any papers or shit. Looked like I knew it too, when I took it out and got the crumples out of it. And my name was on it too! Addressed to Mickey Collins at our old address – the place we were in before Winchester, like. Down by Murder She Wrote's, when I was still a teenager, like!

I opens it up anyway straight away and starts reading and I got some shock off it, I tell ya when I seen it and read it. I read it all, right there and I couldn't even understand most of it, cos my brain wasn't working, but I got to the end and I understood it more then, but I kept thinking of it and thinking of it the whole time. And I read it a few times, but it was all wavy and going in circles after a while.

I was dizzy from thinking of that letter, I tell ya, when I was standing up and coming down the stairs. And I got out by the front door and I tries to look at it again, the letter like, but it's too dark inside there and my eyes were watery a bit, even. I have the letter in one hand now and the knife in the other one, so when I'm getting down on my knees to crawl out the door, I turns the blade of the knife back towards me, so I don't stab my face, like when I'm crawling out.

Next, I pushes the board and gets mostly out and two big lights flash-on straight in my face. Car lights, like. And then the blue flashing lights on top too come on. And I hear, Mikey, Mikey! Heh heh, we have you now, Mikey!

And two hands pull me up from behind, cos one shade was standing there by the door, waiting for me the whole time. And he pulls me up by locking-on tight around my arms and pulls me straight up. And he pulled the knife up too, in my hand, when he done it and it went straight into him, like. Into, like the top of his legs, like. Up near his balls, I'd say like, and might of even gone into his balls. It went straight in, I barely felt it myself, like, go in.

Even after he pulled me up and the knife went in, he gave one more big tug upwards. And that was it then. We both went down after that. The other shade is running towards us, but when I looks at yer man, I knew straight away he was dead alright, like, just about.

Wasn't me at all! It was himself, like, if anyone! And I'm dizzy from that and dizzy from the knife and the letter that I just read has me totally dizzy the whole time. And the fella running towards me is a skeleton or a rat and he's coming to bite me and everything else. All of it. Next thing I know (or don't know, like),

I collapsed then, fainted or something. And that was the last thing.

All black.

Dear Mickey,

I don't know if you'll ever get to read this, but I wanted you to know you are *a very good boy*. None of what happened between me and your mother is your fault. You must believe me when I say it has nothing to do with you. I hope you don't blame yourself in any way. You are such a lovely young man, I have no doubt you will grow up to be a *great adult*. Your natural charisma lights up every room, bringing a rare Zest For Life that is nothing if not contagious.

BE CONFIDENT, Michael. You have the intelligence, the ability and certainly the inner beauty to succeed. I know this might make you laugh or smile, but it's all true. In our short time together I have seen you grow and I know the love you have to bring to the world. You will make some lucky girl very happy one day.

Our time together was pure gold and *I regret none of it*. I spent my working life as a social worker, as you know, but I never took-in a foster-child before you. I know I said I had (I lied), but honestly I'd have never coped with all the rules and regulations it had been my job to keep others beholden to. In that I am like you, Mickey. All those rules can be impossible at times, I know, but what is important is we do our best to follow at least the good ones.

The main reason I never fostered, of course, was my marital status. We don't need to look very far to see how easy it would always have been for someone with ill-intent to twist any relationship between a single male and a child such as you still are, but *we* know the truth and that's all that matters.

I was diagnosed in September, the year before last, with Stage 4 Terminal Cancer and on that same day I was told about

371

you, how there was no place for you anywhere, and asked if I could take you in for a few days until somewhere suitable was found. To say my initial response was not very nice is an understatement. I couldn't see past the news I had just received. But again that evening, a former colleague, Suzanne Murphy, called me to say they would have to send you to an adult prison or worse perhaps, back home, if I couldn't take you for a bit. And I thought, what did I have to lose?

Anyway, as they say the rest is history. You brought Light to my Life, Mickey, at a time when I had only Darkness. You gave me a reason to get up in the morning and never failed to bring a smile to my heart, no matter the weight that was pulling it down.

I wanted you to know, all the rest... the lawsuit, the court appearances, the newspapers... it doesn't matter. None of that has anything to do with you and <u>it is not your fault</u>.

I'm leaving instructions with my brother for this letter to go to you after I'm gone. Hopefully you'll have a chance to read it. We are unlikely to meet again, but I hope the time you spent in my home brought a little lightness to your heavy heart too. Goodbye Michael.

Life, as we know, can be cruel, but look around and you'll find beauty in the strangest of places. I know I have.

Love always,

Desmond Mulcahy.

From the same author:

Nothing More (previously published as *The High Kicking Kung Fu Soccer Playing Bunny Rabbit Tree by K. Michael Forde*)

The Empathy Stone (as *Stanley Rumm* – previously published as *OOYAY*.)

The Leaving Cert (previously and still published as *The Leaving Cert* by Kevin Forde)

All highly recommended by the author.